PARIS IN THE PRESENT TENSE

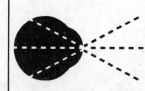

This Large Print Book carries the
Seal of Approval of N.A.V.H.

PARIS IN THE PRESENT TENSE

MARK HELPRIN

THORNDIKE PRESS

A part of Gale, a Cengage Company

Farmington Hills, Mich • San Francisco • New York • Waterville, Maine
Meriden, Conn • Mason, Ohio • Chicago

**LIBRARY OF CONGRESS CIP DATA ON FILE.
CATALOGUING IN PUBLICATION FOR THIS BOOK
IS AVAILABLE FROM THE LIBRARY OF CONGRESS**

ISBN-13: 978-1-4328-4746-3 (hardcover)
ISBN-10: 1-4328-4746-5 (hardcover)

Published in 2018 by arrangement with The Overlook Press, Peter
Mayer Publishers, Inc.

Printed in the United States of America
1 2 3 4 5 6 7 22 21 20 19 18

For Julian Licht, Jules Hirsch,
and Francine Christophe
With thanks to William Winston —
Poet, Critic, Friend

CONTENTS

I. RISING AND ALOFT

Air France 017 13

Paris in Recollection 25

The Insurance Salesman
Armand Marteau 64

François Ehrenshtamm, *Philosophe* . . . 77

This Jack Person 101

Writing a Jingle in Saint-Germain-
en-Laye. 128

Jacqueline at Sparta 148

The Past Upwells 166

The Policeman Is Your Friend 214

Million Swimming Pools 236

Amina Belkacem 248

A Thousand Lawyers. 261

Lights Corruscating Through
the Dusk 284

Touching Down 301

II. BLOOD WILL TELL

DNA. 307
Cathérine and David, François 319
Jacqueline's Photograph 340
1944. 356
The Music Lesson 391

III. *LOYAL À MORT*

The Sun Comes Out for
     Armand Marteau 427
Spring Fire and Smoke 443
As Light and Warmth Put France
     at Ease 454
If, at Its End, Your Life Takes on
     the Attributes of Art 484
The Patient, Barely Alive, Had
     Collapsed on the RER 498
Élodi, Jules, Duvalier, Arnaud,
     and Nerval 525
Élodi Alone 558
August 567
Amina 591
On the Grand Terrace at
     Saint-Germain-en-Laye 619

Jules Lacour was born in 1940, while his parents were hiding in an attic in Reims. His mother prayed that he would not cry, he seldom did, and in the four years that followed neither he nor they spoke above a whisper. That was the beginning of a long story.

I.
RISING AND ALOFT

AIR FRANCE 017

A disintegrating airframe offers little in the way of second chances, and because this sometimes happens, taking to the air tends to heighten one's awareness of that which has come before and that which may come yet. Though travelers convince themselves that statistics watch over them, tension flows through airports like windblown clouds, and as an aircraft rises to 13,000 meters those within it may be drawn to assess what they love and what they hope for in the time left.

And when autumn weather on land may be pleasantly crisp and permissive of wearing a suit in perfect comfort, the North Atlantic is deadly cold and unforgiving. Swells that normally run at three or four feet can easily rise to ten or more, and even as freezing wind draws long lines of foam across the wave crests at thirty knots it isn't called a storm. Delicate airplanes constructed of a million discrete parts fly far above such cold and dark seas for hours as meals are served, movies

13

screened, telephone calls made, and lights turned down while passengers sleep under soft wool blankets. But should the plane break up in the air or crash into the waves, death will have its way most horribly. Surprising for most, but not for all.

A huge, dark-gold, reddened sun had almost set. Manhattan's skyscrapers and tenements, painted in flame on their south and west sides, stood in impenetrable shadow on their north and east faces. And in business class on Air France 017, Kennedy to Charles de Gaulle — who, before they became airports, knew one another and were in power at the same time — a window seat awaited Jules Lacour, who found it, settled in, and assessed his quarters with less enthusiasm than they were supposed to elicit. Low walls that curved to provide privacy and call attention to their design allowed him to see the procession of boarders passing through: tourists and Egyptians, Philadelphia housewives and graduate students, a baby or two, but mainly, in the business and first class cabins, jaded men of affairs who an instant after taking their seats opened newspapers, laptops, or spiral-bound books full of tables and charts. That is, if they were not engaged in cell-phone conversations projected with the stiff self-importance that was their oxygen.

The flight wasn't full, it had boarded quickly, and traffic on the runways was such that the crew wanted to pull from the gate as fast as possible to be slotted-in for takeoff. As the plane was pushed back from the terminal, Manhattan came into view from the Battery almost to Hell Gate. The palisade of buildings was pitch black on its eastern face, but light from the sun side broke so hard upon steel and glass that its coronas roiled over the rooftops like waves breaking over a sea wall.

Although it was for him the scene of bitter defeat, Jules Lacour could not hold his own failure against a city that — unlike Paris, but like life — was beautiful both in spite of itself and as the sum of its ungainly parts. Manhattan was a gift not of form but of light and motion. From a distance or on high the persistent sound that rose from it, a barely audible hum that never ceased, might have been the whispered stories of all its inhabitants, even the dead. He couldn't dislike New York, no matter the petty injuries and humiliations he had suffered there because as a foreigner he could neither fully understand it, nor fight the way it fought, nor speak the way it spoke. Nor could they speak the way he spoke. They didn't even say his name correctly, pronouncing *Jules* indistinguishably from the English word *jewels*.

He never quite got used to this, as in French the S was silent and the J pronounced "zh." They did almost alright with *Lacour,* coming close to the second syllable's *cooor,* and not quite making it, but *Jewels* drove him crazy, as if every time someone addressed him they called him *Bijoux*. Not that Jules' English was that precise — he had a strong French accent — but no one in America seemed to know how to pronounce any foreign word.

And apparently no one had ever heard of anything either, and Jules Lacour was so constantly explaining references and allusions that eventually he gave up. De Gaulle? Churchill? Renoir? Winslow Homer? Cavafy? Not a chance. Set (invisibly when it was off) in the bathroom mirror, a hotel television nearly scared him to death when he accidentally turned it on and saw Mick Jagger staring back at him. On the same machine he witnessed interviews with American beach-goers who thought that in 1776 America had won its independence from California, that the moon was bigger than the sun, that you could take a Greyhound Bus to North Korea, that Alaska was an island south of Hawaii, and that the Supreme Court was a motel in Santa Monica. How could the United States have become so rich, powerful, and inventive? Or, rather, how long could it remain so?

Raising the rpm of its enormous engines, the pilots smoothly and slowly moved the Airbus forward. Ailerons and flaps were exercised at a stately pace as spoilers popped up like

16

prairie dogs and then retreated. The deep harmonies and a slight treble weaving amid and yet overwhelmed by the bass said that despite the immense power already evident, the turbines were still at rest, with the counterpoint of bass suggesting that they were yearning to come up full. Music even of this kind was everywhere the bearer of messages from an unreachable but always beckoning place out of which perfection spilled easily and without limit.

In his deepest despair — when his wife died, when his only grandchild was diagnosed with leukemia (the reason he had come to America) — Jules Lacour might still hear music arising from unexpected quarters: from the rhythms of steel wheels on train tracks, though this was now rare in France after the joints in the rails had been bridged by welds; from the clickings of elevators moving in their shafts; the unpredictable harmonies of traffic; wind in the trees; the workings of machines; and water flowing, falling, or surging in waves. Even in desperation, music would sound as if from nothing, and wake him to life. He was a cellist, and could never have been anything else. The world had courage, faith, beauty, and love, and it had music, which, although not merely an abstraction, was equal to the greatest abstractions and principles — its power to lift, clarify, and carry the soul forever unmatched.

After a steady roll, the plane reached the end of the runway and stopped before final check and permission to take off. The stewards and stewardesses, who as if they had no sex were now called flight attendants, had taken their seats facing backward and at their charges, whom they surveyed unobtrusively. The plane almost pivoted, the tip of the port wing tracing an enormous arc as the tip to starboard backed up as carefully as an intimidated animal. The engines were pushed to full. Just as he had as a young soldier in a troop transport rising on a course for Africa, as the plane sped down the runway and lifted off, Jules forgot his troubles. The war in Algeria had ended so long before, that, when asked about it he would simply say, "That part of my life is now a museum."

They rose with great speed and the mounting force of gravity. Off to the right, Manhattan sparkled, its shadowed side gleaming with uncountable lights. These were mainly white and silver, but some blinked red at the tops of smokestacks and masts, or made the illuminated triangles and summit caps of skyscrapers green, gold, or pale blue. The sun had fallen into New Jersey, which was now nothing more than a burning red rim.

Soon they gained enough altitude to catch a glimpse of a thin line of molten silver — the Hudson — which dropped away as they banked northeast into the night and continued to climb, now more steadily, with less roar. The cabin lights came up. The flight attendants undid the buckles of their seatbelts and stood. The clicking of aluminum sounded two full bars. With a minor adjustment it could have been the opening and theme of a Flamenco. Jules gave it rhythm and orchestration until, for him, but only for an instant, it filled the cabin. When the music stopped, its gifts returned whence they had come.

The genius of the designer notwithstanding, it had taken millennia to fashion the tailoring of an Air France stewardess' uniform, every line and angle of which knew with affection the beauty and charm of her body and the loveliness of her face. The richest possible navy fabric opened gracefully at the neck as if in love with the complex anatomy it complemented. It was almost impossible not to be struck by the brilliant red bow at the waist, the slight bell at the hem of the coat, and the perfect fall of the cloth. Principles as intricate and mysterious as any in the seven arts were present in the cut, a rich simplicity being the secret not only of French fashion but perhaps of France itself. At their best, the dress, the coat, the *maquillage,* were there to call attention not to themselves but to the woman they graced, just as the architecture of Paris, the pattern of its streets, its garlands of trees, and the design of its gardens — every cornice, rail, lamppost, and arch — were there not to call attention to themselves but to be part of a chain of beauties leading to unseen realms. Not dissimilar to the composition of a painting, the deft placement of words upon a page, or music unfurling through the air, a golden proportion enlivened the flow of the cloth as it moved with her.

From within the off-white eggshell of his seat/bed, Jules observed the stewardesses as they moved throughout the cabin. Even if plain, they were beautiful. The scents of the cosmetics, different from those of perfume, and, to him, more exciting, suggested an almost theatrical preparation. The beginning of the flight was a stage for these women. When expectations were greatest and the passengers most awake, they were at their peak. Tentatively separated from loyalties and attachments by the fact of travel, the speed with which land was left behind, the potential for disaster, and having risen into what for most of human history had been called heaven, many of those on board, witness to this play of light and motion, imagined a new life with someone encountered like an angel far above the earth. Though economists, executives, and bureaucrats might have seen it differently, this was an influential effect of business travel.

A stewardess approached Jules, bent gracefully, and, addressing him in English, asked what he would prefer for dinner. Because he had been in America for weeks and was lost in how she held herself and how she spoke, he answered as he was addressed. At first they failed to recognize one another's accents, but with his perfect pitch he soon heard in her English the telltale markers of their native language, in which he then spoke to her. Had he been younger he would have fallen in love. She was beautiful in her way. He hadn't seen it at first. Then he did. So even though he was not younger, he did begin to fall in love, for a moment, a minute or two, and in an afterglow when she left. Then he resisted, as had she by the time she bent to speak to the next passenger. Jules would often fall in love this way, intensely and briefly with women who justly deserved it and often elicited it. But these infatuations would quickly lead to his deep love for Jacqueline, who was now gone.

"I thought this wasn't allowed," he said to the stewardess when she came back. He pointed to a knife on the tray she had just placed before him. The reading light made the silverware gleam.

Rather than give a formal answer, she shrugged her shoulders, which lifted and lowered the beautifully cut collar along the curve of her neck. "The doors to the flight

21

deck are impenetrable," she said. "There may be sky marshals; and although no one ever seems to think of this, the other passengers also have knives on their trays, and there would be more of them than there would be terrorists." His expression acknowledged her point and that he hadn't thought of it. She smiled, turned, and disappeared up the aisle.

He turned his attention to the food. He always ate lightly and suspiciously when in the air. There before him on the plate was a square of some kind of fish, which looked like a piece of yellow pastry. He hardly drank alcohol at all and never when flying, but now made an exception of a split of Pol Roget, studying the bottle as he ate, rather than staring at the partition. The label was admirably modest: some graceful penmanship set against a plain white background. Unlike other brands, Pol Roget was bereft of shining foil at the neck. Champagne was made to go with sparkling and reflected light, and there was no gleam from the bottle itself. But the reading lamp illuminated the bubbles as they rose in undulating silver lines through a sea of gold.

In this little thing and things like it — the perfect and complex ascent of the tiny orbs, all exactly the same size and flawlessly spherical; the uncountable molecules of air that with unvarying obedience to fluid mechanics kept the plane aloft across thousands of miles of ocean; the fuel that burned without a hiccup; the turbines that spun without flying apart life's secrets were beyond calculation or understanding. Not merely the three-body problem, not merely physics, but rather the faithful consistency of nature. The light was invariably precise as it shone upon the tiny, reflective spheres in the Champagne, moving exactly according to universal laws. Just as the plane was held miles high by air that even in the light was invisible, so the most discrete effects betrayed the most fundamental truths.

After the Champagne and before he knew it, the tray had been removed and the cabin lights dimmed. Somewhere over the sea, ignorant of how many hundred kilometers they were off Halifax or in how many hundred Iceland would be directly north in the darkness, Jules Lacour put his seat back a quarter of the way, checked his watch, and looked out the window. The cabin had grown quiet and the stewardesses had retreated. Standing in an alcove, illuminated from above and framed in black, they spoke softly and sometimes laughed. Most of their work was done until morning. Perhaps the one he liked was thinking of him.

Of the seven hours and twenty minutes of flight, almost six hours remained — six hours in which to think of how to plan revenge, save a life, and give his own. With stars all around, the plane split a path through the

23

night, rising and falling more smoothly than a boat on a gently rolling sea.

PARIS IN RECOLLECTION

Rowing on the Seine is difficult and can sometimes be dangerous. The current is strong, especially after heavy rains when the water is high and the river can run so fast a good oarsman fighting the flow as best he can stays in place or finds himself moving backward. Barges that are anything but nimble, *bateaux-mouches,* motorboats driven too fast by men who have had too much wine, and semi–submerged tree-trunks, pallets, or winter ice threaten the narrow and delicate single shells. Add to that the whirlpools, bends, abutments, and unforgiving walls past which the water is inflexibly channeled, and it isn't a rower's paradise, especially if you're old.

But having rowed on the Seine for the sixty years since he was fourteen, Jules hadn't lost his touch. Long experience gave him an almost perfect knowledge of the eddies, ricochets, and fast water of the course as it wound past bridges and islands, and barges tied to the embankments. Nonetheless, he was a little afraid each time he went out, because although everyone flipped over now and then, his balance was uncanny, and never once having gone in the water he didn't want to mar a perfect record of more than half a century. But more than that, he felt stalked by probabilities. If he did lose his balance, without having done so ever in his life, would he know what to do? That he was an excellent swimmer was irrelevant. He might panic if the water were cold, his heart might stop, he might be crushed by a speeding barge.

Not this day in August, a few months before he knew he was going to go to New York, when he glided in on the current to a perfect landing at the dock. Had anyone seen him on the river, glistening with sweat in the August heat, he could have been mistaken for a muscular athlete in his late forties or early fifties. It took work, a lifetime of discipline, showing up when miserably cold and rowing or running through snow and sleet, never eating quite as he might like, and losing precious hours he might have spent in furthering his career. But Jules had resolved from early on, even before he knew it, that until the day he died he would be strong enough so as never to be unable to defend himself.

The shower in the rickety boathouse, a barge illegally moored to the embankment, had a floor of eucalyptus planks so saturated with fragrant oil that it neither rotted nor grew slippery. Though the stream of water was thin and the austerity of the boathouse difficult to exaggerate, he didn't need luxury. He wanted neither an elegant locker room nor a stand piled with thick newly washed towels, nor a Mercedes waiting for him outside, but only to know that, refreshed and clean, he could sprint up the stone stairs to the street and be not even slightly out of breath.

After Jacqueline died he had clung to routine: rising; breakfast; the walk to the RER A; transfer at Châtelet Les Halles (rough and dangerous); the RER B to Luxembourg/*Boul-Miche;* passing through the portals of the old Sorbonne and noting with appreciation their ancient form; then, later, in the hideous new facilities at Clignancourt in the northeast of Paris; the start of class; music in the presence of young people animated by energy, vigor, and struggle; lessons and critiques in which he was carried away by the mystical reach of sound; then punishing exercise on the river; wonderful relief as he walked through the city; the train back; shopping; dinner; reading; practice; reflection; memory; prayer; and sleep.

Taken together, these were the metronome of his life, and he was comforted by their steady procession, like the ticking of a clock, that eventually without fail would bring him to the woman he had loved for most of his life. But today would be different. Because the rhythm of the days that would see him along and bring him to her was imperfect, marred by his weakness and his will to live, today he would arrive later than usual in Saint-Germain-en-Laye because he was going to seek solace not in music or in memory or in a synagogue or church, but in something quite different. He was going to do the impossible. He was going to see a psychiatrist, in Paris, in August.

There was one left, anyway, in the Villa Mozart, three flights up in a building so quiet that to walk into it was like becoming deaf. His waiting room had sea green walls and *Empire* furniture of mahogany and cherry. Jules had hardly had time to sit down when the doctor appeared. A short, bearded man with glasses — the fashion after Freud — he stood at the soundproofed door to his office and looked at his prospective patient, who was older than he was, though not by much. Despite the fact that he was one of the few psychiatrists present in the city in August, Dunaif's prestige in the profession was legendary. Ignorant of that, Jules had found him in the telephone book, his fourteenth call.

Dunaif stood in silence, studying Jules as one might study a painting. People see so

28

many other people that they look at faces
without seeing them. But so much is written
in the face — of the past, of truth, hope, pain,
love, and potential — that each man or
woman deserves a Raphael, Rembrandt, or
Vermeer to see and express it.

What did Dunaif see? He supposed that the
man standing before him, like so many —
but here it was carved to an unusual depth
— carried within him and would not abandon
the life of the past, his love of those who had
come before, a store of vivid memories, and,
not least, the wounds of history. A smart,
brave, and defeated old man sitting in front
of the doctor, reticent as he might be, was
more interesting than listening to the sexual
travails or career disappointments of a
twenty-eight-year-old.

After a few minutes, Jules asked, "Do I
come in there and speak, or do you just stand
in the doorway and stare at me?"

Gesturing with his right hand sweeping
toward the interior, Dunaif invited him in.
Two *portes-fenêtres* facing the street were
open, their white gauze curtains moving
patiently in breaths of summer air. Three
times the size of the waiting room, the office
was full of books — on three walls of floor-
to-ceiling shelves, stacked on tables and his
desk — but still spacious and open. Before
the building had been divided into smaller
apartments at the end of the war, this had

29

once been a family's main reception room.

"Do you live here?" Jules asked.

"Upstairs," Dunaif said, settling into his chair. He interlocked his fingers and tilted his head a little, keeping his eyes leveled upon Jules as if to say, what have you to tell me?

Not quite ready to open up, just as in music the first movement is often quiet and tentative, Jules proceeded gradually. He said, "You seem to be the only psychiatrist now working in Paris. What kind of psychiatrist, no, what kind of Frenchman, would be in Paris in August?"

"I don't like the beach," Dunaif said. "That is, when everyone is on it. And this is what I do. In August the city is quiet and beautiful in its desertion. Although the young residents stay on duty in the hospitals, someone senior has to be on call to guide them."

"Why is there no one waiting? Your secretary? I saw a receptionist's desk."

"She and they are all somewhere else. Paris shrinks as they take with them everything they think they're leaving behind. On the Côte d'Azur the men play tennis as if their lives depend upon it, and the women look at each other's handbags. It's just like Faubourg Saint-Honoré. Everyone's at the beach but me and you. What about you?"

"I stopped going to the beach when my wife died. We used to go to what were then,

30

anyway, the empty Atlantic beaches north of the Gironde. Unlike the rest of France, I'm not afraid to swim in the surf. Helicopters would hover and demand through their loudspeakers that I return to shore. One landed once, and the police tried to give me a ticket. I protested that swimming in the ocean could not be a crime, but evidently it can be. They demanded my papers, which I didn't have of course, because I was in my bathing suit. They asked my name so they could write the summons. When I said *Aristide Poisson,* the cop almost hit me. They looked toward the helicopter, but the pilot moved his head from side to side to say, no, they were already fully loaded. Then they flew away. It was like a dream."

"Yes," said Dunaif. "I had a patient yesterday who had exactly the same dream."

"A common phobia," Jules answered in the same spirit, "helicopters catching you in the sea."

"Go on."

"About the beach?"

"About anything."

"About anything," Jules repeated, looking down.

"Anything that occurs to you."

"All right. It's a shock, and I don't like it, that when I pay monthly, quarterly, or even annual bills, and when I wind the clock each week, I'm absolutely sure that I've done it the day before, not seven, or thirty, or a hundred and twenty days before, but yesterday, as if no time had passed. When writing the year 2014 on a check — do young people even write checks anymore, go to the post office, or read newspapers? It doesn't look like it — I feel like I'm in a science-fiction novel. Sometimes I date my checks 'nineteen fifty-eight,' or 'nineteen seventy-five,' and then cross it out, amazed to write the present date, staring at it like an African tribesman or an American Indian brought as a curiosity to the London or Paris of the seventeenth century. Such a creature, kidnaped from his home, would, no matter what its difficulties, long for his tranquil past. And in the Old World, new to him, his touch would be forever numb, his hearing muted, his sight betrayed and blurred. Whatever the beauties around him, only home — lost over a seemingly infinite sea — would be really beautiful."

"I understand," Dunaif said. "So let me ask what it is that keeps you in the past and prevents you from living fully in the present?"

"Guilt."

"I've heard of that." The psychiatrist was a Jew, and knew that Jules was as well. "This is France, after all. Devout, well practiced Catholics come here to confess. Those who are lapsed come to confess that they haven't confessed — quite a confession. Jews, who have no confessors, are the champions of self-revelation, but telling me your sins, real or imagined, won't wash them away. My job is not absolution but understanding."

"I know. That's why I don't think you, or anyone for that matter, can help me."

"Maybe, maybe not." Dunaif leaned forward compassionately — if this is possible, and it was. "Tell me."

"Rationally or not, I feel responsible for the deaths of many people and even animals. When someone close to me dies, I think that because I couldn't save him I've killed him. It's not logical, but it doesn't go away."

"This started when?" Dunaif asked.

"With my parents. During the war. I didn't save them."

"How old were you?"

"Four and a half."

"I have my job because the life of a man or a woman is forged in the wounds of infancy and childhood. You think, that was then and I can't go back and fix things, and of course you can't. But look at it another way. Now you, a grown man — I dare say, if I may, an old man — are blaming a four-year-old, who happens to have been you, for the inability single-handedly to defeat the Wehrmacht, the SS, the Luftwaffe, the Kriegsmarine, the Vichy police, the collaborators. . . . Would you blame a four-year-old who was not you?"

"Of course not, but you're wrong. Love is absolute. It can't be measured, or contained, or truly analyzed. It's the one thing that you hold onto as you fall into the abyss. When you love, you experience a power close to that of the divine. And, like music, it enables you so far to transcend your bounds that you can't even begin to understand it. So when you love, as a child loves his parents or a parent his child, you suffer the illusion that the limitless power you sense can save them. It can't. I know, but my soul doesn't, and it makes me want to die so I can share their fate."

"Hamlet jumped into Ophelia's grave. But then he jumped out."

"And so do I, figuratively, each time. But let me go on. It hardly ended there. Louis Mignon and his wife, Marie, saved us, for a time. I stayed with them in Reims until I was seven. Then I went to live with cousins in Paris. At the station, Louis and Marie embraced me. They cried. I cried. And Louis tried to press a coin into my hand, *'Pour chocolat,'* he said. But I refused to take it. I was a little kid, a very confused little kid, and I thought that by refusing the gift I was expressing my gratitude. He was deeply hurt, and two weeks later he died. I know I didn't kill him, but you see?

"The next was a dog, my dog, Jeudi. After I was sent to Paris I was bullied a lot in school

— no parents, a Jew who stuttered in the accent of Reims, a child whose unhappiness brought forth a thousand blows and a lot of blood, literally. One day when I was coming home after taking a beating, she ran to greet me. She loved me, and I loved her. Because I had no parents, she was everything to me. But that day, for no reason, I hit her. I'll never forget the sound when she cried out. Sometimes I dream it. Why did I hit her? I know now but so what? Normally I would have taken her in my arms. Her tail was wagging, she was just excited to see me, but I hit her, hard. She's long dead. At times, when I think of that, I come to tears.

"It doesn't end there. I had a cousin, twenty years older than I was, a hero who had served with the Free French. He was tall, he had a beautiful girlfriend, and they would take me to amusements and on long walks. Young people in love sometimes have a kind of practice child. That was important to me, because I wanted to be exactly like him. I was always unhappy when he left, because, frankly, the relatives who took me in Paris didn't want to have anything to do with me. I don't blame them. I was a difficult child. But he saw through that. They had a little garden in which there was a hose for watering the plants and the grass. I played there, or brooded. One day in late September he had to leave, and a taxi was waiting to take him to the station. He came downstairs and into the garden to say goodbye to me. He was wearing a beautifully tailored suit. What did I do? Because I didn't want him to go, I sprayed him with the hose. He got soaking wet and cold, but he had no time to change because he had to catch the train. I was scolded like a murderer, but he intervened and said it was all right. The way he looked at me told me that he understood and still loved me. Two months later he was dead from melanoma. What did I know? I thought he had become sick because of the chill. I thought for years that I had killed him. I know of course that I didn't. It doesn't matter.

"There were so many other occasions of that nature — pets that I had to put down, animals that I accidentally ran over, even a dove that I stepped on as I was coming out of my barracks before dawn. But there are two that loom very large. The time is passing, so I'll tell you those quickly."

"Don't worry about the time. You can come back."

"I don't think I will."

"If it's a matter of economy . . ." Dunaif began. For him, the ability of a patient to pay was not paramount.

"It's not that." Jules paused for a moment before he went on. "I said two more, but it's possibly three. That's the problem.

36

"The first was in Algeria in fifty-eight, on the northern sector of the Morice Line. I was a draftee of eighteen. I had good luck, because I served in the mountains, far from the cities. Our job was to prevent infiltration from Tunisia, of which there was a great deal. That was more straightforward and less morally difficult than most everything else in the war. We were soldiers fighting soldiers who came from abroad to participate in the civil war for which we had come from abroad as well. So, in a sense, we were even.

"I had hoped to be a musician in the army, playing at the Élysée or in parades, but there was no place open for the cello, in marching bands the piano translates to the glockenspiel, and the glockenspiel positions were filled as well. So I ended up on Djebel Chélia, in a pine forest at two thousand meters. It was beautiful there in the middle of nowhere, with snow in the winter; views, from high outcroppings, of hundreds of kilometers; wild horses on the plains below; and heavy, steeply sloped forests.

"Our base was surrounded by mines and wire, and we would patrol the few roads in armored vehicles, which, though rarely, were sometimes attacked. It was a quiet sector, because infiltrators preferred to travel away from the mountain itself, and other units would come into contact with them before they got to us — mostly.

"I loved being in such a place — or would have had it not been for the war — which made me long for home in the same way that one can long for a woman: the deep desire that can be felt, physically, throughout every part of the body. Evidently a lot of people don't experience that, which is too bad.

"Though I had determined to die before I killed an innocent, it was not from idealism. I hate idealism. It was because I couldn't possibly do to anyone what had been done to my mother and father, as simple as that. But there were no civilians anywhere near us in those mountains, where the green of the pines was as deep as the blue of the sky, and I thought I'd escaped that kind of test, which is more common in war than most people imagine.

"I was much stronger than I am now. . . ."

"You seem fit for your age," Dunaif said.

"Maybe, but when I was young I had volcanic energy in surplus and overflowing. So I volunteered. For what? I was already there. But we were vulnerable. During the day, you could hear our vehicles from a kilometer away, and at night you could not only hear them but see their arc-light on top, probably from a hundred kilometers distant. Their ineffectiveness wasn't a danger just because the enemy might have hidden and subsequently passed through, but because he might have massed to wipe out our small post. Not for any strategic reason, really, but just to kill us, take our weapons, enjoy a small victory.

"I went to my commander and laid this out for him. He was one of those people who at the expense of everything else will take any route to his own success. At the end of my strategic essay — I was a young private — he said, 'What do you recommend, patrolling without armor?'

" 'Yes,' I answered. 'Two or three men at a time, going out lightly armed, silently, waiting in ambush.'

" 'Good,' he said. 'Do exactly that, according to your design. Arm yourself as you wish, go when and where you want, hunt in the forest.'

" 'But I thought you would put me under a sergeant,' I told him.

" 'Oh no no no!' he said. *'You're* in command.'

" 'Me?'

" 'You.'

" 'Of how many men?'

" 'One. You.'

" 'I can't take anyone else?'

" 'No. It's possibly a good idea, but I won't risk others. I relieve you of all duties except what you propose. You'll do that and only that from now forward. Twelve hours in the forest every day, whether in the light or in the dark is up to you. Take the armament you need. Obviously, for what you propose, because we don't have the new ones, one of our radios would be too heavy. So be sure to include a flare or two in case you make contact and need help. You've come up with a good idea. Let's try it.'

"I'd spend twelve hours on my patrols — in daylight, at night, or in combination, setting out, for example, at zero three hundred and returning at fifteen hundred, armed with a submachine gun, six magazines of ammunition, two grenades, a pistol, and a bayonet. Depending upon the season, I carried a water bottle or two, chocolate, and bread. It was most difficult in the snow, sometimes impossible, but the snows were rare and would melt fast. And because the enemy knew less of snow than we did, it suppressed his movement better than if we had had two armies rather than just one.

"Nothing happened, until it did. I was patrolling around the mountain in daylight. This was so long ago — fifty-six years now — that although I remember the smallest pertinent details, I don't remember the season. But it must've been either late fall, winter, or early spring, because I know I was wearing a sweater. I'm certain of that, because I have a memory of the images. Our uniforms were brown, as for most of the country that was the best camouflage, but up on the mountain the one good thing our commander

40

did was get us green fatigues. I could stand in the trees, and if I were still, because the boughs in many places were so dense, you would never see me.

"Although at that point I hadn't run into any infiltrators, I was always alert, especially when I moved, which is when one is most vulnerable. Waiting for someone to pass offers an inestimable advantage. When you move, you announce your presence in sight and sound. I moved cautiously and intermittently. It was a beautiful day, under a blue sky, with a breeze. The ground was quite dry. I had my customary armament, the submachine gun in my hands not quite ready to fire (in case I fell). I was unhappy that day probably because of some argument with other soldiers or officers. There was a lot of resentment and frustration.

"I would move, then stop to look and listen. A few meters, then a few minutes of motionless silence. During one of these pauses I thought I heard whispered conversation. It was hard to be sure that it was not the wind. As I readied the gun, my pulse raced and for a moment it was deafening as blood pounded through my arteries. But I let myself calm down, and moved forward a step or two at a time. Straight ahead, I saw through a mass of pine boughs the shape of two people, their clothing illuminated brightly in the sun. That was stupid. In the woods you have to avoid pools of light. They were talking in low whispers.

"I scanned all around. The last thing I wanted was to be shot or knifed by others whom I hadn't seen while my attention was focused elsewhere. After a while, I was satisfied that the two who were talking were the only ones present. I don't know how long it took, but I moved toward them very slowly, making no sound, until I was on one side of a thick pine and they on the other. One of them was an old Arab, armed with a pistol holstered on a Sam Browne belt. The other was a girl of about twenty, French, at least European, with blue eyes and blond hair. She was wearing a black-and-white checkered *kaffiyah* draped around her neck, the way so many young people in Paris do now. The image will never leave me. I was eighteen. The moment I saw her I not only desired her, I actually fell in love, and it knocked all the fear out of me. How crazy can you be at that age? I don't know, because I think I could do it now."

"Falling in love?"

"Yes, even with someone who wants to kill me. The Arab was sketching a map, the girl drawing a picture of our base. Both would point up at the fortifications, comment, and make adjustments to their work. This was in a military area that was clearly off-limits. I knew they were the enemy, but I couldn't see

42

her as that. I can still feel my attraction to her.

"They were so absorbed in what they were doing that they didn't see me until I was right in front of them. I didn't do anything special, I just walked to where they were. Then, when they saw a French soldier, his submachine gun pointed at them, two meters away, their shock and fear bled into sadness and despair. But the old man was clever and experienced, and his despair vanished when he saw how I was looking at the girl.

"At the same moment that I commanded them, in Arabic and then French, to put their hands in the air, he rose, pulling her up and ahead of him. Though she was still shocked and scared she held tightly onto her pad and pencils. This all happened quickly. He drew his pistol, slowly raised it, and pointed it not quite at me. I took aim at him as best I could, but she covered most of his body. They began to walk backward, occasionally almost tripping.

"Though she was distressed, she was not a hostage. I followed, my finger on the trigger, as it had to be. I was afraid that if I tripped I would kill both of them, and I couldn't see where I was walking, because I couldn't take my eyes off them for even a second. Again and again, I commanded them to stop, but they wouldn't. I wanted to shoot him. He was armed, a spy, disobeying my order. But they were moving, all I had was a fairly inaccurate submachine gun, and the only target was a portion of his head.

"Not only had I resolved to die myself rather than kill an innocent, but although she was hardly an innocent I loved her. I was as unhappy that I wouldn't get to speak to her as I was unhappy that they were getting away. I followed for a while, but then I let them go. To have shot them would have been horrible. I knew what it would be like to see her dying on the ground. Even him. I couldn't kill them.

"You can imagine how distressed I was as I walked back to the post, not at all cautiously, debating whether or not to report it. I did report it and was punished: two months in military prison. Prison was rather difficult, to say the least. But that was nothing compared to what followed, and what has stayed with me ever since.

"While I was imprisoned, the outpost was attacked in force. They came by routes through the forest that had been carefully mapped, undoubtedly by the old man and the girl. Who she was I never knew. French? A *colon*? A German, Swede? I was uneasy from the start about what I had done or not done, but in the attack five soldiers were killed. Some had been my friends, my age or close to it. Their lives stopped in nineteen fifty-eight, or early fifty-nine, I'm not exactly sure. It was much warmer there, and as I've said, my memory of the seasons is confused. Am I not responsible for their deaths? Perhaps they would have died in the attack anyway, even had there been no intelligence, but I can't say that I'm not to blame.

"Sometimes I think that this tendency I have, my sense of causation and feeling of responsibility, is as absurd as when a musician I knew banned me from his car because the right, rear tire blew while I was sitting in the right, rear seat."

"Especially when absurd," Dunaif said, "emotions point the way. To get to the burial chambers in the pyramids you have to follow the most twisted, illogical paths. Nothing you've told me is illogical in context, and what you're telling me obviously needs to be told."

"It weighs upon me and always will. Before I sleep and when I wake are the worst. And there are others, but I don't want any of them not to weigh upon me. It would make the sin worse."

"The sin?" Dunaif asked.

"If not sin, failure. Terrible failure."

"I'm struck," said the doctor, "by how strongly each of these reinforces the others."

"I should have died a long time ago, but I've kept on living."

"The year in which you believe you were obligated to die was . . . ?"

"Nineteen forty-four."

"That has almost surely lent its power to the others, and why you haven't described it — perhaps you can't — except to summarize it, as if it happened not to you but to someone else."

Whatever reaction this solicited was not visible to the psychiatrist. It puzzled him. Jules just went on as if he hadn't heard. "I've told you, or you can deduce from what I've told you, how strongly and quickly I fall in love. Whether it's a fault or not I don't know, but I have friends who've never fallen in love, and I wouldn't want to be them. When I met my wife, I fell so hard I thought I'd gone insane. She died four years ago.

"She was sixty-six, in excellent health, and looked at least fifteen years younger than she was. Though perhaps it was vanity or illusion, both of us felt as if we were in our thirties. When we were young, we could walk fifty kilometers a day in the mountains. Even the summer she died, we crossed the Pyrenees, we swam in freezing-cold streams. My God, if you had seen her in the nude you would think she was thirty. Men of my age — I suppose I'm too old now, so I'd have to say men not quite as old as I am — have mistresses and affairs. They want life. That they seek a younger woman is a biological compulsion even if they don't know it, something which, by the way, does not detract from their just appreciation.

"I would never have done that, but also I had no need to. She was beautiful and lithe until the end. The illness struck without warning, just as if it had struck a younger woman. We were old enough to be prepared in the abstract, and had thought about and talked about one of us dying before the other, but even at sixty-six and seventy it seemed remote. That must happen a lot these days, when old people, sometimes as fit as soldiers, are then, like soldiers, surprised by death.

"We were on the terrace and about to eat. Everything seemed perfectly fine and normal. Suddenly she doubled over with pain in her abdomen. Something like that happens sometimes, if rarely, so she said just to let her lie down. But after half an hour it was so bad I had to carry her to the car. When she got in, she wept. I'm sure she was thinking that she would never come back to the house. That's when I felt a terror I hadn't felt since I was a small child. A terror like that of falling. The first time I jumped from a plane, in the seconds before the static line opened my chute, it was that kind of all-possessing fear.

"It was late enough in the evening so that I tore across Paris all the way from Saint-Germain-en-Laye, where we live, to La Pitié-Salpêtrière. I knew it was serious. I didn't want to waste time and referrals, and our doctor practiced there, as Jacqueline and I were both at Paris-Sorbonne and had lived in the Quartier latin. Now the hospital . . . what can I say? It's for the poor and suffering. You feel it. But our doctor was there. He's unsurpassed. The physicians at La Pitié-Salpêtrière have a constant stream of hard cases, so they're truly expert. But I've always thought that I should have taken her to Switzerland, to some gleaming, quiet, expensive place — unhurried, modern, where the walls are clean even on the outside, which at La Pitié they certainly are not. But at La Pitié it's like battlefield medicine. You get the feeling that anything you bring them they've seen the day before and the day before that.

"And they have, but she never did come back to the house, she never rode in a car again. Everything — her walk to the gurney in front of the emergency entrance, the last time she was under the sky, the last breath of outside air — was the last. She tried hard to get me to go home, but I stayed up with her all night. By noon the next day, the diagnosis came in. They said it was cancer of the pancreas." Here, Jules paused to compose himself. "And they recommended that she go to a hospice.

"We said, no, treat it aggressively, experimentally. Fight. They'd heard this so many times before, and I hated their expressions as they tried to explain to us that it was hopeless. How did they know? They aren't God. They acquiesced: which they will if you press

48

hard enough. And in the next few days I pulled every string I could. Granted, I don't have many strings to pull. I'm just an adjunct in music. Whatever powers I have are not practical. Still, we did have the best doctors and they were as aggressive as we had begged them to be. Not so much Jacqueline. She was half gone, resigned. She was by then frighteningly ethereal, tranquil, unburdened, and of a beauty far more delicate than I had ever seen, perhaps because she was vanishing. It was almost like evaporation. I felt her substance fleeing from her, literally rising, as if she were half in another world or had sworn allegiance to a comforting power of which I knew nothing and could not see. I felt her moving toward it and abandoning me, like transpiration, like snow sublimating in the sun. And I couldn't stop it.

"They operated on her for eight hours. They'd told me that it would be at least four, likely six, and that I shouldn't just sit in the waiting room. Too hard, they said, distract yourself. So I walked. There's the little park there, and miles of corridors. You know the name of the park?"

"I've walked through it many times, but I don't."

"Parc de la Hauteur.

"A psychologist must have told them that yellow, creme, and beige promote health and equanimity. Yellow like sunshine. It's everywhere there. The awnings, shades, and panels of Oncologie Médicale, Division Jacquart are yellow. I went to the Seine. Every time I heard a train whistle in the rail yards of the Gare d'Austerlitz between the hospital and the river, I took it as a sign and a prayer.

"And in quiet, hidden places, I did pray. My style of prayer is my own. The Mignons were Catholics, so I sink to my knees, bow my head, and hold my hands like Jeanne d'Arc — like someone, it occurs to me now, about to be executed. And because I'm a Jew I daven. That's how I prayed. I prayed for my wife, whom I loved like no one else. Against a wall of the rail yards I prayed so hard I trembled. A garbage-truck driver saw me. An African. He stopped the truck because he thought I needed help. Then he saw that I was crying, and he put his arms around me and said, 'No no, everything will come right, everything will come right.' I wouldn't have done that to a stranger near a rail yard. Who's the better man?

"I returned to the hospital, in the dark. The operation was to have started in the morning but there had been emergencies and it was delayed. At nine they came to me. There wasn't much left of me by then. Two of them burst through the doors, their operating gowns open and trailing in the breeze of their forward momentum, their masks dangling.

"They were smiling. A miracle. 'We made

50

the most thorough exploration we could,' one of them said, 'and did quite a few biopsies on the spot. We'll have to wait a few days for absolute confirmation, but we've found nothing. It seems that Madame Lacour has pancreatitis, from which there is no reason that she will not recover.'

"Everything changed as I imagined her recovery. I would do the cooking. It would still be warm enough in September to eat on the terrace. By Christmas we would be swimming in a tropical sea. I thought of Polynesia and determined to spend the money. You know, in that hospital city there are banana trees flanking some of the streets on the eastern side. Right out of Africa or South America, what do they do in the snow? Perhaps the point is that they survive when everyone would think that they would not. Probably that's too subtle, but I got it anyway, and all I could think of was bringing Jacqueline to some warm, breezy, sweet-smelling place with blue-green water. I'm not good at vacations. It's hard to pry me away from Paris, my work, and my routine. I had deprived her of a lifetime of vacations because I was always worried about money and the things I had to do. I'm one of those people, you see, who have perfect attendance records and precise schedules. I don't think I've ever forgotten an appointment or not completed an assignment. What good is that now?

"For two weeks, she recovered in the hospital, but she was never herself. The operation had caused major trauma and damage, and she couldn't eat. Then she began taking liquid meals, and strengthened. I set up everything at home so as to care for her. My prayers had been answered. I would keep her close from then on. We would go to the South Seas, we would sit on the terrace, and she would wear her straw hat, because she didn't like the sun on her face — an aversion that made her skin seem like that of a much younger woman. I, on the other hand, well, look at me.

"The evening before she was to be discharged I ate the dinner she couldn't eat, while she had her dinner through a straw. The doctor had said that when home she could start on rice cereal and gradually proceed back to normal. Having been in the hospital for so long, she was weak but no longer confused. In the days after the operation she had imagined that a wall of her room was a vertical front of agitated green seawater with whitecaps and swells, and that dolphins were leaping from it and falling back — horizontally, as if gravity went sideways rather than up and down. This pleased her. I tried to disabuse her of it, hoping to bring her back and keep her. I didn't want her floating away from me again even if on an exquisite vision. That was a mistake. I should have let her go to the ocean, and I should have been pleased to go with her as far as I was able.

"I had rowed that day. It was my only break. I wanted to keep up my strength, because I felt that we were as much under attack as if we were soldiers in a besieged outpost or sailors in a storm. So I worked hard to keep things going at home and stay healthy. What if I had gotten sick as well? In early September the temperature was perfect, and the water, although not still, had been smooth. When the water is smooth and dark and the current is fast you feel as if you're floating through the air. Especially if the breeze is right and things are quiet, with at best only distant traffic sounds, it's as if you're in another world. I was elated that she was coming home.

"At about eight-thirty in the evening I got up from the chair by her bed in the hospital and began to gather my things. I wanted to get home to finish preparations for her return. Our bedroom had always been austere. We only slept there, rather than, as some do, using it as a retreat. But Jacqueline would be spending a lot of time in it, so to surprise her and make it comfortable I bought a Persian carpet (because she had always disliked the coldness of the parquet), a comfortable chair with an ottoman, an adjustable reading lamp, and one of those big flat televisions. I hadn't yet mounted the television and was somewhat anxious about it because it weighed about forty kilos, so I would have to make sure the bracket was screwed to the studs, and I've never been good at locating them in the wall.

"I was going to pick her up and drive her home the next day, but she was seeing the ocean again, and was distant, which I attributed to exhaustion. I kissed her lightly, straightened, and said almost triumphantly that I would be back in the morning to take her home.

" *'I'm going to die,'* she said. I heard it, but it was as if she hadn't said it. I was very well aware of what had happened, but I continued on as if it had not.

" 'It'll be wonderful at home,' I told her. 'I fixed it up. You'll see. The fall will be beautiful, and in late December we'll go to the Pacific.'

" 'Jules,' she said, in a whisper, looking straight ahead, 'I'm going to die.'

"Operating on a completely different plane, I smiled, kissed her once again, and said 'See you in the morning.' Then I left, happily. Never in my life had I been aware of something and yet totally unable to assimilate it. And never since. I drove across Paris that evening, listening to the radio, dancing in my seat. It was as if I were two different people, each in his own world. I suppressed my terror and grief to live in the illusion of the joy I

54

had expected.

"Seldom have I been so euphoric, and yet all the while I knew. It was like Macbeth, only the opposite, as if a dagger were before me but I couldn't see it. At nine-thirty I was in the middle of putting in the bracket for the television, when the phone rang. They made sure it was me, and then they — a nurse, someone whose voice I did not recognize — said, 'I'm sorry to tell you, but your wife has passed away.'

"I was holding a drill in my hand — a drill. The shock was no less than if I had been shot at close range. And yet I managed to call a taxi — I could not have driven — I managed to melt into the back seat, to tell the driver the address, to state to him that I didn't wish to speak. I gave him fifty Euros and didn't even turn around when he left his cab and pursued me to hand over the change.

"They allowed me to stay in the room with her for a while." For a long moment, Jules was again unable to speak, but then he went on. "They had crossed her hands in front of her and tied them together with gauze so her arms wouldn't fall to the side. And they used the same type of gauze to prevent her jaw from dropping. It was tied on her head so that she looked like the way people with a toothache used to be characterized when I was young. The nurses and the residents were not old enough to have seen that, unless they read old magazines. The knot was at the top of her head with two wings of white gauze sticking out into the air. It made her look like a rabbit. There should be a better way, when someone dies, to do what they did. They shouldn't have done that to her. She wouldn't have liked it.

"I kissed her, and, of course, she stayed still. Just as I had known and not known, I was split then, as I have been ever since, between wanting to follow her wherever that might be, and wanting to fight for life so that she would continue to live in my memory. I suppose the balance in the struggle between the two is what brought me here, because the state that it leaves me in is difficult to bear. But the fact remains — and although not a day goes by when I don't dwell on it, not a second goes by when one way or another it does not run my life from an impregnable fortress within me — the fact remains that my wife, whom I love above all, told me she was dying, saw me walk away, and died alone. How can I ever make up for that? I can't."

"I understand," Dunaif said, "why you might be set on punishing yourself for the rest of your life, and I'm sure that even if you don't know it you've found many ingenious and imaginative ways of doing so."

"I'd have to punish myself for eternity, and still that would be insufficient. They put a sheet over her and wheeled her away. They

56

wouldn't let me get into the elevator. Yet the doctor was kind, and said he'd stay with me as long as I needed him.

"When I left, it had started to rain. I didn't know what I was doing. I wandered around La Pitié-Salpêtrière for hours — as you know, it's like a small city — until in the middle of the night, without any plan whatsoever, I found myself on the Rue Bruant, leaning against the hideous, rough stone wall of the mortuary. It's made of slag. The edges are sharp. I stayed there, in the rain, until morning, my hands pressed against the wall until they bled, because she was on the other side and I didn't want to leave her. How can I have done what I did?"

After a long pause, Dunaif asked, "Have you thought of suicide?"

"Is that a suggestion?"

Dunaif could not help but laugh, however sadly. "No, just the logical question."

"I can't count the times — whenever I look down at a river from a bridge. But I'm too strong a swimmer. I'd have to shoot myself before falling in, and having spent several years with the keen objective of not being shot, that's something I'd never do. I detest drugs. I'm too neat and orderly to slit my wrists. You've seen what happens to the bathtub and the floor? It's horrible."

"I haven't seen."

57

"In the cinema."

"Yes, in films. But is it just the method that deters you?"

"No. I'm immune. I tried it once, when I was seven. I thought I'd find my parents, and I was unhappy. In the house in Paris the attic was unfinished: my cousins dried their clothes up there. I took some clothesline, made it into my notion of a hangman's noose, threw the line over a huge beam, slipped the noose over my neck, mounted a chair, and, with hardly any hesitation, jumped off. But it was always so moist in the attic that the line had rotted and it broke. When I hit the floor, that was the last of my suicide attempts. They're out of the question, period. If I haven't done anything of that nature by now, believe me, I'm not about to start."

"It's off the table?"

"Entirely."

"Are you sure?"

"Absolutely. No suicide, just loyalty. To them all. Loyalty is the elixir that makes death easy, but it's also the quality that gives life purpose. I don't mean to speak in epigrams, but I'm French: I can't help it."

It wasn't so much from what Jules said as in his expression that Dunaif knew his not-quite-patient was not in fact suicidal.

"Besides, I can't leave now. My grandson, a baby. . . ."

Dunaif was used to newly divorced or

unemployed patients who then made the discovery that they were depressed; to wives and husbands who had fallen in love with an outsider and could not decide what to do; and to intellectuals who had thought themselves into dark and narrow caves. This was different.

As if to stall or avoid, Jules looked around and read the room.

"Another death?" Dunaif asked.

"I hope not."

"But?"

"It's not up to me, not up to my prayers, not up to anyone except an immense tangle of facts, events, processes, mysteries — from the behavior of individual cells, compounds, molecules, and atoms, to the embrace of a mother or a nurse, to the scudding of clouds above a hospital where the life of a child hangs in the balance.

"If you think it either a matter of pure science, or of prayer, you're wrong. It isn't just that a treatment will be applied, like fixing the brakes of an automobile, or just that God will decide, like a judge or a king, or just a matter of chance. It's all these things, and many that are hidden. It's the operation of the whole, in more dimensions than we know, that must flow together in perfect harmony and with perfect rhythm. On occasion, perfection like that is apparent. It overflows in Bach and Mozart and it's what's in miracles, epiphanies, and great events. It's what made Jeanne d'Arc sink to her knees. It's what made Dante see light so bright it was all-consuming. The same visions possessed the prophets. The age we live in would call it madness."

"I don't think it is," Dunaif said. "It's just that so few are touched by it that others have no choice but to call it so. It would be madness, however, and you would be mad, if what you've just told me were simply free-floating, and had no object."

"It has an object," Jules told him. "My daughter's only child, a boy two years old, has leukemia. At first, he would scream and cry and try to wiggle away when they approached the hospital. Then whenever he was taken to the car. They had to tranquilize him. As things progressed, his struggle to get away would quickly tire him and he would sleep. Now, he no longer protests. I've prayed that I would die so that he can live, but it doesn't work that way. I know, because I received that instruction when my wife died. But, if I could, do you know how easy it would be to give my life for his?"

"How far along is it?"

"Not that far, but the prognosis is not good. They soften it for the mother. Still, she knows. When he got sick, she had to leave nursing school. She knew the implications."

"I understand."

"I'm in good health. I'm seventy-four, but I want so much to join my wife. If what she knows — or doesn't know — is oblivion, I'd like to know it, too. Why must I have the strength of a twenty-four-year-old, and this child be affected so? To see him with the tubes coming out of his tiny body. . . . He's had so many blood draws he's not afraid of them anymore, and he's two years old. His mother and father. . . . His mother is my child. They'll be destroyed. What can I do?"

"Perhaps nothing."

"Yet again?"

"Yet again."

"I blame myself because I have very little money. Were I rich, I could bring him to the United States, to Texas to the MD Anderson Center; or to Cleveland, the Cleveland Clinic; or the Mayo Clinic; or Harvard; or Johns Hopkins. They're the best. Kings, sheiks, and presidents go there. America has almost a lock on Nobel Prizes in medicine. When I was younger I just didn't think that I should work to get money so that if something like this were to happen I'd have the means."

"We have excellent medicine here. You shouldn't hold it against yourself that the child is in France."

"Not like there. And in a hard case it's the margin that can make the difference. The fraction of effort, the new treatment, the inspired physician might be the saving grace. In medicine, I suppose, there's also, as in music, a straining for perfection as if to call down the presence of God, or, if you have another nomenclature, beauty, mercy, and grace.

"But no, I was lost in music. It was enough for me. I never fought for position or cared about money, I didn't even complete my doctoral degree. All I cared for was the music itself."

"What, exactly, do you do?"

"I teach in the faculty of music, Sorbonne. Cello, piano. A *Maître,* not a professor. I know theory but I teach to the sound and the emotion, which places me very low on the academic ladder. Not only that, but unless someone moves to adjourn, the committee meetings last until a bunch of skeletons are sitting around a table. I'm the one who always breaks first, and though everyone else is grateful that I do, it makes me the blackest of the black sheep. I can't stand the bureaucracy and the politics, but I help my students become masters of their instruments and love the music. I'm paid poorly, and always have been. I compose, but my music isn't modern and isn't in demand — to say the least. The flock of birds all bent so easily and at once both this way and that. But I kept on straight, and now I'm quite alone. A failure is how I would put it.

"If I'd had the discipline to be even a professor — not a tycoon — I might now have enough to help the child. His name is Luc. I've thought of robbing a bank: I was once, and in some ways am forever, a soldier. I'll bet I could do it. But what if someone were hurt or killed? And, soldier or not, I'm old."

"Please don't rob a bank," Dunaif said. "It seldom works out well."

"You needn't worry. But this is my last chance. I really would do something like that. I would. He's home now, but he was in the hospital for two weeks, and I couldn't visit him, because of bone marrow transplants, and infection. . . ."

Dunaif nodded.

"The next time I was allowed to visit, a nurse brought him to us. His hair was gone, his face swollen, the cheeks very red. She held him aloft in her arms, and as she walked toward us he saw his parents and me, and he squealed in delight. Pure pleasure, joy, as if nothing were wrong.

THE INSURANCE SALESMAN
ARMAND MARTEAU

The little satisfactions in daily life — a cup of tea, the swirling snow, Christmas lights on a dim afternoon, a bird singing at the end of summer — can be unavailing if they take place within a crown of failure. As Jules Lacour was running out of options, Armand Marteau was running out of excuses. It was true that many potential clients would stay abroad or at the beaches well into September, and some — the richest, the oldest, the least anxious — even into October. Most people, however, even in the rarefied client base that he was assigned to serve, wanted to be and were in Paris shortly after the end of August.

August itself was full of hints of early fall, and by September the sun was low enough to make possible the ethereal blue sky that was characteristic of the city when the sun was not so much overhead as in summer, a kind of north light but in all directions. The air was crisp as often as not. Storms that blew in from Normandy and the west fought the blue with huge thunderheads rolling upward in gray and black. In the minutes before they arrived, the air they charged and their distant yellow lightning made Paris the most exciting city in the world. Everything that in summer had been an obstacle suddenly took on new life in air that was cool and promising.

The rich had gone home or to their offices and were in the mood to purchase and invest. Yet, having sold only one small contract in August, and although his co-workers were now as busy as ever, there was nothing for Armand Marteau at the beginning of September. He was so anxious about his job that he arranged for his wife to call him several times a day so as to fake sales conversations — "I would be happy, as you request, to contact you upon your return to Paris in October." — and he spent hours tapping at his computer and carefully reading old dossiers that he had surreptitiously put in the red cardboard jackets that meant *pending*.

So much of his income was in commission that the corpulent *pater familias* and his wife had begun to eat less, and the whole family had given up excursions, movies, and dessert. They would do without almost anything for the sake of school supplies and decent clothes for the children. This was more than a matter of pride. For the Marteau children the only exit from the gray and dirty *banlieue*, where one could not safely venture out at night, was education. Had Armand gone on assistance he would have been allowed several hundred Euros a month more than he was taking in by trying to sell insurance to Parisians who would disappear in August. But no one in his family had ever been on the dole, and the dole seemed to him to be a kind of death.

His father, a farmer in Epaignes, thought that anyone behind a desk in Paris had an illegitimate lock on success and could by decree dictate prices and shares, whereas he himself was always at the mercy of the sun, the soil, and wind that blew in from the sea. Which is why Armand, who had been an unusually good student with a ready talent for math, had left the farm and now was on his way to a glass building in La Défense, a high tower in which the windows did not open and he didn't have one anyway, although he could see some sky and some daylight across the floor and over the heads of a score of brokers bobbing at their desks.

The huge, pale *place* at the center of La Défense was like a desert. Armand Marteau would look down from the outside windows when he was near them in hallways and the offices of his seniors, and note that because the dominant color of dress in Paris was black — the color of retreat, protection, closing in on oneself, hardness, cynicism, hiding, and anger — the people moving across the windblown, open space seemed to scurry like ants. The speed at which they moved relative to their apparent size and the distance between him and them was undeniably ant speed. And as they were office workers like him, loosed momentarily from the giant ant hills, in one of which he himself was trapped, this was not a happy reflection, as tiny at a distance as it might be, of his whale-like self.

The morning train slowly filled up with people who, because they knew that other people thought they did not belong in France, looked at blond and blue-eyed Armand as if he were the enemy. He glanced back, convinced by what he saw that they, even if born in France, might choose to be forever alien. Were they friendly and in good spirits, it was easy for him to accept them without qualification. But so often they were oppressed, sullen, tired, angry, and in despair, just like him. And so often they seemed automatically hostile to him, a giant, ruddy farmer who would stare back at them in puzzlement. Their eyes seemed to burn, whereas his, he knew, were as cool and transparent as aquamarine.

At the office were plenty of North and sub-Saharan Africans, but they were kinder and friendlier to him than most of their "French" counterparts, who said that for Armand Marteau the best part of the day was the sandwich — a double cut, because of his weight and

67

because he couldn't afford to go out with anyone to a restaurant or even a café, which they did every day without fail. When he first heard the epithets he had heard many times since, such as hippo, whale boy, and elephantus, he had laughed along with them; but nothing followed, no flattery, sympathy, self-deprecation, or inclusion. It was deeply hurtful, for they sat by him all day, and they said these things with neither affection nor respect.

The world is full of men and women with souls like swallows and bodies like buffaloes, and, for no good reason, in the end it is much more likely that the soul will have followed the body than the body will have followed the soul. In between is the tragedy of happiness and delicacy sinking into a sea of slights. For a woman it is far worse than for a man, and had Armand been a woman he would have suffered even more or perhaps given up long before.

But giving up would mean many things, including a retreat to the farm, which in its present state could not support six. And he had no savings with which to expand it. A neighboring farmer had already sold out, and from their house the senior Marteaux saw not only plains of wheat and hay but, less than a kilometer distant, a truck park and warehouse (the distribution center for a hypermarket), with lights that blazed from dusk to dawn. Once there had been camps of Roman soldiers on the same spot, the berms still visible, and their lights had been oil lamps that would have been lovely as they flickered in the distance like fireflies.

Although Normandy was beautiful and was what he knew, and he loved the rain sweeping in from the sea and disappearing as it was chased by sunlight through sparkling mist, he hated the milking before dawn, the lowing of cows leaving for slaughter, the ever-presence of manure, hosing off his boots many times a day, the humidity, uncertainty, cold, and strain.

But the city, which his father thought was escape and relief, had proved in its own way just as difficult. His train whisked him past streets where he could not set foot for fear of his life. Salesmen at his company were not allowed to wear the relaxed, almost universal blue blazer of Paris, but had to spend the day in suit and tie, a torture for someone of Armand's size and weight. La Défense was not like Paris anyway, but just a bleak machine fraying with wear. He hated it. Riding up in the elevator, he prayed for a client or any new business that would take him out into the trees or along the boulevards, into a room, a house, a mansion with a garden. It was becoming more and more unlikely. None of his colleagues referred business to him as they did to each other. Although he could not prove it, even the switchboard operator seemed hardly ever to route new calls to him according to his just share.

Long before, the director had come down hard on the saying of "Moo" when Armand appeared on the floor, but when the elevator doors parted and the salesmen glanced at him, turning their heads like a school of fish, he heard it even if it did not sound.

Maroon acoustic panels floated like space-ships above the work floor. For a Norman whose world had been open to the winds, maroon was a color as claustrophobia-inducing as black. Perhaps lurid purple, the paralytic color of death, would have been worse, but maroon had all the charm of dried blood.

It's difficult to pretend you're working for eight hours every day when there isn't any work to be done, you're in full view of forty or fifty hyperactive drones who don't like you or who are at least made uncomfortable by your presence, and you are both very tall and fat, so that although your desk might conceivably hide behind you, you cannot conceivably hide behind it. The best part of Armand's day was the forty-five minutes when he could bolt from the building and walk to the Seine to be near trees and water. There he would sit, his back to the massif of glass and steel behind him, and eat his lunch alone.

Lunch itself, his chief ally, was in the right-side bottom drawer of the desk, sending messages of friendliness, loyalty, and support. How often he would glance down at that drawer for comfort. He wished he had a puppy to hold. A stuffed animal might do, but he would never hear the end of it. Bathroom breaks were wonderful, although he couldn't take too many or he would never have heard the end of it. Out of the presence of others, he could breathe. And before he went up to the office he would stand in the enormous train station beneath La Défense and stare at a fruit store. Inhaling deeply, he would imagine he was in the tropics, where no one hated him, and he was safe. When he tried to convey to his wife, a much more social person, the extent of his suffering in the office, she could not comprehend it.

"You exaggerate," she had said over dinner in the little box within the horrid box of concrete warrens in which they lived, entombed in gray, smelling the smells of a hundred kitchens cooking, and hearing screams at night. "They can't be thinking of you all the time."

"Only when I move. They forget me when I stay still, I think. It's like hunting. Anything in the forest that stays still almost certainly will be unnoticed."

"Unless," his wife said, "it's shocking pink or international orange."

71

"Quite so."

"They have their troubles, too," she said. "Why would they be thinking of you?"

"Because I'm an irritation, a recreation, a work in progress, a source of constant entertainment. My desk is directly under a spotlight and in the center of the floor, so I loom above them like a fountain in Las Vegas, or a giant butter sculpture. I'm telling you, there are eyes upon me, and twitters. There's hardly anyone I can talk to. True, not all are hostile, but except for a few no one is kind. They're like the men in the trading pits, who make jokes about the handicapped, the Holocaust, and plane crashes. We all compete with each other like gladiators. If you don't meet the quota you're out, and if everyone meets the quota they raise it. With the economy as it is they're shrinking the department. Everyone is afraid of losing his job. It's a bunch of snakes."

"We can go back to the farm."

"It won't support six."

"Still," Madame Marteau said, "clients will come. You'll see. You'll have clients."

"You have no clients," said Edgar Auban, Armand Marteau's chief and the director of the division. Auban was polite. Everyone was polite, with an edge. They mocked him, but not for nothing had they named him hippopotamus and elephantus. Everyone knows that when the poor, ungainly, pathetic hippopotamus finally becomes enraged, as he runs at you, fat shaking, steam-shovel mouth open, log-stump teeth arrayed, there isn't much you can do. So, although you cannot dismiss from your mind his muddy ugliness, and your very expression as you behold him is a taunt, you are always made anxious by his powers, and you keep your distance. In Armand's case, it was a resentful politesse.

"Well," said Armand, staring over Auban's head the way boys called into a headmaster's office stare at something — their feet, the floor, a pencil sharpener — as they are reprimanded, "I have *some* clients." He was staring not at a pencil sharpener but out the window at the rising terrain of Saint-Germain-en-Laye in the distance.

"One." Auban held up his right index finger like a cop stopping traffic. "In August. The next-worst associate had five. How can you have one? You know, there's no law against selling insurance in August." Auban shuffled some papers on his desk and looked up. "Or in the summer. In June and July you had three, total. Three? Gilbert went to Nice in August. He had a very nice time. He told me. He went out on yachts, slept with three beautiful women. . . ."

"At the same time?"

"I don't know. That's irrelevant. He swam, he ate glorious seafood, got a tan, and sold twenty-three contracts!"

"Well, he's our best performer."

"Do you understand that he doesn't sell so many contracts because he's our best performer, he's our best performer because he sells so many contracts? Do you comprehend the difference?"

"It's subtle."

"No it isn't."

"Maybe not."

"Look," said Auban, "I'm forced to this."

Armand knew a blow was coming, and felt very sad. All he could think about was his children. He mustn't fail them, and yet. . . .

"Your August performance was the absolute minimum. A five-hundred-thousand-Euro contract, with an unusually small premium."

"He was young and ridiculously healthy, like a saber-tooth tiger."

"You're a contract employee. If in September you don't meet the minimum, you'll go off salary in October. You can stay through the end of the year — commissions only — but if you don't sell enough to go back on salary by the thirty-first of December, I'm afraid we'll have to give your desk to someone else."

"Oh," said Armand, lips trembling.

"Marteau, they want me to reduce the size of our shop. They specifically identified you. What I got you was four months of probation. There's a lot of pressure on us. You know, they got killed in trading derivatives. The government bailed them out in America. There's so much blood on the floor there, you can't even imagine."

"Who are 'they'? Who identified me?"

"London, New York."

"But we're one of so many subsidiaries. They concern themselves with an individual salesman? With me?"

"They have long reports and people who go blind going over them. Probably there were many lists, and probably someone took twenty seconds to look at one and flicked with his pencil a line or check next to your name, without either looking at your name or knowing your name, but just taking in, for a fraction of a second, the numbers to the right."

"Just like that? Someone flicks his pencil and I, my wife, my son, my daughter . . . are cast to the waves — with the flick of a pencil?"

"Monsieur Marteau, all life is like that. Someone checks his watch, his car veers across the line, and a family is wiped out. A mechanic applies the wrong torque to a nut, which insufficiently tightens the seal, which allows fuel to leak, which starts a fire that crashes a plane and kills three hundred people. God flicks his pencil, a cell goes wrong, and the story of your life ends. This is just a job. Granted, other jobs are hard to find these days, but they exist, and, who knows, you might just get lucky."

"You mean while I'm still here?"

"Yes. There are sixty-six million people in France, each and every one subject to the flick of many a pencil, each and every one potentially in need of life and disability insurance. Sell it to them! That's what we do."

FRANÇOIS EHRENSHTAMM,
PHILOSOPHE

François Ehrenshtamm, *philosophe,* had a trick that for the sixty years since he was fourteen he had used to seize the audiences of his lectures, speeches, monologues, dialogues, and his dominating appearances on panels. He would stare at the crowds as if he would not be able or would choose not to speak, for long enough, sometimes minutes, to hypnotize them with suspense. Then he would explode into brilliance they would never forget. If he were on a panel, it didn't matter who else was on stage. Like a magician, Ehrenshtamm would make them disappear. Those unwise enough to have a go at him would end up as mute as swans, mere decorations on either side of the ferocious, passionate engine that was Ehrenshtamm. His effect on the imaginations of his listeners was like that of an arsonist in an excelsior factory.

The trick? First, it is important to understand that though charisma often masquerades as brilliance, the two seldom go hand in hand. With the passage of time the charismatic disappoints as soon as, like an egg, his smooth surface is pierced and broken by his dullard essence seeking a way out. But Ehrenshtamm, Jules Lacour's closest friend, was as charismatic and intelligent in combination as anyone could be. Although neither as smart as Einstein nor as charismatic as Rasputin, he was a lot more charismatic than the former and far smarter than the latter.

This and his bee-like industry enabled him at a very early age to secure for himself the premier position at *Sciences Po,* the *Major,* and later an unprecedented dual professorship there and at the École Normale Supérieure, followed by a dozen well-received tomes that passed academic muster and were devoured by the intellectual public as well, election to the Academy (of course), and an electronic ubiquitousness across Europe that made his face familiar not only in French and Danish living rooms but at German truck stops, Italian Alpine huts, and Greek poolside bars. His books alternated in fours: totally inaccessible philosophical works such as his *Fluxion and Élan Vital in Bergson's Dissent from the Homogenous Medium;* much less puzzling tomes on Voltaire or Bastiat; serious political books addressing the most controversial questions, such as his *To Be French, The*

Meaning of Liberal Nationality; and looser, best-selling, inflammatory works such as *What's the Word for Stupid People Who Think They're Smart? There Isn't One But There Should Be Many.* He covered the waterfront, and traversed the spectrum.

Phenomenal energy, zero reticence, extraordinary memory, faultless courage, consistent accuracy, mesmerizing delivery, and high eloquence. He read at least one book every day, not superficially, and he could turn out a captivating essay during a taxi ride from his house to whichever was the first of his scheduled interviews. He might have been wealthy but for the stunted scale of monies in the intellectual world, his four ex-wives, one current wife almost forty years younger than he, and seven children, including a newborn, one at Harvard paying full tuition, one living on the beach in Goa ("Please send 120 Euros"), one very neurotic banker, one ophthalmologist, and so on.

He never had enough money, a condition that led him not only to a constant frenzy of activity but actually to borrowing small sums from Jules Lacour, whose income was not even a tenth of his, but who spent very little and saved at a rate that though hardly possible given his earnings still had not led to much accumulation. Nothing like Ehrenshtamm, Jules was rather like the friend of Yeats whose work had come to nothing.

Although he had composed steadily, little had been performed, and that only long ago. The rest had found its way onto several shelves of neat red binders as motionless as the dead. There was no money in what he did, and, despite its unquestionable power, the final product — music sounded out — whether as a result of teaching students or his own playing, was born into the air only instantly to die.

The relative positions of the two men in society didn't impress an imbalance upon their friendship, which had begun when they were children who knew innocently the true value of things and one another, and that over time the strains of living — like cataracts, or storm tides that smother low-lying green fields in floods of gray — were the cause of a gradual blindness to life and color. When Jules and François were together, they were sometimes as fresh and full of enthusiasm as boys, even though these days they enjoyed not only their left-over and intermittent vitality but, as well, the quiet resignation that comes from approaching the end of the line.

Ehrenshtamm's trick was simply that he saved the best for last. It was most important, he maintained, to release the *frappe de foudre,* the lightning strike, just before the close. This was appreciated not merely because one tended to remember conclusions, but because it was the opposite of life itself, which closes most times in gradual loss rather than in a strong light flashing through golden dusk.

Justifying his technique, he would say, "A dim light at the end does little to illumine the profound darkness that follows. A lightning flash, however, has intriguing potential even in relation to eternity. After all, in theory, light can travel infinitely far."

In the early evening, as soon as Jules got home after rowing, François Ehrenshtamm called and Jules went out again. François' new wife and baby were in Biarritz, where he would join them in a day or two. "I have to stay until Thursday afternoon," he said. "In the morning I have an interview with Polish television. The Poles are serious, capable, and we've always underestimated them. Anyway, my books sell extremely well there, and God knows, I need the money. Would you like to have dinner? I can't come out to Saint-Germain-en-Laye: I have a radio interview later this evening — Japan — but we could meet in Neuilly if you can do it."

In travel time, Neuilly was equidistant from both of them, as François lived amid the hives of the Sorbonne. Although Jules was tired, he said, "I can."

On the Rue de Château in Neuilly was a restaurant that was inexpensive and not at all the kind of place where people looked around to see who else was there. François often succeeded in avoiding recognition, especially when with his wife and the baby. They were great camouflage, as were ordinary business clothes, and doing without the philosopher's garb of tortoise-shell glasses, open shirt, velvet jacket, and wild hair. Looking around the first time he had abandoned his spectacles, he said, "Everything's a nauseating blur, but I don't think my own mother would recognize me. My glasses are as much a trademark as Jane Mansfield's *poitrine.*"

Jules pulled out onto the A14, going against traffic. The lights flashing by in the tunnel were soporific, and he was grateful to exit in speed over the Seine, in a tight two lanes with no shoulders, and glass panels that made him feel that he was rocketing through a pneumatic tube. This road, he thought, will be ideal for self-driven cars, which, thank God, will not proliferate until after he's dead. Jules had no desire to see a world where one was guided by machines rather than vice versa.

Then to the N13 and exit into Neuilly, where the pace had quieted and the lights had come out. It was difficult to find a parking place after people had come home and packed the streets with their cars. But he found a space, locked the car — how delightful to walk away from one's automobile — and went to meet François.

The restaurant seated only twenty-five or thirty. It was quiet and dark, perfect for

François, in a corner, reading a newspaper a few centimeters from his face, his back to the other customers. "Do you ever just sit and think, or sit and not think?" Jules asked as he sat down across from him.

"Not in a restaurant. If you sit alone in a restaurant and fail to distract yourself they think you're a madman about to rob them or blow up the Eiffel Tower."

"How do you know?"

"You'll recall that I used to work in a restaurant. I've seen it from the other side."

A waiter came over. François ordered fish and the various recommended accompaniments. Jules asked for *Boeuf Bourguignon* which he (and François, were he to have done the same) pronounced in the accent of Reims rather than Paris, although either of them could have done it the other way. "Only a half portion, please," Jules said, "a salad, and *vin ordinaire,* white."

The waiter made a slight bow and left. "White?" François asked.

"I don't drink red anymore. You know that."

"I haven't noticed. Why?"

"My teeth."

"Something wrong with them?"

"I don't pretend to be young, but there's no reason to have stained teeth. That's not an artifact of age but of wine. And I've never drunk coffee or tea, or smoked, so I had to cut out only one substance . . . and certain berries."

"Open your mouth," François commanded. He did. His teeth were quite white.

"Now you open yours." François did. He looked like a pumpkin.

Both men, friends since they were six, stared at one another. A diner to the left who had seen them opening their mouths doubted they were sane.

"It won't be that long now, François." François knew exactly the antecedent of *it.*

"Every human being in the history of the world, Jules, except those who are or were younger than we are, has been in the same situation, and everyone has been able to handle it one way or another. You can't get kicked off the bus because you're afraid. You'll ride all the way to your last stop wherever it is that you get off."

"I know, but my regrets alone easily overshadow that kind of speculation and philosophy."

"I know, too. I hate philosophy," said François, France's leading *philosophe.* "I'm supposed to be a philosopher, but I believe that if you properly balance sensation and thought, disallowing either to dominate, that's all you need. To be alive is not to be systematized, and to be systematized is not to be alive. Regrets such as what?"

"That I've spent my life in pursuit of art rather than money. It was self-indulgent and

84

I enjoyed it day after day. Once you become really fluent as a musician even the continuous work to stay proficient is rapture. It follows you. After you finish playing, you can hear it all day and in your dreams, in perfect fidelity, but something is missing. Riding home on the train, walking, working in the garden, the music is there, and it keeps you in a high emotional state even though the essence of music is that it, too, is mortal. Because when it stops, its real power disappears. Although the pleasures were pure, in my immersion I was almost a sybarite. Music is like the inconclusive testimony of a temporary visitor to a wondrous world. As it plays, you have everything, but when it stops you are left with nothing."

"Which is exactly like life itself. Jules, you live in one of the most magnificent houses in Paris. You were always healthy and strong, and Jacqueline was wonderful and stunningly beautiful. Why would you care about money?"

"The house is not mine, as you know."

"Yes, but for forty years. . . ."

"Soon to be over, and I can't say that I'm not used to the place. Jacqueline is gone. I'm on half-time in the faculty and that's charity that won't last. Once, I was animated by ambition. Not only have I failed, but part of the reason ambition has fled is that the people I had wanted to impress are dead. Though my own stature is in no way increased, their places have been taken by midgets, idiots, and mediocrities. Impressing such people, even if I could, would be worse than failure."

"You exaggerate as usual. Granted, one can exaggerate in art, though different ages set different limits, but you can't justifiably exaggerate in fact or sense. Since you're trying to talk sense, you mustn't overdo it."

"I'm not overdoing it. When civilization turned a corner or two, I didn't. So some people look back and pity me. But it isn't that I couldn't make the turn. I *wouldn't* make the turn. I'd rather be a rock in the stream, even if submerged, than the glittering scum on the surface, desperately hurrying to be washed away. No offense, François."

"No offense taken. I like being glittering scum. But why, Jules? Why the attraction to loss? Because that's what it is."

"Loyalty."

"A recipe for dying."

"There's joy in dying the way you want, by your own standard, in faith to what you see as self-evident. Enough joy to lift you over death as it comes at you. Though this applies, unfortunately, to Islamist martyrs, it also applies to us."

"Where exactly is it written?"

"It's written, François, *in* exactly, in music. That's how I know. But it's okay. When I was young I wasn't, like many others, foolish enough to think that I or those I favored could remake the world. Now that I'm old I'm not disappointed that the world is un-remade as once I would have liked to remake it. Revolutions, if not started by the inexperienced young and finished by their psychopathic elders, are started by psychopathic young and finished by psychopathic elders."

"You would prefer not to have benefitted from Seventeen Eighty-Nine?"

"Maybe political evolution would have been less catastrophic: no terror, no Napoleon, no emperors, who knows?"

"Fine, but Jules, money? Why suddenly?" François had what Jules thought was a strange and inexplicable smile.

"Luc."

"He has the best medical care."

"No. That's not guaranteed. I want to try America. It could mean his life. I want Cathérine and her husband to have the option of leaving France, and not as poor refugees either. Now Jews are kidnaped, tortured, and murdered here. Dieudonné mocks the Holocaust. Jewish students must hide their religion in school. The far right, far left, and the Arabs have found a common enemy in us. Our synagogues are desecrated and our shops are burned. I don't have to tell you that my accountant son-in-law is Orthodox. He's spat upon in the street. You know what happened to my parents, and I know what happened to yours."

"It's not that bad. Hollande has been a champion of the Jews, up to a point — the president of France! I write and speak against anti-Semitism, and although I've been shouted down and threatened, that can be the result of holding any political opinion in public. Maybe I shouldn't show you this, given your frame of mind, but maybe I should, given that I don't take these things as seriously as you do."

"Show me what?"

François pulled from his pocket a folded, two-page print-out from the internet. As Jules opened it, the first thing he saw was a picture of François in a montage with an enormous Star-of-David clothing patch in sickly yellow, with *Juif* in the center. In the background was a menorah and the flag of Israel. In the picture, François was smiling: his likeness had been taken from a book jacket photograph. The caption was, *His yellow star is his skin.*

Strangely enough, the first thing Jules said was, "You have a color printer?"

"The department has one. Doesn't yours?"

"We have really good music software. We don't have a color printer. What is this?"

"Read it. It's only two pages."

Jules began to read. "The Breton Liberation Front? France is oppressing Brittany?" As he read, he didn't know whether to be fearful or dismissive. It began, "The Jew

88

François Ehrenshtamm, who has the timidity of joining a French name with one that stinks of the Ashkenazi sewage effluent," and went on to call Judaism "a syndicate of crime," and "a biological insanity tolerated for no reason by Aryan-Christian civilization." Throughout, it referred to François' body, associating it with filth. Jules stopped reading after the paragraph that stated: "Ehrenshtamm should be a vegetarian. Imagine a digestive tract at the summit of which is his grotesque Jew head. No animal, even the most vile, would deserve to exit the sphincter of this Hebrew filth that tries to pass as human."

"Perhaps you should put them in the undecided column."

"I've had worse."

"Their hatred is visceral. They see us as a kind of infection. These are the people who have a horror of sharing a swimming pool with blacks. They think we and blacks are irredeemably, physically disgusting and dirty. In the army once I shared a bunker with two soldiers who, as the night wore on, went from one thing to another: We control the banks. We make wars. We shrink from war. We're communists. We're fascists. We betrayed France. We betrayed Germany. We always come out on top. We're impoverished vermin. We cheat. We're greedy. They told me that you could always tell a Jew because he was so clean. An hour later they were going on about how we're so filthy and disgusting."

"What did you do?"

"Nothing. It made me feel helpless and sad, because otherwise they were perfectly nice people."

"But you see, Jules, these are just the crazies and the idiots. They've always been around, and always will be. You mustn't be despondent. Let them spark. There isn't sufficient tinder. I really don't think we're in a replication of the thirties."

"Not yet, maybe never, and I myself would never think of leaving. But in the years to come I would want Cathérine and David — with a healthy child — to be able to go, if they want or if they must, to a safer place."

"Surely there's no more lovely a place in its life and art than France?"

"But safer."

"Where?"

"I don't know. Switzerland? America? New Zealand?"

"New Zealand. I hope they like Chinese food. The country is totally incapable of defending itself."

"No place has to be the last stop. You go where you can live."

"And that's why you regret not having been a businessman?"

"Had I been, my life might not have been as ecstatic, but now I'd have the means. I'll leave behind a shelf of compositions that no one cares about and no one will ever play or hear. Instead, I could have helped them."

"Can't you ask Shymanski? He's been your patron for forty years."

"I can't. He's ninety-four. His sons, who've hated me since I first tried to teach them piano, have taken hold of all his assets. Physically, he's almost at the end, though when he's not in too much pain his mind is sharp. The boys — they're half reptile — have their own places in the Sixteenth, and think Saint-Germain-en-Laye is for old people. They're moving him to the villa in Antibes and selling the house."

"When?"

"I don't know. They announced no date. He protests. Nothing to be done about it. They're vermin come home to roost. They have heavily pomaded black hair down to their shoulders. They drive Ferraris and are married to ultra-long-legged Russian fortune hunters. These women are so tall your eyes are level with their navels, and they wear ermine hats, dresses with huge cutouts, and several kilos of ugly jewelry. If you can catch a glimpse of their faces way up on the tower of their astoundingly thin bodies, you see two eyes as blue and vacant as opals, set into heads the size of grapefruits, without the charm of an Eskimo dog that pulls a sled."

"I take it you don't like them."

"No, I don't care about them. They're just accessories. But the brothers are billionaire, adult, juvenile delinquents. They have lots of girlfriends but they keep their perfectly vacant wives because they're, to quote one of the brothers speaking about the mother of his own spawn, 'explosively fuckable.' "

"They sound like it," François said.

"You like grapefruit? I can get you their numbers," Jules replied.

"I thought the old man was married to. . . ."

"He was. He lost her during the war. Much later, he married a Brazilian, their mother, who left him after a few years, took them, and transformed them into Latinized Eurotrash, *rentiers nonpareils.* Shymanski no longer has access to a *sou,* and I'll have to leave when they sell."

"But you're a tenant. They can't. . . ."

"They can. I'm not a tenant, but a guest. At first it was music lessons. Then just looking after the house when the old man was away, which was most of the time."

"Then you're an employee, which may be even better."

Jules shook his head. "Not an employee. The taxes were never paid. I was just right for the spot. I could give his boys music lessons, protect the house, and keep it quiet and orderly. He knew I had been in the army, that my parents had been killed by the Germans just as his wife had been, that I was a studious academic, compulsively neat, and that the only noise I would make would be Mozart and Bach."

"What about Cathérine?"

"She was always quiet and contemplative. The sweetest girl. Full of *weltschmerz* well before her teens."

"If it's any comfort to you, Jules, I'm not a businessman and I have no money either. I talk and talk and talk, and people listen. But what's left?"

"Books and writings."

"All my books and writings will sit, paralyzed and mummified, on the shelves of the great libraries, taking up less space proportionately than that of a single skull in all the catacombs of Europe. Come to think of it, soon there won't even be libraries but only digital electrical charges that no human can touch, in some Never Never Land where no one can go. I wish that, like you, I could have spent my life transported aloft, as it were, every day, in music. Instead, I've lived like a caffeinated parrot. After my interview with Polish TV, I'll take the train to Biarritz, and although the baby and Michelle have given me new life, still, if it's hot enough I'll lie in the sun and feel at least three types of despair: despair that life is mostly gone and I've wasted it; despair that I cannot feel now what I thought I would if I saw all my struggles through; and despair that, because I don't know any other course to take, nothing will change. Tomorrow I'll speak for three hours to Polish television. I'll try to be brilliant and charming. They'll edit it down and propel it through the ether for twelve minutes. Then it will disappear. It will mean nothing."

"How's your health?" Jules inquired.

"The stent is holding, they say." François was tall and gangly. He had dark curly hair now half gray, and the various parts of his face seemed to have been added to it by different agencies at different times and in a great hurry. But despite this Picasso-like disorganization common to many Jews of Eastern-European origin, the force of his intellect shone through every aspect of his appearance, and he was as physically intimidating, in his way, as a bull. Those brave enough to debate him felt like they were facing a Tiger Tank on the Western Front. It was not fun, and some actually trembled as they stared at him. He was a man like a fortification. He faced you directly, heavily, talked rapidly and clearly, and every word was like a well placed shell taking effect with a deep concussion. "And your health?"

Jules, not as tall, was fit, his hair blond and gray, his face boyish, his features even. Despite his strength and gravity, he had an air of kindness and hesitation — which had always drawn women to him, disproportionately he thought, if not miraculously. François

94

conquered women. Jules loved them. "I'm fine," he said. "In fact, it scares me. Nothing's wrong, which at our age can't be good. I fear that when I row or run I'll drop dead without warning. I thought of tying myself to the boat so my body wouldn't be lost in the Seine — so if they find the boat, they find the body — but then if I did go over, which in all these years I haven't, not even once, I might be trapped by the line and drowned."

"Jules, I just wanted to know how you were. I didn't need a treatise on death and rowing."

"I'm fine. I think."

When they had dessert, with his mousse François had tea. With his cake Jules had Badoit.

Just before they left, François said, "Oh, by the way, would you be interested in writing some music, a theme, for a giant international conglomerate?"

"What? What kind of music? A theme?"

"For commercials. Telephone hold music. Their signature sound."

"Telephone hold music?"

"Hundreds and hundreds of millions of people would hear it every year, and who knows? They might keep it going forever. You might get royalties."

"What company?"

"Acorn and its many subsidiaries, probably the world's largest insurance company —

reinsurance, an investment arm, trillions of dollars. Literally, four or five trillions. At a reception and dinner at the American Embassy, I was seated next to one of their executives. His name is Jack something. I have his card at home.

"They've already asked Steve Reich, Philip Glass, Jean Michel Jarre, Hans Zimmer, Yann Tiersen, and I don't know how many others. They went through an agent. Jack was complaining and hurt, because they all said no."

"Telephone hold music? Why wouldn't they say no?"

"But what's the difference if the music is beautiful?"

Jules thought for a minute. "You're right. There is no difference. If the music is beautiful the context is irrelevant. If it's truly beautiful, it can't be pulled down. Rilke wrote for a butcher's trade magazine. Perhaps they should have known that."

"They're all so busy, you know, and rich."

"How much money can you get for a jingle, anyway?"

Having saved the best for last, François smiled.

"And besides," Jules added, "they didn't ask me."

"Of course they didn't. No one's ever heard of you. You never cared to build an image. But I talked you up, and this Jack person thinks you're one of the most famous composers in Europe."

"That's ridiculous."

"He doesn't know that, and he's the one who'll bring the music — ninety seconds worth, but 'strong, brilliant,' he said — to the board chairman."

"And who is that?"

"You won't believe his name. It was Polish, and he shortened it."

"Jewish?"

"Yes, and the chairman of maybe the biggest insurance company in the world. Fifty-five years old. If he likes what you bring him. . . ."

"What's his name? What is it, a secret?"

François started to laugh. He looked up at the ceiling, then looked at Jules' as if confessing: "His name is, truly, Rich Panda."

"You made that up."

"I didn't. It was Pandolfsky or something. Crazy parents must've changed it to Panda, and named their son Richard. Rich Panda. I bet they do a lot of business in China. You can't necessarily understand these people — they're Americans — but that's beside the point."

"Okay, then how much would a Rich Panda pay for a jingle?"

"That's it precisely. This Jack something was drinking a lot of California champagne, and I'd seen him take down half a bottle of single malt at the reception. He told me how much. I don't think he knows he told me, but I do know what they'll go to if they like it. They've already decided. Assuming they're pleased by what you might give them, you need only hold your ground and they'll roll right over."

"If in fact I get it, and I haven't decided that I'll do this, but if I do, you should have a percentage, as a finder's or agency fee."

"Okay. Pay for this dinner."

"I was going to do that anyway."

"And the next ten."

"Would that be roughly ten percent of the fee?" Jules asked a little nervously as he put his credit card back in his wallet and began to make out the slip that the waiter, almost unnoticed, had left at the table. François was not above making an advantageous deal for himself.

"I don't think so."

"More?"

"No."

"So how much are they willing to pay?"

"Hold onto the table with your other hand. A million Euros."

Jules' pen froze on the ticket. Had it been a pencil, the point would have broken. "If this is a joke," he said, only mechanically, for he knew that François didn't joke that way, "you're very cruel."

"It's not a joke. I'll call him if you want. You can go see him. He's at the George V.

98

He thinks you're Mozart."

"How do you do things like this? You're like a magician who produces birds from an empty hand."

"You know how they do that, Jules?"

"No."

"They dehydrate them so that they're almost flat, and pack them in their sleeves. It's cruel, but the birds don't fly away, because they know the magician will give them what they want the most, which is water. And he always does."

"But a million!"

"It's their worldwide branding and representation. They pay that to companies that come up with a single stupid name for one of their companies. A million Euros for thinking up a name like *Unipopsicom* or *Anthipid.* How about a beer called *Norwegian Backlash?*

"I just now pulled them out of the air, and I wasn't paid a million Euros. These people make so much money they're disconnected from worth. They think that if they don't overpay they won't get something good. Isn't Shymanski like that?"

"No. He knows real prices. He made the gardener return fifteen sacks of fertilizer because they were overpriced by a Euro apiece."

"Not these guys. People like this have houses with bowling alleys and candy rooms."

"What's a candy room?" Jules asked.

"Like a Godiva shop."

"In their house?"

"Yes."

"This is true? They eat so much chocolate?"

"I don't know. Maybe they have parties."

"They're idiots," Jules said.

"Yes, they are."

"But to get all that money and keep it, they must be clever idiots."

"I assure you, cleverer idiots have seldom walked the earth. But this Jack person is not necessarily an idiot. You'll have to judge for yourself."

THIS JACK PERSON

Jules was neither a theorist nor a critic. Though he was fully expert in the technicalities of musical composition and notation, neither he nor anyone else thought he was an intellectual. In fact, apart from François, who was considered by many to be the leading intellectual in France (and, therefore, if you were French, everywhere else), Jules was allergic to intellectuals, who he thought did not quite live in the world and were often incapable of appreciating it. He likened them to condemned men who would analyze their last meal rather than eat it.

But as a *Maître* of the Paris-Sorbonne music faculty he was surrounded by intellectuals. Almost everyone he knew was one. They depended upon the label as if it were an iron lung, and by more or less continuously checking its motor and other parts they strained to demonstrate their intelligence at every opportunity and in almost everything they did, as if failing to do so would explode a bomb inside their chests.

When he was young, Jules was relaxed about admitting that he had no desire to be, and was not, what everyone assumed he would want to be. It was a shock to one associate after another, who within a short time would become mysteriously unavailable, decline invitations to play tennis, or fail to return his calls. He understood that he had exiled himself and was no longer in the pack. It hurt, but he could not have done it any other way, and the music was enough. It flowed through him like a river flooding with snowmelt. It had only to be recognized, liberated, illumined, and it would fill the air like rain in the beam of an arc light. Just as the electrons of radio transmissions saturated the entire world, music was present in everything, but, unlike radio transmissions, it was elemental, present at the creation, and lasting without diminution even past the end. Superior to reason, analysis, and fact, it darted around and above them, playing like Ariel above the sea.

So it was that on his way to meet this Jack person, one Jack Cheatham, at the George V, Jules didn't analyze what he saw, he heard it and he felt it. That is not just to say that he merely listened to the noise of traffic, the wind, aircraft straining at a distance, barge horns, sirens, chimes, and the surf-like rustle of leaves now stiffening before their October deaths. Somehow he heard Paris itself, and was able to apprehend it through a musical lens. That evening, as rain blurred the lights seen through his windshield, Paris sounded like Couperin's *Les Barricades Mystérieuses.* To him this was as real as if there had been a harpsichord in the backseat.

What it showed him, bidden by an image aforethought of the magnificence of the George V, was Paris moving through centuries in which all time coexisted as if it were water poured into water. The city seemed as alive as an organism, with much flowing through it — river, people, birds, clouds, cars, lights, trains, boats — all of which glowed like living cells glorified upon a microscope stage illuminated by the sun-like light underneath. He knew that what he would encounter in the hotel was likely to be the clash and compromise of his necessities and his principles, something he would have avoided had he not been driven to it by Luc's ordeal.

Jack Cheatham, a Tennessean risen from Alabama, was older than Jules by three or four years but in appearance by ten. His great success and high position in business was attributable primarily to the fact that the sight of him inspired confidence and trust. He was tall. His hair and mustache were thick, the color of charcoal (almost blued like a gun) and the white of sea foam. His face was chiseled and square, eyes blue. He looked like he could have been a Sargent portrait made not with a brush but a palette knife. Some painters paint that way, rough and appealing, and sometimes God makes men that way and they become leaders, whether or not they should be. Jack looked like Pershing. He was not handsome, he was arresting.

Jules immediately fell under his spell. Here was a man's man whom he could trust, who was powerful and who — it was hardly irrelevant — might give him a million Euros merely for doing what he loved to do most. This spell was cast not only by the magician but also by his audience and by the set — as Jules had known it would be, having been there before.

The George V was actually richer and more elegant than even the Élysée, where Jules had been as well. The first time at the Élysée had been when François had been the *Major* of *Sciences Po.* Jules had met de Gaulle, if only momentarily as so often is the case with heads of state. He went twice on his own steam, once to give a recital and another time to receive one of the very few honors he had been able to collect. But the George V was on an even higher plane. Disassociated from real, political power, its force was confined to the purely material. Its every detail was perfect, its colors rich, its marble polished, and its proportions exquisite.

In preparing to meet Jack Cheatham, Jules had looked online and found the cost of the suite to which he had been invited. With tax it was almost 10,000 Euros a day, and Jack had been there already for nine days. When Jules walked into this extraordinary suite, Jack greeted him warmly and informally in the American style. A thin, too-efficient-looking young man in an expensive suit stood unobtrusively nearby, oozing so much competence it made Jules think of rotting fruit. This precision flunky was not introduced, and before anyone could really say anything, his phone rang. He spoke discreetly. Then he said, one hand covering the tiny phone, "Sir, it's the pilots, checking in."

"We're okay. Not going home tonight certainly. Probably not tomorrow either. We'll see. Besides, I hate to take off in the rain, and it's raining heavily." They were on the top floor, and the beautiful sound of the rain could be heard tattooing the roof. The young man faded into the background to deliver the reply.

"Pilots?" Jules asked.

"Yeah, my pilots. A couple'a pilots, a couple'a engineers, and a stewardess. You're supposed to call them flight attendants now, but I call them stewardesses because that's what they are. The crew is always on call, but of course they need downtime. They're away from their families, but we pay them very well and it looks like they'll get two weeks in Paris. All they have to do is check out the plane once a day and make sure it's ready to go. There's no reason they shouldn't enjoy themselves as long as we don't need them."

"They stay near the airport?"

"No, they're downstairs. Each one has a room. It's in their contract. You know why? The insurers wanted to make sure they were well rested and in good shape to fly, so they said they have to stay in the same hotel as the employer, which is us, and we're the insurers. Beat that. Not at the same level, but the same hotel. This is the George V. They don't have cheap rooms. That's maybe sixty room nights. You can imagine the cost of the meals and telephone calls. They buy their own goddamn souvenirs."

Jules could see that Jack was doing the math faster than he was, and that Jack regretted hinting even indirectly at the hand he had already given away, without knowing it, courtesy of the American Embassy's Scotch whiskey and Sonoma champagne. When Jack realized he had spoken too freely, for a moment he looked mean. Then it disappeared. He offered Jules a drink, perhaps wanting to lessen resistance, which, from experience, he knew could be lessened a great deal. As he was pouring, Jules did the math.

The cheapest room, he had discovered shortly before, with tax and extras, was about

2,000 Euros, times sixty-eight, with meals and transportation, plus a room for the assistant and perhaps others, plus parking the plane, ground transportation, tips, gifts, restaurant charges, communications equipment, fuel, the amortized cost of the plane.

He assumed that they had come to Paris not merely to find a jingle composer, but, even so, this trip had cost them close to half a million Euros. That information, plus the intelligence François had gleaned at the embassy, made Jules confident that were he chosen and his composition accepted, he could indeed get a million. This was so far out of the realm of his experience — money like that does not come from teaching young people the fine points of the cello — that he wasn't even nervous.

Jack gave him a glass of scotch and sat down opposite him. Jack's glass, unlike Jules' was three-quarters full. He whammed it down. "Want some more?" he asked.

"I haven't had any yet."

"I do." Jack got up and drifted toward the bottle. "It's raining. We were going to go to that restaurant, you know — I don't know what it's called. I can't remember names anymore. But why don't we eat here instead? Would you like room service, or shall we just go down to the restaurant downstairs? I think there are a couple of 'em."

"Whichever you'd like."

"Let's go down then. The rain makes me restless."

Jack's young aide, who styled himself "a concierge without walls" and behind his back was called by Jack "a concierge without balls," literally ran ahead not to secure a table in one of the restaurants but to arrange for a whole room, which he was able to do perhaps because the weather had made for a quiet evening. Although the aide had smoothed the way, he wasn't available to escort Jack to the proper place. That — and because Jack, who had been drinking before his drink with Jules (he drank a lot when it rained, and when it didn't rain), and because he was not used to finding his own way, and because he had a poor sense of direction — was the reason Jack led Jules at high-speed all around the public rooms of "this goddamned hotel."

"Shit!" he said upon opening a door that he was sure would lead to their destination but revealed instead a room full of Ghanian laundresses ironing napkins and tablecloths. "That's not the restaurant. Where the fuck is the restaurant?"

"I think it's on the other side of the lobby," Jules volunteered.

"We were just there."

"No."

"Where were we?"

"We were at the swimming pool. Remem-

108

ber? Water?"

"All right. I'm sorry, I thought it was here."

"It's over there. Look, there's your friend, standing at the door."

In the *Salon Régence,* paneled walls, a blue-and-gold carpet, a marble bust, sparkling crystal, silver, and a centerpiece of white and purple flowers in profusion upon a gold damask tablecloth were lit to gleam and effulge in waterfalls of luxury. The curtains were a deep indigo that Jules had seen once before, when he was playing in a string quartet at the French Embassy in Rome, and a similarly deep-sky-colored cloth had floated in as the gown that embraced the athletic body of a young Italian *principessa.* Though Jules had dropped a couple of notes at the sight of her, no one but the musicians had noticed.

The purpose of this room was to make anyone in it think he had arrived, or to assure someone who was already there that he hadn't left. If only briefly, it imparted as if by magic a powerful sense of well-being. The staff in such a place knew exactly when to appear and when to serve. Out of nowhere, one of them, clad in a morning coat, came over as silently as a mantis and filled two tumblers halfway with fifty-year-old Glenfiddich. At 2,000 Euros a bottle, it was something Jules hesitated actually to drink even though Jack wolfed his down as if it were a

Dr Pepper.

"Ha!" Jack said. Having observed that Jules was aware of all the money vacuumed out of Acorn's treasury as standard operating procedure, he wanted to counter the impression that he would be an easy mark. "You know that kid Mason Reese?" he asked.

Jules shook his head to communicate that he didn't. Naturally he didn't, and, besides, Jules' English was entirely formal, and he thought Jack was referring to a goat.

"No kid in the world looked like this. He was a grown-up kid, but he looked like a baby."

This seemed reasonable to Jules. A *chevre* could look like a *chevreau,* but, still, he had no idea what Jack was talking about.

"In fact, at the time the kid was most famous, our Chairman had recently had his own son. So Rich says to me — that's our chairman. . . ."

"Yes, I know."

"He says, 'On the retail end, we sell insurance to families. Do our commercials appeal to families? No. What the hell does an eagle have to do with families? We've got an acorn and an eagle. Great, but we're not recruiting for the Marines.' "

"Eagles sometimes carry away kids," Jules said.

This made Jack hesitate. "Well, yeah, I guess so."

110

"And eat them."

Jack pulled back.

"The meat is very tender."

Completely at a loss, Jack resumed. "Anyway, Rich says, 'get that kid Mason Reese. No one could ever forget his face. It's one in a trillion.'

" 'But, Rich,' I say, 'he's probably fifty by now.' "

Quite relaxed by the Glenfiddich, Jules felt a little like a tycoon. "They don't get to be that old," he offered. "It's impossible."

Jack looked at him in amazement. "What's the average life expectancy, in France?"

Jules, who still thought they were talking about goats, said, "That's not something I know. I would guess maybe twelve or fifteen years."

"No," said Jack. "We have actuaries. It's our business. You're wildly wrong."

"You know?"

"I would imagine it's at least eighty."

"Maybe in America," Jules said, "but not here. Even if they could live that long, the meat would be much too tough."

"So you write music?" Jack asked.

"Yes."

"Are you sure?"

"Of course I'm sure. That's what I do."

Jack took another drink and continued his story. "We got a kid, a really great-looking one — red hair, blue eyes."

"Really. I've never heard of that."

"Yeah. His mother was gorgeous, too. That helped. We put them in commercials: sitting around, eating dinner, on a roller coaster."

"On a roller coaster," Jules echoed.

"Uh huh, it was a huge hit. It said, 'Protect your loved ones.' And we made out like bandits, but then, through his agent, the kid tried to milk us."

"*He* tried to milk *you*? And he was a he?"

"Yeah," Jack said, looking suspiciously at Jules. "I don't quite understand you, but, anyway, he knew how much money we were making and how successful the commercials were. We were willing to get milked a little, but he wanted the moon. Rich called him in.

" 'You can't get rid of the kid,' the agent says. 'He's too young to go to college. What are you going to say if suddenly he's off-screen? *He left his family to open a surf shop in La Jolla? He went up the river to Sing Sing?*'

" 'We'll get another kid,' Rich says.

" 'Good luck. Nobody looks like this kid. It's like Mason Reese.' "

"So what did you do?" Jules asked, completely confused.

"What else? Rich threw him out of the office. He hires another kid who doesn't look anything like the first one, and wraps him up in bandages like the Invisible Man. No announcement is made, no explanation, nothing. Do you know what a sensation that

112

caused? And how that put our name on the lips of everyone in America? That's what's great about Rich. He's really tough, he's daring. He's unorthodox. And that's what's great about America. Look at Hollywood. A zillion-billion-dollar industry — well, not really, it's extremely small compared to us — built on a mile-high pyramid of jiggling bosoms, dead bodies, exploding cars, and all kinds of other crap. It makes no sense at all, and yet people crave it like heroin. Can you beat that?"

"No, and I don't know what's wrong with us in France. We still tolerate drama."

"Yeah," said Jack. "Europeans are like that. I don't know if it's good or bad."

The menus had appeared before them as if placed by magic. They opened them in perfect synchrony and studied them. Because he couldn't imagine that he would be hired by such people, Jules was content to enjoy the dinner and see what would happen.

Jack, on the other hand, furrowed his brows until he looked like a high school student in a calculus exam. "What's this?" he asked, shoving the menu to Jules.

"*Pâté chaud de Bécasse à la Périgourdine.* It's a *pâté* of woodcock bird with bacon, truffles, foie gras, and toast."

"Woodcock bird. Is it good?"

"I have no idea: I've never had it. I'm going to have a steak."

"Oh," said Jack. "I think I will, too."

It didn't take long for the food to arrive, and after Jack inhaled his steak, he said, quoting Hemingway, "It was good." And it put them in good spirits, as the other spirits had already. And they were pleased.

"So, Jack, are you here just to arrange for a theme?"

"Oh God no. I came to see Hollande. It's funny that your president has the same name as the country almost next door, as if we had a President Canada, or Mexico, or Honduras. Not so strange I guess. You know who Grover Cleveland was?"

"Yes, I do."

"Before he became president he was the mayor of Buffalo. If he had been the mayor of Cleveland his name might have been Grover Buffalo. But I don't know any history. What I do know is that the Socialists are squeezing Acorn, so I went to talk to Hollande. What does Acorn do in France? We relieve pressure on your system of social welfare, and you need that relief especially now. We write more high-end policies than anyone else in France, but that's only a quarter of our business, because we take care of the middle and lower-middle class, too: shopkeepers, *musicians.*" He swept his left hand toward Jules in a gesture that said, *voilà!*

"If we pull out, your insurance and reinsurance markets go bananas. Sometimes even presidents don't think of things like that, and it's their job, isn't it? The welfare state here needs all the help it can get, and right now Acorn is carrying much more than a bundle of straw, only one or two sprigs more of which could break the French camel's back. He got it."

"You threatened him?"

"I wouldn't put it that way. I just laid out the facts. Nobody fools around with us. We have under management more money than the GNP of any country in the world other than the US, China, Japan, and Germany. Our *assets* are greater than the GNP of all but the top thirty countries. And the man in the street, do you think he knows this? Governments do, they can't help but know, and if, as sometimes happens, they tighten the screws on us, we don't break down in tears, we seek alternative markets. We don't have to fight, we just have to move, cast our eyes in another direction. That's a luxury most people can't even comprehend. You've heard of the expression 'too big to fail'? Well, we're too big to fuck. And that's that."

After they finished dessert, Jack leaned back in his chair. No one was going to eject them from this room, and he was in an expansive mood. "We've searched all over the world for what we need. We hired expensive music consultants — what the hell is a music consultant? — and they brought us crap. I don't know anything about music, but even I figured out what was wrong with the American stuff. You know what they do? They take up to eight bars from really great songs of the fifties and sixties, orchestrate them a little, and start off that way. You think something really good's coming, and suddenly the melodic line disappears, the tempo gets weird, and they start with a lot of off-key tricks. The thing I hate the most, the stressed surprise high note followed by an immediate drop. It sounds like. . . . Well it sounds as if they were saying '*I*!! don't, *You*!! can't.' Get it? Like a roller coaster, suddenly way up, then a sudden drop, then repeated. They think that's deep or maybe interesting. It's just stupid. You know what I mean?"

"Yes. I'm familiar with that. I hear it on the radio in my car."

"Is there a term for it?"

"Yes. Music for morons."

"We had a few things — from New York, Boston — that were close but too academic. And the big shots have no interest. They think it's below them."

"Rilke published poems in a butcher's magazine."

"Whatever. Our signature theme will reach hundreds of millions of people again and again and again. We hope it will express us into the hearts of those hundreds of millions. That's what's important. Maybe I'm so set

116

on this because it was my idea, and it arose from my analysis. Rich was not entirely convinced, and he said, 'Okay, but I'll have final say over the music.' I said, 'Why?' 'Because it's so important,' he said. 'Oh? Why is it so important?' And you know what he said? He said, 'This won't be the face of the company, it'll be its soul. If people love you for your soul, your face doesn't matter and you don't have to be perfect.'

"He doesn't usually talk that way, because he hides that kind of thing so that he can disarm. I was really impressed, until he said, 'Yeah, it's like a chick, except with chicks it's not true even if they have a great body.' He's really unpredictable. Still, I knew I had him. He'll give final approval, and then present to the board. What have you got?"

"I've got nothing," said Jules. "If you tell me what you want, maybe I can translate it to music."

"Well, Monsieur . . . tell me again?"

"Lacour."

"That's right, Lacour. We need sixty seconds that can seamlessly loop, end to beginning, for use in television, radio, and internet advertising, to play in retail centers that are coming — banks have them, why not insurance companies — for telephone hold music, and for any other commercial purpose that may arise."

"I don't mean that, although it's helpful. I

mean what, or how, do you want people to feel?"

Jack thought for a moment before he spoke. "I want them to feel as if they're riding across a sunlit plain, on a buckboard. . . ."

"What is a buckboard?"

"Like a flat wagon with a bench seat in front, and the back is for cargo. Pulled by horses."

"I see."

"Under an immense blue sky in a John Ford Western. I want the music to make them feel young, with the world in front of them, as if they can do anything and the best is yet to come. Like when you've just fallen in love. I want to make them see their own lives as a story worth telling. For them to feel courage and love upwelling within them. I want to focus their attention and make them happy, but with the trace of sadness that comes with anything beautiful."

Jules was silent. He had not thought Jack capable of what had just been said. It was always tempting to see Americans as half-baked idiots, but it was just that, like Australians, their style was so peculiar and brash.

"What I'm trying to say is that I want the music to easily place something of high value in the immediate consciousness of the listener, something that will make an indelible impression and create gratitude. Look, I'm surrounded by all the crap" — he swept his

118

hands in a motion that looked like he was clearing away gnats — "that money can buy. But I'm happiest when I'm home, fly fishing in a clear river in the woods, standing thigh-deep, the dark water rushing around me. That sound cleanses my life of all the crud that has stuck to it since I was six. It tells me who I really am — I'm not this — and I love it for that, and remember it like someone you love who's lost. Can you do that with music?" Jack pressed. "I know that Bach, Mozart, and Beethoven could, but their kind of music would be inappropriate. The feel wouldn't be right. Gershwin and Aaron Copland would have been great, but too recognizable, and anyway United beat us to the punch with *Rhapsody in Blue.* Fantastic."

"United?"

"United Airlines. Yeah, they did that. It really worked. We'd like an original composition. I want people to say — the public and journalists both — 'Who wrote that?' In short, I want it to be ours exclusively, as if it had sprung from Acorn itself. Can you do that?"

"I can try."

"How long will it take?"

"I could get it while I was driving home, and write it up by tomorrow. Or it might take months."

"Months won't do it. We've got to get rolling on this."

"I can't guarantee that I can do it at all. It's not mechanical."

"I understand. Would you like to discuss the terms?"

"Before I've written it?"

"Yes."

"No. I'll write it, and if you want it, then we'll discuss the terms."

Jack smiled. "Were you in business?"

Jules touched the center of his chest, sort of like a squirrel, and said, "Me?"

"No, the woodchuck in the corner."

At first Jules didn't get this, sarcasm being inappropriate for a Frenchman in such a setting, and his English vocabulary not including the word *woodchuck*. Then he did. "No. I was never . . . never even vaguely."

"You should have been. Can you email me a demo?"

"I haven't yet learned to do that kind of thing. I can make a tape. . . ."

"No no, you gotta email it. We have a board meeting in October. If we get a theme, it has to be orchestrated, recorded, copyrighted. You'd have to go to L.A. to conduct the orchestra."

"Which orchestra would it be?"

"I don't know, the Los Angeles Philharmonic or some movie orchestra or something. Music consultants said that in L.A. you can knock out something like this quicker and better than in New York. I think everything's ready to go. All we need is the music. Even if you FedEx a tape it might take too long . . . Look, we've got to bounce this thing all over the world. Can't you get someone to help you with email? This is how things are done now."

"Maybe my daughter can do it for me. She mocks me because I have no interest in that sort of thing. Now she can say, *I told you.*"

"I told you *so.*"

"I told you *so,*" Jules repeated.

"No. No stress: 'I told you so.' "

"I told you so."

"Perfect. I have to warn you, though. There's no guarantee. If you wanted to talk about terms, we could put some money out front. That way, if it doesn't work out, you won't have done it on spec. Okay, it's true that if you come up with something we really want, you're in a much better position — in theory."

"Not in reality?"

Jack snorted. "You're talking about Rich Panda. I'm his second. I've got enough money put away to buy a few countries and I'm way past retirement age, but Rich Panda can still make me shake in my boots."

"I don't think anyone can make me shake in my boots, anymore," Jules said.

"Maybe so, but don't count on getting on the other side of Rich Panda in a negotiation. And don't assume he'll like what you come up with. He's extremely sensitive, like a bomb on a hair trigger. And he does what he wants."

"I see. So do I."

"Oooh! This could be very interesting. But let me give you just a little, minor example, not by any means the most revelatory. I shouldn't tell you this. I'm only telling you because I've had a bit to drink. Sometimes I overdo it, you know. And so does Cheyenne."

"Cheyenne?"

"She's Rich's third wife, a Pilates instructress thirty-five years his junior, with a body like the fucking Statue of Liberty. If she shows up at a garden party in a sun dress, there isn't a man within a mile who doesn't go into drugged heat. You should see her. It's unbelievable.

"She and I were riding in the helicopter out to their place in East Hampton. When Rich was a boy there were no Jews in Southampton. He went there once when he was sixteen and was ill-treated, so he vowed never to set foot in the place again, and built his estate in East Hampton instead, on Further Lane. I have a house nearby. Rich was going to follow us later. Cheyenne, who was already drinking in the helicopter, was talking about leaving him.

"We're not dealing with Isaac Newton here. She likes what she calls 'romance.' To her that means candles, rose petals, and a bathtub. I don't understand what this thing is that women have about candles. All I can say is that there must've been a hell of a lot of sex in the eighteenth century. But Rich, on the other hand, is not a candle-type guy. She told me, and she was quite upset about it, that when he wants to have sex he starts ripping off her clothes and says, 'Rig for torpedo impact.' "

"I suppose some women might like that, maybe," Jules said.

"Yeah, but she says his hands are like monkeys."

"Like monkey's hands?"

"No, like monkeys. Two monkeys, running up and down her alabaster body."

"I suppose some women, in the heat of the moment, might like even that."

"Maybe in France."

"Not to my knowledge. Did she leave him?"

"She's still with him. I don't know why. Maybe the prenup." Jack clutched his stomach. "Shouldn't have drunk so much. You think you can have something by ten a.m. the day after tomorrow?"

Jules moved his head slowly from side to side. "I don't think so. What you want is extraordinary, and I'm not Mozart."

"According to Ehrenshtamm you are."

"He's very kind."

"Because if you do, you can hitch a ride with us. Wheels up at ten."

"From Le Bourget?"

"Charles de Gaulle."

"I thought business jets used Le Bourget."

"We have a seven-fifty-seven. It's treated like a commercial charter."

Jules thought about this. "Then why only one stewardess?"

"Sharp. You sure you don't want to be in business? We came over light. She's on staff. We're going back for the fall conference, with a bunch of people from our European subsidiaries. The plane will be about half full. So we'll ferry Air France stewards and stewardesses to New York, and Air France will cater the flight. They get paid and ferried, so they make out well, and so do we."

"The plane is yours?"

"It is, with an acorn on it in gold and brown. But you'd have to go to Los Angeles anyway, so it's probably better to fly direct. If it works out, go to L.A. Fly business class. Stay at the Four Seasons there and in New York, eat anywhere you want, rent a nice car in L.A. because you'll need it, and save your receipts."

"Okay, but aren't you getting ahead of yourself?"

"I always do. It's one way of getting ahead of everyone else." Jack looked around at the room, which was so gorgeous and unmarred that it created a strong sense of benevolence. "Nice, huh," he said, and fumbled in his left inside jacket pocket for the cigar he had left

124

in his room.

Jules drove home without anxiety in rain that was no longer heavy. He could see a kilometer ahead, and yet the windshield was wet enough so that the wipers didn't drag across it. The lights of Paris — headlights, red taillights, street lamps, the muted glow from restaurants and apartments, lights on barges moving through a gauze of fog on the Seine — sparkled on the glass like sequins, with sharp edges unlike the out-of-focus raindrops on car windshields in films, that enlarge to the size of watermelons. He had always sighed in the theater when they swelled on screen, a trick so common that all it said was, 'This is a film in which you are now looking at an artful cinematographic technique.'

Same thing goes for gauze, he thought as he drove, disapproving of gauze in front of a lens. Suddenly he was angry at himself and a little scared. Now he might fail, which would be worse than not being able to help in the first place. Luc would never know. Neither would Cathérine or David, her husband. But Jules would.

And why did he tell Jack Cheatham that Cathérine would email the demo, as Jack called it? There was no possibility of that. He could not ask for a favor at this time in her life, when her child was slowly dying, unless it was in an effort to save the child, which it was. But if she knew, and her hopes were raised only to be dashed, it would be unconscionable. He would have to get someone else to do it.

He had now to compose a sixty-second piece that would magically elevate the spirits of people waiting to speak to a telephone representative or eating popcorn in front of a television set. The prize was, perhaps, the life of his grandchild, the happiness and safety of his daughter, and a proper end for him. But the judges of his success or failure would be people who, though powerful and clever, seemed like they might have come from another planet. They flew around in their giant airplanes, drank too much, had wives with names like Cheyenne, were used to skinny assistants who wore ten-thousand-Euro suits and apparently stayed up twenty-four hours a day, and who thought that he, Jules Lacour, was one of the leading composers in all of Europe and could work miracles on order, when in fact he had such performance anxiety that the last concert he had given, thirty years before, had been a spectacular failure.

He had thought then that he could play Bach's *Sei Lob und Preis mit Ehren,* because he loved it so much and often played it when alone. But, in front of almost a thousand people, he could not. He froze, dropped his bow, bowed his head, and wept. People said it was a nervous breakdown, but it wasn't anything of the sort. Still, it was the beginning of a trajectory that fairly quickly rendered him unknown.

WRITING A JINGLE IN SAINT-GERMAIN-EN-LAYE

As the Seine Coils through lower elevations it is forced by the terrain to mimic a wave. That which it avoids and works around are the hills that rise above it. Some sites near Paris afford a better view than the heights of Saint-Germain-en-Laye: Mont Valérien to name just one. But although in Saint-Germain-en-Laye one cannot see the whole of Paris, nonetheless the tops of its towers old and new, Eiffel and La Défense, are visible to the east. At the bottom of the slope is the river. The trees bend right into it at high water, their leaves brushing the glassy surface as it slowly glides by. And at the top of the slope, looking over Le Pecq on the opposite bank, are the park, the long terrace, the gardens, and the great houses.

The gardens — where part of the palace where Louis XIV was born still stands — are superior to those of Versailles. Here, Le Nôtre was not driven by the royal megalomania that in Versailles rises at every turn to compromise the genius of the design. Instead, what he accomplished in Saint-Germain-en-Laye is the perfect marriage of man's skill and nature's glory. Simple, almost minimalist planes that mate with the horizon, long allées of soldier-like trees standing at attention, and in the fecund gardens flowers as healthy and bright in October — blooming in red, yellow, and a hundred other shades — as in May. In the sheltered market square at the center of town, palms in huge boxes remain well into autumn, as if, on its little mountain just a few minutes from Paris, Saint-Germain-en-Laye thinks it's Taormina.

Sometimes it seems that all the children of France have come to Saint-Germain-en-Laye, with parents fleeing the dangers and disorders of Paris, or as students in the *pléiade* of the many schools located there. On the streets and in the squares, adolescents flock like birds, their movements and exclamations sudden and explosive as their energies overflow and ignite. Jules didn't think that when he was an *ado* he was anything but quiet and contemplative, and though he wasn't sure, he was right.

Younger children are not only quiet but less predictable and more interesting, in that they are fascinated by the world rather than straining to make the world fascinated by them. In the winding shopping streets laden with fairy-tale rows of luxury-good purveyors, there are always little children, morning and afternoon. Jules once counted the number of times a small boy turned in a complete circle as he walked a short block — twelve, and as many jumps and skips. But the most wonderful were the infants, their angelic beauty reminding him of Cathérine when she was wheeled around in a carriage or a stroller. He imagined that to see these children every time he went out was worth a hundred days in a Swiss health spa. Saint-Germain-en-Laye will never be fashionable or dazzling, but there is no end to the praise of a good and peaceful place high on a hill.

Shymanski had bought the greatest house on the crest of this hill and added to it with better taste and judgment than he had exercised in picking his second wife. A dowdy and inconspicuous gate in ill-repair, its squares of sheet metal almost as rusted as if it led to a junkyard, opened onto a two-hectare private compound completely invisible to neighboring streets, a lovely island floating high above the river and partitioned off from everything on every side, its high, long, eastern retaining wall creating an elevated terrace resting upon a secure battlement. The view east was open and stunning, almost an ocean view when the trees were in leaf and the wind moved through them.

In the compound were the main house and a guesthouse one-fifth its size, a small pond, gardens, a tennis court, an enormous swimming pool, and expansive lawns. The main house was as big and as elegantly furnished as a ministry or a museum. A huge, cobbled courtyard at the end of the driveway afforded enough room for the comfortable repose of a dozen automobiles if necessary, but it was usually empty, for a garage disappeared beneath the house. On the lower floor of its eastern side — five meters over the lawn, overlooking the river and out toward Paris and the sunrise, Jules had lived for many years.

On this side of the house, the architect had provided, as Shymanski was fond of saying, enough terraces to grow the rice for Taipei. The Lacour living room, behind an expansive wall of *portes-fenêtres,* opened onto a terrace almost as big as a tennis court, with a stone balustrade, a view toward Paris, chaises, potted pines, a dining table, an herb and flower garden, even a metal fireplace for chill evenings. Every Lacour that had ever lived loved the smell of wood smoke. Especially after Jacqueline died, Jules would sit by a fire there for hours. He had a fireplace inside as well, but a fire *en plein air* was best.

The wood was consumed, and in the morning would be ash, but its burning was a miracle of surprising and insistent animation in the creation of light and heat; in the ballet of rising smoke; in the sound of cracks and reports as in a battle. And before it died it became a glowing, red city pulsing at the end of life like a failing heart. A neighbor newly rich from doing something tiny and invisible with smartphones had complained about the smoke, but Shymanski had put off the authorities with a bribe. The neighbor then came to speak to Jules, who agreed to have fewer fires, but not to do without them.

"The smoke is carcinogenic," the man had insisted.

"So is your telephone: brain cancer. And you don't have to worry about the smoke unless you inhale," Jules had replied.

"It's not like smoking a cigarette. Just the remnants in the air are harmful."

"That's also true of cigarettes," Jules told him, "but I'd give years of life just to have the company of a fire now and then." It was almost true. At least he would have wanted it to be so.

Off the terrace was a room equal in size to the outdoor space. The Lacours had lived mostly in this room. One side was an enormous bookshelf. In the center were a grand piano and space for a string quartet. A dining area and kitchen were on the north side, and a hall led to tiny bedrooms to the south. Cathérine's was now a playroom for Luc, the object being to lure him to his grandfather's with a paradise of toys, just as Jules had wanted to make the house a paradise when his family was young and it seemed that nothing would ever change.

But it did change. Jacqueline was gone; Cathérine visited, but lived out to the northwest, in Cergy; Luc now slept when his mother brought him, and didn't have the energy to play with the toys. Living alone, Jules, like most widows and widowers, talked to himself. But it wasn't quite so. Never once, ever, did he speak to himself, but always to Jacqueline, to his mother, to his father, and to none other. His affectionate reports were even in tone and unemotional. He didn't think that anyone would actually hear them, although he allowed that somehow, by hope and through mystery, they might. It wasn't that he thought they were listening, but rather that, whether they were listening or not, he wanted to speak to them. His loyalty had not in passing time been diminished by the slightest fraction, and he loved to summarize for them all that had happened since they had left. Although he wanted their opinion, and never got it, he spoke as if expecting it. For in their complete silence and immobility, and with the patience of eternity, the compassionate dead looking on were infinitely wiser than the living, so many of whom never stopped for an instant as they thrashed through life like fish in a net.

By the time Jules returned from the George

V, the rain had stopped. He pulled up to the garage, pressed a button in the car, and the door was swallowed by the ceiling as if the house were inhaling a scarf. He drove in as the door closed behind him, and left the car, not bothering to lock it. In the spacious garage were a Rolls-Royce, a Maybach, and two lizard-like Italian motorcycles as black and swept back as the hair of their atrocious owners. Those self-idolizing idiots loved the dreadful sound of their expensive engines. The whine, like that of a huge blade encountering exceedingly hard wood, was their music. When, encased in leather and helmeted like bugs, they rode these machines, they gunned them as they came out of the garage and roared up the drive. You could hear them a little later racing across the Seine at Le Vésinet-Le Pecq, the sound they made like that of Stukas subduing Poland. The lizard boys seemed not to care about waking a thousand babies from their afternoon naps, or, at night, whole populations formerly asleep in what they had thought were quiet villages.

In good weather, the Rolls and Maybach were taken out twice a week for exercise. The family chauffeur would arrive in uniform to spend eight hours attending to them, which is why they were as clean and polished as the day they were born. The smell of their wood-and-leather interiors was worth paying for, especially as it was accompanied, if faintly, by the lingering perfumes of the elegant women Shymanski would often have ferried to his house for business meetings. He was in a wheelchair, unable to dash around the way he did when constructing his empire, which had sprouted with electric vigor from a little pharmacy in Passy. Now the modest shop had become a multinational combine with factories all around the world, producing not only drugs but jet engines, perfume, elevators, telephones, naval vessels, and Champagne.

Jules could have placed a hundred photographs of Jacqueline in the house, but he knew that she would disapprove. So he had only five. It was a big apartment, and five photographs were not overwhelming. He could've had a thousand pictures of Cathérine, but she was alive and young, so he had only two, and there was one of his parents, their sole surviving image. These photographs had become as much his world as the world itself, perhaps more so, for in them he found comfort and invulnerability. Like certain music, were it done right, they could be a window beyond life.

With a revulsion that had cost him dearly, Jules had shied away from a theoretical approach to music. Never could he rise in the faculty, because he preferred neither to analyze the miracles within music nor to question its natural flow. He had taught a small corps of great musicians, even if as the classical music audience disappeared none of them had had either the inclination to hire a publicist or the personality to appeal naturally to the public — and thus break through to fame and riches. They labored in obscurity. He was capable of expertly teaching the technicalities. With his long experience these came easily, and as a *Maître* he was unchallenged. That was not however the essence of what he provided to his students. First he made sure that they played flawlessly, and when he was assured that they did, he bid them disengage. That is, analogously, to close their eyes and take their hands from the wheel or let go of the reins.

"Music," he told them, countering their education and the ethos of his country, his continent, and the century, "is not made by man. If you know this and surrender to it you'll allow its deeper powers to run through you. It's all a question of opening the gates. Of risking your disappearance and accepting it. If you arrive at that state you'll be effortlessly propelled, seized, and possessed by the music. Paradoxically, your timing will be perfect as time ceases to exist. All matter, and even we, are a construction of energy, and all energy is pulse and proportion. Within the most stolid block of granite, electrons have never ceased to circle and speed. Perhaps if you could see them they'd look like

136

stars. Whether or not they pulse with light, they are animate. In us, animation is body and soul. We move, we sense, we see, all by the organization of irrepressible primal pulses. When music is great, it's coordinate with those. You can't engineer this: it's too fine. You just have to accept it."

"How," they would ask, in their expressions.

"Give it everything, work 'til exhaustion, exceed yourself, risk, and it will come to you. And then, if you've done your homework, it will be beautiful."

Delphine — tall, fine featured, with brown hair pulled back and beautifully braided — was like so many musicians of her sex highly intelligent and always quietly judging. Her violin and bow had been resting on her lap but secure in her hands. Then she straightened, and held out violin and bow slightly to each side, lifting them as in a question. "And what is beautiful?" she challenged.

"I realize," Jules answered, "that anyone your age has had a relativistic education. I realize as well that Croce produced a thick volume attempting, even if sideways, to arrive at a definition of beauty, and couldn't. Just because you can't catch and stuff it doesn't mean it doesn't exist or that you can't see it. And it isn't in the eye of the beholder but rather that people see differently and some are entirely blind. The keen, the myopic, the color blind, and the blind looking at a moun-

137

tain range from different angles and in different light would see or not see many different things, but the mountain range would be the same.

"For me, beauty is a hint, a flash, a glimpse of the divine and a promise that the world is good. And in music that spark can be elongated long enough to be a steady light."

Often they heard what he was saying but couldn't allow themselves to know it, such was their education. Furthermore, they didn't think he would actually say what they feared he would say, and what some of them longed for, unless he were pressed and cornered. But they didn't know him. They didn't know that he was only the latest of untold generations that had not failed to assert what current generations denied, and that those to whom Jules was heir had done so for thousands of years and at immediate pain of death, which often followed. At the age of four this ancient, stubborn confession had been thrust into his child's heart as if by cauterizing steel, and neither force nor fashion could turn him from it.

They would think that, out of fear, he would go no further, for in university faculties there is a kind of terror to which they were highly attuned because they were young and still had far to go. But then he would shock and surprise them as much by what would appear to be his tranquility as by what

138

he would say. "Quite simply, and make of it what you will: music is the voice of God."

They had to reject this, or at least they thought they did, to make their ways in the world. They had to make a living. They had to support families that, though they did not yet exist, would come. How could they own up to such a thing, something that could not be proved but only asserted or, according to Jules Lacour, experienced? So they kept their distance until — if they worked hard enough and were devoted enough, and could, without design, flow through a piece without effort — when they were at home alone or in some cold and drafty practice studio, or on a stage, blindingly lit, their selves would disappear, gravity and time would cease to exist, sound and light would combine, and they would know that their sacrifices had not been in vain, that their poverty had been riches, that the world was not only what it seemed, and that what Jules had said was true.

Thus he would make clear to his students and to himself time and again that he preferred waves to wave theory, that, in his view, a porpoise understands wave theory better than a physicist. "Look," he would say, "at home I have a stainless steel drain strainer, which when struck with a spoon produces a perfect, unclouded C with fifteen seconds of sustain. Were I younger I might be able to hear thirty seconds. The quality of beauty is implicit in my kitchen-sink strainer despite its uninspiring form and function — implicit in the steel, implicit in the form, and brought out by what? Accident? Perception? Illusion? Or perhaps by something greater, waiting to spring, that would sound, and sing, forever."

But then, contradicting himself, he did have a theory about the power of photographs. God knows, he spent enough time looking at photographs and paintings: that is, portraits. Landscapes could be exquisite, but in painting it was the human form that, like music, lent itself to transcendent powers. Facial expression, the way a body was positioned — these were language beyond language that could communicate an infinite variety of messages, coexisting even if contradictory, until their power was intensified beyond what intellect could describe.

His theory of photographs was so simple as almost not to be a theory, which pleased him in that he didn't want it to be. It stemmed from a movie he had seen. He couldn't remember which, but in it a detective solved a crime by looking carefully at a photograph and noticing something or someone in the background, that, caught by a shutter speed of hundredths of a second, otherwise would have passed unnoticed.

Like everything else, time is infinitely divisible. In the motion of things, therefore, we

140

miss most of what is present. So might it not be that in freezing an interval we cannot otherwise perceive, a photograph allows a liberation of powers we do not know we have, a window into truth that exists at every moment and everywhere but that in our continual distraction we do not see? What else could explain the power and truth of expressions frozen long ago but in which the camera had captured an elusive truth that nonetheless is always present? Somehow, Jacqueline's young eyes held complete knowledge of what was to come, and her smile held sadness.

The photographs of his wife and child, his mother and father, would, with concentration, come alive. Jacqueline in a canoe in Canada, her head turned toward him as she sat in the bow, her flowing deep red hair, long magnificent back, and shockingly beautiful face, young and smiling. Jacqueline, age twenty-seven, the first, formal, faculty portrait of her, in a Chanel suit. Her youth, her openness, kindness, and willingness shone through as if she were really there. Cathérine, in a gorgeous portrait of her asleep as a baby, in complete innocence and flawless beauty, her deep red hair, like her mother's, splayed magnificently on the pillow, or as a mischievous sprite that he would forever love, making a face, in a ridiculous Bolivian hat. And the tattered, cracked, sepia photograph of his parents at a beach in the thirties, when they were less than half his age now. Perhaps he read too much into it, but it was as if, despite their expressions, they knew, and as if they were looking at the child who was yet to be born and who was looking back at them from the future they understood then better than it would be possible for him to understand now. Such is the power of photographs, the power of music, and the power of love.

The next morning, he arose naturally at six-thirty. There had been not a single note of music in his dreams. When he was young he would hear whole symphonies there, grand pieces, long cadenzas derived from Mozart, Beethoven, and Brahms. He never wrote them down, because though they were variations with many an original theme or phrase, they owed everything to what had inspired them. And rarely did he play his own music for anyone but himself, for it always brought him back to the same thing, and he often had to stop in mid-phrase.

By seven o'clock he had shaved, bathed, and was out the door and in cool sunshine. Unlike many runners, who had colorful clothes, shoes engineered like Ferraris, and various accessories — water bottles, visors, pouches, pedometers, music players — he had a pair of old white tennis shoes, military surplus khaki shorts, and a gray T-shirt. That was it, except for a swimming pool pass and goggles pinned at the waist to the right side of the shorts. Although he was no longer fast, he was steady. A slow, five-kilometer run, kilometer swim, and fifteen minutes of weights and calisthenics outdid all the accessories in the world. In the army he had learned that he was happiest when stripped of everything but his own strengths. All the rest, purchased, was never truly to be possessed.

Easy breathing didn't come to him in the compound, on the Rue Thiers, the Rues Salomon Resnik, Le Nôtre, Boulingrin, or the maze of streets on top of the hill, not even along the Allée Henri II in the park itself, but only when he had rounded the circle and faced the long, open straightaway of the Chemin du Long de la Terrasse, the Grand Terrace, its narrow white paths engraved as if by a rule and disappearing north in the open air.

The forest of Saint-Germain-en-Laye was enormous, the trees thick, the allées mainly level. You could run any route you pleased, a hundred kilometers even, and hardly pass the same place twice. But though far cooler in summer and less used than the Grand Terrace, it had so much less wind and light that Jules, who could no longer run great distances as once he had, preferred the terrace and the immense gardens of the Chateau de Saint-Germain-en-Laye.

Averse to death by cardiac infarction, he had accepted for almost two decades the humiliation of being passed by girls, who probably thought it miraculous not that someone like him was running, but that someone like him was still alive. Though he could go much faster, solely out of caution he didn't. In fact, with the musculature of a much younger man, he could easily have run until his heart gave out, and he knew it. Running high above the river at a good but easy pace, newly harvested fields to his right, and trails of mist sparkling in the sun as they rose from the Seine, he waited for music, but nothing came.

Today, Tuesday, was the only day of the week that the pool was open at eight. As was his custom, he arrived in just enough time to do a thousand meters before the nine-thirty closing. After passing through the turnstiles, he elicited from a frog-like little gatekeeper who dressed remarkably like Clemenceau a greeting not necessarily to be expected from a professional attendant: "You again."

"Why do you always say that to me?" Jules asked.

"Say what?"

"*You again.* Do you say it to everyone?"

"Yes and no."

"That answer is impossible in response to the question."

"I don't think so."

"I know so."

"Intellectuals are all the same."

"I'm not an intellectual, and intellectuals are not all the same."

"Some of them are."

"That means not all of them are."

"That's what *you* say. *I* say they are."

Having lost, if not on the merits, and given up some minutes in the pool, Jules surrendered. Now he would have to swim faster, but the risk of death such as it might be was still preferable to swimming not a thousand meters but 975, or 950, or, God forbid, 875. And, unlike others — doctors, lawyers, beefy finance guys who wore lots of rings — all of whom were finishing up and would head for the showers, the mirrors, and the hair dryers, Jules did not have to change. He shed his shoes and shirt, not bothering to lock them up, unpinned his goggles, and dived into an empty lane as the last of the other swimmers cleared the hall.

Warmed up by his run, he began slowly but then increased the pace, going a little faster than usual. Even with the water rushing by as he moved through it, in the empty hall the sound made by all indoor pools had not failed to gather beneath the ceiling — a sound like a continuous soft crash; or the crumpling of tissue paper; or the extreme extension of a breaker as it recedes and its abandoned foam sinks into the sand; or, heard from a distance, a forest fire minus the crack of exploding trees; or a cathedral in which a large number of supplicants mumble prayers that mix together beneath the vaults before escaping on the wind. Because sound had been his profession in adulthood and his love for as long as he could remember, he had a lot of analogies for it and a lot of memories of it.

At 550 meters, his rhythm strong and steady, his strokes powerful, at each turn of his head to breathe, he looked up to see the three replica dolphins suspended over the pool as if leaping from the water. The dorsal fin of the first one almost touched the ceiling. The other two followed in a slightly imperfect arc. It was beautifully done, realistic but with a touch of artfulness and impossibility. They were such admirable creatures and in their flight so wonderful that his strokes came in line with and were perfected by their inspiration.

As he caught their flawless rhythm, it came to him, a simple phrase of two bars, repeated with ascending and descending variations so as to make it forward sounding, rising, gathering, open, sunny, and optimistic. But for every two steps up it took a sad and commemorative step back — a look at what had been left behind, an acknowledgment of what had been sacrificed to lift the song into the present, and an expression of love for all that had been lost. As soon as the core of the piece was established, the accompaniment came to him, a string section playing elongated notes to shepherd forward the progress of the two bars in their alternating rise and fall.

At first he thought he should get out of the water lest he forget, but the music would not and could not leave him. It filled the echoing swimming hall as if the Orchestre de la Suisse Romande were playing at full volume in the bleachers. He knew that it would follow him through Saint-Germain-en-Laye to the obscure little café where he would have a scalding hot chocolate and a brioche. He knew that were music playing there it would not drive the piece from his head, for what had come to him in a moment of need was exquisite and good. At the very least, it was telephone hold music. He had it. It was beautiful. And now he might get money from Acorn, to give, along with his prayers, to Cathérine and Luc.

JACQUELINE AT SPARTA

On his terrace at Saint-Germain-en-Laye, as summer rose from the grave to give Paris a last reminder of itself, mating with the autumn air until the offspring of the two seemed like the first days of spring, Jules was pleasantly exhausted from his run. In weak sun shining through white haze as cool and dry as smoke, he half-slept, half-dreamed. Sometimes trains tooted like toys as they crossed the Seine at Le Pecq, but other than that it was quiet enough to hear the passage of soft winds.

Summer, 1964. Jules Lacour is twenty-four, looking forward to prestigious graduate studies in the fall. The reputation of the faculty where he will study is like a crown of invincibility, and, thus assured and to his everlasting shame, he behaves badly.

Trapped for days in a cheap, ancient hotel in Milan, the bleak hallways of which echo with the lost sounds of German soldiers quartered there twenty years before, he and his friends naively wait for the car they have shipped from Paris by rail to be offloaded at the freight yard. It takes them four days to understand that this will occur only with a bribe.

Jules, Serge, Alain, and Sandrine each have a single room much like a prison cell. On the wall above Jules' bed, as if in the previous two decades there had been no such thing as paint, is a crude portrait of a German soldier, with a penis the size of the Hindenburg, facing a presumably Italian woman with legs spread and her dress held up above the waist. This is somehow appropriate, because the three young men, idled in heat and the incessant diesel fumes of Milanese traffic, are crazed with sex. Sandrine, pretty only from certain angles, is the subject of their lust. As in a French or Roman farce, they swift through the halls at all hours of night, thinking that the other two have not done the same, and knock at her door.

At first she is flattered, but this quickly wears thin and she begins rightly to detest them. "I hope you all had fun last night," she says during breakfast the next day, "but from now on don't knock on my door, or I'll call the Italian Masturbation Police."

Jules is mortified, Serge amused, Alain counterattacks, and it gets uglier and uglier as the days go on. By the time the car is

149

ransomed and the four of them are stuffed into it riding through the heat and dust of Southern Italy, they want to kill each other. Sandrine abandons them at Bari for the boat to Greece, stating that they should all go fuck themselves: "literally," she says. When they reach Brindisi, Jules, who wants no part of this, embarks on the boat to Patras prior to the one with reservations for the car.

On the short voyage across the Ionian Sea Jules sleeps at night on the cold, moist, sooty, rolling deck, and is almost dangerously sunburnt there during the day. Never in his life will he forget how as the ship rolls in the sea the stars seem to move back and forth across the sky, how brilliant they are, and how the black smoke from the funnel struggles to blot them out, but they emerge in untouched perfection. Before landing, two commanding German lesbians station themselves at the foot of stairs that everyone must use, and rate each man who passes. Jules is tall, slim, and blond. They give him the highest rating. Embarrassed and flustered, he has no idea why they are doing this so publicly and demonstratively, and never will he be enlightened as to their motives, but it is the first time in his life that a woman — two, actually — has told him that he is attractive. It will happen only twice more in seventy-five years: once when a sweet, mouse-like woman accidentally sees him naked in a beach cabana; and once, indirectly, when a woman on a bus comments to Jacqueline after he has kissed Jacqueline before she boards. Even once every twenty-five years on average it will shock and discomfit him, but this time, the first time, it's lucky as well, in that it whittles away some of his shyness.

The sun is setting in Sparta in July. Tourists of many nationalities overwhelm the town, and Greeks are visible only as they work in souvenir shops and restaurants. Hardened and sunburnt from walking most of the way across the Peloponnesus, eating little, and sleeping on stony ground, Jules is happy that now he carries no weapon, there is no need of weapons, and the war is over, even if not a hundred percent in France itself, where the OAS is in its last death agonies. He is walking east on Sparta's main and more-or-less only street. The sun is setting behind him, bathing everyone he faces as they pass in the deepest, richest light he has ever seen. Coming toward him, caught in this light, is a girl of twenty. She's tall. She wears a white leotard top and beige skirt. A camera strap crosses her body. Her posture is royal, her back straight, hair deep red and alight in the sun, her eyes green. Deeply tanned like everyone else in Sparta, she seems to Jules to be so extraordinarily beautiful — as, he comes to know, twenty-year-old young women

151

almost always are and sometimes remain —
that he falters as if he had tripped. Seeing
this, she smiles. He begins to take stilted little
steps so that he won't fall. This amuses her
even more, and she suppresses a laugh. Her
teeth are shockingly white, her beauty dizzying, but her expression is neither patronizing
nor haughty. Rather, it is kind and warm, as
if they are equals and have known one another for a long time.

But Jules cannot believe that he is fit to approach such a magnificent woman, and
against every impulse he forces himself to
walk on. He returns to his *pension,* agitates
for an hour, and charges out, hoping to find
her, but he doesn't, even though he walks up
and down the main street many times. He
tries to imagine what he might say to her,
and decides on no formulation, because he
knows that if he meets her he will be too
stunned to remember what he had decided.

Unable to get her out of his mind, as the
cicadas grow louder and the night grows
cooler in Sparta, he says to himself over and
over again two lines in English from a poem
by John Betjeman about an infatuation during a tennis match and after, and perhaps
forever:

Miss J. Hunter Dunn, Miss J. Hunter Dunn
Furnished and burnish'd by Aldershot
    sun. . . .

He likes Betjeman's poems. He likes Voltaire's: *"Les 'Vous' et les 'Tu' "*. Both men know love so well that they capture it in the imagination even as it eludes them, as now in Sparta it has eluded him.

Greece is full of French, German, and American tourists — the French and the Germans because the exchange rate is favorable; the French because they want nothing to do with Franco; and the Germans because, to the discomfort of everyone else, they have pleasant memories of Greece in the war. The Americans, whose exchange rate seems always to be favorable everywhere, have come in droves even prior to the release of the movie *Zorba the Greek* and subsequent sales of books by Kazantzakis. Bouzouki music is popular around the world, which delights Jules, who despite the opinions of snobs in his faculty has great admiration for Mikis Theodorakis. For them it's perfectly acceptable for Beethoven and Liszt to assay upon traditional dances, and Smetana to use an ancient folk song for *Má vlast,* but not for Theodorakis to reawaken the soul of Greece — perhaps because he was, presumably, making so much money. Five years later, in Itea, during the dictatorship of the colonels, Jules will witness the arrest of a merchant merely for playing Theodorakis' music in his shop, but Greece is happy now, at least on the surface.

Two rooms have been reserved in an Athens *pension* on the assumption that by the time the four friends reached Athens someone would have become close enough to Sandrine to share one with her. But because she's gone and Serge and Alain are in one of the rooms, Jules finds himself the sole occupant of the other. Except for a terrazzo floor, it is all white. Two single beds with white sheets and no blankets are the only furniture except for two chairs and a small table on a terrace overlooking a minute plaza at the juncture of Aristotelous and Kamaterou streets. The bathrooms and showers are off the hall.

Jules walks into Serge's and Alain's room, puts down his knapsack, and sees them sitting on their beds, feet on the floor, heads bent in dejection.

"You look depressed," he says. "Did Sandrine come back, or is it because you anticipate that I'm going to insist that you share in paying for my double room — because I am."

Serge and Alain are cousins. They shake their heads in unison. "That's not it," Serge says.

"What is it then? What happened?"

"We're leaving tomorrow, flying back."

"What about the car?"

"We sold it at a loss. It doesn't matter."

"Why?"

154

"My sister has cancer," Alain tells him.

Jules has never met her, but he feels part of the blow. "I see. I'm sorry."

"We don't know where Sandrine is. She's not here. You're on your own."

"That's nothing. Don't worry. I hope your sister gets better."

Alain looks up. "She won't. That's the point."

The next day, they're gone, and, no singles available, Jules is paying for a double room. He goes to the Acropolis, and because it's as mobbed as the Eiffel Tower doubles back and decides to return either very early or very late to avoid the crowds. The heat is exhausting. He sleeps until evening, when his room is slightly cooler, especially in the breeze of the fan above his bed. Awakening, he hears conversation on the terrace next to his. Half asleep, he staggers to the threshold between his room and its terrace. A partition of wavy glass divides his outdoor space from the one that had been off the room of Serge and Alain. Through it he sees two indistinct forms moving as gracefully as fish in an aquarium. They aren't fish, but two women, speaking in French. One has an extraordinary, bell-like, clear, and musical voice. Jules is a musician and sound is half his world. He falls in love with the voice just as he has fallen in love with the girl in Sparta. He can hear in it high intelligence, care and modulation of thought,

155

essential goodness, vitality, enthusiasm, freshness, charm, and innocence. The other voice,
while not unpleasant, is unentrancing.

The beautiful voice says, "I had no idea.
How can you love him? We spent three hours
with them. I'll bet he's in the Piazza San
Marco right now with two other French
girls."

"Not Gianni."

"Not Gianni!" the beautiful voice says,
gently mocking.

"No. He's wonderful, beneath the surface."

"I'm not sure that the surface and the
subterranean are not the same. And the
surface counts, too. In Gianni it's as slick as
oil on ice," says the beautiful voice.

"It's because he's Italian. *Bella Figura*.
When he spoke to me privately, he was different."

There's a pause. The woman of the beautiful voice, knowing when to choose her battles,
asks, "When are you leaving?"

"The boat from Piraeus leaves tonight at
nine. There's a bus, but I'll take a taxi to be
sure."

They disappear from behind the wavy glass,
and Jules, still groggy and suddenly crazy and
daring after his nap, runs to the railing. He
looks around the partition. The girl he saw in
Sparta, now in one extraordinarily quick motion, like a move in ballet or martial arts, lifts
her blouse from the hem and rockets it above

156

her head and into the air. There she stands for a moment in the light, in a white brassiere that seems to glow in contrast with her flawless, suntanned skin, her body as beautiful as her face, before she pulls on another blouse. Jules falls back into the darkness of his terrace so as not to be seen. Never has he felt the fusion of desire and necessity as he feels it now. But all he can do is sit on his bed in the shadows and feel his heart beat.

Their door opens. He rushes to the door periscope, through which he watches them leave. Each one is carrying a piece of luggage. He won't know until later, perhaps until morning, which of the two will foolishly return to Venice in search of "Gianni." Jules already detests Gianni and imagines that he's a pickpocket and a gigolo. The most beautiful voice he has ever heard will stay, and he wonders if it belongs to the most beautiful woman he has ever seen. If he had to choose, he would choose the voice.

Jules is awakened by sunlight flooding the western half of his terrace. As he pulls on a pair of khaki shorts he hears beyond the wavy glass the civilized clink of silver on china, or, given the level of accommodation, the slightly more relaxed but still civilized clink of stainless steel on ceramic. One of the two women is gone, and the other is at breakfast on her terrace. Without even putting on a shirt, he goes to the railing and looks around the partition.

The most beautiful woman he has ever seen is in fact in possession of the beautiful voice. This makes him so happy that he begins to laugh. Startled, she turns toward him. After a moment's inspection, with a neutral expression and not a ruffle of surprise, she says, "When I saw you in Sparta I didn't know you were a lunatic."

This makes him laugh even more, until he recovers and says, "I'm sorry. It's just so . . . nice to see you."

"Why?"

"Because when you smiled at me it wasn't flirtatious, it wasn't coquettish, dismissive, misleading, or false in any way. It was you, and it was kind, intelligent, innocent, and good. I had hoped to see you again, and now, by accident, there you are."

"An accident?"

"Of course it is."

"Okay. Now what?"

"Nothing, unless you have no plans and would like to go with a lunatic to the Parthenon before the crowds spoil it, because in ancient Greece people probably didn't walk around in T-shirts that said 'Heineken' or 'University of Missouri'.

She looks at him. As he knows her, she knows him. From his voice, his face, his expressions and bearing. She knows that he

158

is a good and serious man. There is perhaps more than that, as she feels the giddiness of falling in love, and although after she saw him at Sparta she thought of him a lot — even at Epidavros, even at Corinth, even in Athens — she finds it hard to believe that this should come so early and so hard.

Already far gone in the walk from Omonia to the Acropolis, they sit together on a block of ancient white marble and look out at the sea beyond Piraeus. He is in love with even the clothing that clings to her, her hands, her eyebrows, every detail, movement, gesture, and word, her perfume, the subtle embroidery at the neck of her blouse. She feels enveloped, loved, and excited by this young man who seems older than his age, wounded, strong, and even somewhat dangerous. But no matter, she knows she is protected and safe.

They speak all afternoon, and as the sun crosses the sky and the heat begins to subside he notices how her dark red hair throbs with color, and next to her glowing skin and Breton freckles her green eyes are preternaturally striking. She seems not to know how beautiful she is, or that speaking with her is electrifying. She is unmatched in the fluidity, richness, and brilliance of her conversation (Jules wonders how someone so young knows so much and judges its pertinence so well) except perhaps by François. But unlike

François she doesn't press with the weight of all that has occurred to her as Jules speaks, eager to release it in a spectacular allegro. Instead, with the perfect and natural charm of the Frenchwoman, she presses at times and she draws back just as often, she has deeply held beliefs and is sometimes grave, but she also smiles, laughs, and makes him laugh with her. This extraordinary young woman does not photograph like a model (so many of whom seem unalive, unpleasant, and stupid), because her beauty is not fixed but the result of what she is as she moves and speaks. The life within her is what makes him love her, and he thinks how lucky he is to have met her when both of them are so young.

They are astounded to discover that they live close on the same street in Paris. "It will be easy to visit you," he says, "when we get home."

"We'll see," she says, plunging him down a hundred-storey elevator shaft, instinctually barbing the hook so that it will never come out, and enjoying it immensely as soon as she realizes from his expression that she has done it. "But, you know, we've been speaking for hours, evidently — I didn't realize that — and we seem to have left something out."

"What?"

"Our names."

He pauses, realizing that he has neglected

the most obvious formality. "Jules Lacour," he says.

"Jules Lacour," she repeats. She likes it. "Jacqueline Blanchet."

"Blanchet is so often a Jewish name. Are you Jewish?"

"Yes. Are you?"

"I am. Not that it would matter?" he adds.

"No," she says, very seriously, for the first time indicating commitment. "It's convenient, isn't it, amazing actually, but you could be the Pope, and it wouldn't matter."

"You could be the Pope's daughter and I would still. . . ."

"You would still what?" she asks, interrupting. She knows what she is doing, she knows what is happening. So does he.

They have known one another for fourteen hours and not parted for a minute. That evening they return to the hotel and descend again to the tiny plaza below it. In the center is a news kiosk with three chairs inside, a microscopic kitchen, and a smoking brazier. "I've never seen a smaller restaurant," Jacqueline says. "It will be just us, assuming the other chair is for him."

The owner beckons them in. "Sit you," he says, in English. "I make best dinner in Athens." He holds up two fingers, "For price of two *Paris Match* magazine. Okay?"

"Okay," they say together.

He begins to cut up cucumbers, tomatoes, and feta. He puts four skewers on the grill. It isn't donkey meat. Fragrant smoke blows back into the interior. At evening, people have come home, lights have come on, it's cooler. "Retsina extra," he says. "Two big glass for price of *Time Magazine,* international edition. Okay?"

"Okay," Jacqueline says.

"How old are you?" Jules asks her.

"I'll be twenty in August."

"You were born in August of forty-four?"

She nods. "In London. I'm a British subject as well as a French citizen. My father was with Leclerc at the time. After Paris was liberated, it took a while but we returned. And you?"

"Twenty-four. My parents were killed the year you were born."

"Both of them?"

"Both of them, yes."

"I'm sorry. You must remember."

"I do. Your parents are alive?"

"Yes," she says, smiling. She has deep, happy affection for them. This means a lot to him. "My father," she says, "was a banker before the war. He's spent the last twenty years trying to get back what they took from him. It's useless, so he works for a salary at Crédit Lyonnais. Small banks aren't able to compete anymore anyway, and many of his clients were *exterminated.* I use that term because it was the term that was used, and even if others may, I shall never forget it, and never cease to understand what it means about who I am — now, in the present tense — and who I'll remain in the future."

"And yet you're not afraid or bitter."

"We have what was denied to them. We would betray them were we not happy to be alive. It's nothing less than an obligation — to see as they cannot see, hear as they cannot hear, feel as they cannot feel, taste as they cannot taste, love as they cannot love."

Nineteen until August, Jacqueline doesn't know what she will do. She has always been a superb student. She will have her choice. He wonders if she is too good for him, too subtle, too deep, too regal, certainly too beautiful. Men will be smitten with her throughout her life, she will always have her choice of whom to hold, and she's very young now.

The news vendor is right. His is the best if least pretentious restaurant in Athens, and he has tossed away his profit to give them a whole bottle of retsina, which they finish as they eat, and which brings them even closer and puts them more at ease.

"My friends left," Jules informs her, "because the sister of one of them has cancer. They sold their car and flew back. They're cousins."

"My girlfriend left to go back to Venice, where we went out with two Italian boys who only want to have sex with English-speaking, French, Teutonic, and Scandinavian girls. She doesn't know that, but she'll find out."

"I'm paying for a double room."

"So am I," Jacqueline confirms.

"If we combined?"

"After less than a day?"

"I wouldn't take advantage. I wouldn't even try."

"Everything has happened as fast," she says, "but this is different. I know it is. And I trust you, I much more than trust you."

"Of course. You should. I have such high regard for. . . ."

"Shhh!" she says. "I trust you more than not to 'take advantage'. I trust you in everything. And it would be highly stupid and wrong if we didn't make love. I'm not that quick. Absolutely not. I'm very old-fashioned and guarded, and always have been. But not now." She rises.

In the *pension* they consolidate their things quickly. The management is cooperative, and ten minutes after dinner, at around ten o'clock, they are sitting on one of the beds in what was hers and now is their room, the door locked, the neighborhood quiet, the air sensuous.

Jules embraces her, and the sides of their faces touch as they hold close. Perfectly content, they remain in one another's arms for a very long time. He is in love with her delicacy and hesitation, and she is in love with his. They fear only that it is an illusion that will not last, but it does, and it will.

In Saint-Germain-en-Laye, yet another train sounded its horn as it crossed the Seine, tooting as if it were part of a model railroad, and Jules awakened. In memory he has been to Sparta many times, and although Jacqueline is gone, she is still there in the reddening sun as he saw her the first time, somehow still alive, more alive and vivid, with each day that passes, than even the present. Everything he loved, he loved in her.

THE PAST UPWELLS

In the fortress in Algeria and the forests
around it, the young soldiers had learned that
everything was at risk every hour of every
day. As it had been for most of mankind since
the beginning, and continued to be so in
regions of pestilence, famine, and war, life
was tenuous and unprotected. For Jules, this
was not a revelation, and yet throughout his
life the dangers had been primarily episodic
— in infancy and early childhood during the
war, during the late forties and early fifties in
severe illnesses just before the dawn of truly
modern medicine, then in Algeria, in France
when the Algerian war was brought home,
and, in a minor way, during the crisis of '68.

In regard to even the most protected and
stable lives in the protected and stable West,
a car crash, cancer, or a child gone missing,
to name just a few of many catastrophes, gave
lie to the general assumption of safety. Jules
lived, nonetheless, like everyone else, in the
illusion of security that modernity affords to

166

advanced nations. He understood the absurdity of his minor complaints, and yet despite what he knew and had experienced he could not put them in their place: clothes at the cleaners not ready; the Métro hot and crowded; a cold rain soaking him as he rowed; receiving a wildly inaccurate and impudently demanding bill; the sink leaking; a dog wailing all night.

Irritations like these would vanish in the face of illness and death — when Jacqueline died, when Luc became ill. And it was happening slowly (true, he had a special sensitivity) as French Jews felt the fear and darkness of the thirties rolling in, differently this time, but in some respects a close copy of its early phases.

He fought as best he could, but the more he planned the more he realized he was not in control. Had he not gone to the George V and been engaged purely by luck? And had he not discovered only in the rhythm of swimming the song that might help to pull his family through?

All this was so, but the day after the theme had come to him on the air over the water, the stakes were raised, and whatever remained of the illusion of control was completely shattered. For in the morning of the day he would record the song, send it off, and row happily on the Seine, he would (entirely against his wishes) begin to fall in love. And by nightfall, violence would change what was left of his old age.

The teaching of music was spread all over the city. Because Jacqueline had always been based in the Quartier latin and Jules had started there, he had made a tremendous effort to stay in place after his faculty was moved to Clignancourt. Long before that, when the Conservatoire National was moved to the Cité de la Musique, he stuck like a limpet to his tiny office in a quiet building in the Sorbonne. But to teach he had to fly almost from one extreme of the city to another, in traffic, dodging trucks, speeding by endless litter and explosions of graffiti in the weed-choked allées that paralleled the busy highways.

To record his thirty-two bars, he had to go to the Conservatoire in the Cité de la Musique on the eastern side of Paris. Arriving in mid-morning, he was able to round up half a dozen violinists, two violists, and a student to act as engineer. It would take only half an hour. But he was in need of another cellist, and none was about. As he handed out the music to his little improvised orchestra, half of whom had been or would eventually be his students, he said, "We need another cello. Is anyone around? We really shouldn't go ahead without it."

"Élodi," said Delphine.

"Who?"

"Élodi. She's not yet in the program," meaning the joint program with Paris-Sorbonne in which all of Jules' students were enrolled. "She just came up from Lyon. I saw her a minute ago and she has her cello. She's a little strange."

"How do you mean?"

"Maybe I shouldn't say, and it's hard to express, but she's tense yet disconnected. You'd think that she'd grown up in an old house, all by herself, with just books."

Wanting to defuse this, Jules said, "Maybe she did. There's nothing wrong with that. You've heard her play?"

Delphine nodded. "You can't help but be jealous."

"Then go get her." He expected an odd-looking, awkward, and unattractive girl, and decided, charitably, to protect her from the others.

They set up. The drafted engineer, who wore distinctive rectangular black glasses he'd bought in New York, went through his checks. The students studied the music and tuned their instruments. Jules loved the promising, not-quite random sounds that come before a concert, like animal sounds in the jungle, which startle you and then disappear.

"It looks nice," one of the violists said, "very nice, simple, and hypnotic."

"Telephone hold music," Jules stated. "A

169

job. And thank you for your help, all of you."

They waited. Some studied their parts, some actually played them briefly, ending abruptly so as not to trespass on the prerogative of the composer to decide how the piece would be conducted. Jules wanted to get started and had begun impatiently to tap his left foot. Then Élodi walked in. His expectations had been wrong. She was extraordinarily attractive, captivating, and graceful. One could tell that despite her striking and unorthodox beauty she was, and might always be, alone. Only part of it may have been that she was so radiant as to be unapproachable.

Here was not only great complexity, but mystery. Jules felt that she had no interest in making a connection with anyone beyond what was minimally necessary, perhaps, to make a living — if indeed she had to, given that she possessed the air of someone who does not. Not a few women are so wounded that they seem similarly ethereal ·and detached, but she seemed not at all wounded. In fact, she radiated confidence bordering on contempt, but without demonstration of either. She was tall and slim, with a long, straight back and an almost military posture. A mane of sandy blonde hair combed back from her high forehead fell in a wave below her shoulders. Her features were even, her cheekbones high, her nose fine and assertive: that is, like her posture, there was an exciting thrust to it. Most distinctive were her eyes, which to Jules seemed illuminated by the kind of storm light that slips in under a tight layer of cloud. This may have occurred to him because, steady and guarded, her expression was almost like that of a sailor peering into the wind.

She was wearing a navy suit jacket with simple white trim, a plunging but narrow neckline, no blouse beneath, and heels that made her tower over everyone else, to whom she gave not even a glance. Her perfume was fresh. Although she seemed unhappy, it was impossible to tell if either happiness or unhappiness were pertinent to her. She found a seat, un-cased her cello, took the music handed to her by another student, and looked at it intently, seeming to take it in both deftly and expertly.

"Do you have to tune your instrument?" Jules asked after she failed to do so.

With a slight smile of either conceit or otherworldly detachment, she said, "I was playing it moments ago."

She didn't deign to glance at him. Everyone else looked to him for direction, but she stared down or ahead as if no one but she were in the room. He understood — Jules knew himself — how, suddenly, he could desire her as strongly as he had desired or loved any woman at first glance. And yet he felt no sexual attraction. Perhaps after its absence or secret containment it would surface explosively, but not now. Now all he wanted was proximity. The greatest pleasure he could imagine would be to face her a hand's breadth away, merely to be close, actually to look in her eyes or, even if not, to look at them, to watch her, the pulses in her neck, her blink, her smile. He would have been content with just that. To kiss her would either have broken the spell or been unimaginably transcendent. He tried not to stare or give himself away, but he was breathing more deeply than he should have been.

How could he have fallen in love so quickly, beyond his control, and stupidly? Although she looked much older, she was probably twenty-five, certainly no older than thirty. It was impossible and undesirable. Even were it possible it would have been impossible. He had had, of course, like any man frequently in the presence of young women, many temporary infatuations, but never like this. Had he touched her, just shaken hands, he would have been gone forever. But he had always put an end to such things and come back to Jacqueline, his infatuations calmed.

"Okay," he said. "Thank you for your time. This is what the Americans call a demo. It's a theme to be used in commercials and for telephone hold music." Because he was smiling when he said it, they laughed. Élodi looked at him sharply, as if she understood that something, perhaps his dignity, or more than his dignity, was in play. "I've recently dealt with some very rich, strange, crazy, and perhaps dangerous people. They commissioned this and I agreed to it. They probably won't be happy, but let's get on with it."

Everyone positioned themselves. That is, everyone but Élodi, who didn't move a centimeter. When they were settled in, the engineer gave a thumbs up, Jules nodded out the count to three, and all the bows began to move simultaneously. Very quickly, the students were taken up by the music, lifted out of themselves and into the better world that was the reason they had become or were becoming musicians, a world into which they were given entry with just a few strokes of a bow. It was so easy and yet so wonderful that it left them as if among angels. When after a day at work they would go home, they would float above the sidewalk, the sky would come alight, everything that moved would dance, and the faces of people in the Métro would be like the faces in Renaissance paintings.

Now they were gliding along the rhythmic ascending and descending waves, locked in the repetitions, and moved by the violins' commentary — a loving but sad validation — upon the more active cellos and violas. The entire cycle lasted only a minute, and they went through it four times, five times, six, and seven. The engineer kept on giving the cut signal, but they were entranced. Their expressions were elevated and alive with optimism. They were happy, but with the regretful underlayment that makes happiness real.

Glancing at them, Jules recognized the beatific expression musicians sometimes have when they play the allegro of the Third Brandenburg and do not want to stop. He had never heard his own piece played, never seen how it could affect others. He thought that, as in all good music of every kind, he had been privileged to allow the escape of — in this case — the tiniest sliver of an ever-present perfection that presses invisibly against the heart of all things. And he knew that were they to go through the cycle too many times, as they might, something would be lost. There was only so much of the gift of music that the soul could support until exhaustion. So he stopped it while they were still vibrating almost as much as their strings.

"Beautiful," said a violinist as the instruments were cased.

"American telephones," said another, "will now surpass ours. You're a traitor."

"It's for our telephones, too."

They liked it, but would the Americans? After all, it had no "Bop bop, sheh bop!" Or anything like that. America was a giant country that seemed always to be racing ahead and bouncing up and down. Very violent Europeans had clashed with very crazy savages in a place where geysers popped out of the ground, and what you got was "Bop bop, sheh bop!" At least that was the view of the French. His piece would have to pass muster in Los Angeles, which was sunny, pastel, green, and unreal. Jules didn't even know how to send it there. "Can you make this into an MP9?" he asked the engineer.

"An MP3? Sure. Do you have an email address?"

Jules didn't like having even a cell phone, but Cathérine was able to attach one to him by arranging a beautiful aria as its ring tone. Sometimes Jules would call himself on his landline so he could listen to it over and over. And often he missed calls because he listened rather than answer. He didn't remember his cell number, and most of the time left the phone off. Of the engineer at his bank of equipment, he asked, "You can do it right here, now?"

The engineer, knowing that Jules was of several generations past, nodded tolerantly. "This is a computer," he said.

"It records and it mails? It's all prepared?"

"All prepared." With some rapid keystrokes and mouse movements, he set it up. "What's the address?"

It was *jackcheatham@acornint.com.*

"What would you like to say?"

"I would like to say, in English, *'Dear Jack,*

175

here is the music you asked for. I hope it pleases you. Please let me know at your earliest convenience. Jules Lacour.' "

"That's all?"

"What else?"

The engineer hit send. "It's done."

Jules thanked him. Things had gone wonderfully, and for the moment he was not thinking of Élodi, but when he turned she was right there, staring at him. She couldn't have been either more forward or more inexplicable. He almost started. Now he could see directly into her eyes, and never had he beheld a more elegant and refined woman, not even Jacqueline. This pained him, but he couldn't escape either the truth of it, the traction, or the feeling of euphoria as he stood by her.

She broke the silence. "*Bonjour.* I'm going to be your student," she said matter-of-factly, extending her hand. He reciprocated, they shook hands, and when they stopped they failed to disengage — for perhaps five extraordinary seconds.

After a moment, he came out with, "I don't think you're on my list." It was all he could manage to say.

"I'm not, but I will be," she replied.

He was astounded. Among other reasons, this did not happen. But though placement was not up to the students, he had no doubt that in fact she would be on his list.

"I may have to go to America for a few weeks," he said.

As if he were an idiot, she replied, instructionally, "You'll be back, and I'll be here." Then, without looking at him, she lifted her cello, turned, and walked out. He might as well have been hit with a shovel.

At the beginning of fall, cool nights at Saint-Seine-l'Abbaye (the source of the Seine, near Dijon), and in the Haute Marne and other regions descending from the lower parts of Switzerland into the Île-de-France had sped up the flow of the Seine and made it suddenly cold. At no preset date, but as September wears on, it is as if a switch is thrown to banish summer. The strength of the sun is equivalent to that of March, the leaves begin to turn, with many having fallen already in August, and the scent of burning brush, floating up the hill in Saint-Germain-en-Laye, hints at the wood fires that will arrive with winter.

Jules had put his boat in the water and begun to row upstream against the stiff current that just before he got in his shell had tried to rip it from the dock. For half an hour he would fight the flow, moving slowly, and then shoot back to the boathouse in less than ten minutes. The turn at the Bir-Hakeim Bridge would be tricky, for when the current was perpendicular to the boat, swinging the stern around required force greater than that which pushed against it from upstream. He had seen single shells swept downriver sideways, totally out of control, until they were either fortuitously turned in an eddy, thrown against the embankment, or capsized.

Unlike many who found themselves once every few years struggling in the water, Jules had never gone over. Not only was he anxious of maintaining his perfect record, but, for him, capsizing would be dangerous especially when the water was cold and fast flowing. So he tried to concentrate, but found that he couldn't. Possessed by excitement, fear, and regret, his mind raced as he strained at the oars. Thinking of the young woman, Élodi, who had appeared and disappeared, leaving teasing words that echoed through him, he felt what he had felt half a century before when he had fallen in love with Jacqueline — a dizzying, euphoric, internal rocket launch.

But it was impossible and it was wrong. Though Jacqueline was dead and by the world's standards far more than a decent interval had passed, she lived in his memory, and to replace her would be to silence her. He spoke to her many times a day. He brought back her image and could see her in color, moving and three-dimensional. He was able to feel her touch and retrieve the scent of her perfume just in imagination. Little was left of her except in the fidelity he dared not compromise.

Had Jacqueline never existed, falling in love with Élodi would anyway have been ill-advised. He was not François Ehrenshtamm, who could leave even a living woman he had once loved and start all over again with someone else young enough to be his daughter. Jules had always thought that this kind of desire for a much younger woman was a vain play against death — which, because it of all things could not be denied, would end the gambit in hellish suffering not in an after-world but this one, when the aged man who had become a repulsive husk would despair upon the sight of a young woman who wanted and deserved others.

Élodi was young enough to be his grand-daughter and probably had no interest in him at all. He hoped he had misinterpreted her tone and her words. He didn't want, like François, to tilt against aging and death but rather only to spar with them, striking here and there, evading their blows as much as possible, but always aware that they would win. In that dance they would take the lead and he would accept it if only because courage was worth more than trying to hold on to youth.

Although at first his astounding infatuation had had no sexual component, now he felt such immense heat in imagining her that he quivered. He was possibly fit and capable enough to keep up with her for a while, but how long would that last? It simply could not be, so he tried just to concentrate upon the rhythm of his strokes as he strained at the oars. But straining at the oars was like making love to her, and in a parallel he didn't particularly like, he couldn't strain for as long as he wanted against the new volumes of water flowing inexhaustively from the foothills of the Alps.

Remembering the calming scent of smoke rising up from the slopes of Saint-Germain-en-Laye was not enough to distract him. Nor were the prospects of his song in America. All he could think of was this Élodi, in whose presence he had been for only twenty minutes, whom he had hardly touched, and with whom he had spoken only a few uncertain words. Then, at Bir-Hakeim, he made the difficult turn while he was distracted, and was almost swept sideways downriver. But because there had been so many turns over so many years and he was not quite ready to fail, he recovered and was soon speeding back to the dock, fast and straight, liberated for a moment from everything except his rapid progress on the water.

Ten years before, after sprinting without pause for half an hour he would have been awakened as if by caffeine, but now after rowing or running he had to rest. A twenty-minute nap usually would suffice, or just sitting quietly on a bench. No one else was in the boathouse, as often was the case when he rowed. The few people left in the club almost always came only in the morning or on weekends. He paid ever-increasing dues keyed to the ever-declining membership, kept his boat and oars in good order, cleaned up the dock, and tidied the desk where the logbook rested. Though he was the most senior member of the club, if not the oldest, many of the newer ones, never having seen him, thought he was fictitious.

He took a long, hot shower, and dressed. A cot wedged between the boat bays was covered in a white towel. Someone may have used the towel to wipe down a boat, and it was filthy. He seized it, threw it into a hamper, took a freshly laundered terrycloth from the top of the dryer, and laid it out. Then he sat on the cot and looked over the dock and across the water.

Though the fast-flowing Seine was the color of gunmetal, the sky was Parisian blue and early autumn wind made trees across the water glitter in continuous palsy. Because of the wind, the velocity of the current, and the surge of barge traffic in mid-afternoon, no one would be rowing. Also, participation fell off at the end of summer, when people were busy once again, and who could blame them? Streets, gardens, and colors were at their most beautiful in the cool air, dimming light, and the shadow of a weakening sun. The club was neither incorporated nor allowed in Paris itself, but the barge had been moored against the Quai du Point du Jour since before the war, and during the war was used by the Resistance. Every mayor of Paris since had told them that if they kept quiet, didn't expand, publicize, or make a fuss, they could stay.

Jules swung his feet onto the cot, lay back, and turned his head to see barges as they raced by. The wind coursing through the leaves sounded like a river running through a weir. He breathed deeply, intending to sleep for twenty minutes or so but no longer. As he thought of one thing after another, all took flight and he was released into sleep.

When he awoke it was dark except for lights on the opposite bank. He had slept so deeply he knew neither where he was nor when it was — not merely the time but the decade. After a few seconds, he got his bearings. The boathouse didn't have a clock, his watch didn't have a luminous dial, and because he was never there at night he didn't remember where the light switch was.

As he sat up he felt the cell phone in his pocket, pulled it out, and flipped it open. It illuminated his face in such a deathly way that it was fortunate he didn't see himself.

Nonetheless he was shocked to see that it was after eight and he had slept for more than five hours. Then he remembered Élodi, and a wave of pleasure and pain coursed through his body. Without even thinking, he used the phone to call Ehrenshtamm.

"Have you eaten?" he asked.

"Who?"

"What do you mean, *who*? Who else?"

"I'm about to go out. I gave a speech, got home late, and they had already eaten — with nothing left for me, thank you very much. I think that's a message, but anyway I was going to go to Renée. Why? Where are you?"

"Rowing."

"At night?"

"No. I slept. See you in half an hour." Jules disconnected.

They still frequented the undistinguished *Boul-Miche* bistros in which they had practically lived when they were students, but now when François finished a speech in which he was adored by the audience — especially the attractive women — and pocketed a fat check, he liked to go to Chez Renée on the Boulevard Saint-Germain. Not only was it excellent, it was the kind of place where if François were recognized he would be ignored, because many of its patrons were, or thought themselves, of equal or superior status. He was an intellectual, and they were intellectuals, but because he was famous and

183

could be seen on television, they looked down on him as much as they deeply envied him. Also the restaurant served Purée Crécy, for which François had had a weakness since childhood. He had been going there for a long time, it was doing badly enough to suggest that it might close, and he wanted to help.

"You slept for five hours? Are you sick?"

"Tired."

"Usually a good reason to sleep. Shouldn't you have gone home first? You're not a narcoleptic."

"Perhaps not, but when I nap in the afternoon I find it hard to wake up. I'm still not fully awake. What was your speech like?"

"It went well, filled the hall, lots of beautiful women, especially one in the front row. I couldn't stop looking at her."

"What was the subject?"

"Accident and design."

"I may not have the heart for controversies anymore. There have been too many, and I'm too old."

"It was on a different level, apart from controversy. I observed that sometimes accident is so perfectly aligned with purpose that it seems impossible that there is no design, but I didn't push for a conclusion. Hamlet tells Horatio that sometimes our indiscretions serve us well, and then concludes that it's because a divinity shapes our ends — and I can't believe that Shakespeare, of all people, was unaware of the rather broad pun. I left that to the audience and dwelt instead upon the many circumstances when that which either you never could have dreamed or that which you fight against surprisingly delivers you to your exact intended destination. You know those film clips, of explosions or natural catastrophes, that are run backwards?"

"Yes, the billion fragments of a vase that has fallen to the floor and been smashed, but all the pieces fly up and reconstitute themselves perfectly."

"Exactly. That seems to me to be one characteristic of reality that we tend to ignore. In math and physics the three-body problem shows that it's impossible to predict the behavior of, for example, the components of a fluid. Yet its uncountable, autonomous particles will always align properly and perfectly to flow through a restricted channel, and then break out into seeming anarchy in a bay. It happens over and over again, all the discrete parts of reality hewing to one another, eventually, to make a whole: *eppur si muove.* Put it this way: sometimes the things you want the least end up saving you, in a flow of time and events that's impossible to predict and yet ends with all the disparate pieces making something perfect, beautiful, and just."

At this moment, half a dozen motorcyclists roared past on the boulevard so loudly that Jules couldn't answer, and both he and François turned to look. "The police don't do that," Jules said. "Their machines are just as powerful if not more so, but they're much quieter. I hate barbaric motorcyclists. Ninety percent of their machines are black, as is their clothing. Their helmets completely hide their faces, making them look like space insects, erasing their humanity. They ride around like the Black Knight. I detest knights. Except when I played with lead ones, I've always detested knights."

"Even Sir Launcelot?"

"Even Sir Launcelot."

"I'd have thought a traditionalist like you would find them admirable."

"Admirable? The agency that kept all of Europe in a system of slavery? I'd have been with the peasants who pulled them off their horses and killed them as they wiggled like turtles in their heavy armor."

"What's going on? Were you just hit by a motorcyclist?"

With a quick shake of his head Jules indicated that he had not been.

"Why then this volcanic eruption? It's not like you." François checked himself. "Actually, it is, if you remember Sophie."

"Sophie who?"

"The little girl when we fenced."

186

"Oh yes. I had forgotten her name. I remember, vaguely."

"I'll never forget. She was tiny, about twelve, maybe eleven. Whenever a man was paired against her, we went easy. It was the beginning of paternal love for us — perhaps a little early for university students, but we wanted to protect her."

"Except that bastard . . . where was he from?"

"I don't remember, and I don't remember his name. He was huge, and he whacked her until she folded up into a fetal position. You ignored all the rules, jumped in, and even though it wasn't a match but real fighting, you beat him down until he begged you to stop. *And you didn't.* We had to pull you off. Had they been real sabres, you would have killed him twenty times over. What's up now? Why motorcyclists? You loved Steve McQueen. You wanted a BMW."

"Steve McQueen's jacket was brown, not black. No helmet, you could see his face, and the motorcycle was to get to a safe and beautiful place away from the Nazis, not to try to be like them. Not to oppress and terrify everyone else. That's what it is. The motorcyclists these days, most of them, seem like Nazis: the arrogance, the distance, the assertion of power, the wish to intimidate and the enjoyment when they do. I hate them."

François hesitated for a moment, took in a

breath, and said, "I know."

"And I guess I'm upset. I don't know what to do."

"Me either, and I've been that way for seventy years."

"Yes, but I'm in love."

"Oh no," said François. "That's ridiculous. Please, not that. You'll sing like a loon until you finish the soup. Then you'll slowly become a miserable turkey in a tragicomic farce. Upon starting the salad, Jacqueline will return. By the time the plates are cleared you'll be staring at the last quarter of your second beer, speaking to me but begging her for forgiveness. You'll go on to explain to me, indirectly of course, that the life I myself have chosen lacks integrity and maturity, that your present suffering and denial will amount to less than mine at the end. You'll say, 'I love this young woman but it's impossible and inappropriate, so I'll let her go.' But Jules, she's probably no more aware of you than of the location of the nearest fire hydrant. . . ."

"Oh, but she is!"

"She tracks fire hydrants? I don't think so. And it's likely she thinks of you as a kind of walking Egyptian mummy, and that you just ginned her up in your imagination. You don't have false teeth or a big belly, but unless she's seen you naked or done a dental workup she's got to assume that you do. When she arises in the morning she doesn't look like a punching bag, does she. But you do. Her breath is sweet, her skin tight, her eyes have sparkle. Give it up."

"I don't understand. What about you?"

"Me? I'm in worse shape than you. I smoke for Christ's sake. What an idiot, I know. My teeth are wine-stained. *I* can't run ten kilometers. You could probably run a hundred."

"I wouldn't ask you to."

"I know. So why do you think I, the male equivalent of a decayed strumpet — if my hair gets any whiter I'll look like Colette — wake up every morning next to a fresh, nubile, fertile, charming, young woman?"

"Because you're famous . . . you have. . . ."

"You don't have to be famous. It helps to be rich, which, because of alimony and child support, I'm not. The difference is that I'm not, as you are, the caretaker of another soul. Jacqueline is always with you. She hasn't quite died, has she?"

"No."

"You can still love her even if you love someone else, but not if you remain the way you are. You're more devoted than a priest, Jules. You have only one life, at the end of which there may be nothing. Why must you be so faithful? What is it about you?"

"I try, no matter how vainly, to keep them alive."

"Who's them?"

"All of them."

189

■ ■ ■ ■

After François returned to the domesticity for which Jules, rather than he, had been born, Jules walked through the Quartier latin as it started to rain. At almost eleven he crossed the Champs de Mars, which were deserted because of the hour and the weather. His intention was to tire himself so that when he reached home sleep would outcompete worry. If he could, he would go all the way to Passy, where he had grown up, and depart from there for home after touching the façade of the house his parents had lived in before they were forced to hide in Reims. The Jews fled either south to try to cross the Pyrenees, or southeast to Switzerland, but the *Famille* Lacour went instead to Reims, where the ordinariness and lack of importance, as well as the fewer Jews than in Paris, might have afforded them a contrarian chance. Many of their friends, diamonds sewn into the seams of their clothes, had been captured or turned back at Annecy or Pau. Jules had no idea who lived in the house now, and had never wanted to know. But every once in a while, especially when he was troubled, he would go there and touch the wall.

He walked through a downpour that had started after the Champs de Mars, and headed for the Pont de Bir-Hakeim. Bir-

Hakeim was where the free French, by holding against Rommel, had begun to turn the tide and restore the dignity of France. It was the symbol of springing back from defeat, and though the bridge named in its honor was a fairly hideous structure, it was his favorite, because it was where he turned around after struggling hard against the current. Ugly and ungainly, the Pont de Bir-Hakeim was a symbol of redemption, which made sense, as redemption seldom comes without suffering.

Hardly used even during the day, the walkways were now slick and deserted. He walked in the center, between columns that supported train tracks on the upper level, as here was some protection from the rain. Almost at the midpoint, where a staircase led down to the long and narrow Île aux Cygnes mid-channel in the Seine, he heard a commotion of angry voices echoing amid the columns and fading when an occasional car went by and the wash of its tires on the wet roadway muffled all sound.

The closer he came, the more he knew that something was terribly wrong and dangerous. He didn't run to it, but his pace quickened. It was like being in the forest in Algeria at night and in bad weather. He was unseen, perfectly safe, with surprise and the lack of fear to his great advantage. Though he had no weapon, he had these and he had experience. By the time he saw what was going on near a buttress at the midpoint, he had partially returned to a soldier's state of mind.

Three young men, one of whom had a knife, were beating and kicking another one, who was rolling this way and that on the ground in trying to protect himself. Jules hadn't been afraid, but he was now — because they were three, they were young, he was old, and he was one.

Surprise itself could deliver him the first. His experience and strength might give him the second. But what of the third when Jules would be winded? So he held back. If this were between them and they were all the same, why intervene? Maybe the police would come, but now they were nowhere in sight. What could he do but watch, ashamed to retreat but unable to take action.

They kicked and pummeled the figure on the ground until it could move only agonizingly, rising into a low hump, collapsing, trying to sidle away but stopped by the buttress. Then they stopped, drew back, and the tallest one, who had a knife, approached the body on the ground, staring at it while drawing the hand that held the knife back past his shoulder.

Jules was by this time so torn between two imperatives that he trembled, though not out of fear. Then what he saw stopped his trembling. The young man on the ground, now

192

risen to his knees and covered in blood, was wearing a yarmulke. Though he didn't speak, his eyes were begging. What he didn't know and surely could not have imagined, and what his tormentors did not know and surely could not have imagined, was that watching from the shadows was Jules, a man who was thrown back seventy years as if no time had passed, whose whole life had been a compressed spring in wait for just the trigger they had pulled. He knew not himself of what he was capable.

Although it was true, he wasn't aware that here was a chance to kill in just the way as all his life he had wanted to kill, and to die in just the way as all his life he had wanted to die. They hadn't noticed him, until, running at full speed, he burst from behind. He knew they would freeze momentarily, and they did, all of them. Before they moved, Jules was on the tall one with the knife and had opened his hand to grasp the assailant's head and hold it as tremendous forward momentum pushed him against the stones of the bridge. Guiding the head against a sharp edge of masonry just above a more rounded course, Jules used the buttress as a weapon, killing the first one instantly.

The other two attacked even before the first one hit the pavement, windmilling their fists, because they didn't know how to fight. In the split second in which Jules determined how to deal with this, he also managed to wonder what a Hasidic Jew was doing on the bridge at night, alone. Perhaps he was just walking, or they had dragged him there. He limped off toward the Left Bank as Jules shielded himself as best he could from the blows and struggled toward the stairs. Punches were coming fast and hard from every direction. He couldn't keep up with them, but instead of boxing — he was no boxer, even if they weren't either — he waited for an opening and, with a scream, seized one of them by the neck, turned his whole body, and as if diving into a pool pushed off hard into the abyss, out from the stairs, riding the one he had seized down the twenty-one steps as if on a toboggan. When they stopped, the stunned young man pushed limply against Jules, trying to get up. From above and behind came the footsteps of the other one, who now had the knife and was closing. Aching and winded, Jules understood that he could no longer deal with two, or perhaps one, so he waited until the boy struggling beneath him was in a completely unguarded position as he tried to rise, and punched him in the throat, which he knew would — and did — kill him.

At this point, the boy with the knife lost his courage. Not knowing this, Jules looked at him, expecting either to die or perhaps to kill again in what seemed like a dream and what for an instant he thought must be a dream. Then the boy threw the knife into the Seine.

Exiting the trees on the Allée des Cygnes were a man and a woman walking beneath an umbrella. They froze. The boy who had thrown away the knife inexplicably picked up and pocketed a piece of paper — as if at this point he was fastidiously concerned with litter. Then he began to scream in a high-pitched, threatened voice. "He killed my friends! He killed my friends! *Raciste! Raciste!*"

The woman pulled out a phone, but she was shaking too much to use it, so the man grabbed it from her as the umbrella he dropped began to roll around in the breeze. The Hasidic Jew was by this time long gone, and the two witnesses had seen only that Jules was standing over a body as a frightened boy cried for help.

Jules knew that even if his explanation were accepted or somehow proved, which it might well not have been, and even if they could locate the Hasidic Jew, they would never find the knife, and Jules would be condemned for overreaction. How he was supposed to have fought three, one of whom had a weapon, didn't matter. Well protected citizens, who would not themselves have intervened and would have allowed the unknown Jew on the bridge to die, eschewed violence so passionately as to close their eyes and wish to be done with it all equally and without the labor and risk of judgment. Prosecutors would prosecute him with single-minded professionalism. If the assailants were Muslims, and it was likely they were (*"Raciste!"*), pressure from one side and the desire to appease it from the other would almost certainly send him to prison, and never could he have afforded to go to prison, most especially now.

The sound of sirens came from the Right Bank as a chain of cars with flashing blue lights began to ascend from the west onto the ramp leading up to the bridge.

Rather than run and thereby telegraph guilt, Jules began to walk west at a pace that suggested he hadn't been aware of the events that had just occurred. Though his manner comported perfectly with his shock, to the witnesses it looked like indifference. He glanced back at the Pont de Bir-Hakeim, at the center of which dozens of lights flashed hysterically in blue. Police were running down the stairs.

Which meant that Jules had to run, too. He ran every day that he didn't row, sprinting intermittently, and now he sprinted much faster than usual. As the police following him saw him pulling away they received the clear impression that he was a young man. They couldn't catch him, but what would he do when he reached the end of the Allée des Cygnes at the foot of the Pont de Grenelle?

196

It was late, and raining. The streets were empty and would be saturated with police.

The running and his desperation felt much like war. He had no fear, because, as in war, the feeling that he was already dead freed him. It had been like that in Algeria, a kind of joy at writing himself off, which left him free to act in a way that by stunning and confounding his enemies might have saved his life.

Ahead, the Pont de Grenelle was lit in a garland of flashing blue lights. Closed in, there was only one thing he could do. He had always loved to walk or run through the Allée des Cygnes, but now he would have to leave it. He went to the fence, put one foot on the bottom rail, and vaulted over the rest. Then he slid down the steep masonry, taking care not to sprain an ankle, and without the slightest hesitation or making much of a splash, launched himself feet first into the river.

Everything continued to happen fast and numbly. Still, he was able to realize that he was tasting the spattered blood of the first man he killed when he had smashed him against the wall. But going into the river washed away both the blood and its taste, which was like a piece of raw iron that has not rusted but, somehow, rotted. The river took him as he knew it would. It was painfully cold, but not enough to confuse him. In less than a minute he grew used to it, and by that time he was level with the ramp and stairs leading from the Pont de Grenelle to the Allée des Cygnes, down which police were running, the straight beams of their flashlights sweeping jerkily from one side to the other as they moved. Some of the police were keen enough on the chase to skim their lights over the river on both sides of the Allée. Swept downstream on the north side, Jules submerged himself.

He had rowed here for sixty years, and knew the river's every trick. Although he had to check visually, he could fix the stern of his boat on a landmark and row without looking back for many strokes, and then turn the point of the stern to another landmark to round a curve or avoid a bridge pier. Just where he had now gone into the water was the point of greatest danger when rowing, and he probably knew this particular patch of river as well as anyone in the world. The wakes of the *bateaux mouches,* although miraculously less than that of a powerful outboard, often filled the cockpit of his shell, and it took some skill not to capsize as they passed. On very windy days, one couldn't row safely on the Seine, which was a muscular river that had always refused to be completely conquered, even by the great mass of Paris. The *bateaux mouches* made their astounding turns here, pivoting at their centers, whirling like blades. This made the biggest waves. To be caught in them was extremely difficult. To be hit by an immense, twirling *bateau* was death. West of Bir-Hakeim it was quieter, the main threat being commercial barges. But now there were no barges or *bateaux mouches,* and had he been in his light boat he almost could have run the whole river blind. After he counted slowly to twenty he knew the current had swept him beyond the westernmost point of the Allée des Cygnes, and he surfaced with a gasp.

Flashing police lights on the bridges at either end of the Allée lit them more brightly than Christmas trees. Carried by the Seine into a new life dictated by chance, he felt electrically alive and excited, even as or perhaps because he thought that everything was headed to the kind of cataclysms and death he had been spared all his life — of the Jews, his parents, the Mignons, the soldiers and civilians in Algeria, Jacqueline, and now Luc, and himself. But the river carried him west, death still at bay.

He knew the current veered south, hit the left bank, and ricocheted north, which would carry him to the dock. He had observed this every day, traced by detritus on the surface. Letting the current carry him, he felt it move south, bounce off the south bank, and head north. It slammed him against the north end of the dock as if he had been shot out of a circus cannon.

He climbed into the much warmer air. It was completely quiet — no sirens and no lights. He couldn't be seen from the street, no one ever came to the boathouse at night, and he had the key. After a moment's rest, he went in, stripped off his clothes, and threw them into the washer to rid them of all traces of blood and the Seine. Wrapped in towels, he sat on the edge of the cot where he had slept not long before, and, as the washer agitated, he rocked slightly in the dark.

His mind racing, he stayed awake until the washer finished. Then he threw the clothes into the dryer. The tumbling sound and light escaping from inside were soporific. He lay back, noting to himself again and again that he must get up in the morning before others came early to row. He didn't know who came then or exactly when they did or even if they did, for he rowed much later, but he had to arise before the light so as to be dressed and waiting. He would leave only when Paris was busy, the streets were full of early risers, and the cameras would be sucking up the imagery of thousands, tens of thousands, and hundreds of thousands of people making their ways, blurring, moving, innocent or not, an indistinct mass of men and women pressing hard upon the pedals of their ever-disappearing lives.

Awakened by first light reflecting off the gray

river, he tried to go back to sleep. There were two worlds now, as perhaps there had always been: one of sleep without dreams, where anxiety did not exist; and the wakeful world in which fear came in paralyzing surges. Because it was impossible to sleep, he faced what had become of his life.

This was just before six, when someone might come to row, though it was unlikely, as the river flowed faster than it had the day before, and local rains had scattered garbage and tree limbs, sometimes whole trees, across the surface of the water. The weather was cold, dark, and foggy. Still, someone might come, so Jules rushed to prepare. He knew that later he would have to think very carefully about what to do, but what he had to do within the boathouse itself was obvious, and he moved fast. He threw the towels he had slept on and used as blankets into the hamper, and laid down a fresh covering, just as he had done the day before. Next, he went to the sink and cupped his hands to carry a little bit of water to sprinkle on his boat to make it look as if it had just been used. He turned on the shower and poured a little shampoo on the floor so that it would appear that after going out on the river he had bathed. The scent wafted through the rows of boats. Then he rushed to fix a light to the bow of his boat. He never rowed in the dark, so he fumbled with the unfamiliar attachment, but soon fastened it.

Should someone arrive now, the evidence would point to Jules having been out on the water early. He wasn't yet dressed, as someone who had just finished showering would not have been. Probably no one would show, but whoever might wouldn't notice anything out of the ordinary. The next step was to dress, and as he did he thought through one scenario after another.

His life had been saturated with and overwhelmed by ever-present guilt for the deaths of people he hadn't killed, people he had loved, whom he would have done anything to save. Now, in regard to the two men, or boys, that he was fairly sure he had actually killed, he felt no guilt at all. The very fact of feeling no remorse made him feel remorse sufficient to set him in an argument with himself even as he desperately tried to strategize a way clear of capture.

Was what he had done a crime? Was it murder? There were three of them — and at least one was armed with a deadly weapon. Might he have been more measured? He was not a boxer or a street fighter but a seventy-four-year-old musician. Had he tried to moderate his response, they probably would have killed him, or at least they might have pushed him aside and killed the Hasidic Jew. Should he have abstained, as required of a good citizen, leaving the monopoly of violence to the state but allowing the murder of an innocent man? Years before, a woman had been raped and murdered in the park at Saint-Germain-en-Laye. And not that long after, another woman, both with extreme brutality. The neighborhood was literally terrified. And the response of the good citizens had been to hand out orange plastic whistles.

At the neighborhood meeting, imagining a bunch of frightened, impotent people watching a crime unfold as they provided the musical accompaniment with their whistles, Jules had asked why they didn't hand out revolvers instead. A hundred people summoning another hundred more would be of absolutely no avail if not a single one was willing actually to intervene. He stated this, perhaps somewhat un-diplomatically, by referring to "sheep whistles not for calling sheep but to be blown by them." He was ostracized forever by everyone present, an indignant crowd bravely determined to be militantly helpless. His last words before he left were, "One must have the courage to save a life." They thought he was crazy, and now he thought that perhaps they had been right. He was so shaken, unsure, and fearful that it grayed his vision, and things would fade in and out as he tried to think of what to do.

"Steady yourself," he said out loud, "hold through." It began to work. He would be all right even if someone came in, and no one did, giving him time to think. In the quiet fog of early morning everything was muted in gray, and the vigorously flowing river, powerful and unperturbed, was a model for his thought.

For whom would they be searching? The three witnesses would undoubtedly think he was taller and heavier than he was. Just as children imagine monsters, and seafarers once returned with exaggerated tales of gargantuan creatures, the witnesses would most likely endow Jules with strength and size appropriate to their fear of him. That he could outrun young police officers suggested that they would estimate his age to be lower than it was, given also that he had been able to take on three young men and quickly kill two of them. The heavy rain that night had soaked his hair, turning it dark and plastering it down. And he had been wearing a distinctive saffron/marigold-colored rain jacket over his blazer. He had bought this in Switzerland many years before. Its color was unforgettable. The company that made it was Japanese, and the Japanese vision of the spectrum was somehow different from the European. He had seldom worn it, but that day he had pulled it from his closet in response to the weather forecast.

The first action he took, therefore, was to wrap the jacket around one of the small cinder blocks used at the boathouse to prop open the doors on windy days, and tie it up with nylon boat twine, which would take years to rot. He then dressed, seized a broom, and went out to sweep the dock. At the edge, he inconspicuously dropped the weighted jacket into the water, which he knew to be about twenty meters deep beyond the dock, with a strong, scouring current. He carried the broom and swept in case there were distant traffic cameras across the river.

Instead of a taller, heavier, dark-haired man of between thirty and fifty, in a bright orange-yellow jacket, leaving the boathouse and exiting onto the street would be a man of lesser build in his middle seventies, with thick hair that was blonde and white. Leaving a place he had habituated for more than half a century, he would be dressed in a blue blazer. The blazer had come through for him in that it was made of a certain kind of fabric that simply would not wrinkle. The boast of the manufacturer was that you could stuff it into a thermos, if you could find one big enough, pour in hot water, leave it for a week, and it would come out as good as new and ready to wear. Why do this would be anyone's guess, but the point was made, and despite the fact that it had been in the river the perfectly pressed blazer was an important element in disguising Jules as himself. Thus transformed, he would be anything but the man who had had the confrontation on the bridge, although of course he was.

Before he got dressed, he inspected himself. He had bruises on his arms and shoulders but his face was clear and he had no cuts or abrasions whatsoever, meaning he had left no blood. His hair had been matted by the rain tight against his head, so there was little chance that a hair had flown away as, when it is dry, it can. Nor had he left anything on the bridge or the Allée, for he still had everything he had had with him. At his age, the bruises would take two weeks to disappear, but none was visible as long as he was dressed. There were no cameras on the road near the boat-house. This he knew because he often parked longer than he should have, and in judging his chances of getting a ticket he had taken into account the lack of surveillance. Of course, there were cameras all over the place, and had someone actually dissected his comings and goings they might see that he had not returned home that night, and that his outerwear had changed while he was still out and about.

But there were millions of people in Paris, and the skein of their transit was a tangle of a billion threads. It would take an impossible brilliance or amazing luck to focus on his whereabouts specifically, especially given that he didn't resemble the man the witnesses would describe. All he had to do now was walk calmly into Paris as if nothing had happened, buy a newspaper, sit in a café, read while having breakfast, and take the train home. The trick was not to shake and not to flutter, and, if he did, never to let anyone see.

When he got home he was tired because he had walked to l'Étoile to get the A line west. In Saint-Germain-en-Laye he had picked up something to eat, and now, with a sandwich and a bottle of beer, he sat on the terrace. The sun began to burn away first the clouds, and then the mist that had lingered over the Seine far below.

Not long before, it seemed, a young family of three had moved into these splendid quarters. The wife was vital, quick, statuesque, and erotic, but what was most wonderful was the way she loved her child. It would remain the most beautiful thing Jules had ever seen. Watching Jacqueline with Cathérine gave him a purpose and defined his life. He knew that educated people, who strove above all not to be commonplace, would mock his feeling that the child was an angel. Once, and only once, he had innocently and happily declared it. The robotic contempt that had ensued had spurred him to strike back. "You think it's trite?" he asked. The unspoken answer was absolutely clear. "And that angels are only an embarrassing figment of the medieval imagination? Let's stipulate, then" — the person he was addressing was a lawyer

— "that there are no such things. But we do have evidence that for thousands of years people have believed in pure and blessèd intermediary beings close to God. So, what do you think fed their perfervid imaginations? Where did they get the idea? What were their models?

"Children, of course. And when a parent describes his infant as an angel, he's referring to the source and inspiration of the word. The children came first, and the word, with all its connotations, is truly specific to them. It's an accurate, exact, and original description with which one flatters the Pope's angels by associating them with one's child. And why must you react with such bile to such a lovely and wonderful thing even if it isn't true?"

When Cathérine was an infant even Shymanski had been fairly young and his children not yet old enough to be horrible. Jules could run fifty kilometers then, and row twenty almost as fast as an Olympian. He was flush with his new academic appointment, and would sometimes awaken in the middle of the night to write down music that came to him in dreams. In summer they traveled throughout the Mediterranean, light and on the cheap, and they were sunburnt, well rested, always near the sea. When Cathérine was a little older, they went to the Atlantic beaches of the Gironde. Paris in the fall was the most glorious place in the world. Jacqueline had a gray Chanel suit that she had bought for her lecturing. To see her in it took her students' breath away. And, famously, for her hour they hardly stirred in their seats.

At least as he now remembered it, life had been close to perfect, but then it began slowly to erode — imperceptibly at first and now almost gone, with a few years left of shortness of breath and difficulty sleeping as his body predictably and inevitably failed. But perhaps he could make one last reach, for Luc. That was his task, the last run, now more complicated than ever.

After the war, when he was still a child, Jules had no desire to live, and thought of death as his sole comfort. As he grew older, the will to survive was welded inextricably, in a slowly forming braid, to his love of beauty. Just the streets of Paris, the way they flowed pleasurably one into another, and the musical life of a city that was itself a musical composition seduced him at first modestly and then irreversibly.

For most of his youth, until his inherited talent and devoted work slowly led to greater ambition, he dreamed of living in a small, quiet place in a poor neighborhood, with a pretty wife, a cheap car, and perhaps a city job: clerk, sweeper, motorman, guard. He would be unheralded, undistinguished, and unambitious, but alive to every little thing, appreciative and observant of all the frictions of life, happy to live in the shadows, free to cultivate memory and devotion as busy people who grasp at the future seldom can. And now when he passed through the gray concrete cliffs of the *banlieue,* although he would never choose to leave his magnificent lodgings, he wondered what it would have been like, and was almost envious.

There would be nothing in that day's papers of what had happened on the Île aux Cygnes, so he threw them away. No matter what was occurring in Africa, space, or the Middle East, not to mention all of France, there was only one story he would have the patience to read. Although in regard to Luc and his own health time was against him, in regard to the Île aux Cygnes it was salvation. No matter how devoted and programmatical were the police, time would dissolve evidence, passion, and motivation. Even in the relatively short term, after a month or two, he could not possibly be expected to come up with an account of his whereabouts or actions thirty or sixty days before. That clock had just begun to run.

On his terrace, far from the center of Paris, shielded by distance, riches, the trees, and the top of a fortress-like palisade, every slow breath marked the increasing seconds in which there was no knock at the door. But then the telephone rang. He started, and was frozen as it rang eight more times. Of course, the police would not have his telephone number, and wouldn't have called him if they did. When finally he answered, the line was as clear as it would have been had someone been calling from next door, but the call was from New York. A woman's voice asked in English if he was Jewels Lacour. "Please hold for Jack."

"Hey Jewels! Hey!"

"Jack?"

"Jewels! We love it! Rich loves it! You didn't get my email?"

"I haven't looked. I don't really like the email."

"It's all in there. We're taking it. Isn't that great?"

Jules hesitated. "Yes, yes, it's great." For some reason, he was fearful. He felt it in his stomach, but then he overruled it.

"Look, we want to use it for the Super Bowl, so we've got to get going. There's gonna have to be a big change-over throughout the world. It's a rush. We need you now in L.A. to orchestrate and record. Can you come right away?"

"Yes."

"That's perfect. It's all in the email, a deal memo, which is a sort of contract. You know, emails, they never go away unless you're Hillary Clinton. Get back to us, and we'll see you soon. Any problems, call me."

"Okay."

"Great, Jewels. I won't be in L.A. but I'll see you in New York."

"Okay, but. . . ." The line went dead as Jack had something else to attend to.

Jules didn't bother with a few other emails but opened Jack's directly. It read: "Acorn International Ltd., A subsidiary of Acorn Holding Company, London and The Hague, accepts the composition forwarded by M. Jules Lacour as of this date, and will pay Euro 500,000 upon completion of orchestration and recording in units of varying length to be used in different venues and media throughout the world for the purpose of promoting Acorn's products, corporate image, and good name, without further payment or restriction."

Already living far more dangerously than even a bank robber, Jules wrote back, "I cannot agree for less than one million Euros," and hit send. He remained staring at the screen, not expecting anything. But then, in less than a minute, the answer appeared.

He opened it. "Agreed. One million Euros." The phone rang. It was the secretary again.

"Hold for Jack."

Jack came on the line, and without even making sure Jules was there, he said, "No problem, Jewels. We accept. When will you be in L.A.?"

"As soon as I can get a flight. Where in

L.A.? Is there a person to contact?"

"Just go to the Four Seasons in Beverly Hills and get a room on a high floor, not on the entrance side. At night the bar gets really noisy, believe me, I know. Look east and over the back garden if you can. Better yet, south and over the pool. We'll get in touch with you when we've got the personnel lined up. We're working on it, but it may take a while to get an orchestra together, because the studios take precedence. Still, you should be there so that when they're ready you'll be available. Save your receipts and we'll take care of everything at the end. Fly business class. We're no longer allowed to deduct First, but don't stint on anything else. In L.A. you'll need to rent a nice car, so you'd better reserve it as soon as possible. They don't always have them."

"What kind of car?"

"I don't know, something nice. A Mercedes or a BMW. Try a convertible. It's L.A."

"But that would be so expensive," Jules said.

"A business expense, Jewels. Go for it." Jack hung up abruptly, as usual, as if Jules didn't exist.

"Okay," Jules said to the empty ether before he put down the phone.

THE POLICEMAN
IS YOUR FRIEND

Cathérine, David, and Luc lived half an hour to the northwest, if there was no traffic. If there were, that would be something else. Jules usually visited in late morning when the roads were clearest. He didn't like to drive at night, so in winter when he went for dinner he would take the RER. Jules thought that Cergy looked like Germany. Despite that, his daughter's house, with a roof of bright-orange terra-cotta tiles, was the typical little French villa advertised in the back of magazines. These houses were always very neat on the outside and rectangular in shape. They were somehow French and yet not French at all, too Mediterranean for the North, but not Mediterranean enough for the South. The orange roofs and white stucco exteriors had the effect both in photographs and in reality of bringing up the greenery around them and making the leaves in the bushes and on the trees seem waxy even if they were not. Jules thought that probably inside every such house was a washer-dryer combination that loaded from the front through a Nemo-like glass door, and that because of this, generations of children would be calmed by sloshing water and tumbling clothes.

Her father was crippled by doleful allegiance to a time and events with which, not wanting to saddle her, he kept from her. Thus, Cathérine resented him for being, without apparent explanation, so much unlike other people. The fathers of other children in school at Saint-Germain-en-Laye had been businessmen or functionaries of government. They went to offices, were members of clubs, danced, drank, took vacations on fashionable islands, and dressed sharply. They were happy in groups, schools, flocks, teams, and herds. Although Jules, always athletic, would play tennis with Jacqueline and François, he did everything else alone — running, rowing, swimming, even riding (except for the horse). Jacqueline was that way, too. At a time when Cathérine needed to fit in with classmates or suffer their rejection, her parents had few friends, avoided social engagement, were awkward when they couldn't avoid it, and spent most of their time reading, playing music, doing punishing exercise, or, like crazy Zen monks, sitting for hours in the garden or on the terrace doing absolutely nothing.

They and especially Jules were not only

incapable of imparting to her the skills necessary for a happy life among others, but for the rest of her life she was angry that they had never seen the need to do so. Her time at school was immensely painful because they had failed to protect her by at least making an effort to be like everyone else. They were not materially rich. They were not normal. Different as well for being Jewish, they were allergic to overt religiosity and ritual, and had no home even among the Jews.

When Jules was about to debut his music in the most important setting possible and at the start of an exciting season, Cathérine came with Jacqueline. Before they left home, Jules looked at his wife and daughter, both of whom had dressed beautifully, even little Cathérine, who was so young he could carry her in the crook of his arm. He loved them so much at that moment that he was diverted from ambition and felt guilty for having indulged it. Later, as they and a thousand other people watched, he began the concert with a Bach piece, the *Sei Lob.* Cathérine knew it well by sound, but was so young she didn't know that music was composed by people, and thought it was just there. The public never heard Jules' music, and Cathérine, who at first had been proud, was suddenly frightened and ashamed because, as a thousand people held their breath in embarrassment, her father wept.

As she grew older she separated from them as much as she could. She became religious. She dressed carefully. She married an accountant. She had many friends, and was comfortable in their society. When Jacqueline died, Cathérine asked her father point-blank why he had lived the way he had lived, why her mother had been that way as well, and what it was that kept him apart, even from Jews, who were themselves forever condemned to be apart. He didn't really tell her, because it was so much what he was that he was unable to identify it as an outside force. And he had never wanted to make her like him, but rather to keep her from the details of his affliction so she would not repeat it. He wanted her to be successful and to thrive, to shed the past. So he answered indirectly.

"Because your mother and I," he said, "are like Thierry."

"Thierry? What does he have to do with it?" He was one of their few friends, and they saw him probably no more than thrice in her lifetime. But they often spoke about him.

"He's one of the greatest photographers in France, and when he was younger he was quite famous and getting quite rich. Unlike many others, he was an artist of lab work, and did all his own. Photographic printing is an art in itself, and other photographers would turn to him for it. He was so good at this that he decided to build the finest lab in the world, to train protégés, and strive for better and better work. He mortgaged his house and went deeply into debt on all fronts to build a magnificent facility.

"Just as things were solidifying well, photography began to embrace digitization. Now the embrace is complete. But Thierry stuck with the old processing and printing. In five years, he lost everything. People begged him to switch while he could, but he didn't. There's no mystery in digital. It's all asymptote and no curve; binary code, unvarying, with no imperceptible bridge between its discrete elements. Thierry's prints, especially the black and white, had worlds between those elements. They gleamed as they retreated into dusk and darkness, like mother of pearl in fading light. In photographic printing, art lives in the variations of chemicals, paper base, enlarger lenses, bulb filaments, and processing permutations. He stuck with that art because, even though it was as defeated as if a tank had rolled over it, it was beautiful, it was better, he loved it, and he was loyal to what he loved."

"But he suffered because of it."

"He continues to suffer. But loyalty is like magic. It makes suffering immaterial."

"You're loyal to what? Being peculiar?"

"No, I'm loyal to a world that was destroyed."

Their differences had by necessity receded into the background when Luc got sick. Now Jules was in Cergy out of love for his child and his grandchild, and to say goodbye before he left for America.

"David is working?" he asked Cathérine.

She nodded. She was worn down from living with the threat to Luc far more than she would have been had she herself been ill.

"I brought Luc a book." He held up a thin, broad, gift-wrapped slab.

"I hope it's not about going to the hospital. One of our friends gave him a book like that before I could intercept it."

"This is a picture book in which there are hundreds of chubby little people in helmets and bright uniforms. They build roads, climb ladders, fly planes, and collect garbage. They all look like Hollande, they live in a world where everything is colorful, rounded, and kind, nothing sharp or dirty. Danger is everywhere, but perfectly contained. They're safe because they wear harnesses, hard hats, and reflective vests. I'll read it to him before lunch."

Luc trailed in absentmindedly, but when he saw his grandfather he rushed to him and hugged his leg. Jules lifted the child onto his lap, kissed him, and said "Ah! Luc! What a good boy! And, you look less swollen!"

Luc, who knew what swollen was only too well, said, "Less swollen."

"Here's a book for you. Would you like to unwrap it?"

Children unwrap presents either three times as fast or three times more slowly than adults. Seldom is there an in between. Luc did it slowly.

"He's going to be an archaeologist," Jules said to Cathérine. "Look how carefully and thoughtfully he's peeling off the layers."

When Luc was done and he saw the bright colors, he smiled. Looking slowly over the cover and taking in all its great detail, he put an index finger — like a cat using its paw to pounce — on a little white police car in a corner of the frame. Then he wiggled off Jules' lap and ran to his room, returning proudly with a toy car just like the one in the picture, only it had a yellow rubber dome at the top that, when depressed, made the car beep. Both the plastic and drawn cars were unthreateningly bulbous, non-aerodynamic, and taller than they were long.

Back in Jules' lap, Luc held the toy upside down, showing his grandfather the undercarriage. Jules knew that this meant, what is it?

"It's a police car," Jules said. "See the policeman inside?"

Luc nodded. He thought for a while. Then he turned to Jules with an expectant, skeptical look. "Are they good guys or bad guys?" he asked. At two and a half, he thought the world was divided that way, and it was, though not as clearly as he imagined.

"Oh!" Jules said. "They're good guys. They help people. The policeman is your friend."

Two *APJs Adjoint — Agents de Police Judiciare, Adjoint —* were stuffed into a tiny white police car almost as high as it was long, driving southeast toward a dangerous Alphaville to interview one Raschid Belghazi, the only survivor of the victims on the bridge. The police had left from the Quai des Orfèvres, in the car of Duvalier Saidi-Sief, who was attached to and worked out of the *Commissariat de Police du 16é Arrondissement,* Passy, because the other officer, Arnaud Weissenburger, had taken the Métro. Duvalier Saidi-Sief was from the *Brigade Criminelle,* taking the lead on this double homicide, although of course reporting above to his *Officier de Police Judiciare,* or *OPJ,* whom he did not like. Arnaud Weissenburger had been pulled from *Les Mineurs,* the *Brigade de Protection des Mineurs,* because one of the victims was under eighteen. He had wanted assignment to the *Brigade Criminelle, La Crim,* and hadn't been chosen, but at least he's been posted to Paris.

"Next time," Arnaud said, "let's go in my

car. It's twice as big."

Duvalier, who was slight and wiry, said to Arnaud, who was tremendous and heavy, "Next time bring your car, but meanwhile this one's fine." He knew what he was doing.

"No, it's not. My knees are in my teeth. And we should decide where we work. We can't work out of two places. We should work out of the Fifteenth. Our building is bigger and there's a restaurant right next door, Le Saint Florent."

"That's nice, but at the foot of our *Commissariat* is a *bar à huîtres;* and catercorner to that a *boulangerie/patisserie.*"

It was true. The police went in and out of the *patisserie* like bees at a hive. Their other hive was the station itself, which opened onto the tiny Rue Sergé Prokofiev and a tiny circular park, the *Place du Préfet Claude Érignac,* the *Préfet* of Corsica assassinated in Ajaccio in 1998. The station itself was a two-storey glass box projecting toward the back of the apartment building of which it was the base. The windows didn't open.

"The streets are less congested in the Fifteenth," Arnaud asserted. It was true.

"Yes, but Passy is nicer."

"Nicer?"

"More fashionable, a finer finish. Right next to our front entrance there's a locksmith, which is sometimes very convenient. And, really, the restaurants in Passy are superior to those in Montparnasse."

"If you'll pay for me," Arnaud said. "They're more expensive, at least at our price level."

"No no. Can't do that."

"Then how are we supposed to decide?"

"Do you have a coin?"

"Who has coins in the morning? I drop them in a box at home at the end of the day."

"What about for parking?"

"We're policemen, Duvalier. We park where we want."

"Maybe, but I pay."

Arnaud looked at him in disbelief. "When you're driving a police car?"

"Absolutely."

"You don't have to."

"I know I don't have to, but I do."

"What for?"

"Honor."

They were together because the dividing line between the 15th and 16th *arrondissements* ran right down the middle of the Île aux Cygnes. The bodies and pools of blood literally straddled this line. Duvalier Saidi-Sief had been transferred to Paris from Marseille, Arnaud Weissenburger from Nancy. They didn't know the city that well.

"So how are we going to decide?" Arnaud asked. His knees really were almost touching his chest. "If this thing crashes we're both dead."

"Do you accept *this*?" Duvalier asked, continuing. "When the minute hand on your watch passes the next five-minute mark, count the cars coming at us for one minute. If less than twenty percent are white, we work from the Rue de Vaugirard, and we eat at Le Saint Florent. If more than twenty percent, we work at sixty-two Avenue de Mozart, and we eat at the locksmith."

Worried that perhaps his new partner was touched, Arnaud checked his watch. He had three minutes before the next five-minute mark. He said, "Let me think about it." For two minutes he counted cars, trying not to give away what he was doing.

"I know what you're doing," Duvalier said.

"I'm not doing anything."

"Oh?"

After two minutes, when fewer than ten percent of the cars that passed were white, Arnaud said, "Okay, I'll take the bet."

In the minute remaining, Duvalier said, "It doesn't matter. I saw you. You were moving your lips. Had you done it ten times that would be one thing, but the sample was too small."

"I don't know what you're talking about."

After they started the count, it was as if a white-car convention had just broken for lunch and everyone was headed for Paris to eat. "Okay," Arnaud said, "we work out of Passy. But we use my car."

"Good. A bigger car is better. You can take a picnic, and if you have to move a body, there's room in the trunk."

"Duvalier," Arnaud asked, "now that we share this case, what is your background? Frankly, you sound like you come from an insane asylum."

Duvalier smiled. "I'm in the police, so that answers the part about the insane asylum. What about you?"

"Me? I don't like oysters. They remind me of Dominique de Villepin: hard, abrasive, salt and pepper on the outside, soft and gutless on the inside. But I asked first."

"Not too much to tell. My grandfather came with his family from Algeria. As you can figure from my name, we weren't *colons*, but, still, I'm second-generation French and I don't really speak Arabic. Well, a little. I have two degrees: from Provence Aix-Marseilles, and ENA. At Aix-Marseille there are twice as many girls as boys. It was paradise. Not ENA. I know you'll ask why the police after ENA? The answer is so someday I can head the police, maybe."

"You're crazy if after the ENA you came here. I was going to ask what you studied as an undergraduate."

"Korean."

"Jesus Christ," said Arnaud.

"What's so bad about Korean? What about you?"

"Université Nancy Deux. Mining engineering, but I dropped out and went to work in the blast furnace at Saint-Gobain. I'm not going to head the police."

"Why'd you drop out?"

"We didn't have the same boy-girl ratio you did."

"It was better in the blast furnace?"

"The blast furnace is formidable enough to take your mind off even girls. The next exit's for us."

As they continued on, Arnaud, who had missed much of the briefing, and couldn't turn enough to reach the thick folders on the back seat even if the back seat was practically the front seat, asked, "What have we got?" He expected an intelligent summary, if only because Duvalier's bright eyes brightened even further.

"First of all, Houchard, the *OPJ,* is an asshole."

"I did pick that up."

"He left Marseilles before I came in to the police, but he couldn't take his reputation with him. He doesn't do any of the work, then hogs all the credit. His reports hardly mention the people under him, so your prospects are dimmed in proportion to his as they brighten. Notice how he made himself a barrier between the judge and us. Okay, we're working for him, but there's no reason we can't talk to the judge. I like talking to judges: they're usually quite bright and interesting, and they often help a great deal. I don't see why people in our position are afraid of them. Did you see that when we were finished I disappeared?"

"Yeah," Arnaud answered. "Why did I have to meet you in the garage?"

"Because I ran after the judge. I asked if we could contact him directly. He said, 'Why? You're supposed to go through Houchard.' I said — I took a big chance — '*Monsieur le Juge,* I want to put this as diplomatically as possible. Houchard is an asshole.' The judge laughed. I said, 'He'll ruin the investigation. I'm not looking for credit, but we want to do our job without undo obstruction. Each of has to wrap up our other cases, but this is by far the most important. We're going to have to work like hell to fit everything in.' After thinking about this, he said, 'First go to him. If you can't reach him immediately — let's say after two rings? — give me a call. The important thing is that we get this done, and although I haven't worked with him before, I've heard things about him. This is not to be repeated.'"

"You should have asked me before you did that," Arnaud said.

"You're right. I apologize. I'm not good at

227

procedure, and I didn't have time. Sorry."

"It's okay. The *OPJ* is an asshole. We'll go around him when we need to. It can be done. Who knows, he might even leave us alone, and the best time to risk your career is at the beginning, when maybe you can do something else. But what about the case? Which is what I asked you."

"Okay, nine forty-five on the Pont de Bir-Hakeim, a weeknight, rain and wind. Three skinny 'Arabs,' two of whom are dead, one we'll meet shortly. An assailant who, according to the survivor, killed the first victim by smashing his head against an abutment after charging out of nowhere while screaming racial slurs in German."

"Does he know German? How does he know they were racial slurs?"

"We'll find out. Second victim, according to the survivor and the preliminary autopsy report, was ridden down the stairs like a magic carpet and punched in the throat expertly and hard. Airway collapse. Two witnesses, unconnected as far as we know, saw the assailant standing over the body and the panicked survivor screaming for help. When our men arrived they saw the alleged killer, chased him, and lost him in the river. They came from both ends, so it must've been that."

"The body fished out?"

"Not yet."

228

"Surveillance cameras? Along the river?"

"That'll be our life for who knows how long. Just you and me, because we can't trust eyes not invested in the case. They'd almost certainly miss something. We don't have final autopsies, or DNA, but we do have blood typing. The first victim, one Firhoun Akrama, was Type B negative. Amire Bourrouag, victim number two, and the survivor, Raschid Belghazi, both A positive. But there was blood at the site of the initial encounter up on the bridge. It painted the pavement, left spatters, and some pooled and congealed into little recesses in the concrete where there had been cut-off pipes or the ends of rebar or something. It was pried out in thick, maroon circlets, and didn't match the victims or the survivor. O positive. That's our assailant."

"Maybe they attacked *him.*"

"Self-defense or not, he went at them hard enough to kill them. Because of the severity of the crime it's an expedited case. If there's no defense of necessity it's an aggravated homicide — homicides — if only because one of the victims was a minor. The judge allows that a defense of necessity may exist, but suspects that it would be disallowed on the principle of disproportionality. He suspects it's a racial crime. And he hopes not."

"Maybe," Weissenburger speculated, "there was a fourth person."

"Occam's Razor," Duvalier said. "What are

the odds?"

"Occam's Razor," Arnaud replied, "is not sharp enough to exclude them. What is this supposed German's description?"

"I spoke to the two witnesses who were walking on the Île aux Cygnes, and I really don't think they're connected. The man is a high-school geometry teacher, his wife a salesgirl at a Monoprix. They said our guy looked like Gérard Depardieu only he wasn't as fat as a hippopotamus, his nose wasn't flat like a spatula, and his hair was shorter and darker."

"So how did he look like Gérard Depardieu?"

"That's what I asked. Then they said, 'Oh, the *young* Gérard Depardieu, when he was about twenty or twenty-five, and after he dyed his hair blond.' But this guy was about fifty. The woman said he had the look of someone in shock. He didn't speak in their presence, so we have nothing more on his language or nationality."

"When does the surveillance come in?"

"As it's collected and formatted we'll get everything available on both sides of the river downstream all the way to the bend north."

"The bridge. What about the bridge and the streets leading to it?"

The cameras there have been out for more than six weeks. Lightning in August."

"They couldn't fix them?"

"They don't have the money. It's like the Third World here."

"Duvalier, the Third World is going to pass us soon, not because it's fast but because we're racing backwards. Were you named for Papa Doc?"

"No."

"Baby Doc?"

"I hope not."

As he stuck to his narrative, Raschid Belghazi was noticeably nervous. They were up on the roof, having left his mother's apartment not only so she could not interfere in the interrogation, but because the apartment smelled very bad.

"As I told them, we were walking to the station when he attacked us on the bridge, from nowhere. We went to the Comédie-Française and had dinner, and were going home. We had to walk to the Gare de Montparnasse because we didn't have enough money for the Métro."

The detectives were stunned, and for a while they said nothing, until Duvalier asked, "You went to the Comédie-Française?"

"Yeah. We go there a lot."

"You do?"

"Yeah."

"What did you see?" Arnaud asked.

"I don't remember the title."

"You don't remember the title of a play you

231

saw two days ago?"

"What play?"

"That's what I asked you."

"They don't show plays there," Raschid told Arnaud, as if speaking to an idiot. He laughed.

"To the contrary," Duvalier instructed. "That's where you see Molière, Racine. . . ."

"Who?"

"What did you see there?"

"A pornographic movie."

"At the Comédie-Française?"

"Yeah."

"Where is the Comédie-Française?"

"On a side street in Pigalle. It doesn't have a sign because the movies are so dirty."

"Okay, okay, but what was the title?"

"In pornographic movies the title is unimportant," Raschid Belghazi said with the authority of a professor.

"We have to check it out. What was the plot?"

"The plot? This chick goes to a tropical resort and everybody fucks her, even the women, even on the airplane."

"You mean in the airplane, unless they're all wing walkers."

"I don't understand."

"Never mind. Tell us a detail you remember."

Raschid laughed. "I know!" he said. "This you can't forget. She goes into a hut on the tropical island and has sex with a guy, but through the window you can see the top of the Arc de Triomphe, covered in snow. I don't think anyone noticed but me, because when I yelled out they all told me to shut up."

"Duvalier," Arnaud said, "you realize, you're going to have to see that movie."

"We'll both go. Maybe we can arrange a screening at the Comédie-Française."

Raschid then told the rest of his story.

"Describe the guy," Arnaud commanded.

"He was very tall, heavy, bald, a mustache. He yelled at us in German."

"Do you know German?"

"No, but I can recognize it."

"You said he made racist insults. In German?"

Raschid nodded.

"How do you know?"

"*Arabische Schweinen?* That sounds racist to me."

"Is it grammatical?" Duvalier asked, turning to Weissenburger.

"How should I know?"

"Weissenburger?"

"You don't speak Arabic."

Duvalier pressed on. "Your description of him is completely different from what the two witnesses say they saw. Why? Don't you want us to find him? Was it a drug deal? Was he someone you attacked on the bridge?"

"So why did he run?" Raschid asked indignantly. "I didn't run. He killed my two friends. I swear, we didn't attack him. We didn't. I can take a lie detector test. He just came out of nowhere."

"Did he look like Gérard Depardieu?" Arnaud asked.

"Are you kidding?" Raschid asked. "This guy was an athlete. Gérard Depardieu is as fat as a hippopotamus."

Duvalier turned to Arnaud and they both stepped aside to where Raschid couldn't hear them. "I like the kid," he said. "He's kind of an idiot, but so was I at that age, in a different way I admit."

"I like him, too," Arnaud said. "It makes me want to find out who did this even more. Why kill some jerky kids who think the Comédie-Française is a pornographic movie house?"

"None of them has a record. We'll have to make some inquiries, but I don't think this kid is attached to a gang or anything. He's too dumb. Okay, the gangs use dumb ones, but they're always afraid, and he isn't, unless he's dumber than anyone I've ever encountered. Granted, he's a tabula rasa, but I don't think he's mixed up enough in drugs or the underworld to have had anything impressed upon him yet. I mean, maybe when the cars were burning he threw a brick or two, but I'm not even sure he'd know how."

"Informants?" Arnaud suggested.

234

"Do you have any? Because I don't. We can ask the local cops, but so what. These guys are the victims. Let's not forget that."

They asked Raschid a few more questions about the details of the encounter, and the interview came to an end as a giant Airbus, forced by traffic and the wind to make its turn southeast of Paris before setting a near-polar course, roared overhead so loudly that it sent the forest of television antennas on the roof into aluminum hysteria.

A MILLION SWIMMING POOLS

Like remnants of Pacific spray sparkling in the sun, a million swimming pools were sprinkled across the hills, ravines, and flats of Los Angeles, glinting sapphire and aquamarine from Mexican-tended foils of green. Veins of blinding molten silver in newly burgeoning watercourses testified to a recent October rain. And the unstoppable, inescapable traffic, never ceasing, coursed through arteries everywhere. As the plane made slow and methodical turns that with baby G forces pressed Jules against his seat, he strained to stay close to the window.

Wheeling now over the Pacific, now over villa-covered hills, Jules was able to sense that the lightness and ease of Los Angeles arose as if the whole city wanted to float up and be carried away on the wind. But though held down by a netting of freeways, roads, streets, fence lines, canals, high tension wires, telephone and other communications lines, and tens of thousands of radio and microwave rays that, were they light, would have encased the city in a gleaming, golden skein, Los Angeles, perhaps more than any place in the world, pulled buoyantly against the threads that tethered it. It was balmy, sunny, happy, and unreal.

The car Jules had rented was not available, so he was promised it at his hotel the next day. In the taxi ride from LAX to the Four Seasons on Doheny, he was shell-shocked by the Persian horde of traffic, the massive construction, the ceaseless and insane maneuvers of cars, the cranes, helicopters, road workers, pedestrians, police, the desperate commercial density, and the radio.

"I know who that is," he said to the taxi driver as a giant plane roared overhead after having almost given the Getty a haircut.

"Who who is?" the taxi driver returned.

"Erre, e, esse, pé, e, cé, té."

"What?"

" *'Respect.'* Aretha Franklin. She's excellently popular in France."

"That's the oldies station. I can change it."

"No, I like it."

"Aretha who?"

"Franklin."

"I think that's from a long time ago."

"How old are you?" Jules asked.

"Twenty."

"Oh."

"Are you a pilot?" the taxi driver wanted to know.

"A pilot? Why do you ask?"

"I picked you up at the airport. Air Ethiopia. Did you ever jump out of a parachute?"

Jules thought, so this is America. Then he answered. "I jumped out of an airplane. I was a paratrooper. How did you know?"

"Because I'd like to be one. I'd like to jump out of a helicopter into the ocean. With a surfboard. That would be cool."

"You could do that, maybe minus the surfboard," Jules told him, "if you set your mind to it." They were passing a Bank of America at the edge of Beverly Hills. Although Jules was the same careful, honest man he had always been, he was also now a different man, on the run from the police, freer, crazier. So he said, "How about helping me rob a bank?" It was a joke, of course.

The taxi driver was silent for a block. Then he said, "When?"

"We'd have to plan it. The hard part for me would be getting the money back to France. But you don't have that problem." That also was a joke.

"Just one?"

"Just one what?" Jules asked.

"Just one bank?"

"Oh no, but we stop at six . . . banks, not o'clock."

"That's right. You don't want to press your luck."

As they glided along now green-swarded boulevards columned by fifty-foot palms, Jules breathed somewhat hard for someone just riding in a taxi. Before the Île aux Cygnes, the last time he had been an outlaw had been in Algeria, because when he was there, where he was there was no law. Something about being an outlaw was the same in music, and in dying. The words *flying, falling, disappearing in light,* and *rising* occurred to him completely absent framework or order.

They pulled onto the crescent drive of the hotel. Instead of allowing Jules to square with the taxi driver, get a receipt, and put back his wallet, the doorman opened the cab door and stood expectantly, as if used to greeting tycoons and heads of state who neither carried money nor took taxis. This put pressure on Jules, who gave the taxi driver an enormous tip. As Jules was struggling to exit, the taxi driver jumped out, ran around the front of the car, and pushed the doorman from the door. "Don't touch my cab," he ordered, "and don't mess with a guy like him," he said, nodding proudly at Jules, "unless you want a dead donkey on your bed."

"What?" the doorman asked.

As Jules stood up, the taxi driver whispered, "My cell number's on the back of the receipt. Let me know when it's time to roll."

As Jules walked toward the hotel's acres of highly polished marble, carpets' as soft as marshmallows, gardens echoing with chamber music and the sound of fountains, and people dressed beyond the nines, he passed a young woman walking alone the other way. A bright yellow silk print dress tightly embraced her from the waist up but flowed at the skirt. She had a mass of genuinely golden hair that was like a halo or an unruly crown, and she was beautiful in an intelligent, entrancing way. As she passed, she smiled at him and her eyes widened — as Jules, now in his seventy-fifth year, well understood — with interest as genuine as the sun color of her hair. To say that he was electrified would be an understatement. He was practically electrocuted. Once again, now in Los Angeles, it was as if his emotions had leapt from an extremely high diving board. That he might encounter her later gave rise in him to equal measures of hope, numbing pleasure, and terror.

He wondered what was happening as his face flushed so hard that he stopped in his tracks and people had to walk around him. A bellboy asked if he might take the bag, and was refused with a vacant shake of the head. Then Jules saw the bar. He hadn't had anything to drink on the plane. He hardly drank at all, and he never went into bars. What's more, he was always so buttoned up and responsible that he normally would have checked in and placed his clothing in the empty drawers and closets. He would have organized his papers, laid out toilet articles neatly along the side of the sink in their exact order of use, washed, and visited the fire stairs, counting the steps from his room so that he could escape in the dark, possibly crawling along under the smoke, dressed in wet towels, like an ancient Egyptian. But instead he went into the bar.

At first he thought he wanted a Martini, because he had been served one once and it was so clear as to be invisible, but after a sip of what seemed like dry-cleaning fluid he realized that he was really after the olive. Here he would have to have something else. For him, this hotel bar was as dark, elegant, and beckoning an adventure as if he were sneaking in at age twelve. The bartender came over.

"*Bonjour.* In the Caribbean," Jules said, "I once had a drink with soda, rum, sugar, and lime. I've forgotten what it's called in French. I never knew what it was called in English."

"That's a Planter's Punch," the bartender told him. "I can make you one."

Five minutes after he started drinking it, not yet having checked-in to the hotel, fleeing Paris after having killed two people, and very recently proposing to a crazy kid he had just met that they rob banks together, Jules was floating with the same lightness that had always defined Los Angeles. He had wondered what people did in bars, how for half an hour, an hour, or more they could sit silently and immobile on seats from which it was surprising that they did not fall. And now he knew, because, for an hour or more, soaring like a condor on rum and sugar, he thought of the woman in the yellow silk dress — her hands, her hair, the magic of her face, the way she walked, the scent of her perfume, her eyes, her smile.

Although he couldn't stop thinking of her, he understood that she had been just a brilliant, sudden, overwhelming flash, an imagined perfection that left its imprint upon the eyes even after it had vanished. And this, he realized, was the essence and object of Los Angeles itself, a work of the climate, terrain, vegetation, sea, and light. How wonderful that it could be found in the beauty of a woman apprehended in an instant as she smiled and passed by.

He went to bed early without dinner and the next morning was at the swimming pool at dawn. Never had he seen such a clean pool. He tried to find a leaf, a speck, perhaps a discarded peanut, but couldn't. How did they do it? Was the water distilled? Stacks of rolled towels and tables with pitchers of lemon water flanked every entrance. Solid chaises with thick cushions lay unoccupied all around the pool. Nothing stirred, and the water was flat until he broke the surface and swam his accustomed kilometer, trying not to lose count of the laps.

After he went back upstairs, he shaved, dressed, straightened up the room, and made the bed. He always did that, and then tipped and thanked the maids, who wondered what he was up to. His room was plush. Two balconies overlooked the pool to the south and Los Angeles to the east. It seemed peaceful and green, although he knew there was more to it than that, and that he was holed up in a privileged enclave.

As he drove toward the Getty, palm fronds passing above like the fans that cooled the pharaohs, he tried not to think of the woman in the yellow dress, who had appeared like a blinding sunburst with the promise that it could put an end to longing and lay the past to rest. She was just a symbol, but he was sure that her splendor was not merely superficial. In her expression he had seen modesty, love, intelligence, and kindness.

He wished he had a billion dollars, or just a hundred million, perhaps even just fifty million. Then at least he would suffer for a time the delusion that he could outwit mortality. He would fly Luc in an air ambulance to the Cleveland Clinic or the MD Anderson Cancer Center in Texas, or Harvard or Johns

Hopkins, whichever was the best. He would settle Cathérine and David in a nearby Four Seasons or Ritz Carlton. He would visit them frequently. And he would buy a house on a mountainside so as to look out over the whole expanse of Los Angeles, comforted by the flat blue of the Pacific disappearing calmly toward the joint between water and sky, the fine-line gate to infinity. In this city, disconnected from everything but the present, he would live with the woman in the yellow dress, the woman who had such full-bodied, wavy, astoundingly gold hair, if she would have him, until he was eighty, when he would die and return to Jacqueline forever, if she would forgive him.

Had Jacqueline lived, life would have been even more peaceful than the natural narcotic of Los Angeles could make it. She had a talent for happiness, and the patience, gentleness, and feminine power that allowed her to hold through without fighting. He, on the other hand, knew how to hold through only by fighting, and when he could no longer fight he would be done.

Since her death, his many infatuations, which had radiated like burning infrared into the hearts of younger and inappropriate women, were nothing more than a confused and pathetic attempt to reach beyond the veil, and by touching, embracing, and loving the beauty of another, to touch, embrace, and love life once more. Although he hadn't misled the subjects of these infatuations for more than an instant, and although what passed between them was as pure as it was powerful, he was ashamed nonetheless. As honest as were his impulses, he could not act on them. He had full license to do so, for widowers can remarry. But not Jules. He could kill two men, evade the police, and perhaps rob a bank or two, but he dared not seek out the woman he had seen leaving the hotel, speak to her, embrace her, kiss her, and chance to stay with her for as long as he could.

As the days had passed in beautiful weather and he had heard nothing, he had presumed that Acorn was making arrangements for an orchestra. He was so much absented from his own world and so put at ease by Beverly Hills — its drunken blue and green night lighting that made jeweled caves of almost every pocket of vegetation; its highly waxed cars gliding over streets as clean as new cloth; its population, desperately, but slowly, on the make — that he spent money as if he actually had it. After all, he was going to get a million Euros, and his living expenses would be covered by Acorn. He felt free to buy a thing or two: sunglasses for $750; a deep blue silk tie for $300; a cashmere blazer for $2,000. Then, after he hadn't heard anything for five days, and thinking that he might have been hung out to dry, he stopped spending promiscuously.

After parking his car in the Getty's spotless underground garage, he took the train up the mountainside. Perched above the sea, the museum's many levels, terraces, fountains, courtyards, gardens, and galleries hung dreamlike in the sky.

As he sat on a bench overlooking the Pacific — its sparkling, its Technicolor blues, its beckoning and hypnotic disappearance at the horizon — his phone rang.

He fumbled it out of his pocket. "Hey, Jewels."

"Yes?"

"Jack. Come to New York."

"When?"

"Now."

"What about here? What about the orchestration?"

"They did that already in New York."

"Why am I here?"

"You mean why were you born?"

"Why am I in Los Angeles?"

"I don't know. It was supposed to have been done there, but they must have found a quicker way to get it done here."

"Who are *they*?"

"The people who manage this kind of thing, whoever they are. No big deal. Hop on a plane and come here for the board meeting."

"Okay," Jules said. He wondered how he would fare with these people, who exhibited the carelessness of great wealth.

AMINA BELKACEM

Jules chose a window seat on the port side of the aircraft so that on his way east he would be able to look across the expansive landscape in north light. At 40,000 feet, two miles higher than Everest, the world below would seem at peace. In clear weather, the silent action — as if to confirm an intractable state of beneficence outside the realm of human affairs — would be of clouds and their shadows moving slowly across deserts, mountain ranges, prairies, and endless farmlands punctuated by thin exclamation points of almost immobile white smoke.

When the plane was airborne with wheels retracted, but still in tight maneuvers before setting its course, a disembodied voice filled the cabin. Half the passengers looked into the air. As Moses could testify, rich, authoritative, disembodied voices are both comforting and disturbing.

"This is your captain speaking," it said with the ease and authority of practice and command. "We have some weather in the Southwest, so we're going to take a more northerly route to New York today. We think we can make up for the time that would normally be lost, by getting a boost from the jet stream, which is farther north than usual, and why on the southerly route there's the heat and humidity making those storms. We'll be in the jet stream twice as long as we would have been, and hope to get you to New York on time.

"Meanwhile, we'll be flying right up the center of San Francisco Bay, almost as if we'd departed from San Francisco International. Those of you on the left side of the aircraft will get a good view of San Francisco and the Golden Gate." The microphone clicked. Then he came back. "And, on the right side, the Oakland section of the Bay Bridge, and Berkeley. Then the valley, the Sierra, and we'll be on our way. Thank you for flying with us today. I'll be turning off the seat-belt sign in just a few minutes."

Not long after, they started up San Francisco Bay. Jules could see the shadow of the plane speeding along the water, and to the west, from their fairly low height before the climb to transcontinental cruising altitude, the Peninsula came into view. First the glittering water, wrinkled and refracting; then industry and highways; then a light-green residential area patchworked with houses

249

overshadowed by trees; the wide open, less green, but still verdant Stanford campus; rolling hills with dry, golden grass, almost silvery white; deep-green, fog-watered mountains; and beyond them the frigid blue of the Pacific, ending at a thick wall of fog that seemed as big as a continent. The land below appeared to be a paradise, the kind of place Jules had seen in his mind's eye when he wrote the piece, a place where with luck the burdens of history might be left behind. He fixed his eyes upon the garden spaces and great trees between the university buildings and the town. He was often enthusiastic about beautiful places, but this was something more. He felt inexplicably that he might have a chance there unlike any he had had in his life, and as the plane quickly carried him away, he yearned for it.

"Why am I going to my office? What am I going to do in my office?" Amina Belkacem said to herself aloud, confident that no one would hear, because there was no one. She squeezed the brake levers of her bicycle so hard that its rear wheel left the ground for a moment, and the front wheel skidded on the path for three or four feet. She enjoyed this because she had done it out of anger, and it was decisive. But anger immediately gave way to the despair of someone who has been abandoned. And in her case, it was after thirty years of marriage.

She dismounted from the heavy English bicycle, its tubular frame a deep cobalt blue, and walked it to a lone bench. Long ignored by the groundskeepers, the bench was covered in dried eucalyptus leaves and surrounded by piles of them blown its way by passing bicycles. Amina leaned hers against one end of it, swept the leaves off the other, and sat down, staring ahead at the deserted grove of pale, massive trees. Anger, then to the brink of tears, then strong feelings like those of first love, came and went, one following the other in a terrible beating.

She cried, and afterward felt a little better, but her emotions were like maritime weather — small storms, squalls, sudden clearing, a ray of sun disappearing, all very confusing for the sailor who nonetheless tries to keep her prow headed into the wind. Students rushed past on their bicycles, oblivious of her. She regarded them maternally, knowing what they did not know and remembering how youth had carried her through gales of chance. They lived in a blind world that was yet wonderful. Sayyid, at sixty-seven, was insane to think he could make a new life with a twenty-four-year-old. When and if he would be eighty and in need above all of compassion and possibly diapers, she would be thirty-seven, running marathons with her long legs, not even at her sexual peak. Then what? Serves him right.

Amina, sagacious and lively, sixty-one but looking no older than forty, was still beautiful in a way that was inimitable and lasting, even if not to a shallow man. She had crow's feet at the corners of her eyes, but these combined with her smile to make her even more alluring and attractive than when she was younger. She radiated happiness, love, intelligence — and mischief. Though practically children, her male students by the score fell in love with her, and, long before, she had learned to put them off while simultaneously comforting them. Sayyid had had no such experience, so when an astoundingly leggy and vacuous graduate student — her doctoral thesis was on women and bus stops — had fallen for him, he was as gone as if he had jumped from a cliff at Yosemite. He had never given Amina children, because he couldn't. Despite this, Amina had stayed with him.

They bought the house in 1998, at the peak of the dot-com boom, for $550,000. While still in France they had put another $200,000 into it before they moved in the next year. Stanford gave them both tenure when they transferred from Paris-Sorbonne, and even with California taxes, the vastly higher salaries plus a federal tax rate lower than what they paid in France made them feel rich for the first time in their lives. The dot-com bubble deflated and, later, in the crash of 2008, they thought the house value would lessen commensurately, but were incredulous to find that Silicon Valley was an exception to the rule. By 2014, real estate agents were pestering them every week with offers of $2.5 million and more. The house was in her name, and even though California was a joint property state, Sayyid was a son of a bitch and she was sure that he was so crazy now that he would just walk away from it — as he had walked away from her that morning to move into the rental hovel of his seductress and sit there for the rest of his wretched life on a beanbag chair. After everything found its angle of repose, Amina would have, one way or another, three or four million, some Social Security from the U.S. and France, and either a pension or, if she continued working, her considerable salary. But money was not relevant to a broken heart.

Though the cycles of conflicting emotions would quickly come and go and were terribly taxing, still they pushed her slowly and steadily forward, and with time were not merely cycles but spirals. Pain would lead to recognition, and recognition to resolution as the hours passed on the bench. For example, at first she was hurt, and then angry, to reflect upon how much he had changed, weakly floating on the tides around them even as she held fast. She had watched him move with the times so that now he would approach

253

with reason and detachment something like a love story, and exercise indignant, overloaded passion in politics and economics. What had happened to him and others that they mocked sentiment in the love between men and women and treated public policy with the drive and resentment of spurned suitors? Sayyid had become a different person. Whereas he let the world in everywhere, she had never done that, and never would, preferring a life of her own.

Because he had changed so completely, he was in no danger at work. But she had loyalties she wouldn't betray, and she knew that, tenure or not, she might not last long, perhaps not even until retirement, although having seen the quiet desperation of professors emeritus she wanted to work until she dropped. How could she communicate the reality of war and its effects — her field was twentieth-century France — without upsetting some Alice-in-Wonderland student who, having experienced nothing and been hypnotized into victimhood, would demand a trigger warning? It was a madhouse, made even more difficult for her in navigating the shoals of what was her second language after French, the third being a childhood Arabic fortified by some later study.

To her astonishment, she was forbidden to describe atrocities against white people or men. At first she thought this was a joke, but it wasn't, and she quickly came to the re-alization that such a regime was merely a mechanism to give power to one or another struggling political faction in the highly infected, incestuous bloodstream of the university. She had been protected by her Arabic name. Her father was Algerian, as was her mother, but her mother, blonde and blue-eyed like Amina, was a French *colon.* What did these idiots, these self-appointed little commissars, who swerved from one angry lunacy to another almost daily, know of the mixture of blood, of race, existence, history, and love?

Despite her many transgressions against orthodoxy, Amina was in a sense paroled because she was an Arab and therefore in their view not white; and because she was a woman, an intellectual, and a foreigner. On the other hand, she was blonde and blue-eyed, magnificently dressed (she bought most of her clothes in Paris when she returned home), and elegant by nature, which screamed elitism and privilege, although she had never been privileged in the accurate or even the common and false understanding of the word. She was not confident that she would be able to work in the American university system much longer, as she was guilty of what had become its gravest sin: she thought and spoke freely.

Things began to clarify much faster than

she had expected. In fact, they raced, and the afternoon was not even over.

Riding into the Arboretum at high speed was rather dangerous, because at lunch she had had too much to drink. Which is to say that she had twenty-five fluid ounces of Japanese beer, almost enough to put her under the table. She never drank, not because she was a Muslim — she hadn't been devout even as a child in Algeria — but because she didn't like it and didn't need it. But after Sayyid had knocked the wind out of her when she came home from class at eleven, and walked out of the house with a German rucksack slung over his shoulder, never to return, she couldn't stay a minute longer. So she got on her bicycle — she really loved her bicycle — and by accident found herself at a University Avenue Mexican restaurant called "The New Original Celia's."

It was a reincarnation, to the letter, of the previous establishment, and like its predecessor highly air-conditioned, welcome that day at noon in Indian Summer. She ordered a ceviche salad and a Kirin Ichiban, thinking that Ichiban meant "little." It came in a huge glass mug that had been in the freezer probably since 1969, and was so cold that it almost anesthetized her. By the time she left the restaurant her head was spinning in the bright sunshine and, for the first time in her life, at age sixty-one, she was a drunk driver on a bicycle. This was dangerous, exhilarating, and the reason she went so fast and was so relaxed about doing so.

She was sufficiently unused to alcohol that she hoped the delirium would go away after she paid her check and went to brush her teeth — thirty seconds for each quadrant, faithfully as always. Everyone in California had — well, everyone in Palo Alto — glacially white teeth. So did she, although she could not compete with fluoridated youth whose smiles were as blinding as locomotive headlights. But then, locomotive headlights or not, they could not compete with the gentleness, wisdom, and warmth of her inimitable smile, preserved since childhood in all its innocence despite the infusion of a life's-worth of strength and good graces. As she would note on the bench, the intoxication would take all afternoon to dissipate, it exaggerated her emotions, it filled her with love, longing, and regret, and it sped her decisions and made her recklessly and satisfyingly resolute.

In France, Sayyid had reminded her, men his age had mistresses. "Fuck you, Sayyid. You need another woman when you can't even give me a child? And fuck them. I don't care what they do in France. They're greedy bastards who should be killed, every one of them. If I had someone on the side how would you feel? What if I took up with one of

257

my graduate students, a young man of twenty-four who could father a child? How would you feel?"

"You can't have a child, Amina," was the reply.

"Not now, but I could have."

"I have to go."

"Yes, Sayyid, *you have to go.*"

When he actually walked out, not looking back, with a spring in his step, she knew it was really over. It was the lowest point, and she almost fainted. Then came the cycles, which, although she didn't know it, were part of a spiral that would lead her to a new life. Even while at The New Original Celia's she fell in love with a man, a handsome, professorial, quiet man who sat at a table by himself reading a medical journal. It was a heady feeling, and dangerous, soon exaggerated by the alcohol. She loved him, and saw him as her salvation. They would marry. He would be perfect. He would be divorced or a widower, and he would have wonderful, beautiful children, to whom she would be a substitute mother, and who would love her as much as she would love them.

But in an instant she understood that she was like a free radical that out of necessity and compulsion would dangerously bond with the first available atom, and she resolved not to, not to hop from one ice floe to another, but soberly — although she was sitting at the counter at The New Original Celia's, increasingly not sober — to let time pass. Time did pass of course, and all afternoon she stayed on the bench, which was now so firmly her own that if anyone had tried to sit on it, even the Dalai Lama, she would have punched him.

When it began to cool, as it does in the evening all along the Peninsula even in summer, she found herself clearheaded and calm. She would accept her new status, live with her independence while neither glorifying nor regretting it, and, after a decent interval, keep her eyes open in the time she had left, refusing to discount the prospect of love. She had never been indecisive, and although modest she had always been courageous and she had always known her own mind.

The sun was setting, the fog beginning to roll down from the hills. The sky to the east and above was perfectly clear, dim, and almost golden. To the west, the fog bank descended, gray, moist, and white. Amina Belkacem, a most wonderful woman, who deserved to be loved, resolved to go back to France. California was in many respects a beautiful dream, but in France the beauty was awake and alert. France was her home, and there was a great deal to be said for going home.

With the sunset came the sound of a mourning dove somewhere in the trees. As in

Algeria and as in France, it had waited for the tranquility that comes in heat or fading light. Its call was not a lament. Neither of happiness nor sadness, it rested perfectly upon the edge where these met, as if upon the ridge of a roof, superior to either, overlooking both, with the clearest sight and highest, most open view, which is that of acceptance. The cry of the mourning dove is beautiful because it wants nothing.

A Thousand Lawyers

Had Jules been jerked around in France from one end of the country to another, he might have been resigned. A powerless semi-academic, he had been defeated even in infancy. Though in his youth he had had episodes of energy and luck, such flares had faded with age. In Paris, he might have simply bowed his head and let them work their ways with him.

But this was the New World. Floating on the jet stream, his plane roared toward the night in fearless confidence. The sun set across the plains, casting a deepening shadow until east of the Mississippi the land below was scattered with the sparkling of cities great and small. To the north, perhaps all the way into Canada, a continental storm front flashed with lightning as constant and surprising as raindrops bouncing on a lake.

The immense turbines spinning within the aircraft's engines didn't miss a beat. Like the heart, they had to be constant and reliable until the end. He could hardly explain whence his sudden energy and optimism came, but on the red-eye into New York he neither slept nor read. He felt that something from the vast substance of the ground over which he flew was penetrating him insubstantially. If a hundred invisible particles with strange names, and radio waves, cosmic rays, and magnetic fields were at any moment and without detection bathing him, everyone in the cabin, and indeed the whole world, with their unknown, mischievous, and mystical transits, who was to say that the land, air, and light over or through which he shot could not give strength where there was no strength, luck when luck had vanished, defiance in the face of defeat, and life where life had been running out?

He couldn't have slept even had he wanted to. Running through him like an electric current was the empowering conviction that he himself did not need to live. It was Luc who needed to live. Without fear, Jules could take any chance. Understanding and accepting that he was expendable gave him strength as steady as the power that propelled the jet over one diamond-lit city after another glittering in a sea of black.

Nothing from the night flight vanished or dissipated. By the time he went to his tower room at the Four Seasons New York, he needed sleep but was neither exhausted nor demoralized. The image of Luc appeared, as often before, but now more lively and happier. He didn't think anymore of Luc dying but only of Luc living.

Luc didn't understand leukemia, but he understood crocodiles and was hysterically afraid of them. Once, when putting him to bed, Jules saw that the child would be kept up in fear, so he said, "Look, crocodiles live in Africa, which is far away from here, and they don't even know that this is where you live. If they knew, they wouldn't know how to get here. And if they did know how to get here they wouldn't be able to cross the jungle and the desert to get to the sea. And if they could cross the jungle and the desert, they couldn't swim the Mediterranean. But if they could swim it, they couldn't walk from Marseilles all the way to Paris. If they could walk to Paris, they wouldn't know how to take the RER to Cergy. And if they did know, they wouldn't have the money to buy a ticket, or know where to get off, because they can't read and speak French. And even if they had the money and could read and speak French, once they got off in Cergy they wouldn't know where you live. Even if they did, they couldn't get in the front door. Even if they broke down the front door, they wouldn't know where your room is. If they knew where your room is, they couldn't get in the door.

And even if they did, I would shoot them."

Needless to say, this did not have the desired effect, as attested by Luc's open mouth, widened eyes, and the fact that he hardly dared breathe. "Wait wait wait," Jules said upon seeing this. "Forget what I just said. That was pretend. This is what it is really," and he then went through the sequence in reverse, banishing the crocodiles back to the Blue Nile, and watching Luc relax as they grew farther and farther distant, comforted enough so that before the crocodiles had even finished struggling across the Sahara he was fast asleep.

Jules hoped that if parents and grandparents truly loved and tried their best, the children would forgive the mistakes even when those who had made them were long gone.

Acorn might have hundreds of thousands of employees set in the tectonic foundation of several trillions of dollars. And in comparison to Jules, Jack Cheatham and Rich Panda might well be like advanced space aliens with brains and social senses so much more capable than his that in the arena of their type of calculation and maneuver he would be as ill-equipped as a crocodile on the Champs-Élysées. But if he didn't fear and didn't retreat, if he simply stood his ground and dared, he might cut through the webs made by people who spent their lives spinning them.

The meeting about the music was set for one o'clock the next afternoon. The board of Acorn would consider the rollout of what would be their international signature for a decade or longer. Jules had reserved his room for three days afterward, in case there were adjustments, contract signings, complications — of which he now suspected there would be enough to overwhelm him until there would be none, and, worn down, he would give up. Then his flight back to Paris, like the room in the hotel, prepaid and non–refundable. Including what he had spent in Los Angeles, he had parted with an enormous amount of money. Ordinarily he would have been more than anxious that the nearly €40,000 would be a loss if, as seemed possible, he would not be reimbursed. That amount could have gone a long way in regard to Luc, and was a substantial portion of what he could give to Cathérine were he to give her everything. He would do precisely that of course, but it wasn't enough. Still, he wasn't anxious. Acorn owed him the money, and without the vaguest idea how, he was confident that he would get it and — if Acorn proved difficult, dishonest, and dishonorable — more than what he was owed, as either interest or penalty. He wondered why he thought this, because he had no basis for doing so. How could Jules Lacour even accounts with Acorn?

For almost twenty-four hours, he slept a deep sleep, deeper than any since his twenties. In Los Angeles he had swum every day. Now he would run, and on a blue, autumnal morning, having studied the running map supplied by the hotel, he set off for Central Park. In Saint-Germain-en-Laye he had the perfect place to run, with the Seine below to the east, gardens and forest to the west, and a gravel path that was straight, level, and lonely. There was no better place in the world. Here, he had to dodge taxis and pedestrians, and when he got to the park weave his way on unfamiliar paths, cross roads stuffed with fat, aggressive automobiles, and leap over potholes and patches of mud. For many years in Saint-Germain-en-Laye he had puffed along, swift only for a man his age. Long before, he had gotten used to people passing him: even children. But now in New York no one passed him. For the first time in many years he ran as if he had no weight, and as the run progressed, instead of slowing down, he sped up.

Attributing this to the long sleep, he knew that he would not tire, and that by one o'clock he would be even stronger and more clear-headed. So he ran faster and faster, slowing of course on Heartbreak Hill just south of Harlem, but racing down the west side of the park on the home stretch. He even leapt low fences, something he hadn't done in decades.

In his room, which often was above the clouds, he showered luxuriously in a Niagara of hot water, put on a suit and the $300 deep blue tie he had bought in Beverly Hills, and left for the meeting, having breakfasted and had a haircut while still in running clothes. In Los Angeles his suit had been a prisoner of the closet. Now, on 57th Street, it happily met the cool air, and his dress shirt glowed like snow in sunshine.

The Acorn tower was so high that in strong winds the top swayed like a pendulum. If they turned pale enough, visitors to the executive floor at the very top were given air-sickness bags. Much smaller Acorn buildings had sprouted around the tower as if it were an oak, because the multi-trillion-dollar behemoth had set grafted limbs to grow until they themselves had to scatter their own Acorns to office parks or glass plinths: in Connecticut (for the criminal trading of derivatives), London (insurance and re-insurance), Washington (pensions, public relations, legislative bribery), Boston (art), Philadelphia (old money), Short Hills (financing new-money monstrosities with one-hundred-car garages, faux mine shafts, and master-bedroom, in-wall, gold-plated popcorn machines), to mention just a few.

The efficiency and wealth of this organization became immediately apparent upon realization that whereas its two-or-three-hundred-thousand-and-change employees managed its trillions, the Federal government mismanaged not much more than twice the sum with four million civilians and military on staff. Of course, Acorn didn't send rockets to Mars or have a navy. It was just a great money machine. Like a whale, it cruised the markets, sweeping up cash in its baleen. Like a clam, it sat amidst constantly mobile currents and strained them for things of value. It produced no wool, wheat, or flax, no lawn-mower engines, apples, or fedoras. It was solely conceptual, the purely intellectual construction of statistics, fears, gambling, demography, predictions, assurances, numbers, and lies. Three things happened in its labyrinthine, magnificently decorated offices. Numbers were sliced, diced, churned, whirled, wiggled, and juggled. Payments came in. Once in a while, payments went out, too, but it was the job of the actuaries, auditors, adjusters, and lawyers to keep these to a minimum. All in all, a happy situation for Rich Panda, who with time kept getting richer and richer — like the rosewood in the boardroom that with time also kept getting richer and richer. But whereas the wood was a rich red, Rich Panda was a rich butter color. His glasses, which he wore for appearance rather than to correct his vision, were a rich butter color. His hair was a rich (thinning) butter color. His skin, unlike Shymanski's, which was sallow to the point of taupe, was a rich butter color, tinged with a rich, buttery red. His suit, of the softest, richest, most glowing wool in the world, was a rich butter color — anything but black and white. His tie — it need not be said. All in all, he resembled the sun setting over Napeague Inlet as it turned from white to a rich butter color. He was very heavy but not jolly; as round as the man in the moon and as deeply menacing, because you could not quite see him. Not because he was blinding like the sun, or hidden in a briar patch of flounces and curls like Louis XIV, but because you could not even vaguely sense, despite his smile, what was going on behind his cold, sled-dog-blue eyes.

When Jules stepped from the elevator and into a reception area adjacent to a most spectacular boardroom, he was met by a stunningly attractive woman standing beneath a huge Picasso. She greeted him and brought him to his seat.

Jules noted the members of the board, their faces, and how they were attired. Three women — one perhaps in her thirties, two certainly over fifty — were dressed expensively and elegantly, with expertly done hair and makeup. Lightly but noticeably bejeweled, they sat with backs as straight as ram-rods, and each one had purses and portfolios of extremely expensive leather in which various electronic slabs were discreetly hidden. He could smell their perfume. They were pretty. But although these women had every attribute of femininity — delicacy, beauty, grace, and more — they were patently un-feminine merely because they chose to be. Suspicion, aggression, self-assertion, and the sense that they were crouched to spring radiated from them quietly but unmistakably. Perhaps they felt that these qualities were necessary in what had formerly been a man's world, but Jules was as repelled by their aura as he was by that of the men around the table, from whom radiated the same suspicion, aggression, and self-assertion. As a board, they were supposed to have been guiding the company with its best interests in mind. To the extent that they did this, it was to advance their own standing. They spoke either to show off or to discredit their colleagues without leaving fingerprints. They gobbled at success just as tensely as fancily dressed people in a fancy restaurant.

There were nine men, including Jack Cheatham and Rich Panda. No one acknowledged Jules, but he continued to study them.

He was fascinated by the roll of their lapels. He knew nothing about fashion and had never paid much attention to clothing, especially men's clothing, but now he was hypnotized by lapels. Even the name was strange in English if you said it or thought about it several times, although in French (*revers*) it seemed more sensible. If you knew French, the English word was even stranger, as it meant *the shovel*. Although Jules had no idea, every suit in the room was a Paul Stuart made-to-measure by Samuelsohn in Montréal, and the roll of the lapels was expressive of much of America: its informality, its riches, its confidence, and even of the curl of waves breaking at that very moment along the hundred miles of wide, windblown beach that ran, broken by surging inlets, from Brooklyn to Montauk Point. Never in Paris had he seen such lapels. In Paris, lapels were flat and bodiless. Here, they were full-bodied, and seemed to give substance. Jules thought, if fabric is soft and rich, it should indeed roll like a wave.

Apart from the rosewood paneling and fine leather chairs, the boardroom had a lot of glass, some etched, some clear, all extremely thick and heavy. This, and a long, million-dollar, walnut table were solid counterweights to the somewhat nauseating sway of the building. Through windows in various directions one could see the Atlantic, Long Island Sound, the Hudson Highlands, and the distant Ramapos.

The board had been at work since eight and

had broken for lunch in a dining room accessible by the first of many staircases descending ten floors through the interior of the skyscraper. Though the dining room was only one storey down, an electric dumbwaiter had carried up a tea-and-coffee service that, before business resumed, was laid for the board by young men and women in French waiters' costumes. Each person had before him a gold-rimmed cup and saucer and an insulated carafe of either coffee or tea. Planted along the centerline of the magnificent table were silver salvers loaded with petits fours and stacks of the kind of cellophane-wrapped, long cookies one is given too few of in an airplane. As people bustled with their papers and partook of their coffee and tea, nothing was offered to their aides sitting against the rosewood walls.

"Okay," said Rich. "To business." He nodded to an assistant, who tapped a key to begin recording. "The first item on this afternoon's various agenda is the proposal to adopt a musical theme as Acorn's worldwide branding signature. He signaled, and the recording Jules had made in Paris swelled to fill the room. Jules heard Élodi. It was so vivid it was as if she were there. When the music stopped, once again no one said anything, or even sighed.

"Well?" Rich asked. "What do you think?"

At the far end of the table, a man who was

so big he looked like he had inhaled a delica-
tessen, said, "Isn't a jingle supposed to be irritating, so it becomes a brain worm, and you
can't forget it? This isn't irritating, it's inappropriately beautiful. These days, people
don't like that."

One of the outside directors raised his hand
briefly and said, "Has this been tested in our
markets all around the world? Differences in
taste and musical perception are vast. Half of
humanity has a non-Western musical system."

"No, we haven't done any testing yet," Rich
admitted.

"As far as I'm concerned," another titan
said, "it's too slow, too referential, and too
demanding of the attention span of the Mil-
lennials who are the market we have to clinch
in the next decade."

"Good point," said another. "It was too
nineteenth-century. You couldn't fit it into a
ring-tone, and anything longer than that is
kryptonite to the young unless they're on
Ecstasy."

Rich nodded as if learning a needed lesson
while surviving a necessary reprimand.

Next, one of the two older women spoke
up. She was astoundingly elegant. Her hair
was gray and she wore diamonds with re-
straint. A university president, she was simultaneously guarded and aggressive, like a bee
carefully hovering before going in for the
sting.

"I appreciate very much that you've made the effort, Rich, but it's not going to work. I strongly recommend against it."

Rich nodded in an accepting way.

Jules was astounded, and stood to protest. "Excuse me."

"And who are you?" Rich asked.

"Jewels Lacour," Jack Cheatham said.

"Who?" Rich wanted to know.

"I wrote it," Jules said. "It's not nineteenth-century at all but firmly twentieth-century."

"We're probably not going to use it," Rich said. "We'll let you know."

"You accepted it. It's written clearly in the emails."

Rich turned to Jack, who shook his head in denial. "As always," Jack stated, "acceptance depends upon getting the product into usable shape, which means that the supplier has to meet our needs and requirements and be willing to work with us, no matter how long it takes."

"I'm willing to work with you," Jules told everyone.

Silence. With a slight, barely perceptible smile, visible at the corners of his mouth, a spider smile, Rich said, "As you've heard, we have to test it worldwide and adjust for each market and culture."

Thinking of Luc and time, Jules said, "No."

"So, you're not willing to work with us?"

"The email said *accepted.* The piece was

agreed-upon."

"The email, Mr. . . . ?"

"Lacour," Jack filled in for Rich, "Jewels Lacour."

"Is not a contract." The attorneys in the room remained omittedly mute.

"I don't think we should have any world-wide signatures," one of the board members said. "And, besides, shouldn't this be left up to the professionals in the ad agency? We're not set up or competent to develop such a campaign."

It appeared that a consensus had been reached, as usual, silently welling up and incontrovertible. "So noted," said Rich. "The next order of business."

"So noted?" asked Jules, at first angry but then feeling as if the ground beneath his feet were falling away from him.

"So noted," Rich replied.

Two hours later, as the brilliant afternoon was ending in the kind of brilliant day that everywhere is the emblem of autumn, Jules was riding in yet another elevator, rising at terrific speed to the top floors of a skyscraper even higher than Acorn's. He had gone to the French Consulate and been directed to a lawyer at a leading firm, someone who knew French and was familiar with French law.

It was yet another building in which the windows didn't open. Whatever the aerodynamical requirements of structures so high that winds aloft flew past them ·at hurricane speeds, Jules hated that huge, complex, and expensive systems were required to ventilate these lifeless boxes built in such a way as to keep out the oceans of air all around them. Better not to build such buildings than to shut out the noise of the wind in the trees, the crack of thunder or sound of rain, birdsong, the murmur of distant conversation, the sound of water in a stream or merely a gutter, and, of course, the many fresh and lively breezes.

Even worse was to be in an elevator. He wasn't claustrophobic, but he did object to being encased in a steel box that played awful music. Time was running out and he was in the midst of a complication such as one in which half a dozen things — appliances, vehicles, plumbing — break at once and each must be fixed in a series of multiple steps, appointments, and waiting for parts. This had always shattered his concentration upon music. Some people like incessant busyness, distractions, games, a million things happening simultaneously, which blocks their awareness of oblivion. But Jules had been profoundly aware of oblivion since the retreat of the Wehrmacht and the SS through Reims in the summer of 1944.

Oblivion and grief, the darkness that gave meaning to light and life, had turned him away from games, respect for status, and the desire for position, influence, power, or even a good name in the eyes of others. These he rejected in favor of his family and the honor of doing what was right — all conveyed and confirmed by the beauty and flow of the world in transient flashes, in faces, and in the way things came together rightly when seen in tranquility and from on high.

He didn't want to play the kind of games that had transformed people like Rich Panda into spiritless husks. He didn't want to embark upon a lawsuit to get money. He was a failed composer, a musician with performance anxiety. To take on a giant corporation run by insanely aggressive, acquisitive, semi-human ciphers was hardly promising of success or pleasure. And yet, as bankrupt as it seemed, it was the only thing he could think to do. He wondered if in fact the semi-human ciphers had once been forced, as he was now, to enter upon this game, if they knew or regretted it, and if even at this late stage he would become like them.

Sammi Montmirail had the patience and fortitude to sit at a desk all day and do legal puzzles under high pressure, but when Jules walked into his office he had been thinking about how his children would like the hat he had made for their dog, a timid and self-effacing beagle who was the baby of the family. It was a surprise for them. When the beagle was naughty, which she was on occasion, she would be sent to her bed and made to wear the hat, a baseball cap with holes for her ears and the word *Cat* embroidered on the front. So much for the United States Code. Nor was Sammi Montmirail the lawyer's original name. Jules knew this upon seeing his face, a wonderful face to which Jules took instantly. "Where are you from?" he asked.

"The Gironde, fifteen minutes from Bordeaux."

"And before that?"

Sammi hesitated. Jules had made him, but he hadn't made Jules. "Israel," he said.

"And before that?" Jules asked in Hebrew.

Sammi relaxed. "Iran."

Jules looked past him all the way to the Atlantic, where enormous ships in great number seemed no bigger than bright little seeds. New York was a water city, close to the ocean, hard by bays, riven by inlets, surrounded by rivers. Just as Paris was surrounded by hills and forests to which many Parisians did not give a thought, probably many New Yorkers never realized how, in their city, land and water intermingled like clasped fingers. "So, a Jew, an Iranian, an Israeli, a Frenchman, and an American. Of the five, which is your favorite?"

"I would say husband and father, definitely. And you?"

"The same, although for me that's largely over."

"How old are you?" Sammi asked.

"Seventy-four."

"And where were you during the war?"

"In France."

"Then we both started rough. How can I help you?" Ready to take careful notes, he picked up a fountain pen and opened a portfolio.

Jules told him the whole story and laid before him copies of the emails promising acceptance. Sammi was slight and dark, his face gentle and sympathetic. He read the documents carefully. When he finished, he thought in silence.

This hesitation impressed Jules, who wanted to trust his thinking, whatever conclusions might issue. But nonetheless, before the lawyer could utter even a word, Jules said, "Apart from whatever the facts or legalities of the case, I have a question."

"Which is?" The lawyer was expecting a query about cost.

"Does the law," Jules asked, "have within it, like music, secrets and keys that unlock it?"

"I'm not sure what you mean."

"Things that, though in the open, remain hidden to most, but if discovered clarify and increase the power of effect — patterns, repeated proportions, and rhythms that when taken as a whole and with sufficient detachment melt into a coherence that can't be properly perceived without them."

Who was this person? At a thousand dollars an hour, the conversations Sammi had in his office were dense with information rapidly communicated, and never philosophical or discursive. "Can you give me an example?"

"Verdi and waveforms."

"Okay," he said, in the way it can be said meaning, *Go ahead.*

"Almost all of Verdi's music comports with the timing and amplitude of ocean waves. Or sea waves: after all, he knew the Mediterranean and the Adriatic. Though this is complex and subtle in an analytical frame, it's easy to perceive in the sound, and if you've realized what it is and how he does it you can ride on those waves instead of letting them wash over you."

"You're a musicologist?"

"No. They would protest what I've just said. I'm a musician. Musicians work in waves. Musicologists work in shards."

"You realize," Sammi said, "that these speculations cost a thousand dollars an hour, or — I like to remind my clients — sixteen dollars and sixty-seven cents a minute, or twenty-eight cents a second?"

"What the hell," Jules said, in for a dime, in for a thousand dollars an hour. "Does the law have waves?"

"Yes, but I don't think waves are as relevant

to the law as they would be to Verdi, especially to contract law, which is all about the definition and legitimacy of specifics — what you would call shards.

"And the shard picture, upon cursory examination, is not encouraging. To be blunt, Acorn has a thousand lawyers floating on a lake of several trillion dollars. In suing Acorn, few individuals could withstand the intense combat that would occur entirely apart from the merits of the case. It would cost you, not including appeals, upwards of a million dollars and at least two years. Bring in French law, and you might not have to double those figures but you'd certainly be in for a lot more than a million, and three or possibly more years."

"For such a simple thing?"

"For such a simple thing: depositions, motions, discovery, countersuit. And Acorn is not invested in it emotionally. Whereas the Acorn principals will never think of it other than at the end, you will obsess and your dreams will be monopolized. For them, depositions will be fun. They're sadists when it comes down to it. You're analytical and perhaps brave. You won't collapse in deposition, but no matter that you might do well, you'll still be angry, frustrated, insulted, and your blood pressure will double."

"But what about the merits of the case?"

"Sixty/forty for you. I would side with you.

But it could go either way. It depends upon the judge and, believe me, we have what my associates here call *doofusses.*"

"So what do you advise overall?"

"Take the blow and get on with your life. You may not thank me if you follow my advice, because you won't know. But if you go ahead with the suit, I promise, you'll curse yourself.

"Do you know why I asked your age? Not just from curiosity and to gauge who you are and what you might know, but because I've had clients, and not just a few, who spent the last years of their lives drowning in the nonsense and unhappiness of a lawsuit. You might end up like that bunch of Jews in California who because they wanted to open a casino called themselves the Snickers Tribe."

"Snickers? For the feet?"

"No, Snickers. It's a candy bar."

"A bar of candy? Why would they . . . ?"

"It's hard to explain, but, needless to say, they didn't get a casino license because they weren't really an Indian tribe."

"So why did they say they were?"

"That's a question I can't answer. You'd have to ask them. All I can say is that they spent a lot of money on legal fees."

"I see."

"Don't be crestfallen. Among other things, this has been half an hour – five hundred dollars — and I won't bill it."

"I insist," Jules said, looking around at the office. "With this kind of overhead, you must have so much pressure to bill."

"I do, but I've never had a client who at a thousand dollars an hour talked about Verdi and waves in the ocean. Tomorrow I'll cut half an hour off lunch."

LIGHTS CORRUSCATING THROUGH THE DUSK

Once again, Jules was running in the park. It was sunny, the weather tranquil and bright. Convinced that the only thing left to him was physical strength, he attended to it. The day before, the music faculty had told him by email that his teaching load and his salary, such as they were, would be further reduced. And Cathérine had written that Luc had a persistent fever, slept most of the day, and cried often, not from pain but for help. Jules was trapped in New York because changing his ticket would cost several thousand Euros more than he had already paid, and as the hotel was irrevocably paid up as well he would stay on until his originally scheduled flight out, economizing by eating at supermarkets and from street vendors. That kind of saving hardly mattered. He'd kept a ledger of his expenses in a little notebook. With the recent change in exchange rates, by the time he walked in the door at home he would have spent nearly €40,000, not a single Euro of which would be reimbursed. Half his savings were gone. In addition to what was left he had some gold coins, Jacqueline's jewelry, and a tiny Daubigny, which together and with luck might bring €50,000. The piano was worth quite a lot, although he didn't know how much.

He could live solely on his pension, semi-impoverished like so many others, and give the rest to Cathérine for Luc, but that would be only a fraction of what was needed. He would stay in Saint-Germain-en-Laye even if not in the Shymanski house. Saint-Germain-en-Laye was his home. Jacqueline flowed through it like air, and to leave it would be to break a connection yet unbroken.

When the Shymanski house was sold, Jules would probably end up in a small room above a store, with loud neighbors, traffic sounds, no view, and persistent cooking smells. It wasn't supposed to be like that. Jacqueline had deserved to see her grandchild, and yet she had not. She had deserved to live, and yet she had not. She had deserved to go gently, and yet she had not. Luc deserved to have a childhood and not to suffer and die early. Jules had failed them and could think of nothing except to keep up his health and strength so that if an opportunity arose he might seize it.

But he ran too hard. He wasn't as fast, and he no longer sailed effortlessly as he had after his prodigious sleep. By the time he reached the northern end of the park, having almost sprinted down the hill, it got easier, so he picked up his pace, all the while trying to think of what might arrest the downward trajectory of his life.

As the road turned south, it climbed what was known, if not to Jules, as Heartbreak Hill. Although he had run it on the first day in New York, in Saint-Germain-en-Laye he was used to level ground or, in the forest, rolling rises. This was different, a steep hill with sharp rock outcroppings. Though everyone tried not to, everyone slowed here. Three quarters of the way up, Jules began to feel lightheaded. It was pleasant, but as it intensified he grew alarmed. If only he could crest the hill, he thought, his lightheadedness might cease. Soon after, it became painful, and the world darkened as if in an eclipse. Apart from the strain of ascending, he felt all right. It wasn't his heart. He was running automatically, and soon he could no longer hear either his steps or the wind. Then he was flying through total darkness as his feet left the ground and there was no gravity . . . until he hit the pavement without even extending his arms to break the fall. First his head struck, followed by his chest, as his body slid forward with continuing momentum. His left cheek burned as it scraped the asphalt, and what felt like warm water gushed around his face. This was not unpleasant, and he enjoyed it until he lost consciousness.

Half a dozen runners immediately came to his aid, and a woman called 911 on her pink cell phone. Someone took off a nylon jacket, folded it, and put it under Jules' head after two other people had rolled him onto his back. "Is he dead?" another person asked, as someone else began to push Jules' chest with the heels of his hands, singing, as he was taught in his CPR class, the song "Stayin' Alive," to time the pushes. The sound of an ambulance could be heard not even half a mile distant, near St. Luke's. All the while, Jules' heart was functioning perfectly well even as it was suffering violent and unnecessary ministrations. And all the while he was dreaming, although the dream was so real he would think upon remembering it that it was not a dream but a visit to another world.

In his dream, fur-clad, pre-medieval warriors met on a frozen strait, far from land. The battlefield was perfectly white and flat, with no horizon but only three hundred and sixty degrees of mist. And there they fought to the death. Hours passed, combinations formed and dissolved, but the battle continued to the last man on both sides, and the two who remained killed one another. Scattered over the reddened ice and its snow were whitened bodies. The corpses, and weapons of bone, wood, and iron were laid out as if by a receding flood, stacked and crosswise, hunched over, the men's faces a gallery of frightened and agonized expressions. Nothing moved or changed. Neither crows nor jackals interrupted the quiet. Silence reigned until spring, when the ice melted and gave way, and in half an hour every evidence of life and struggle disappeared as if it had never existed, all the vanquished sinking into oblivion, their weapons, plans, hopes, and passions easily subsumed in the smooth, unconscious sea.

When Jules awoke he had an extraordinarily strong, almost sensual feeling of delicacy and impermanence. Aware that he might die at any moment, he was like a traveler who, before taking a single step, has in spirit left his home, his city, and his country. He was reconciled and unafraid, sorrowful only because important matters remained unaddressed. Little things ballooned in his perception as if he were once again an infant. The painfully white, waffled, cotton blanket that covered him up to his chest, the almost smooth, slightly threadbare sheets, the top of a copper-clad steeple he saw through the window, murmurs from the hospital corridor, and the cooing of pigeons nearby and out of sight were as comforting as if he were embraced, held, and loved.

He had no pain, and breathed easily. Something had happened, he didn't know what, but evidently he was not yet over the edge. A nurse came in and saw that the patient was conscious, his eyes open. She had strawberry-blonde hair, a big face, and prominent upper front teeth.

"I enjoy this hospital room," Jules declared. It stopped her cold.

"I've never heard that before," she said, "ever."

"Oh yes I do," Jules said.

"Sit tight," she told him, an idiom with which he was not familiar. "I'll get the attending." She went out.

It took fifteen minutes for the attending to arrive, and when he did he announced himself as Doctor Beckerman. "How do you feel?"

"I don't know what happened."

"You were running. You experienced what appears to have been a transient neurological event, and you fell. Before anyone could stop it, you were given unnecessary CPR, which, surprisingly, didn't break your sternum. It easily could have. You went down on Heartbreak Hill. An ambulance was near and got to you very fast. You were brought here in four minutes, which must be some sort of record. You're not in acute danger."

"What kind of danger am I in?"

The doctor was consummately professional but warm by nature. He could have been a rabbi or a priest. Some people are simply born that way. "You know what an aneurysm is?"

"Yes."

"You have a basilar aneurysm. The basilar artery is located near the brainstem, and your aneurysm is unusually large. They tend to burst before they enlarge to the extent that yours has. Did you ever have a serious head injury? That's a medical question, not a taunt."

"Yes, I did."

"When?"

"When I was four."

"Did you suffer the impact in the back of your head?"

"Yes."

"And did you lose consciousness?"

"I believe so."

"I realize that it was a long time ago, but can you recollect what happened? How old are you?"

"Seventy-four. I was told it was a rifle butt."

For a moment the doctor was shocked into silence, but then he calculated. "In nineteen forty-four," he said, as if vaulted back to the war that was over before he himself was born. "Was whoever did this punished?"

"His nation was punished."

"I think I understand. We don't have the best news for you. We did an MRI. . . ."

"An NMRI?" Jules asked. "I know there's no radiation in it."

"That's correct. Most people don't know that, and there's no point in scaring them. Unfortunately, the aneurysm has formed and expanded in such a way that it's partially wrapped around the brainstem. Blood pressure to the brain is consistent and well-regulated, but, still, with the exertion of running up the hill, at your age, perhaps a change in position, the pressure of the aneurysm itself — without leakage, as far as we can tell — mimicked the effects of a hemorrhage.

"It would be very dangerous were you to strain. The aneurysm may not be operable, being so unusually large and because of the way it embraces the brainstem. We're affiliated with Columbia P and S, and later this afternoon our team will consult. The surgeons can do extraordinary things. Meanwhile, you should know that your blood values are truly amazing, unheard of in someone your age. I've never seen every single measure of blood chemistry right where it should be. Do you know that you may have Gilbert's disease? Actually, it's a syndrome."

"I do have it," Jules told him. "Whenever my blood is taken, they tell me that."

"So the bilirubin. . . ."

"Is always elevated. But in my case never to the extent of a negative effect."

"That's it," the doctor said. "There's a strong correlation between Gilbert's syndrome and living past a hundred."

291

"Does it cover aneurysms?" Jules asked.

"Not to my knowledge." He looked at his watch. "I'll come back early in the evening after studying your imagery. We'll know more then. All you need do is rest and be calm."

"In regard to a possible operation," Jules asked, "could there be side effects?"

"Of course."

"Grave side effects?"

"Yes."

"Such as?"

"Death."

"And with no operation?"

"You could die tomorrow or you could live to a hundred. We can't even guess about the probabilities until we have observations over time, to see if there's degeneration and/or expansion. That is, the thinning of the artery wall, and/or the expansion of the aneurysm. Unfortunately, they usually go together. It's a difficult decision. You don't have to make it now."

"It's been made *for* me."

"By whom, or what?"

"By my plants."

"Again?"

"My plants. Every Fall I have to decide whether or not to bring in some of the annuals or leave them out on the terrace. If I bring them in and put them under lights, they weaken, grow pale, and stay deathly still. If I leave them out, they get full sun, full air, and they move in the wind. Sometimes they last even to December, but in the dangerous time of frosts and rain, and what you call Indian Summer, even though they die they may be better off than if they spend the winter paralyzed under lamps."

"What *I* call Indian Summer?"

"English is not my native language."

"Yes, of course. You're French?"

"I am," Jules answered, and an idea began to form, so he said, "I was born there."

"But you live here and are an American citizen?"

"For decades."

This seemed strange to the doctor because Jules' pronunciation was extremely French for someone who had lived for so long in America. But he wasn't about to open the question. "Good. That makes it less complicated. We need to know who you are. Did you have identification while you are running, a license, credit cards? From what was described it seems unlikely that anything was stolen, although it does happen."

"No, I had nothing."

"Not a problem. The nurse will come in to get what she needs for properly admitting you and contacting your family. She'll take care of the paperwork. Right away, we'll need your Medicare and supplemental plan numbers. There are a lot of forms, which you're certainly able enough to fill out, but you can do it verbally — she'll have a computer. All you have to do is review and sign. When we return, we'll do a neurological workup, and if necessary load you back into the MRI once again just to make sure that we're not over-looking anything and to see if in this short time there's been a change. Sometimes these procedures take a while to assimilate, especially when you find yourself suddenly in a new environment. Don't fault yourself for not being quick."

Jules smiled, because he was already quicker than he would have thought possible.

A long time before, he and François had rid-den almost the whole length of the *Boul-Miche.* Missing their stops, they engaged in discussion on the open platform at the back of one of the green-and-creme-colored buses that no longer ran beneath overarching trees as once, to the delight of many Parisians, they had. It was June, they were young, unknown, and full of energy. The diesel fumes on the *Boul-Miche* were actually sweet and so good for the trees that the canopy of thick, glossy leaves dappled the light as if the crowded avenue were under agitated water.

They were discussing the nature of paradox. François told Jules that he had lately discov-ered that the last person to leave the ship is also the last person not to leave the ship. François would ask his professors, point-blank, "What is paradox?" They knew, but were not quite able to define it, at least not easily, and they resorted to the dictionary, repeating that a paradox was, "an absurd proposition true on its face, or vice a versa."

But for François and Jules this was insufficient, even inaccurate, and they had agreed that a paradox was more the statement of two contradictory propositions, both of which, nevertheless, were true. That two contending propositions could be correct was for Jules rather easy to accept in that it was an almost ordinary facet of music, and part of what gave music its escape from worldly friction in its ability to embrace even the starkest contradictions.

So now, in a New York hospital bed, Jules understood. Paradox, the reconciliation of opposites within a theater greater than the world, within infinite time and infinite space, was the solution to his dilemma. He understood now that he could never leave Paris, and he would not. But he had to leave Paris, and he would. He had it. It was all locked up, and he was happy. But it was complicated, painful, and would take some doing.

He could die at any moment or he could live to a hundred, which was as it had always been of course, and was for most people. But now, for him, this common condition was as intensified as if he were dreaming or in a movie in which he was strapped to explosives and had to choose to cut either the red or the blue wire. How much easier it would be for heroes if all such contraptions followed a convention similar to the laws of traffic signals worldwide. The red light always means stop. But was it *stop the bomb from going off,* or *stop, don't cut the red wire?*

Jules threw aside the thin blanket, swung his legs out, and left the bed, thinking that this or any movement might be the end — even opening the closet door or reaching to take his running clothes from the shelf, or bending to grasp his running shoes in his left hand. After he shed the hospital gown, he sat down and put on his shorts and shirt. He was afraid to lean forward to lace up his shoes, but he had no choice. Then he stood up and walked out of the room and down the hall. Fit people in running clothes do not excite the same suspicion in a hospital corridor as, say, a limping, drooping, slowly moving and unshaven old man whose behind is visible from the back of his gown as he pushes the IV stand to which he is tethered.

As Jules walked south on Amsterdam Avenue he was tempted to run but didn't. He had no money, so he walked the three or four miles to the hotel. He was perfectly okay when he got to his room. Contrary to his recent practice of strict economy, he ordered from room service, and his dinner that night — as he watched a million lights blink on in the great palisades of buildings, both close by and at a distance — was consommé, a salad, and grapefruit juice. They even had Badoit. Although he didn't know why, he thought it would be good to drink water in excess of his thirst.

Alone in his room, he had lost or was losing everything at a faster and faster clip. But he was unafraid, excited by the lights, the form of the room, even the form of the bottle of Badoit, and by masses of lights corruscating through the dusk, like stars. From his tower he looked out at dozens of spires lit in many colors as if they were the jeweled tops of *Empire* obelisks. Most comforting was the silence. You could hear neither the street below nor even the air that even on a calm day was undoubtedly whistling past the windows.

It was strange to have a bedroom higher up than the top of the Eiffel Tower, and to see great distances across which were scattered buildings lit in white like Christmas trees, the catenaries of bridges like necklaces of blue lights, and immense ships moving silently across the harbor, slow skaters bearing torches across black ice. But there was no breeze and there was no ground, and he ached for home. The value of all the great construction was nothing when weighed against ordinary things that were modest and humane. He thought not of the magnificent towers so terribly out of scale but of people: of Jacqueline, Élodi, Cathérine when she was a child and as she was now, and Luc.

Firmly in the camp of the elephants, Luc thought of them as protection against crocodiles. He loved Babar, who was as real to him, or perhaps more real than anything in the world. When he was still able to visit, Cathérine had dropped him off with Jules while she left her car and took the RER into Paris to have lunch with David and to shop. Jules forgot everything as he willingly entered Luc's world. They sailed a model boat in Shymanski's pool. They released helium balloons and watched them with binoculars. Luc affirmed that he could see them, but he was pointing the binoculars more or less downward at the Seine. They watched cartoons, and ate the blandest, tiniest lunch Jules had eaten since Cathérine was three.

As Luc and Jules were building with Legos, Luc fell asleep. Jules carried him to the sofa, arranged pillows so he wouldn't roll off, and then brought out the *grand éléphant d'activités Les Papoum,* a wonderful, velveteen elephant with cloth ears and rattles in its feet. He set it next to Luc, and sat in a chair from which he could see the child's expression when he awoke.

Jules was reading an essay about the Roman quest for a quiet life — the monuments, coliseums, *insulae,* and legions had perhaps

298

created the Romans' desire for life as nature laid it out at its simplest — when he heard a little yawn. Still holding the book, he let it drop to his lap. Luc opened his eyes. There was the elephant, from Luc's perspective, towering above him. At first he froze. Then he smiled broadly and his eyes opened wider. Then he laughed, and lunged into his new friend, embracing it. All the great things that man has engineered, the vast cities, the dams, bridges, rockets, and trains, even the breathtaking forest of lights in Manhattan, could not hold a candle to that.

No one in the world but Jules Lacour knew that he had an aneurysm that would carry him away if, for example, he chose to outrun a pretty young girl on the long terrace at Saint-Germain-en-Laye. He could end his life at will, and it would never be taken as suicide. Other than the aneurysm, as far as he knew, he was in good health. He had kept up his strength because he had been sure since childhood that at some point he would need it to save himself or those he loved. Although he had not been able to save his mother, his father, or Jacqueline, he had always dreamed and prayed for the power and courage to do so. He had understood that never would he be able to come to their aid, and yet all his life he had dreamed that he would. And although he had never lacked courage, and had nurtured and come to the aid of others, never had he fulfilled his deepest desire, which was to save a faltering life by giving his own.

TOUCHING DOWN

Paradoxically, flying is the handmaiden not only to fear but to optimism. Lifted above earth and oceans; seemingly higher than the stars close to the horizon; piercing through scudding, moonlit clouds; shot forward at great speed; the cabin carefully lighted; perfumed women circulating among their charges who sleep or read beneath pools of light . . . All this allows fresh starts, new thoughts, and the kind of planning that, once one touches down, assumes a weight and difficulty it does not have at altitude.

As the Airbus raced through thin air aloft, schemes and plans occurred to Jules almost uncontrollably. In the dimly lit cabin, its little spotlights illuminating here and there those who were still awake and working, he imagined thoughts issuing as if from a soap bubble machine and floating about, ephemeral and sparkling. But his speculations, tempted to fly off left and right, hewed to the centerline of necessity.

Disregarding morals in favor of necessities, he would have to abandon a lifetime of caution. For Luc, he would violate the categorical imperative. When things are so arranged, he thought, that observing the law crushes an individual, a family, the truth, then the categorical imperative need not be observed. He had already collided with the laws of the state. What he had in mind was far less a transgression but still illegal. Although in the hospital the first glimmer had appeared, the rest had come to him as he flew.

The plane now maneuvered over Paris grayed in morning light. As it dropped below the clouds, early traffic came into view, its red taillights reflecting off rain-slicked roads. There was a remarkable difference between the struggle below — thousands of cars slowing, skidding, sometimes stopping, all crowded together — and the enormous plane gliding smoothly through the air and aimed at the runway, like a rifle shot.

Despite all the troubles he would find, he was happy to be home. Though not vast, France is a big country, neither elongated like Italy nor broken into an archipelago like Japan, Denmark, or Indonesia. France is solid and centered. In Paris a Frenchman can feel that his world stretches more or less evenly in all directions, uninterrupted by sea or mountains, and yet not with the infinitude of the Russian Steppe or the Australian Outback.

The center of gravity is just right, the country, although known as a hexagon, is like a protective sphere that most times allows the French to discover both the art of living and the perfection of art.

They flew low over fields, highways, and factories. The stewardesses strapped themselves into their seats. Now that Jules was an outlaw, he stared at the stewardess, the *hôtesse de l'air,* who he thought had perhaps expressed a desire — even were it fleeting — for him. And she stared back. Certainly he was too old, but there is a solidity and truth to age, and he was still physically able. Maybe for her he would be a novelty. Or perhaps what was most influential was that, as his inhibitions were overwhelmed by the sight and imagination of her, she felt his intense appreciation. She may have sensed the state he was in, and wanted to be taken to the ground along with him and cleared of everything but essence. Both of them had the same aura that envelops soldiers who fight with neither fear nor regret in a battle they know will be their last: release, abandon, humility, a feel for the earth, the defeat of time. But then, as always, there was Jacqueline, in the separate, inviolable world in which he would join her happily and soon. And that was enough for a constant widower as he wearily deplaned on the grayest of mornings in the city that still held his life.

II.
BLOOD WILL TELL

DNA

Just as a curve is a series of infinitely small angles, and according to philosophers a point cannot exist, logically there is no present but only the infinitesimal and perhaps non-existent space between past and future, as any schoolchild thinking about space and time might suspect. One thing that distinguishes Paris, however, making of it a magnet of attraction, is that it turns all this on its head. In Paris the present dominates the spectrum of time, spreading the otherwise invisible gap between past and future into spacious fields the ends of which one cannot even see. Just as music sounded out is only either heard in time that has passed or will be heard in time yet to come, and yet is solely of the present, Paris is overwhelmingly of the present as well.

The past is present in its reverberations and sustain, and the future is present in the clarity and beauty of its promises. For example, the crowds in '44, surging with joy at the

Liberation, continue to echo with such fidelity that one need not even close one's eyes to see them. The future is also palpable not in pathetically featureless glass buildings but in generations yet to be born who are just like us, recapitulating every emotion and fault and, like us, suffering the illusion that they stand apart from a chain of life unbroken since the beginning of time.

In spring the trees of Paris bloom so lightly they seem to float on the breeze. In summer, its deep green gardens often shade into black and an orange sun revolves in the air like a crucible risen from a foundry. In winter, white silence in the long, treed *allées* and not a breath of wind. And in the fall bright colors and deep blue sky roll in on cool north winds.

After an unsatisfying, late dinner in a restaurant impatient to close, Duvalier Saidi-Sief and Arnaud Weissenburger sat like exhausted zombies in front of two huge computer screens in a cramped room of the *Commissariat de Police du 16e Arrondissement,* Passy, from which by a census of white automobiles they had agreed to work. Police stations, never empty, come alive at night. The two detectives had been staring all day at surveillance images issuing from portable hard drives delivered weeks after the crime. Such was the efficiency of the authority — they didn't know which — that ran thousands of cameras to capture a present that, although the bureaucrats in charge probably didn't know it, someone like François might claim did not exist.

To Arnaud and Duvalier, the inhabitants of the nonexistent present moved on astoundingly fast little legs. You could make them go faster, slow them down, stop them, or run them backward. Although both *flics* had the air of conspirators or people who know a great or terrible secret, they differed in their approach. Duvalier had to discipline himself not to force the images ahead at high-speed so he could watch clouds rushing with mysterious velocity across the rooftops. Arnaud was steadier and more thorough, perhaps because at one time he had had to stare at slabs of glowing steel as he guided them dangerously over giant hot rollers, and this he accomplished while sweating in heavy clothing and looking through a dark glass faceplate.

For hours they peered at the screens, sometimes trying to zoom in on the images of pretty girls so they could forget for a moment what they were doing and why. They didn't even know exactly what they were looking for. There were two contradictory descriptions, but lab work had come back showing that the DNA of the O+ blood belonged to none of the three boys. Perhaps surveillance techniques of the future would chart the DNA of each fast-moving ant in the images, but now they had to find him before they could make a match. They did have a clue. The presumed assailant was male and 98% likely of Ashkenazi descent. So although it was neither necessary nor sufficient to do so, they kept their eyes open for Orthodox Jewish dress, even though they knew that only a small percentage of Jews would be identifiable by it, and that no one had described the suspect in those terms.

They saw such a person in images taken close to the time in question and not far from the bridge, near the École Militaire. The surveillance there was intense so as to protect the vast underground facilities of the GIC as it vacuumed up telephone and Internet communications throughout France. But this was a slight, young boy, hardly visible in the rain and walking in a direction opposite to that in which the assailant was known to have escaped. Although he might have seen something, they could not waste time searching for him rather than for the murderer. But they kept the Orthodox boy, along with many other things, in the back of their minds.

He had entered the Métro at the École Militaire and disappeared. They couldn't check every surveillance camera at every station, even at that uncrowded hour. If he had been on the bridge, why wouldn't he have entered the Métro at Bir-Hakeim?

"If he were there, why would he have skipped a station?" Arnaud asked himself out loud, quickly answering himself. "Maybe he wanted exercise. But it was raining. We know he's not our suspect. What can we do?" They let it drop.

Though they were young, the posture into which they were forced by spending so many hours in front of their computers made them stiff and gave them headaches. They would stretch, complain, crack their knuckles, get up, and walk about. At midnight, Arnaud said, "I've got nothing."

"How many cameras do you have left?" Duvalier asked.

"Something like forty or fifty. You?"

"Seventy or eighty."

"You spend too much time looking at the girls. You can't see anything anyway."

"I can't help it."

"You think you're going to ask them for a date?"

"Some of them I'd like to."

"Good, keep on looking," Arnaud said. "I'm going downstairs to get some coffee if it's open across the street. You want some?"

"No thanks. I don't drink coffee."

"Tea? A cookie?"

"I'm fine."

"Duvalier?"

Duvalier turned to receive the question.

"What kind of Arab doesn't drink coffee?"

There was a pause. "I'm not really an Arab, Arnaud, I'm a French Muslim."

"Excuse me then. What kind of French Muslim doesn't drink coffee?"

"The kind that's looking at you, a French Protestant who does."

Arnaud shook his head in contradiction.

"A French Catholic."

"No."

"Atheist."

"I believe in God."

"Buddhist? Hindu? *Jew?*"

Arnaud smiled slyly.

"They put a Muslim and a Jew on a case where it appears that a Jew killed two Muslims."

"They did."

"On purpose."

"They didn't know at the time that the assailant was likely a Jew, but they did know that two Arabs were the victims. They could have chosen others from our divisions, but they didn't."

"To be fair to both confessions?"

"Maybe just to keep Christians out of the mix. It would be against the law, but who could prove it. And Houchard, you know, is that kind of asshole."

"Arnaud, you don't look Jewish."

"That's right, Duvalier, but you do, and I'll protect you if any Arabs try to beat you up."

"I have a gun."

312

"You would shoot them?"

"I would. You would catch a Jew who murdered two Arabs?"

"For sure."

"Maybe Houchard is not such an. . . ."

"I'll bring you some tea," Arnaud said.

When Arnaud returned much later — because of the hour he had had to go farther than he had planned — Duvalier was leaning back in his chair, a contented look on his face.

"Sorry," Arnaud told him, "the tea must be cold."

"I think I have something."

"In the time I was gone?"

"Look at this. I've been going down the river from the Pont de Grenelle. Nothing, right?"

"I've already done that. The cameras stop before the bend. I saw nothing."

"Ah, but there's a traffic camera on the left bank that stares across the road and, therefore, across the river."

"That's so far. How could you see anything? Unless someone climbed out on the left bank? Was it lighted there?"

"No. And we don't have anyone getting out of the river, at least not in the light. The cameras aren't infrared. The river is cold as hell, so either he got out of the water at night or he's dead."

"So what did you get? The camera's too far

away to see anything, and light would be hours later. We should be looking more at the Métro cameras. The stations are always lit."

"Maybe. But look at this." They went to Duvalier's screen. He ran the video, fast forwarding from the time of the crime until light."

"You can't see anything, Duvalier. The river is completely dark except for the barges that come through. Not even the *bateaux mouches*. It was late and cold. Only barges."

"That's right. You can see the running lights of the barges high above the water."

"Not that high."

"Higher than a rowing shell, the kind in the Olympics."

"Your point?"

"This building," Duvalier said, gesturing toward the screen, "is a boathouse. In the day, they take out that kind of boat. The weather was bad, so only a few. Later, at dusk, two boats were out. They put lights on them. It must be a rule."

"Yes . . . ?"

"And the night of the crime, all night, no lights low on the water, and, then, no boats out at dawn. Then, in the morning, when you can see, no one goes into the boathouse. *But someone goes out.* And before he goes out, he emerges and does something on the dock."

"Who is he?"

"How can I know? Here's him on the dock. Then, a little later, he leaves. You can see if you go to maximum zoom." He did.

Arnaud said, "It's a man. I can see that. What's he wearing?"

"I think it's a blazer."

"Just like every other man in Paris. You'd think this was London. But our guy was wearing a rain jacket."

"Still, did this guy sleep there? If he didn't, he came out of the river. A little before he left, he comes out and goes back in."

"Maybe he's the caretaker, and lives there."

"Possibly," said Duvalier. "Let's find out. Let's say the killer rows from this place. He would know the river, the currents, and that he would be swept to somewhere where he could get out and find shelter."

"How likely is that?"

"I would say, not at all. But if he rows he's got to be strong, like someone who can kill two young men with his hands. We have his DNA. All we have to do. . . ."

"How many people might have access there? To go through them could take forever. Is it worth it?"

"Of course it is. There can't be that many, and what else have we got?"

The next day was cold, but at noon several boats were out. Arnaud and Duvalier could see them up- and downriver. There were other boat clubs, too, but these were near La Défense. The likelihood was that the shells they saw had come from and would return to this boathouse, so the two policemen scaled the gate that was supposed to keep people out, and went down the ramp to the barge. The door was unlocked. They went in, calling out, but no one answered.

Narrow boats were stacked five high on wooden racks that filled three bays. Near the garage door of one of the bays was a counter strewn with lights for the boats, batteries, abandoned personal items, and logbooks. A board on the wall recorded that three boats were out, the time they would return, whether they went east or west, and if they would return in a single loop or would continue past the dock and make a second loop. Looking at trophies displayed on a shelf above the board, the policemen observed that no one had won anything for ten years.

"Hey," Duvalier said, holding up a thin loose-leaf notebook. "The members, their addresses, and contact information." He took a moment to count down the page. "Forty-six."

"That would take forever."

"Not at all. There are eleven women, which narrows it to thirty-five."

"Almost forever."

"But there are two of us. Three a day apiece, six days, maybe less if we go faster.

It's only some questioning and a sample of DNA."

"The *OPJ* won't go that far. It'd be too broad. And no judge would. The theory is too tenuous to get us such an order in regard to thirty-five no doubt upstanding citizens. And what if some of them live outside Paris? There are a lot of places where you can't row. They might come from all over. We'd need clearance."

"We'll go through the *OPJ,* and if we have to interview someone beyond our jurisdiction we'll get it cleared. I'll call the judge and tell him we have people to question, that we'll just ask them for DNA. If three or four refuse to cooperate, we'll have narrowed it down so we can stick on them until we find something. If we narrow it down enough we'll be able to get whatever permission we need from above. But before we do this, because admittedly it's an outside chance, we'll be good boys, and look into everyone, shall we say, informally?"

"Are we going to steal this list?" Arnaud asked. "Or abide by the law and get a warrant?"

"You see that?" Duvalier pointed to the corner, where a copy machine was partially hidden in the shadows. "Maybe at one time, before email, they had seventy or a hundred members. Clubs always have meetings, notes, notices, fund-raising, dinners, whatever. Let's hope the machine still works."

It did, and by the time Duvalier had turned it off, folded the copies, and replaced the originals, a shell glided to the dock and an old man with a ring of white hair around his head such that he looked like a soft-boiled egg in a cup, struggled to debark and take care of his boat and oars. He neither saw them nor heard the click of the gate as they left.

"I like it when it's like this," Duvalier said. "No warrants, no questioning, all the information we need on a list, and none of these guys even knows we're coming. It gives you a sense of accomplishment."

"Yes," Arnaud said archly, "like building the Panama Canal."

"I'll bet he's on the list. Millions of people in Paris, and maybe the name of the man who committed the crime is on a piece of paper folded in my pocket. Sometimes being a *flic* is not bad."

CATHÉRINE AND DAVID, FRANÇOIS

For a day or two, Jules had little feeling for home. Though far more splendid than the hotels, in comparison the house still seemed worn and improperly decorated even if he would have had it no other way. When he awoke he thought he was in Los Angeles or New York, and for some minutes he wanted to be, in the kind of retrospective yearning that, though it quickly fades, may last a lifetime in dreams.

But soon enough he was his previous self, almost forgetting that he had been away. He went shopping to replenish the kitchen, attended to his mail, went swimming, and ran gently and slowly, as if finally his years had caught up with him. Having an aging body is like living in a big house. Something is always going wrong, and by the time it's fixed, something else follows. Very old age is when the things that go wrong cause other things to go wrong, until, like sparks racing up a fuse, they finally reach a pack of dynamite.

Soon his nearly truncated teaching schedule would put him in a Cité de la Musique practice room alone for fifty minutes with Élodi. After trying unsuccessfully not to think of her, he rehearsed what he might say. He would keep his distance, but convey — safely from behind the barrier of his experience and age — that the moment he first saw her he fell in love as strongly as at any time in his life. That when he shook her hand, formally, reining in his feelings, he hadn't wanted to let go. That he could remember and re-create over and over in memory every second they were in contact. That he knew her virtues and her beauty and her ability to excite, but that he loved her, nonetheless, inexplicably, independently of splendor or sex, with neither knowing nor having to know why. And he would convey as well that the tremendous difference in age made it impossible, and nothing could follow or result. When he went through this little speech, intended to clear the air and yet a way for him to move close to her even if just for a moment, he couldn't see beyond it. Because when he imagined the end of his declaration, he imagined that he did not move, and she did not move. He could never get to the point where they parted.

On Saturday he would have lunch with François. Though the last thing he wanted was to confess to François about Élodi, he knew he would, and that François would smile and say that it was right, that Jules had the obligation to live, that Jacqueline would want him to, and all the other predictable nostrums one might think France's premier *philosophe* might surpass, except that, as common as they were, they were true. Jules couldn't accept them even if they were, just as he couldn't envision himself walking away from Élodi, as demanded of him both by his ability to see the future and his deeply felt concern for Élodi herself. François was not the proper confessor — far too lenient. It would be like confessing to a heroin dealer that one had had too much to drink. On the other hand, a priest would be severe, inflexible, and inappropriate to say the least. The psychiatrist already knew too much about Jules, and he had to be paid. François, therefore, while not the only confessor available and likely not satisfactory, would be the best.

That would be Saturday, an ordeal but also for Jules the pleasure of describing a beautiful young girl and his love for her. Confined to description, he was safe. And tonight, Friday, he would have Sabbath dinner with Cathérine, David, and Luc — another kind of love, and another kind of suffering.

When he walked from the RER to the little house with the terra-cotta roof so inappropri-

321

ate to the North, the streets were cold and dark. The wind cut through his clothes, but still he hesitated before he went in, staring at the yellow light of the windows. Yellow was the old Jewish color: dim light from shtetl windows of parchment or imperfect glass, weakly shining in yellow; the color of chicken fat and chicken soup; the candle flame; the yellow Star of David. Yellow was the color of weakness, resignation, defeat, and feeling. It was also the color of gold and the sun.

Cathérine had been gone for more than two decades. When she was a baby the family had seemed to be as unbreakable as the nucleus of the atom. Jacqueline, Cathérine, *et* Jules. The ones he loved the most were always there, the ones for whom he would do his best and, if necessary, die. He knew at the time that it could not last, but was unable to imagine its end, perhaps because when it was over his purpose would have been served and nothing truly important would be left to him.

Their daughter was central to both of them. She was as nothing else had ever been or would be, just as Luc was now central to her after her own parents had, of necessity, receded. Her own identity and new life demanded it. But, secretly, they still had the same devotion and were ready to sacrifice themselves for her if required, on the instant and without the slightest hesitation. This she never knew and they never said, for not having been in the world long enough to have been taught, she thought such things entirely imaginary, at least in the France of this century, so safe, modern, and just.

Jules was suddenly startled when, from behind, in the dark, David put a hand on his shoulder. "You scared me," he told his son-in-law.

"That's impossible. I'm an accountant."

"True."

"What were you doing?"

"It's not quite six."

"So? In fact," David said, after looking at his watch, "it's six-fifteen." His tone was affectionate, his unspoken language stating that whatever it was that Jules had done, it had something of the unpredictability of age.

"Anyway," Jules said, "we missed sunset by a lot. Is that allowed?"

"No, but we need the money for Luc, the firm is secular, they're laying people off, and I can't risk my position. If necessary for Luc, we would light the candles at midnight or not at all. If God wouldn't forgive me then He'd be wrong and I would tell Him so."

"We never lit candles. But if we had, I would have to agree."

Almost forty, Cathérine had no idea how her father valued her even for her imperfections, which had come mainly from him, which he could trace to the charm of her face when she was a baby, and which now and always would fill him with love. She didn't know the terrors and humiliations he faced, nor should she have. It was not her role. She had to be distant now, as he had never had the chance to be distant with his parents — who were forever vulnerable, and who had to be cared for in perpetuity and protected in retrospect, if only in the imagination. And, whatever she did and however she acted, he had to do for her and for Luc whatever he could.

She had wanted to greet him with love, but when she saw that he held a wrapped present she said, angrily, "Not again. You'll spoil him."

Recovering from this dart, he looked at her as if to say, "So?" It meant, of course, that he recognized that Luc might die, something of which she was aware more than anyone, but to which she fiercely would not allow anyone, including her father, to allude even subtly.

"Shall I put it in the closet?" Jules asked.

She sighed. "No, put it by his bed so he sees it in the morning. You can give him a kiss, but don't wake him. He had a bad day, lots of crying. The fever is back and he hardly ate. It's okay to put it by the bed."

Jules went into Luc's room to leave the present. A dim light came from a night-table lamp in the shape of two sheep lying next to a tree, the crown of which formed a lamp-shade printed with glowing green leaves.

When Jules saw how hard the child was breathing he had to fight back tears.

Faithful husband, good father, and flawless auditor, David pulled a yarmulke from a pocket and put it on. This was an excellent excuse to change the subject.

"You don't wear that on the street?"

"No."

"Since when?"

"A lot of people don't, and it's been that way for a long time. I kept on wearing it despite the risk. But while you were in America I went to Lyon to do the accounts at a parts supplier for Airbus: they were padding. On my way back to my hotel after dinner, in the center of town, I was attacked. I wouldn't have been terrified had there been one, or even two" — David was as big as a bear — "but there were about a dozen."

"A dozen! What happened?"

"It started with words. They got more and more excited and started to kick and punch me. Of course, I ran, but I couldn't have outrun them, as they were quite young. A truck driver saw me, stopped his truck, and told me to get on the running board. The truck had huge mirrors, so I held on to the mirror bars, and he drove through *centre-ville* at fifty kilometers an hour, right through a red. Then I got in the cab, he circled around, and dropped me at my hotel."

"Did you tell the police?"

"No point. It was a crowd. They weren't out for it, and weren't together in the first place. They collected spontaneously."

"You should have done something."

"What was I supposed to do, kill them? I don't have a gun. I was never a soldier. I wouldn't have done that anyway."

"Didn't you feel like it, though?"

"I just wanted to get away. I have a mortally ill child. I can't solve this problem for France. I don't think anyone can, but certainly not me. Even if I could, my efforts and attention must be elsewhere."

Jules had always been numb to the lighting of candles and the procession of ceremony. In his first years in the attic in Reims it would have been difficult to mark the Sabbath and holidays. They might have done so, as did others, with matchsticks for candles, but they didn't. Since the mid nineteenth-century, with a temporary reversion during the Dreyfus Affair, the Lacours had been fully assimilated. Even had they not been, in hiding during the war they were stunned enough to exist in many kinds of silence until its end. Their hope was merely to stay alive. Ceremony might begin afterwards, but until then it seemed like something only for those who were not hunted. Throughout his life, Jules had always refused any kind of celebration for himself, and though he tried his best he was present only half-heartedly in celebration of others. As for religious ritual, he was embarrassed by the weakness of rote public prayer, perhaps because when he himself would pray in silence, his simple, improvised prayer was worth a thousand set pieces.

"How do you think it'll go?" David asked him as they were eating.

Jules knew what he meant, and that he was supposed to know how "it" might go, given that he had lived through the war. "David, I was five when the war ended, a shell-shocked child who couldn't speak. That warped me for the rest of my life, as I'm sure Cathérine has told you."

David nodded.

"I've never been equipped to live in peace and judge dispassionately. My reality was real then, it may be real in the future, and it's partially real now. As much as it grants me clairvoyance, it also cripples my judgment. So I can't tell you how it will go."

"Of course not," David told him. "I'm just as uncertain, but unlike you, I don't have the benefit of experience. I know you can't know, Jules, but what do you feel?"

"What do I feel? I feel that you should get medical treatment for Luc in the United States or Switzerland, and establish yourselves there. What about Geneva? The lake is cold and blue, the shadows deep, the streets quiet and clean, everything well ordered, peaceful, and rich. The medical care is expert and precise. They speak French, it's high up, protected from war and conflict. You can have a life there."

"Really."

"Really. Yes."

"It's expensive," Cathérine said. "We couldn't even begin to afford it."

"First, consider it," her father asked.

"Jules, you speak as if there could be another Holocaust in Europe," David said. "Do you actually believe that?"

"I don't. But the smell of it is in the wind, the taste is in the water. That's enough. Why should you live your lives in continual anxiety? Why should you or Luc be beaten in the street? Why should he have to hide his identity at school? Why should you fear that he'll be massacred in his kindergarten, or that you'll be blown to pieces in a synagogue or restaurant? Except for me, your parents are gone. You have no siblings and neither does Cathérine. You should move. I don't want to worry that when I'm no longer around you might have to replay the story of my own life."

"Not that we could go anywhere else," Cathérine said, the spoon in her hand having been motionless since David's question, "but if we could, if it could happen, you'd have to come with us."

"No, Cathérine."

"Why?"

"Because, for me, France is the world, too synonymous with life. To quote a British politician, *J'adore la France, les Français sont charmants, la langue est à mourir.* Your mother is buried here, as are my parents, somewhere, in France. Everything I know, have done, and felt is tied to this country and laid down indelibly. Keeping faith to the theme of my life is more important than living itself. There can be changes in tempo, but one must always preserve the tone. You know how you read sometimes in the papers that old people stay behind even as the barbarians approach?"

"Yes, they do that."

"There's a reason for it, and it's not just that they're tired and have no chance for a new life." He knew that she could not quite understand such a thing.

"What is it then?" she asked.

"When you're of that age you're given a certain kind of bravery that perhaps you had when you were at the peak of your powers. I don't think it's just because you don't have much to lose that the calculation runs in favor of daring. Rather, you get a level-headed courage that allows you to make death run for its money even though you know it must win. I'll never leave France, but you're young, so you can."

"We can't afford it," David said.

"I forgot. You're the accountant."

"That's the reality."

"It can change."

"How?"

"For one thing, I'm going to give you everything I have," Jules said. "I have some savings. There's a bit of jewelry, and I'm going to sell the piano. A Bösendorfer concert grand, beautifully cared for, might bring a hundred thousand Euros."

"Forgive me, Jules," David said, "but even that would be hardly enough."

"I'm working on other things, though nothing is certain."

"What other things?" Cathérine asked. "And how will you live? You can't even stay at Shymanski's. Everything will be gone."

"I'll live on my pension."

"You have something up your sleeve," Cathérine said, almost as if she were a child. She knew him well enough in that regard.

As he might have done when she was a child, Jules made a show of looking at his forearms, raising first the left and then the right. "No I don't."

"If you're going to stay," Cathérine said, "whether we go or not, you should be more observant."

"Religion again."

"Don't say it like that, it's insulting. How are you Jewish? You're French. How would anyone know what you are? How will the Jews survive in France, or anywhere, if they break

330

the chain of five thousand years?"

"Who's breaking a chain?"

"You are."

"No. You're the next link. You do all the stuff, I'm expendable now, what's the problem?"

"It's not enough just to be born Jewish. What have you done to keep the tradition alive?"

"I stayed alive myself. I managed to survive well enough so that I could work, have a family, and love my wife and my child. It was a closely run thing when I was little. I didn't feel then that I deserved to live. I consider it an achievement that I didn't die, or kill myself, or become even crazier than I am. What about that? Survival. I look at it as miraculous. I'm proud of you and David for reviving observance in our family, but it's not for me. God is too immediate, splendid, and difficult for that."

They looked at him in silence. Then David said to Cathérine, "Maybe your father's one of the *lamed vavnikim.*" It was only partly sarcastic.

"What's that?" Jules asked.

"Never mind," David told him. "If you are, you don't have to know. In fact, you can't know."

"So why did you say it?"

"I was just trying to tell Cathérine that you're okay, and that compared to you in regard to being Jewish, we're amateurs." David was older than his years, and kind.

Even if his intuitive notions sometimes passed as brilliant flashes of theory, Jules had no theory of music or anything else. The potential to love abstraction had been blasted out of him forever in a single shock that had then defined the rest of his life. He thought it just as well, for the things he valued, things great and everlasting, were mysteriously self-evident yet elusive of explanation. He was loyal to the secret power of that which blessed the homely and unfashionable, the failures and the forgotten. Where theorists saw mathematical relations in music — sometimes clearly and sometimes with foolish complexity — he saw only waves and light. When sound could find and conjoin with these invisible and ever-present waves, it became music. High resolution images through great telescopes showed magical colors and heavenly light that the eye perceived only as a blur of white in the impossible distance. But there was much more to them than a pinpoint sparkle, and in the roseate clouds of effulgent galaxies was music in what was supposed to be silence.

This was, anyway, what he thought, felt, and sometimes saw, although he could neither bring it back, nor, it goes without saying, prove it. Waiting for François in the Gardens of the Palais de Chaillot he saw the same thing in the undulating spray of the fountains as the wind struck their jets. A hundred million droplets shining in the sun moved in synchrony like schools of fish or flights of birds, rising suddenly to a crest and snapping back in explosions of silver and gold against a field of blue. Jules read this and heard it no less than the *"Ma di"* of *Norma,* which was like a boat running with the wind, rising and falling gently on the sea. He never tried to explain music more than in its craft. He thought that music was almost like a living thing, that it had a mischievous character, and that, like a spirit or sprite, it would know when the trap of explanation was set for it and craftily disappear. Like electrons, it, too, was allergic to measurement.

François descended the staircase, a plastic bag suspended from his right hand. On what promised to be the last warm day until spring they were going to eat in the Gardens of Chaillot even though the crowds there looked like they were staging to tear down the Bastille. François had suggested that the masses of people would lend them comfortable anonymity, and he knew a place nearby on the Avenue Kléber that made the best sandwiches in Paris. They had had this kind of lunch all their lives, *thon* or *jambon* on *baguette,* with beer, outside on a bench, in a park, on a terrace, or by the river.

They couldn't sit at the edge of the water, as the masonry was either flush with it or blocked by hedges. The benches were occupied, and the steps had too much traffic, so they had to get up onto the wall behind the benches, where the spray didn't reach even on the windiest days. The lower part of the wall, nearest the Seine and the Eiffel Tower, was easy of access and occupied. Only as it rose, eventually taller than the tallest man in the world, was it not taken up. Jules and François chose an empty section in the middle, where in their youth they would have been able to jump up, twist in the air, and land firmly planted in a sitting position. Now they were too old, stiff, and heavy to do that, but they managed by making footholds of the iron eye bolts that ran in lines all along the wall.

No one would ever think that François Ehrenshtamm would be sitting here eating a sandwich from a plastic bag. One might conclude only that these were two old guys — maybe retired motormen or very low-level bureaucrats of the kind who thought the whole world could fit into a pencil — who, passing into the restful indolence of retirement and onto the easy ramp down which, forgotten by others, one slides into death, had nothing better to do than drink beer and eat tuna sandwiches. They were invisible to the young, who, assuming that even were they wise they would be useless in new times, were in most cases correct. In the gardens of the Palais de Chaillot, where they began their conversation, they were relaxed and well worn. Who ever thinks of an old shoe? There is no need.

As François laid out the lunch, Jules asked, "Why are the fountains of Paris more exposed to the wind than those of Rome? You know how many times a change in wind direction has soaked me in Paris? In the Tuileries, here, all over the place. But not in Rome. Roman water is disciplined as if by Mussolini. It behaves. It goes up, it goes down. But in Paris the water comes at you like machine gun fire."

François thought before he spoke, not merely as the habit of a philosopher but because all his life when he didn't think before he spoke he got into trouble. "You realize," he said, "that the water in Rome is older, and doesn't have the energy to attack. The water of Paris has sharp elbows and jumps around, like monkeys or adolescents."

"Really," Jules said.

"Do you have a better explanation?"

Jules thought. "Yes."

"And what is that?"

"What surrounds Rome?"

"What?"

"Hills. Rome is almost in a bowl. Therefore, less wind."

"Of course I knew that."

"No, you didn't, because you're a philosopher, and philosophers aren't concerned with wind and waves."

"Jules, I'm not really a philosopher, I'm a *con* who talks on television."

"That's not going well?"

"It's going fine — Polish television, Russian television, Brazilian television, African television. It sells books, but it's like bleeding in the water. Though I don't want to do it anymore, I have a young family. I wish I could retire to a cottage by the water's edge in Antibes and put a line in the sea. All day."

"Five million Euros would do it," Jules said, "although you wouldn't have a guestroom."

"I have to keep on working, but really, television makes me sick."

"Why not just stop television?"

"My income would decline by seventy or eighty percent. You're lucky. Believe me. Privacy is royal."

"I know," Jules said. He did.

"What are you doing in your privacy, of which, truly, I'm envious."

"There's a difficulty."

"What? The girl again?"

"She's a student, my student."

"Nothing wrong with that. I married one. If we were lake dwellers in four hundred B.C. and I was a chieftain in white furs I'd have an even younger wife."

"François, this is not four hundred B.C.,

we're not lake dwellers, and I'm not a chieftain in white furs."

"How can you fault yourself for being in love?"

"Because obviously I'm crazy. I lose all sense at the first appearance of a lure. I'd be a terrible fish. I fall for images, voices, and, God knows, women I meet sometimes just for a moment. Not because I'm frivolous, but because I see in them their true qualities. I penetrate too fast, right to the core — which is so often angelic. It isn't that every woman has this, but that so many do."

"You know that a lot of them would snarl at you and deny the entire proposition. I don't mean to pun," François said.

"Perhaps the ones who would, would be moved by rage that they themselves aren't angelic. When jealousy finally cracks, it releases insatiable anger. And people who aren't innocent don't believe that innocence exists. People who aren't good don't believe that goodness exists. Alcoholics believe that everyone drinks. Thieves think that everyone steals. Liars think that everyone lies. And those who don't lie, believe even liars."

"You see the beauty and goodness in women. So what else is new?"

"I didn't say I discovered anything, but the fact remains that they're superior to us — not by action but by existence. They don't have to work at it, as we do, and as far as I

337

can see, we do so mainly to be worthy of them. Anyway, what am *I* doing? I'm trying to re-create something that was lost, to make perfect something that was imperfect but still the best thing in my life. Nature has brought me to where I am, and will allow me peace only if I accept it. But leaving them behind is really difficult."

"I'll bet that as many hours as you've spent imagining it you haven't even kissed her."

"No. Nor should I. Even if at this late hour it was not foolish to love anyone else, I still couldn't be unfaithful to Jacqueline."

"It's not as if she was always faithful to you."

For Jules, it was as if a bomb had exploded nearby and knocked the wind out of him. (This had happened once, in Algeria, and he knew what it felt like.) "What?" he asked, as he recovered, observing in François a moment of panic quickly made unobservable by his long practice in debate.

"I mean, she died, Jules. She left you."

"That's not what you meant, because you said *always,* and that doesn't fit."

"It is what I meant."

"No, it isn't. It's not as if I haven't known you forever, François. I know what you meant. Why did you say that? Who told you?"

"Do you really want me to say, Jules? Because it would be better if I. . . ."

"Yes. You have to."

"Do I really?"

"If you ever want to see me again."

"Then I won't see you again, ever, because no one told me," François said. "No one had to. Jules, it was a long, long time ago, and we were all so young."

Even as he dismounted from the wall, Jules reeled. It was as if he were falling off a cliff and nothing was left of the world. After he jumped down, he couldn't look in François' direction, much less at him. Instead, he turned and blindly made his way up the hill, the fountains on his right still bursting forth unpredictably.

Jacqueline's Photograph

Though often diverted as the streets connected and meandered, Jules went on foot all the way west to Saint-Germain-en-Laye, dreading the moment he would arrive home, except that he knew the many hours of walking would make sleep easy when otherwise it would have been impossible. Were he not continually moving through fresh air and light he would have no escape from fear and despair, as only the walking put off his nausea and helplessness.

Months before, as if the war there were not enough, huge mudslides had made whole villages in Afghanistan disappear in a trice. It was the kind of thing, like ferry sinkings, that appears regularly in the newspapers, eliciting a second or two of abstract sympathy before the reader goes on to news of sports, business, and celebrity. Grief for one person is almost unbearable. Grief for hundreds or thousands is beyond the capacity of the emotions. So such things glance only briefly against them before they migrate to the faculty of reason.

But in May, just after the mudslides, the newspapers published a picture of an Afghan woman — her entire family, her house, her village, as the newspaper said, "lost to the earth." God knows how many infants and grown sons and daughters had already been taken from this woman, and now she had nothing. She was pictured kneeling on endless bare ground with not a feature left where once had been the village where her life had unfurled. She was dressed in red and purple flowing around her in profusion, hiding everything but her face.

Because her skin was as cured, brown, and creased as old leather boots, it was impossible to tell if she were thirty-five or ninety. Beneath her left arm she cradled what a Westerner might have thought were bath mats. Upon closer inspection, Jules realized that they were enormous flatbreads, all that was left to her. Where would she go? How would she live? You could tell from her expression, particularly from her eyes, that she expected not to live. Jules understood only too well that this was the ever-present foundation upon which rests all that is done to remain above it.

As he neared home he found that, despite the walking, nausea finally overtook him in direct proportion to the fading of his hope.

341

What if François, like Iago, had hated him all along, and Jacqueline was innocent? This proposition, which he excitedly presented to himself, brought no relief. Was François justly punishing him for having fallen in love with Élodi? Or was François projecting upon Jacqueline his own promiscuity and transgressions — of which she would be innocent.

Or was Jacqueline, in what Dante would have called "her second age," when she had risen from flesh to spirit, reprimanding him for having turned away as if he thought that, her mortal life finished, her good had died with her? That we can merely sense the soul and prove it only by beauty and indirection allows it the possibility of life when all the things that can be proved are gone, and now it seemed that they were.

Had the ghostly Jacqueline observed, disapproved, and set François to lie? That could not be. But how could Jules have betrayed her when, in the beauty of Élodi, he partly found her? That was a poor excuse. What he had done was cruel to Jacqueline, who was betrayed and replaced, and cruel to Élodi, who deserved better than to share her finite existence with the ceaseless calling of the timeless dead.

He dared not admit that Élodi was in love with him, for fear that she was not, but he knew she was. She could not feel, as he could every day, that which was in store for him quite soon. Age, mortality, and the past standing in his way made what might have been simple infatuation all the more compelling. If Jacqueline had betrayed him, he ought now to be free, but he was only bound to her more strongly.

When had it happened, and for how long? Jules had never strayed, taking control of his attraction to students who were at the time not much younger than he, mastering it so that it fused with and dissipated its energy in the music. Was it then, as his infatuations were transforming into art, that Jacqueline was in their bed with François, or others? How could something so tawdry be so painful?

Upon reaching Shymanski's gate, Jules found himself in the dusk. Alone on the street in the remnant light of a dark red sunset and in lovely weather that once would have enthralled him, he froze in place. On the wall, drawn as large as a man, was a swastika, although it was not accurately reproduced, as the right-angle extremes pointed down in the nine-o'clock position rather than up. The Nazi swastika was like a waterwheel that would catch water if it turned counterclockwise. But not this one, which despite its inaccuracy was no less powerful.

He told himself not to be overwhelmed by the strengthening cascade of events, because although sometimes things happen all at once, seldom does everything collapse without some part of it springing back. Were he to hold through he might see a break in the line, and something good arise. Still, he was frightened beyond reason of just a symbol some imbecile had drawn on the wall, frightened of crossing his own threshold, of seeing Jacqueline's photograph, of sitting in the silence of his rooms. Now she was truly gone, and he could no longer take comfort in his wish to join her.

But when he did cross the threshold, and when he did force himself to sit down opposite her photograph, raise his head, and look straight at her, she was the same as she always had been. You could see in her face that her beauty arose from her purity and goodness. It had lasted from infancy to and through her death. Her photograph showed that no matter her faults, she was yet irreproachable, which made it intensely more difficult for Jules, who might never put the contradiction to rest as long as he might live. He still loved her. Even with the hollowness he felt — which was defeat — he loved her.

Just as it had been after her death, returning home to silence was impossible to sustain. He wanted never to speak to anyone again, and yet he desperately wanted a confidant. The Bentley was parked in front of the house rather than in the garage, which meant that

Shymanski was home. For years — like a servant who must trade on function as the passport to his betters — Jules had gone to speak to him only about practical matters, and now he had just such a practical matter.

He went the outside way, through the dark. The beige pea gravel on the driveway made a sound beneath his feet like several truncated chords, or the sound of a brushed snare drum disciplined by a felt damper. Though the light in the huge *porte cochère* was off, it was probably too early for Shymanski, even at his advanced age, to have retired. After Jules rang the bell, a servant whom he didn't know came to the door. He had to tell her that he lived in the lower part of the house. She was with Shymanski in the South, and knew little of what went on in Paris. "It's late," she said.

"It's seven-thirty."

"It can't wait until tomorrow?"

"Is he up?"

"Yes."

"Is he dressed? I know his reluctance to see people, but he knows me."

"Yes, he's dressed, but he doesn't even like to see people he knows, even those closest to him."

"It's always been like that, and I imagine it's worse now. I understand."

She was beginning to close the door, but Jules said, "Is he busy?"

"No, he's not busy."

345

"Is he well?"

"As well as can be expected."

"Then why shouldn't I see him?"

"All right, I'll ask."

After a while, she came back. "He says okay."

"Then if he says okay it must be okay," Jules told her, his tone conveying the message that she might think more for herself.

"I don't make decisions for him," she shot back. "I'm not his keeper, and he's not that far gone."

He was at least a little gone, sitting in an armchair that could have engulfed a Sumo wrestler, much less a tiny, ancient Jew with so little time left he was afraid to wear a watch. His head seemed as big on his body as the head of an infant, and was shaped like an egg. The large part of the egg was uppermost, narrowing as it descended to the chin, where it met a body that widened as it dropped to the heavy, broad ballast of the buoy of his hips and his behind, from which extended two short legs that seemed as thin as lollipop sticks. Thanks to a magnificent terrace on the Côte d'Azur, he was the browned color of expensive leather. Because of his bald, egg-like head, a nose like a door handle, and huge, careful eyes, he looked not quite human but rather like a creature from Dante or Lewis Carroll. Before he was confined to chairs, wheelchairs, and the back

346

seats of Rolls-Royces and Maybachs, he had walked like a goose, pivoting to left and right before catching himself to return to center, setting each foot down as if on a stepping-stone. The wonder of it had been endearing.

Opening onto the glow of Paris, the salon where he was ensconced was masterfully decorated — in gray, silver, and yellow — to soothe and impress. On one wall was a tapestry, its dominant colors yellow, rose, and gold. On another, a Fragonard portrait of a woman in yellow silks, like the one in the National Gallery in Washington. How beautiful she was in every detail, not least her fine concentration. Though gone for centuries, she was fresh and lovely enough so that every time Jules came into this room he fell in love with her. That she was, at most, powder in the grave, made no difference. By the flash of her indestructible soul in the painting, forever still, he knew and loved her. So did Shymanski, who sat across from her, frequently glancing, kept alive.

Only the tapestry and the painting were lit, by tiny spotlights out of sight behind a reveal. When Jules' eyes adjusted to the darkness, he said, "There's a swastika on the wall near the gate."

"I saw it when I came in," Shymanski said. "It's not really a swastika. It's backwards. Must've been drawn by an idiot."

"Who else would draw a swastika?"

347

"Maybe Hitler, who was no idiot, and he doodled them. In conferences with his generals and when he was talking on the telephone — 'Hi, it's the *Führer*' — he drew swastikas. Unfortunately, those people were not idiots. They were capable enough to destroy my family and yours. And although you and I are technically alive, they destroyed us too, didn't they?"

"Yes, but not entirely, and it was different for me. You were old enough to have known and lived in the world. My universe was a dark, one-room attic with three vents and one high window to which I was sometimes lifted at night. That and my mother and father were all I knew. In the first minutes that I left that world it was destroyed. I've done my best since. I've loved, I've tried but failed to protect what I've loved. The only way I've been able to go back has been in music, and only teasingly. It brings me, as Moses was brought, to a height where I have a glimpse of the Promised Land. But I can't go in."

"I understand," Shymanski said. "For me the war was an aberration, and I knew what it was that I wanted to find again. That kept me alive. For you, they would say it was trauma, but I wouldn't. I'd say it was simpler, that like everyone else you have a paradise you long to restore, but your paradise is also hell. Although getting back is dark and dangerous, you won't be deterred. Love draws you back. You can't escape."

"Escape is only for my daughter."

"But maybe not, not in France, not now," Shymanski told him. "Throughout my life I've observed that old men become wonderfully optimistic, and yet I'm not. What is France but a once magnificent house now occupied by ignorant squatters. By no means the majority, but enough to destroy the culture and the law. After all the confused, tragic, costly work through war, plague, famine, revolution, and wrong turns, the house stood beautifully nonetheless and with potential unmatched in history. And now they write on the walls, break the windows, and make fires on the floor. Perhaps I see it that way because I have no strength left. You have a grandson, isn't that right?"

"I do."

"I hope he won't suffer, your daughter, too. I don't know. Now I'm leaving everything behind. My children. . . ." He made a dismissive gesture, as if throwing something away. "They're Brazilians, like their mother, not really French. They think life is cocktails, watches, and cars. It's my fault: I couldn't feel for them what I feel for my children who were lost. It was a sin, because, half Brazilian or not, they're my sons. I made them what they are. I was cold to them. I pushed them away, and the more I did so the more they became what repelled me. I lost them when they were young and now they're getting their revenge. They've stripped me of everything, but that's all right. I deserve it, and what is everything anyway? Things? I know how to die. I've never left the war, not for one second. You too, I think, though I don't mean to presume. I know the facts but I really don't know enough about you. As for me, I'm not afraid of the swastika. Let them come. They came before. Most of them are dead now, and I'm alive. I'm just sorry for the youth. For them, no Holocaust, just the mist of it that every day they can read in the eyes of others, which is enough to color a life forever."

"Unlike you, I didn't experience the beginnings the last time. If it's a mist, it's opaque enough that I can't see behind it."

"I think it's more like Dreyfus," Shymanski said. "French anti-Semitism is immortal, but not strong enough by itself to make a holocaust. For that dance, the Germans must take the lead, or maybe now the Arabs."

"In July," Jules said, "I had to buy a part for my car. It's an old car, and the part was cheaper in a little store near the Gare du Nord. So I was at the edge of the Quartier de Barbès when the disturbances began. There were just a few police, but the battle lines had begun to form.

"I was in Algeria during the war, but in the mountains. I've never seen anything like this.

Hundreds, no, thousands of young men, muscled and trim. . . . They don't have jobs. What do they do all day, lift weights and look at jihad videos? They had overturned cars and buses to build barricades. They tore up paving stones, made fires, and looted stores. The heat and wavy air from the fires mixed all the colors — green, red, black, metal — and smoke hung over everything. They were covered with sweat, screaming with rage, their eyes like coals. Bitter and unreachable, they wanted to kill and they wanted to die. Half of them were fitted out with iron bars, chains, clubs, knives.

"They had so much energy and were so worked up that when they weren't charging they would jump up and down. They were an army, and I've never seen, even in photographs, so much hatred in so many eyes. Focused on the police, they paid no attention to me. Had I been identifiable as a Jew I'm sure they would have killed me. This happens all over France. It's not just a mist."

"It's not the Wehrmacht, either."

"No, but France is helpless before it, and when France is helpless, one way or another, it surrenders."

"It hasn't yet."

"What scares me is that, on rare occasions, unable to overcome one another, the right and the left fall in love and make common cause against . . . guess who? You saw that with Dieudonné. He filled the theaters with Arabs and the FN. Don't you have powers?" Jules asked, hoping that somehow Shymanski could summon these and set things right.

"Jules, no one has. The higher you go, the more constrained you are. Real power depends on the ebb and flow of events. It comes from riding and floating on them, but it doesn't matter who you are, you're just a passenger. Eventually you're thrown off or you sink in. I was once the third-richest person in France. I succeeded in building this lovely tomb, and I'll die in comfort. The best doctors will come. The drugs will float me away. The nurses will keep me clean. The room will be quiet and beautiful, with many flowers sent by people whom I never really knew.

"How did my wife die? How did my children? I don't know. In a cattle car? A gas chamber? Shot? Raped, my little girls? Beaten? I don't know, but I do know that when I die I'll be just like them. The lifetime I've spent insulating myself will disappear in smoke, as they did. The swastika on the wall is a sign that at last I'm to join them. And when I think of this, I feel peace and joy such as I've never felt in all my life, through all my successes."

"I know exactly," Jules told him, "but I have a daughter and a grandson. I don't want to part from them. I can't leave them yet, because the child is seriously ill."

"The child. I'm sorry."

Jules dipped his head in acknowledgment. "Not even a year ago," he said, "seventeen thousand people marched in Paris and chanted 'Jews out of France,' and 'The gas chambers were fake.' Children are massacred in Jewish schools; we have to hide on the streets; throughout the country there are 'Israel-Free Zones'; some authorities instruct shopkeepers that they cannot carry 'Zionist' products."

"You think next is *Judenfrei*?"

"It feels like that now. I myself am safe when I walk through Paris only because people think I'm a Norman, or a German. My coloring. My face. To pass was always exhilarating, and gave me a feeling of freedom and acceptance. Even now. Then I see Hasidim, I see their expressions, feel their tensions, and I think, why am I hiding? I'm hiding for good reason, but I'm ashamed even as I continue to do so. After the Holocaust we were free for decades. That freedom felt light and good, and I still experience it, but only because I'm taken for something that I'm not.

"My daughter's husband is Orthodox. Because he was attacked, he takes off his yarmulke when he's on the street. My little grandson doesn't know anything about this of course. He may not even live, but if he does I want to get him out — to Switzerland, America, or New Zealand."

"Okay."

"I don't have the money, and neither do they."

"I'd give it to you, Jules, if I could," Shymanski said. "I'd give you a million Euros, two million, whatever it would take. But now I don't have a *sou*. My sons control everything, and they hate you."

"I'm not fond of them, either."

"Jules, your life has been so much better than mine."

"Really?" Jules asked. "I've come to nothing."

"So have I, but on the way you've had music."

"Music is evanescent, not even like a painting. It flees like smoke in the wind. It's just gone."

"Everything is evanescent. Why do you think I offered you the apartment? If there's a God, and I do believe so even if He's become inscrutable to me, music is the finest and possibly the last way of reaching Him. I wanted you to teach my boys so they could escape what in fact they've become, but they've always sought what they should avoid. They're half Brazilian: maybe they have a different heaven."

"Monsieur Shymanski, I could never sustain the elevation of music. When it stops I can still hear it, but the elevation vanishes."

"Still, it teaches you, Jules. You of all people

should know that. It shows you that there is something sublime. When I was younger I used to believe that if there's an afterlife it would be filled with luminous color and gentle light. Now I think that it would be like music. When music, which seems more real than life itself, vanishes, where does it go? Maybe when we vanish we'll go there, too."

As Shymanski was speaking, Jules had caught a glimpse, almost hidden in the darkness, of a new table in a corner. On it was a stainless steel tray with a neat case of phials and another of syringes. After a moment, Jules said, "I see." Seconds passed before he asked, "Are you going to paint out the swastika? I can arrange to have it done. Claude won't do it, because he says he won't do anything but garden and watch the gate. I can do it."

"No. Let the new owners paint it out. I'm content to have come full circle."

1944

In the chaos before the Wehrmacht drove on Paris in 1940, vehicles and pedestrians rushed in all directions, crossing and weaving pointlessly as they sought salvation in places from which others had fled. Like most of the population, Philippe Lacour had taken to heart the lesson written in his own blood as a young *poilu* during the Great War, which was that Paris would not fall, or, if so, only after years of fighting. In the perfect June weather, the speed of the German columns and the collapse of the French army seemed both incredible and inappropriate. It was summer, the season of awakened life burgeoning under clear skies and strong sun. Just days before the panic, Philippe and Cathérine had seen young students celebrating their start into life arm in arm in tuxedos and gowns. As usual in June, Philippe, a cellist, had a full schedule of weddings, graduation ceremonies, and parties. As he and Cathérine rode toward the Gare de Montparnasse, in a taxi for which they had paid five times the normal tariff, he was anxious that he would be held to account and lose income for failing to show up at his engagements.

Though expensive, the taxi ride was short. Because everyone in Paris wanted to escape south, the streets were choked so much that half a kilometer from the station the taxi came to a halt. Every sidewalk was packed with people carrying heavy suitcases, many of which were eventually abandoned to thieves. At first they dragged their loot into the side streets and alleys, but soon they began to split open luggage where it had been dropped, struggling over precious items and littering the street with clothing strewn like entrails after a battle.

"People will be fighting to get on the trains, and how many trains will there be?" Philippe asked Cathérine. For him, her dark red hair had never ceased to be a mystery, endlessly deep, endlessly exciting. Now she was in the eighth month of her first pregnancy. He knew that even if they could make their way to the station and onto a train, the journey south might take their unborn child from them, and perhaps the life of the mother as well. And the rumor was that to stop movement south the Germans were strafing rail lines. As the cellist in a chamber quartet that had toured Europe, Philippe had flown in German civil airliners that had been surrogates for the development of military aviation otherwise forbidden to Germany — planes with metal airframes, ribbed sides, and powerful engines. He didn't merely think of how the Luftwaffe would strafe rolling stock. Rather, he imagined the view from the cockpit as an aircraft easily overtook a train below. He knew that the approach and attack would take only seconds. He saw the steam issuing from the fleeing engine, waving in the wind before disconnecting. He saw the relative motion of aircraft, train, smoke, and steam on and across a landscape of rich green fields, wheat-colored grasses, and blue sky.

"She's pregnant," he declared to the taxi driver, who had noticed and taken pity, which is why they had been able to snare his cab. "We can't fight that," meaning the crowds and disruption visible through the windshield.

"So what do you want?"

"Go left at the next street. Then take us to the Gare de l'Est."

"I was there," the taxi driver told him. "People are pouring in from the Marne and Champagne."

"The trains going out will be empty."

"But to where? The Germans?"

"There'll be a vacuum behind their lines, filled only by supply troops. They'll focus on what lies ahead."

"Bird shouldn't fly into traps."

"All of France is a trap. For the moment,

we'll take refuge in a neglected corner. If you were a German, would you pay more attention to Paris or Reims?"

The point was made, and the taxi driver grunted in assent. At the sooty Gare de l'Est, the least glorious of Parisian stations, Philippe and Cathérine fought their way against streams of people coming from the east. They had had to leave their suitcases strapped to the roof of the taxi, and now photographs, letters, and records, like their home and their past, were gone forever. Cathérine cried as she walked, but they pushed on, because their lives depended upon it.

All Philippe could think of was to save his wife and child. He had his cello and a briefcase with documents and money. Cathérine had her purse, to which she clung as if it were a child about to be ripped from her arms. In the crowds flowing past were many Jews, some Orthodox, their dress ensuring that they would be in the most danger, and some identifiable mainly to other Jews. Though they were assimilated, their eyes told everything. When Philippe and Cathérine passed them they knew each other for what they were, and it was not just Cathérine's red hair, for Bretons and others frequently had red hair, but a certain tentative way in the world, always alert as if expecting what always came.

"The Germans will have flushed the Jews from Reims the way beaters clear a field of pheasants. They won't be looking so hard for them as they will here. Provincial, non-elite troops may not know what to do, or be so inclined."

"One hopes," said Cathérine. "But where will we stay?"

"I said Reims because I don't want to disappoint you, but maybe we can get to Switzerland. Perhaps they would let us in as refugees. I played a concert at the Ministry of Foreign Affairs, and I remember the name of the functionary who took care of us: Von Arx. He was kind, and he may remember me. He wasn't high-ranking, but that was in thirty-four. Perhaps he's risen."

In front of the station, they heard a sound from within like that of a chorus. It was the sound of people in distress, of the past breaking, illusions shattering, and mortality bursting forth from the comfort of ordinary life. It sounded like fire whistling on gusts of air through a burning forest.

Philippe turned to take a last look at Paris. He lifted his gaze to the sky and was astounded to see ragged smoke curling through flawless blue as rich as fresh paint. The smoke was as black and gray as the lines in an etching. Moving both violently and expansively, rising on the wind and racing as if to escape toward the sun, it was composed of the remnants of that which would disappear rather than submit.

■ ■ ■ ■

In the station at Reims, open spaces were packed with anxious crowds that had flowed in from the city streets and surrounding countryside. Gustave Doré could not have drawn people stripped more of comfort and assurance. As would his son, Philippe loved sound, and he stopped to listen as the murmur of the crowd floated above them in a cloud. The station was alive with the electric energy of a thousand desperate people: children in arms (somehow they too knew the danger, and their little faces showed it); men charged with the protection of their families; old veterans and their wives, saddened to see war once again; officials who, though trying to do their duty, were beaten back by the panic.

Having discovered that no trains were moving southeast toward Switzerland, Philippe and Cathérine remained calm. Except for them, no one went from the station to the city, and as they walked against the tides the Parisian cellist and his wife felt that, driven by a kind of madness, they had almost left the world of the living. Not knowing where they were going or how they would end up, they persisted in moving toward the danger, suspecting that they were soon going to die.

On the boulevards, some stragglers were

hurrying toward the railway, but the side streets were empty. "There are no hotels here," Cathérine said as they looked down a long residential street half submerged in summer shadow. Brassy light spilled from the cornices and chimneys still illuminated by the sun, with the effect of blackening the darkness where sunlight did not strike.

"The last thing we should do is go to a hotel, because the first thing the Germans will do will be to requisition them for their officers."

"Then where will we stay? We don't know anyone here."

"We'll ask." From the north and northeast came the muted sound of distant artillery. "We have perhaps a day, certainly hours. We'll find something." He wasn't half as sure as he wanted to sound for Cathérine's sake."

They walked farther into the shadows. Halfway down the last of several streets later, they came to a storefront: *Patisserie Boulangerie Mignon.* Though it was closed, Philippe saw variations of light coming from a room in the back, as if there were a fire or someone were moving about and blocking or reflecting the light of a lamp. He knocked on the glass-paned door.

"They're closed," Cathérine said. "They get up in the dark to bake."

"Someone is moving inside." He rapped on the glass respectfully but urgently. They could hear heavy engines — perhaps of tanks or half-tracks. "I thought we had hours," Philippe said. "We don't."

No one came. "Oh God," Cathérine exclaimed as she saw, at the end of the street, the first vehicles leading an endless column of half-tracks, command cars, and trucks speeding past the gap straight into the sun.

Philippe rested his cello on the sidewalk and put his arms around his wife. The convoy at one end of the street was now matched by the lead vehicles of a similar column at the other end. As minutes passed, thousands of transports, artillery pieces, and tanks went by unceasingly. These were only part of an immense, overwhelming power stretching toward Paris. Philippe had seen such things as a soldier in the Great War, but to Cathérine they were new.

The glass door opened. Standing inside, his left hand still controlling the door lever — for he had yet to imagine much less make up his mind about what might be asked of him — was a short man in his fifties, with graying hair, a mustache of the same coloration, and a white apron, its strings loosely hanging parallel with the pinstripes of his gray pants.

This was Louis Mignon, thrice-wounded veteran of the previous war, baker, chef, deeply devout Catholic, husband of Marie, father to Jacques, and savior of Philippe Lacour, Cathérine Lacour, and their unborn

363

child, Jules.

Risking everything he had, the great-grandfather of Marie Druart Mignon had bought the building during a nineteenth-century financial panic, and now it was hers, three storeys above a shop, a steep Mansard roof with no windows on the street but three louvered vents where dormers might have been. One small dormer window looked out over the back garden, and in the twenties, when business was good, Louis had had a bathroom installed, even before a staircase, when the main plumbing stack had to be redone and the contractor suggested that they take the opportunity to prepare the attic for future habitation.

Hearing trucks and armored vehicles, Louis brought Philippe and Cathérine in quickly, closed and locked the door, and peered out the window, to left and right. "They're not coming down this street," he said. He stared at his guests. "Is she Jewish?" he asked Philippe. There was no hostility. It was a necessary question. Cathérine was beautiful, her face and deep red hair different somehow from the faces and deep red hair of the women of Brittany and Normandy. One could tell.

"We both are," Philippe answered.

"You look Dutch. I would swear you were Dutch." Philippe was tall and blonde. "You could pass for German. You're not a German?"

Philippe shook his head to indicate that he wasn't. "We were Dutch a long time ago before we came to France. There are many Dutch Jews."

"What do you expect of me?" Louis asked.

"Nothing."

"Do you have someplace to go?"

"No."

"Not a temple, or other Jews? They say Jews always come out on top."

"Yes, of course, like us."

"You don't take care of your own?"

"We would if we could. Right now, the richest, most powerful Jews in Paris are headed toward the Pyrenees, maybe walking on the road. Some may have diamonds sewn into their clothes, but that won't help us here."

"What will happen if the Germans see you?"

"I don't know. They don't like Jews of course, and although it's not written on my face, I killed some Germans in Fourteen-Eighteen."

Louis now looked at him in a different light. "I killed them, too," he said. "You've come from Paris?" He could hear it in Philippe's speech.

"This afternoon."

"Why here if you don't know anyone?"

"The trains were empty in this direction,

365

and we thought we might get to Switzerland."

"No," Louis said. "Everything's shut down."

At this point Jacques and Marie descended from the floor above. "Who are they?" Marie asked. She was a little shorter than her husband, with wavy blonde hair. Jacques — seventeen, thin, tall, and dark — saw the arrival of the Lacours as messengers of what life was going to be like. He had already adapted, and for him it was an adventure.

In answer to his wife's question, Louis Mignon said, "They're Jews from Paris. We have to put them in the attic. The hatch is in the ceiling of the closet, and if we stuff the shelf with duvets you won't be able to see the opening. We'll have plenty of food, because the Germans will make us bake for them and we can siphon off whatever these two. . . ." He glanced at Cathérine, "these *three,* need."

Marie thought about this, completely unafraid. "But the Germans will be here for bread and pastry every day."

"That's good," Louis told her. "It'll be as if it's their own. They'll be happy each time they take away what we bake, and they'll never look here because for them it will be pleasant and familiar. If I could, I'd hide Jews across the street from wherever the Germans will have their headquarters. Jacques," his father commanded, "get the ladder." Everyone was enthusiastic, as if they were embark-

ing on something that would neither be difficult nor last long.

Marie Mignon delivered Jules as Philippe
paced on the other side of a sheet hung as a
barrier in the dimly lit attic. Philippe was
puzzled, disarmed, and made superfluous by
the feminine power and mystery of bearing
and bringing forth new life. Jules cried for
only a few seconds when he first came into
the world. As if he had understood, he suddenly stopped. For four years, silence came
naturally at first, then in imitation, and then
as a game in which sound, though desired
above all else except freedom, was the enemy.
They didn't flush the toilet or bathe unless
the shop was closed and the Mignons kept
watch, ready to knock with a broomstick
against the ceiling of the third floor, as a
signal to stop. Even when he was hurt or fell
with a shock, Jules hardly cried, or when he
did it was nearly silent, a disciplined gasping,
then tears and nearly inaudible short breaths.
For four years, like his parents, he didn't
speak, but only whispered, and didn't know
that his and their voices could be full, clear,
and less like wind gently whistling through
imperfections in the window frames of an old
house.

Philippe fingered the strings of his cello and
moved his right hand — always entrancing to
Jules — as if he were holding the bow that he

367

left in the case so as not to be too tempted. Though Philippe could hear the music as if it were actually sounding, Jules could not, but he saw clearly that his father was lifted into a different world that shone on his face and showed in his motions.

Little Jules would try to go there, too, moving his own imaginary bow with great seriousness. For his father and mother this was wonderful to see. "Someday," Philippe told him, "you'll learn to do this with a real bow, and with sound."

"When?" Jules had whispered.

"Someday."

The sounds that the child did hear came from the street and neighboring houses: engines, hawkers' cries, orders commanded through German loudspeakers, thunder, rain and hail on the roof, birdsong, the wind, water running in pipes, muted conversation and laughter, and, eventually, artillery and bombs — bombs on the railheads, bombs on bridges, bombs in the city. The Lacours could never go to the basement during a bombing, where anyone on the street, including German soldiers, SS, even Gestapo, might take shelter. But as time wore on and the Germans didn't show, Louis Mignon suggested that if the bombardments grew heavy enough it might be worth the risk.

For his first four years Jules knew nothing but one big, brown room, with raw, unfinished wood making up the steep ceiling, the knee walls, the beams, and the floor. A taut bedsheet on a wood frame cordoned off his parents' 'bedroom,' where, when Jules was deep asleep, they made love in complete silence except for not-quite-silent, astounded breaths. Perhaps having heard this in his dreams, for the rest of his life, try as he might, no matter how abandoned his lovemaking, Jules was never able to utter an exclamation, a cry, a groan, or a single word.

They had no artificial light, because even with blackout curtains it might have shown through a fissure in the walls or vents. Thus, their hours were decided by the sun, and when the days grew short and the nights so long they couldn't sleep through them, they whispered in the dark. They dared not look out their one window when it was light, so the only part of the outside world Jules knew other than a pinched view of the street through the louvers of the vents was the back garden in moonlight. Because the city was blacked out, he hadn't even been able to see warm lamps in beckoning windows.

Although light came through the window in the day — had it not, they would have lived just like bats instead of almost like bats — Jules thought the world was much darker than it is. He thought the moon was the sun, something he was not allowed to see in the day, when, in his particular cosmology, for some reason the "moon" grew much brighter. The most beautiful things he had ever beheld were the beginnings of sunrise and the reflected remnants of sunset, especially when one or the other struck new copper flashing on a distant roof or steeple and the reflection of what he thought was the moon in its excitable state shot through the darkness of the attic, illuminating white, dancing dust in its beam and painting a portion of the sloping roof in blinding gold. The first time he saw the sun itself he was knocked back in shock, and his father, who was holding him up to the window as he himself stood on a chair, nearly toppled over. In the spring of 1943, a few months after most of the 226 Jews of Reims who had been flushed out of their hiding places had been sent east to die, he saw moonlight on a tree in the back garden when it bloomed into a fixed white cloud that winked on and off as the true clouds above it hid and revealed the light.

Immediately upon Jacques' report of what the Resistance knew about the deportations of the spring, the Mignons had refined their already ingenious system. They would eat their meals and clean up before delivering food to the attic. Thus, when the Lacours had finished and the dishes were brought down, there would never be two sets that might cast suspicion. Jacques would keep watch during the passages. Working for the

Resistance, he, like everyone in the house, was always in danger. Philippe regretted every day that he could not risk for the Mignons what they risked for him. He asked if he could participate in the actions that Jacques reported, taking the boy's place as the obligation of an adult and a veteran. He knew how to use weapons and how to fight. But no, it was out of the question. He couldn't move on the street. Even with false documents he would have been conspicuously out of place as he left and returned to the Mignons, passing Wehrmacht and SS troops and officers who, despite their military discipline, were as weak as anyone else in the face of baguettes and the famous *biscuits rose de Reims,* the scarce ingredients for the latter made available to a rather nervous Louis by an SS officer who, had he known what the Mignons were doing, would have executed the whole family without so much as a thought, rapidly delivering pistol shots to the backs of their heads.

The scheme required that even laundry be matched, so that though Cathérine was thinner than Marie, nothing came down to be washed unless it could be plausibly worn by one Mignon or another. Jules' clothes never came down but were laundered with many of Cathérine's in the bathroom sink, and part of his play was silently kneading them in the water.

In the four years spent in their dark brown room, the things that take up time in a normal life were absent: work, play, shopping, travel, amusements, promenades, visits, appointments. Instead, they read, they dreamed of life after the war, they whispered about what they remembered and loved, and they taught Jules, who as a result of this upbringing was unusually precocious. All day long, they read to him until he himself could read. Forced by circumstance and lack of choice, starting at age three, he read everything passed up through the hatch: Victor Hugo, Molière, even Voltaire, none of which he actually understood, but he loved the sound of the words. His parents taught him the rudiments of musical theory, promising that when it would be filled out with sound he would know one great day after another. Even if it were beyond his comprehension, he was nearly force-fed a child's version of mathematics, philosophy, history, and the sad story of their lives, things young children are not normally required to learn unless compelled to by half-insane parents, or war. There was little else they could do with sixteen hours a day of enforced idleness made otherwise only by learning, talking, and dreaming. And always the drills and the crucial game, which taught Jules how instantly to stop his play and freeze in place without even putting down a foot that had been raised, except so softly he could not hear it himself. Despite what they told him, he thought that this and all the other unusual things were normal. He was happy despite his parents' unhappiness, because he was with them, and because they loved him so much and so well. This was his world, but then, in August of 1944, it ended.

The spring of '44 had been unusually hot and dry, and in June as the Allies fought through the hedgerows and all of France breathed expectation, the weather was unlike anything anyone had seen before. The heat beneath the copper roof in the attic was difficult to withstand. Three vents and the open window facing the garden were not enough to exhaust the air, so Philippe would open the hatch to get a convection current going. It worked so well that the column of rising air was enough to push back Cathérine's hair when she looked down into the third-floor closet. They closed their eyes and imagined it was a sea wind. In Reims, no less than the rest of France, a heat wave arrived in August just ahead of the advancing American troops. By the time Patton's Third Army had pressed the Germans into the city, it abated as if in deference to the expected battle.

On the 16th, the kind of immense convoys that in 1940 had carried the Germans west through Reims now flowed east in even greater volume, for, unlike as in the advance four years previously, the routes of retreat were constricted because, battered in the north, the Germans lost them there. They poured into Reims day and night in a cross between panic and military rigor. Now they didn't merely course down the avenues, leaving only a small part of their mass to garrison the town as they pushed toward Paris, they stopped. There were so many that they had to splay into the lesser streets, which quickly filled with bumper-to-bumper military vehicles, field kitchens puffing smoke, tense and camouflaged soldiers, and defensive positions at key points replete with sandbagged revetments and emplaced anti-tank guns, the infamous 88s, pointing down the boulevards or across the squares to cover fields of fire.

The troops on the Mignons' street looted the bakery in the first half hour, taking flour, sugar, and butter, and from then on the Mignons were unable to go out to replenish. Not much remained anywhere else anyway, except what they could beg of the bivouacked Germans. They had as much water as they needed, the heat had abated, Jacques dared not leave the house, and everyone was more or less still and waiting. At dusk when the shadows made it impossible from the street to see into the vents, Philippe looked out and reported. "There are almost a thousand German soldiers here. Trucks, half-tracks, armored cars. No tanks. We would have heard them anyway. There are four field kitchens belching smoke." Later, the Mignons brought some German rations — potatoes and a small block of cheese — to the Lacours.

As the week passed, the troops in the street would suddenly pack up and leave, only to be replaced by a new column that choked the same space with nearly identical vehicles and equipment. The sounds of arrival and departure were always the same: straps slapping against metal, engines starting, tripods folding, the slides and bolts of weapons exercised after oiling, commands shouted, and, upon leaving, the blast of a whistle followed by the revving of engines as the vehicles rolled off. Each wave would rap on the door of the bakery and demand supplies. Told that they were gone, the corporals assigned to scavenge made forced inspections. Some wanted to check the upper floors for hidden food. This was highly suspenseful, but Marie Mignon, an honest woman of great maternal authority, would inform them that the first formation had taken everything. "We have only what you give us now," she would say, truthfully. "Otherwise, we'd starve. We can't move. There are three of us. We've hardly eaten in a week."

Then came a pause in the retreat. Some units moved back into the city from the east, and those pouring in from the west ceased to depart. In all, twenty-five thousand infantry took up positions in and around the city. The encampment below now had another kind of energy, higher and quieter, as the soldiers made preparations for battle. Communications lines were run from newly established headquarters to numerous subsidiary commands in freshly requisitioned buildings. *Chevraux de frises* blocked streets bristling with 88s and machine gun revetments. Artillery battalions fell into line within range of the Marne, and what was likely a substantial proportion of the remains of the Luftwaffe, two flights of forty fighter planes apiece — or perhaps one passing over twice: no one knew — buzzed the city, as if to fool the waiting troops into false confidence.

One evening during the buildup, Louis Mignon poked his head above the hatch to confer with Philippe. Both had been at Verdun, and they feared that Reims was about to be leveled by bombing, artillery, or both. They decided that when the bombardment began the Lacours would go to the basement together with the Mignons. The Lacours would be cousins from Paris, and their papers would have been left upstairs in the rush to take shelter. Perhaps no Germans would come into the basement. Perhaps even if some did they would not query anyone as they waited out the attack. What a pity it would be if, only days before the liberation of Reims, either the Lacours would be discovered or they and the Mignons would be blown to bits, their flesh and blood mixed with that of the Germans who had driven them into hiding. Civilians who could, fled to the chalk caves beneath Reims famous for holding the major portion of the world's aging Champagne. The Mignons — father, mother, and son — had decided that rather than abandon their guests they would live or die with them. But on Saturday, the 26th of August, the telephone lines that had just been run were re-spooled, the German generals mounted their elegant, nickel-trimmed cars and drove off before dawn, and their formations followed in the light. Reims had been so filled with men and material that it took two days and nights of steady movement to empty it. The Germans completely lost control on the 28th, and those remaining were confronted by the Resistance and an advance guard of Free French. By the evening of the 29th, American tanks were on the outskirts of the city, and would drive for the center just before sunrise on the 30th.

That morning, crowds surged through the streets and into the main squares. The Tricolor was unfurled everywhere. Jacques went out and returned, triumphant and elated, to report that there had been only minor skirmishes and few killed. It was over. Nonetheless, here and there small German units had been trapped or were lost. Some had only now arrived from the south, having made a hook after retreating from Paris. No one knew how many, but it was certain that these were very few and that they were trying to flee via inconspicuous routes before the main roads east were blocked by the Americans.

"What's that?" Jules had asked, hearing the faint strains of the *Marseillaise.* For fear that it might somehow, in a circumstance they could hardly imagine, give him away, he hadn't been taught it.

"That's the *Marseillaise,*" Cathérine told him. "It's the song of France. They're singing because they're happy the Germans have gone away." Having whispered for four years, she whispered still.

As she spoke, Philippe sat down and pivoted his cello into position, but this time he held the bow. This time, he would play music sounded out. And now Jules would hear music not through walls or at a distance or in the abstract.

It would have been appropriate to play the *Marseillaise,* but it was not what Philippe chose. He wanted the first music his son would hear to reflect not a secular glory but something more powerful. Philippe chose instead the choral part of a Bach cantata, which before the war he had transcribed and which he heard, despite the lack of sound, almost every day of their confinement — *Sei Lob und Preis mit Ehren.* Even to a Jew hiding in Reims in 1944, that it was Christian and that it was German was of no consequence, for it had been written as if in divine light, it was perfect, it was joy expressed through mourning, like the darkest clouds when lit by radiant beams. It was as if a mother were singing her last song to her child, confident that, like her love, the melody was invincible and would endure. Hearing music close and immediately for the first time, Jules was astounded, and loved it so that he knew that this was what he would follow for the rest of his life.

But he was not the only one who was moved. The cello had sufficient power to pour forth from the vents and fill the street immediately below, where, at first not hearing it, as the Lacours and the Mignons had not heard them, a detachment of Germans in three command cars and a half-track had come to a halt so as to listen carefully to the movement of armor in the distance. Like hunters in the forest, the SS troops and their commander, splintered from the barbarous 17th SS Panzer Grenadier Division Götz Von Berlichingen, froze, cocked their heads, and strained to determine the location of what they were hearing. The unmistakable rumble of tanks came from the northwest, quite far away. This they could tell if only because they were themselves part of an armored division, from which they had been separated, serving in Paris for two months. They wanted to stay away from the tanks above all, although they knew that PIATs or heavy machine guns could at any moment and from any redoubt or casual position do them in almost as well.

They heard an ocean-like hiss of crowds to the north and east. These, too, were an obstacle, although a way through them could be cleared with a few bursts of fire. And everywhere, they could hear the *Marseillaise,* played from many sources and therefore with a dissonance that was intolerably irritating to the fifteen hardened soldiers seeking escape through backstreets. In their silence — listening, still, stiff and straight they — accurately conformed to their image of themselves. They were self-contained, stoic, and ruthless. They had deliberately ceased long before to wonder about war and death so as to be hardened and unafraid. War was now a duty that, were it not necessary to be highly agile and alert, they would have conflated, even in its most savage parts, with tedium. When they did fight, they fought bravely, efficiently, and without emotion of any kind.

Nonetheless, the retreat had taken an invisible toll. The reality of loss and defeat had opened to them. In a surge of the kind of feeling so often coupled with resignation, they experienced a vision of — and an intense love for — the things of the world. Thus, standing absolutely straight in the lead vehicle, face

380

turned to the sky as he listened for what he had stopped to hear, the major in command was moved, for the first time in a long time, by the music coming from above. For so long having denied himself such feeling, he decided that he would compliment the cellist, not only for his skill, but for being sagacious and catholic enough to play Bach at the moment of liberation, when probably no one else in France was playing anything but the *Marseillaise* or would dare play anything German. The major was greatly and uncharacteristically softened by this. He wanted to be kind, to give a gift, to share with whoever was playing the music, which he recognized exactly, the admission that they were in fact brothers, that the war would be over, that there were higher things.

He dismounted. Shadowed automatically by a corporal and a private each armed not as he was with a pistol but with a submachine gun, he went to the bakery. Not surprisingly, it was closed, but with his riding crop he rapped hard on the door. He expected to be received, and that someone would appear expressly to receive him. One thing he did not lack was authority. The glass nearly broke.

The sound of this startled the Mignons as they were gathered around the radio, listening for news of their liberation. Keeping himself hidden behind the curtains, Louis looked out the window. Then he backed into the room. "Germans," he said. "They're right there." As the radio was switched off and the dial turned from the BBC, he heard the cello for the first time since the Lacours had been hidden. It was beautiful, and for an instant he noted that, but then signaled Jacques to run upstairs and silence it. As Louis went downstairs to answer the door, Jacques raced upstairs and knocked with a broom handle against the ceiling. The cello stopped instantly, and Jules held position as in the game he had learned from his beginnings.

Louis was used to officers, who came often to the bakery — but not so much to the SS. Perhaps his fear showed, although what fear he had was largely neutralized by his natural courage and discipline, the knowledge that Reims was very nearly liberated, and the conviction that the war would end with Germany prostrate. For the moment, however, he could not let this confidence show. In the last act, all they had to do was get through, just as they had come through four years of war and occupation. These were only the few remaining minutes. The major was smiling. It was obvious that he meant no harm.

"I want to compliment the musician," he said, "not only for his talent but especially for playing German music."

"Thank you," Louis said. "I'll tell him."

Still benevolent and unsuspecting, the

major said, "I'd like to tell him myself, if I can." He was polite.

"I'll get him," Louis announced.

"No no no," the major insisted, wanting to save him the trouble. Here, the indelible habit of absolute authority took over. "I'll go myself." He started up the stairs, untroubled by the impoliteness of doing so without invitation. His men followed, and the stairs creaked with their weight.

Louis had no idea what would happen. He waited, thinking that this might be the end for them all. He heard the major encounter Jacques descending from the third floor. "Are you the cellist?"

"Yes," Jacques answered. It was not convincing.

"What moved you to play the *Wach Auf?*"

"It's beautiful," said Jacques, who didn't know that this was not the piece Philippe had played.

"Really," the major said, having changed in an instant. He pushed past Jacques to the third floor. The soldiers flipped off the safeties on their weapons. Looking around, with the pleasure of a hunter, the major asked, "Where's the cello?" Jacques had no answer. He thought that so near the end of the war for Reims, he was going to die, and that he would be unable to protect his parents, who were going to die as well. He hoped they had fled, but knew that while he was in danger

383

they would not.

The major looked at the ceiling just as he had looked at the sky a short time before, but now he felt betrayed, and he was angry. "What's up there?" he demanded.

"Nothing. It's a crawlspace. Too small to enter."

"I saw the vents and the pitch of the roof," the major said. He was both driven and led as if in the chase. The corporal opened the closet door and pulled out duvets and bedding, tossing them over his head. Then he announced that he had found a hatch.

Without an order, the private went over to the corporal, cupped his hands into a stirrup, steadied himself, and gave the corporal a boost to the closet shelf. The corporal then used the barrel of his gun to knock open the hatch, and poked his head through just as Louis had frequently done. When his eyes adjusted to the dim light, he saw the sad, improvised furniture of the attic, the cello, the bow, Philippe, and Cathérine — but not Jules, who had been told to hide among the beams where the bathroom had been built against the rear knee wall, and, as in all the games, had obediently done so.

"They're hiding Jews," the corporal called down.

The major was more disappointed than angry, although he was irritated that he was wasting his time and putting his men in danger for the sake of a generous impulse that, in his view, had been thrown back in his face. He could hear through the walls, if faintly, the chest-shaking vibration of at least several companies of American tanks, and the sounds, like surging water, of distant and exultant crowds. "How many?"

"Two. One bed, two chairs. There are only two."

"Get them down."

With the deepest sadness and boundless fear for themselves and their child, Philippe and Cathérine left the attic they had entered four years before, and awkwardly descended through the hatch. As the corporal and private helped Cathérine down, each of them felt her breasts with their hands. Philippe saw this. His head swam, and the only thing keeping him upright and able to move was the overwhelming imperative of saving his child. He looked at Cathérine, and she at him. In a single glance they said that they loved one another, that they understood they were going to die, and that what they had left to do now in the world was to hope that Jules, overlooked, would live.

Sadism feeds upon itself, and this was the SS. Philippe and Cathérine were not escorted down the stairs, they were kicked and thrown. By the time they reached the *rez-de-chaussé,* Cathérine's ribs and wrist were broken, her face cut and bruised. Philippe was hurt even

385

more, but felt nothing except the exquisite pain that he would not be able to save his wife. She looked toward him, he thought, as if he could save her. The Mignons observed all this in shock, certain that they themselves would be shot for harboring Jews.

As if to demonstrate to the soldiers outside that they were doing their job, the private and the corporal hit Cathérine and Philippe with their submachine guns to propel them out the door and ordered them onto the half-track. They were in too much pain to climb up themselves, so the soldiers hoisted them up, threw them onto the steel floor, and forced them to kneel.

As if to explain why they were not simply shot and left on the ground, and why he was not going to shoot the Mignons, the major said, "We'll have to live with France." Then he mounted the step and got into the half-track. He looked up and down the street. The unmistakable sound of tanks grew louder. His men looked at him as if to receive orders, but he held up his hand, meaning that they should leave their engines off, and freeze. He hoped that as the tanks passed on the boulevard they might fail to notice his small unit parked quietly and half in shade in the middle of the block.

Jules had never in all his life been anywhere but the attic room or without the presence of both his parents for as much as a second.

Their absence was intolerable, and the game was over. At the hatch, he looked down. The shelf was close, but he was scared. He was, however, more scared to be left alone, so he lowered himself. Once on the shelf, he had to jump. He held his breath and did so, closing his eyes as he fell, and rolling when he landed. Shocked but unhurt, he saw the stairs. He'd never seen stairs, much less taken them, and it was difficult for him to do so. He used his hands, backing down, going sideways, terrified of the height. Still, he made his way down the several flights, and though he was confused as to where he was he saw through the bakery window his mother and father kneeling in the half-track, the Mignons outside, their backs to him, and all the soldiers.

He burst through the door, trying to reach Philippe and Cathérine, but Marie Mignon caught him and pressed him to her, hoping in vain that the Germans would take no notice.

"Is that their child?" The major asked.

"No," Marie answered. "Our grandson, a Christian child, a Catholic child, baptized."

The major took a step toward Philippe, who was bleeding from his face and could see through only one eye. "Is that your child?" he asked.

Philippe turned his head to look. Suppressing all emotion, he said, "No." He knew that

Jules would hear this and would not understand.

The major asked Cathérine, "Is that your child?"

It took her entire being not to shake and cry, but she said, "No. That is not my child." Like her husband, she cast no last glance and shed no tears — the most difficult thing in her life.

The major withdrew his pistol from his holster and put it near Cathérine's head. "Is he?" he asked.

"No."

Then he fired.

Philippe's heart burst with powerlessness and regret. Had he not been shot in turn, as he was, he might have died still. It was too much to live through.

Only when Philippe and Cathérine had collapsed, hidden by the sides of the half-track, did Jules speak. It was the first word he had ever said not in a whisper, and it was so loud that it echoed from the façades across the street. *"Maman!"* he cried.

At this, Marie dropped her head, and shed quiet tears. A soldier came and tried to pull Jules away from her. She resisted. Jacques and Louis joined her. The soldiers had rifles and were too close to fire, so they used them as clubs and beat everyone down. The Mignons fell to the ground and waited to be shot. Jules staggered toward the half-track.

As if to prevent the four-year-old from damaging the armored vehicle, one of the soldiers — who had killed many children already — took a quick step after Jules and used the butt of his rifle to smash the back of his head. Jules saw the ground rushing up at him, and then, before losing consciousness, felt the left side of his face hit the pavement.

After the major had shot Philippe, he kept watch up the street, pistol in hand, as if nothing had happened around him. Just as the soldiers remounted their vehicles, pointed their rifles at the Mignons, and waited for the order to fire, the major saw an American tank on the boulevard pass the gap at the end of the street, stop, and slowly backup. "Go!" he ordered. "Drive!"

The engines started, the soldiers dropped behind the armor plate of the half-track, and the SS detachment, still carrying the bodies of Cathérine and Philippe, sped out as the turret of the American tank rotated to aim its gun. The tank fired one round before the targeted vehicles turned onto the boulevard at the other end of the street. The shot hit the second command car, blowing it across the boulevard, but the way was then made clear for the half-track to round the corner, following the lead car. The tank rotated its turret back and continued in the direction in which it had been going.

Marie dragged herself to Jules and pulled

him to her again as Louis tried to rise to his knees. "Is he dead?" he asked his wife.

"No," she answered, the blood from Jules' left cheek soaking into the front of her dress as she cradled him, "but how can he live?"

THE MUSIC LESSON

He did live. Although all his life he wanted to follow his mother and father into realms of which he had no fear if only because they were there, and by sharing in their defeat to know, honor, and love them well, he lived intensely and deeply even so. Music kept him steady on course. Its magic clarified existence, stimulated courage as if from thin air, and illuminated that which could not be understood except in the language of music itself, and of which, when the music ceased, the only remnants were the conviction and desire such as one has when longing to re-enter a dream.

Whether or not the rhythm and syncopation of music matched the pulse, the atomic and subatomic timing within the body, or the symphonic motion of countless electrons in every nerve, channel, and cell, its wavelike melody and narrative elevated all things. Without this, Jules, when he was young, would not have been able to go on. So he sought it out, he studied hard and practiced until he bled, and it saved him.

Through the fifties and into the sixties, when a lucrative career and glory were possible in classical music, his fellow students worked for fame and riches. Moved by ambition — some so much so that they worked harder than he did — they went further. In his field, François did the same, rising to the position of someone respected by his peers and sought by every facet of journalism, even Indonesian TV. Jules was left behind. When whatever talents he could proffer had opened opportunities to rise, he froze, unable to perform in public. He associated the joy of success with betrayal of his mother and father, and as if to be true to them in their darkness as, he imagined, they moved through eternal space, he failed time after time.

But just the music was enough. It made a quiet existence better than that which was royal or rich. Every step and misstep brought him closer to them and made him loyal to all who had come before. Though it never succeeded completely, music promised that sin and suffering might be washed away.

Other cities have been or in time will be liberated, but the nature of Paris is such that when it was liberated in 1944 its beauty swelled as if fed by an artesian stream the Germans had been unable to stem. By coincidence, fashion, or the lack of dyes in wartime, the women of Paris at the Liberation were dressed mainly in white. In their simple white dresses as they marched at the forefront of crowds in celebration, they were like angels. At the Liberation, the impure were made pure, and people who had never experienced happiness suddenly came to know it.

Paris after the war was the creation of Paris before and during the war, and little of the stress and emotion was lost or forgotten. So when Jules was a boy, first in Reims and a few years later in Passy, he was living as much in the war as after it. He always remembered, and often would recall, how at eighteen and brimming over with energy and invincibility — before his induction, before the pine-covered mountains of Algeria, before the experience of exiting an aircraft in flight — he rode on a summer day upon the rear platform of a bus on the *Boul-Miche*, one of those buses that seem to have been part of Paris forever and to be destined to last just as long, but did not. If you were young and agile, you hopped onto the back as they were moving, and smiled at the angry conductor — if he was there to catch you — who then gave you a cardboard ticket after you had paid up.

Jules had just been conscripted and was saying goodbye to the Quartier latin and a way of life he had closely observed but never embraced, as had for example François, who without inhibition gave himself over to study while surrendering his body to wine, tobacco, and frenzies of the intellect. On the bus, Jules looked down the boulevard as the traffic made clouds of almost-sweet diesel smoke. It was hot, and the overarching limbs of the trees swayed slightly in the wind. Nineteen fifty-eight — everything seemed possible.

More than fifty-six years later, the buoyancy of youth long gone, he would make a telephone call to set in motion a series of events that were they to go smoothly or even just adequately would as in the last movement of a symphony unite disparate currents into one stream. Although he himself would never see the braiding of the threads, he hoped that they might save Luc; help Cathérine and David; punish the son-of-a-bitch, lying, dishonorable Jack and the crazy, son-of-a-bitch, lying, dishonorable Rich Panda; allow him to escape jeopardy for what he had done on the Île aux Cygnes; and, finally, achieve at last his greatest ambition.

It would start with a telephone call from which everything else might cascade. Although somewhere south and east of Iceland, eight miles in the air over the darkest ocean, he had laid down the rough outlines of what he had to do, he went over it again and again

394

to rehearse the details and anticipate the unexpected. The dangerous things he had done in his life he had done either in the heat of the moment or as a soldier without choice in the matter. Here, he had a choice, and passion could easily ruin what calculation might achieve.

Before he made the call, to steady himself, clear his mind, and create a kind of alibi, he re-established his routine. It was as if he were two people, one embarking upon something complicated and dangerous, the other quietly going about his business. He would retreat to the routine whenever he felt himself beginning to falter, but, when he regained his footing, go out again.

He began to run once more, gently. He had lost weight in America and now, because of François' revelation, perhaps only a claim, when he could not eat. Blood pressure and chemistry, pulse, and stamina had to be honed to near ideal levels for his age. He would sleep well, eat sparingly, and work as hard on his endurance as he could without pushing enough to trigger the end.

He placed his faith on the frequency of exercise rather than on its intensity or the length of a single session. This made him very, very busy, in that he would run, swim, and do calisthenics and weights four times a day. He ran so slowly that it was almost like fast walking. The swimming was low key as well, as were the calisthenics. In between sessions, he would nap. This regime was so demanding of his time that he had to take regular days off to attend to other business. He did, however, have a lot of time — on the long terrace, in the pool, before he slept, and as he sat in a café for lunch or tea — to work on his plan, which as it grew in detail he kept exclusively in his memory, with nothing written.

Neither tiring himself nor dropping dead, he passed into the new year, during which he would run ten kilometers and swim two every day, and do hundreds of abdominal, stretching, and weight exercises, with much rest, and civilized meals of small portions. He gave up reading the papers and hardly attended to his mail, which would accumulate as if on the desk of the kind of irresponsible person he had never been.

One did not need to read the papers to know about the massacres at *Charlie Hebdo* and the kosher market, or the beatings, boycotts, divestments, and threats. Three years before, after the murder of Jewish children in Toulouse, Jules had come to a conclusion that others were not quite ready to adopt even at present. Now his answer to these events, as most people reacted with surprise, was to maintain a stoic silence and keep up the kind of program common to young musicians embarked upon precompetition: epic, cloistered practice. What they did was like what Olympic athletes do, like the life of a ballet dancer, the charrette of an architect, or the self-isolation and Herculean work of a great scholar. Though Jules had something else in mind, he pursued it with similar devotion even if the months of discipline would no longer be necessary after one single unthreatening hour.

He didn't have much to do with anyone except Cathérine, David, and a few waiters and clerks in Saint-Germain-en-Laye whom he had known for decades. The man at the swimming pool wouldn't even look at him now. He said, once, and only once, after admitting Jules twice a day for a few months, "Congratulations, you now have the body of *Arnaud Schwarzenaigre,* but if you keep this up you're going to drop dead."

"Thank you," answered Jules, as he tossed his towel into a bin and headed out into air so cold it froze the water left in his hair. But, warm and ruddy, he enjoyed the wind.

He still had not made the phone call, but he had the plan in his mind in as much depth and detail as if he had practiced it a thousand times. He had done the necessary research. All that remained to set it in motion was to press the buttons on the telephone. The new term had begun. He paid no attention, because he thought he had left that life behind. But he hadn't quite done that, because no plan is perfect.

Saint-Germain-en-Laye that winter was paler, cleaner, and quieter than Paris. The stones had not been as darkened by soot. As the buildings were lower, more blue sky was visible, and, of course, as it was on a height, it was windier. Except during market hours, the streets were fairly empty, sometimes achieving the winter silence of a country village. Just as the great forest and the long views in all seasons brought the contentment of nature, so did the clarity of winter and the cold that swept cleanly through the town, quieting the streets and returning people to the stillness and assurance of home, with red coals in the hearth.

This kind of winter, the Christmas kind, of lights and joys in darkness, is then often subsumed in the raw, wet cold that kills off the season as it grows old. But rain and sleet can turn into beautiful white snow in the aftermath of which the ground is blinding, the air clear, and the sky blue.

One afternoon in February, Jules was between his penultimate and last exercise sets of the day. He would fall into a narcotic-like sleep in these interludes, and wake up flushed and freezing once he tossed the covers to the side. Going out into the sleet or rain was painful, but he did it time and again. It strengthened him so much that it was dangerous: he was not supposed to live like a young recruit in basic training.

Still in his running clothes, he was cold and he had the fever-like remnants of a nap in winter. Some stretching and calisthenics warmed him up and he was just about to go out when he heard a brutal knocking on his door. This had to be Claude the gardener, who knocked with an identifiable coarseness, as if the cold and wet outside were resentfully petitioning the comfort of a heated house.

It was indeed Claude, whose face was redder than Jules' even though in winter he was not outside that much and spent most of his time in the gatehouse, looking at television and drinking the kind of red wine that comes in square cartons. He'd come through the fog and drizzle. "There's a girl at the gate," he said. "She says she has an appointment."

"What?"

"There's a girl at the gate. She said she has an appointment."

"I don't understand," Jules said, mainly to himself.

But Claude took it literally. "A woman, a female. She's standing near the gate. She says that she, the woman, the female, has an appointment — a meeting, a rendezvous — with you, Jules Lacour."

"I got it."

"You said you didn't."

"I mean, I don't have an appointment with her. I don't have an appointment with anybody."

"I'll tell her that."

"No, no. I may have forgotten."

"What should I tell her? She has a big case."

"Let her in."

"What if there's a machine gun in the case and she wants to assassinate Shymanski?"

"Shymanski's not here and he's not coming back."

"He always says that."

"This time it's for real. The sons are selling the house. New owners on the first of September. Everything changes."

"I didn't know that," Claude said, visibly sinking. You could see it in his face.

"Maybe they'll keep you on."

"If they don't I'll go on strike."

"You're in a union?"

"No."

"There's probably enough time to form a gardeners' union if you start today. Meanwhile, tell the woman, the female, to come in."

"Does she know where to go? Has she been here before?"

"Point to my door. And, Claude. . . ."

"Yes."

"Did you tell her anything about me?"

"No. Why would I?"

"Although what I have in mind doesn't apply to her, that's good. If anyone else comes to me from now on, please tell him nothing about me."

"Him? Who is he?"

"No, if any people come — them."

"What would I tell them?"

"Nothing. That's why I said tell them nothing. And, after this, for everyone who comes to visit me, if you're discrete, I'll give you twenty Euros." It was part of the plan.

"Twenty Euros? Are you sure?"

"I'm sure. Go. Don't let her stand in the . . ." — he looked up — "snow."

The drizzle had become a snow squall when the wind picked up from the west. It drove dark clouds at great speed eastward over the palisade of trees in the park, across the sunken cut of the Seine, toward the tense, ugly walls of La Défense, and then over Paris, which in the thick of the snow was as relaxed as Manet's Olympia reclining on her divan. Large flakes sped nearly sideways in almost parallel lines and were frequently seized by whirlwinds that made them knock about in captured circles, rising, falling, jerking left and right, and sometimes just holding position in the air, like confetti in a photograph. It was almost night, and sometimes the squall was violent enough to obscure the gatehouse. Coming through alterations of light and dark was the tall, slim figure of a woman.

And as Claude had said, she was carrying a massive brown case behind and at her side. In the islands of the squall, color came through like a sunburst — yellow, white, gold, and some black. And as she got closer, Jules thought he had gone mad. For the slim, young figure approaching seemed in appearance exactly the same as the woman in the hotel in Beverly Hills. At first, because of what his eyes told him, he thought it was she.

It was Élodi, dressed in a yellow print silk dress that if not of precisely the same pattern as the dress in California was very close. Élodi's hair, which had been straight, was now buoyant and wavy. Jules didn't really know what women did to their hair — his was cut every month for ten Euros and that was all, except that in the summer the sun lightened it by many shades — but now Élodi's hair, previously a white gold, was richer, almost the color of brass. The silk dress was tight on her body. She wasn't wearing a coat and seemed not to mind the cold. The dress clung to her abdomen as if it were her skin, the silk firm against her breasts.

She walked straight to him, stopped, and paused. Other than that she was carrying a cello, he had no idea what she might be doing there, although just that she was there separated him momentarily from all his concerns. The snow fell for some seconds of silence and accumulated on her hair and on the silk covering her shoulders. A light air of perfume clung to her as a remnant of a formal occasion. Although dressed exquisitely, because she was focused on work she seemed more beautiful than if she had been dressed primarily for show. When she saw him she asked, "Are you going running?"

"I was."

Inside, as the door closed behind them, she said, "In the snow?"

"When I was a young soldier in the mountains of North Africa, I would stay out all night in the snow. You get used to it, and it becomes a point of pride. You don't have a coat."

"I'm not cold. What mountains?"

"In Algeria."

"The snow there must be less snowy, I would think."

"Mostly it disappears the next day with the sun."

"I shouldn't interrupt you," she said, the cello still suspended from her shoulder and not touching the floor.

"That's all right. I can be done for the day."

"Doing what?"

"I run five kilometers and swim one, twice daily."

"Why?"

"I have to pass a very important physical."

"You won't pass if you're dead."

"That's what they always say, but what do

they know? You can put that down."

She carried the cello into the expansive room with the piano. As she put it down she looked about, and through the *portes fenêtres* that led to the terrace. Having taken note of the gatehouse, the address, the grounds, and the Château itself, she said, "I didn't know you were a billionaire."

"I didn't know either," he replied, "because I'm not. You've heard of Henri Shymanski?"

She shook her head to indicate that she hadn't. Had she been older, she would have. Jules thought this was both charming and frightening.

"Pharmaceuticals, jet engines, hotels, ships . . . banks. The house belonged to him, and now it's his sons'. I ran it, watched it, and gave lessons to his Brazilian spawn."

"I beg your pardon?"

"His wife is Brazilian, and the boys are like animals. It's made him perpetually sad. He wanted them to play the piano, to be physicists or artists, to be upright, dignified, honest, and deliberative."

"And they're not?"

"No. They look and speak like drug kingpins, go around with a retinue of bimbos and strumpets, play music in their cars that cracks foundation walls as they pass, beat people up in bars and pay them to shut up, and they sleep until three o'clock in the afternoon."

"Not my type," she said, sitting down on

404

the sofa. "Where *were* you?"

"Where was I?" he repeated. "When?"

"You didn't show up."

"For what?"

"Two lessons. I waited through, the whole time. They don't know," she said, meaning the administration, "so I have credit, but no instruction."

"What lessons? I have nothing until spring."

"No, you're on the calendar, for me."

Jules went to his computer and called up the schedule. She was right. "No one told me."

"How often do you look at your email?"

"I don't, really. If I don't expect anything."

Incredulous, she said, "You don't look at it unless you're expecting something?"

"No."

"Okay, but, on average, how often?"

"Maybe once every two or three weeks. I prefer the telephone or the mail."

Élodi found this funny enough to laugh. Laughter changed her, and, because he really loved it, he found it as upsetting as it was wonderful.

"You're my student now?"

"Yes. I told you I would be."

He read her name in the computer: "Élodi de Challant," he said. It was the first time he had seen it. "Very aristocratic."

"A thousand years ago."

He looked at her from top to toe. She was

not at all, as the other students had said, strange. She was rare, breathtaking. "I don't see," he said, "if indeed your ancestors were magnificently refined, that in those thousand years anything was lost. Did you grow up," he asked, "as one of your fellow students speculated, a lonely girl in a house full of books?"

"I did. I did. From my room you could see the Alps — snow-covered — and we had enough land so that not a single work of man was visible around us. A swimming pool, horses, a tennis court, but neither my father nor my mother played tennis, so I would hit the ball against the backboard — and play the cello, another thing you can do alone, although of course," she said pregnantly and a little archly, "you need a teacher."

"What does your father do?" Jules asked, thinking that her father was probably young enough to be his son.

"Neither of my parents is living. My father tried to make money but lost it. He was never good at that."

"The tennis court? The swimming pool? And the rest?"

"Inherited."

"You're here for the lessons I owe you?" He thought, what am I doing? And he felt a chill and something akin to falling.

"Only if you want to. I had a job in Saint-Germain-en-Laye and thought I would stop by, since you never showed up."

"I'm so sorry. Would you mind if I changed? I don't feel comfortable giving a lesson in running clothes. Maybe if it were summer and everyone else was in shorts."

"I'll set up. Is that yours?" She gestured to Jules' cello leaning in a corner. "Obviously it's yours, but I mean, it looks. . . . Like mine, it's not just off the shelf, is it?"

"No. It was my father's, and it's very old, Venetian. I heard him play it only once."

"Why?"

"Let me change. Did you bring music? Do you have anything specific in mind?"

"Neither."

"Then I suppose it's all up to me."

When Jules re-entered, fully dressed, he looked younger and more dignified than when he was in running clothes. Among other things, in near panic mode he had combed his hair, and the cut and collar of a polo shirt does wonders. Élodi had taken a chair opposite the chair closest to Jules' cello, her own instrument resting as casually against her as a sleeping child, the bow in her right hand pointing relaxedly at the floor.

Before Jules sat down he asked if she would like something to eat or drink. "Thank you. I spent the afternoon at a wedding reception, and the musicians ate for yesterday, today, and tomorrow."

"I remember doing that," Jules said. "Sometimes we drank so much Champagne that what we played sounded Chinese. We were terrified that we wouldn't be paid, but they never seemed to notice, because they had had twice as much Champagne. And young people who have just been married never notice anything but themselves anyway. I remember that, too. It's as if you're in an opium dream."

Élodi seemed slightly hurt by this. He thought he understood, although if it were so it would be very hard to believe. He took both a paternal interest and the liberty to ask, "No boyfriend?" He wanted her to understand that he was too ancient to be exploring with his own interest in mind, but to his embarrassment he realized after he spoke that he was doing just that.

She understood perfectly. She shook her head in an almost imperceptible motion that meant no, and that she suffered.

"Inexplicable," he said. She had brought forth every fatherly instinct in him, and he loved her in that way, too. "Absolutely inexplicable. Except that perhaps you scare them off because they think they can never come close to matching you."

"I'd hardly say that. It's just like everything else. I have refined expectations, a very slim pocketbook, and I don't want to be rescued."

"Someone will come along, someone with

equally refined expectations and an equally slim pocketbook, and you'll fall in love like crazy. My late wife and I — that's her," he said, pointing to a photo of Jacqueline that was on the piano: she was in her gray suit, and devastatingly beautiful — "had the best time of our lives when we had nothing. I know that's a cliché, but you'll see."

Élodi nodded and looked down. She thought after seeing the picture of Jacqueline that what she had assumed and felt about her attractiveness to Jules was both incorrect and presumptive. She was as beautiful as Jacqueline, but she knew that remembrance of things past is the preeminent anchor of the heart.

Jules understood from her expression what she might have been thinking, but rather than explaining to her, as he could not, that the pull of Élodi in the present was no less than the power of Jacqueline in her absence, he changed the subject. They had already waded in too deeply, as they had the first instant they beheld one another, and the first time they touched. Even so, no water was too deep to exit. He'd done so before, and would do so now.

"I've been remiss," he said, "and I apologize. The next lesson will be in the studio in the Cité de la Musique."

"I hate it there," she said. "I hate the architecture. I hate the commute. The Romans made the age of concrete, and it took a thousand years to come to this. . . ." She pointed at the warm, rich wood of her cello. "Look at the patina, like the skin of something that's alive. And now our age is again the age of concrete."

"We could meet in my office at the old faculty. They didn't think about this when they built it, but the acoustics are better. Wood and stone."

"Why not here? Isn't it allowed?"

"It's allowed, but it's so far."

"It reminds me of my house."

This caused him to ask, "How is it that, for someone with a slim pocketbook, you dress as you do?" He meant beautifully. "The suit you were wearing when we recorded. . . ."

"Chanel."

"Chanel. And this?" He gestured toward her sunburst of a dress.

"A young designer in Italy, young but expensive. The only friend I have in Paris is an apprentice — I can't tell you for whom. I promised. They buy these clothes to reverse-engineer the cut, the fabric, the stitching, tailoring. They literally take them apart. She smuggles out the pieces and fits them to me and to herself."

"That's a great trick," Jules said. "And," to compliment her again, "it works."

It was almost dark enough not to be able to tell a white thread from a black thread, and

Claude threw a switch in the gatehouse that sparked on the lights illuminating the compound. Though normally the curse of billionaires, the security lighting now caught and exaggerated the snow, making each gyrating flake glow against the black sky and thickening the snowfall so that it appeared twice as dense as it really was. Student and teacher stared at the storm shining beyond the windows as snow fell almost silently, muffling sound. Because he wanted to love her and knew he could not, there was nothing left to do but begin the lesson.

"I think I can now afford to be direct. If not in absolutely everything, certainly in this. I have nothing to lose, nowhere to go, and I'm just about finished."

She heard in his tone and saw in his expression that this was something, if tinged with regret, that was pleasurable in the freedom it bestowed.

"My duties have been lightened, and are probably in the midst of being lightened further as we speak. I'm not . . . not so much in demand. I was never much in demand, but now there's almost nothing. That's why I don't even check the schedule.

"What I'm supposed to be able to give you is, first, a moderate amount of musicianship, the equivalent of *explication de texte,* say forty percent; then a huge dose of theory, fifty

411

percent; and ten percent of vagary about the philosophy and spirit of music. That is, about the ineffable, of which the moderns think even one percent is too much.

"But I'm deficient according to present beliefs. I give seventy percent to musicianship, ten percent to theory, and twenty percent to the ineffable. That's what makes me vulnerable, because, obviously, the ineffable is ineffable, so it's not as if I can punch a clock and claim a salary for doing what by definition is invisible. But if my teaching and your learning are successful, they'll have effortlessly and undetectably strengthened and purified your musicianship, mating with it so that they'll be indistinguishable both to the audience and to you. That is, together they'll be ninety percent. But, enough, I'm not a statistician. I short-change theory, which is what the leaders in the field crave, because I don't like it. I've never brought myself to assimilate it and I have no patience with it. The language and syntax of music, like the language and syntax of all art, is as imperfect as our bodies. And its relation to mortality is the same as our own. Though the music of language can do this almost as well, nothing expresses so closely human sorrow, joy, and love — in its rhythms, its changes of tone, and changes of tempo — as music. People say God didn't speak directly to us. Maybe He didn't, but He's granted us a powerful part of His language, with which, at the highest, we can come close to dialogue.

"You know Levin of course." Jules had never experienced heroin, but had read that in coursing through the arteries and veins it brought a burst of love and pleasure. He tried not to look at Élodi, but felt intense love and pleasure when he did, so much so that he was unable not to look at her.

"Yes. Who doesn't?"

"You'll have to take his course. He plays like a machine. Never a mistake, never a variation. Have you heard his cadenzas?"

"I haven't."

"And you never will, because he can't do them. The imperfections in how music is played — the small, sometimes microscopic variations in tempo, in pressure on a string, in emphasis — are what give us even in the midst of its perfections the pathos we need so that we can truly love it. It's like a person, whom, though so many of us do not know it, we love as much on account of imperfection as anything else. That's what's so stupid and wasteful about people who pride themselves on their standing, their appearance, their achievements. Love is the great complement to imperfection, its faithful partner."

"What about God?" Élodi asked. "Who's perfect, and yet loved?"

"For Jews God is perfect but imperfect. The God of Israel is jealous, demanding, and sometimes cruel. We argue with Him. It's like a goddamn wrestling match, and exhausting. If you're a Christian — I say 'if' because these days people your age all seem to be proud atheists — your God is split into three parts. He suffered as a man, He was tempted, He even died, just like the rest of us. The more perfect something is, the less it can be loved — like a face, a body, voice, tone, color, or music itself. In playing a piece, don't strive for perfection: it will kill the piece in that it will prevent it from entering the emotions. That's the kind of advice you can't do anything with except perhaps later, when you don't even know you're doing it. It's part of the freeze of counterpoint."

"I've never heard that expression," she said.

"*Stasis* may be a better word — the liberation of the space between two contradictions. Let me explain if I can. If two waves of equal but opposite amplitude meet in water, what do you get?"

"Flat water."

"In sound?"

"Silence."

"Right. From agitation, peace, a perfection that you might have thought unobtainable from the clash of contradictory elements."

"I think you've explained the magic of counterpoint very well."

"Not really. It's inexplicable. I've noted it, that's all. Half of humanity's troubles arise from the inability to see that contradictory propositions can be valid simultaneously. Certainly in music, where the product, in the emotions and in understanding, is superior to the elements that produce it, and has no sound.

"This is nothing new. We have Yang and Yin, Keats resting within the riddle, the Hegelian Dialectic, the whole story of the sexes — and even Versailles."

"Versailles?" she asked.

"Yes. You take it from there."

Élodi felt not only excitement but that she was embraced, loved. She looked up, as if to receive an answer. She always did this upon solving a problem that took some thought. She had done it so often in exams that she was an expert in gymnasium ceilings — their beams, ropes, protected lamps, pulleys, and nets. "I see," she said. "Versailles is simultaneously a crime against humanity in that it was possible only because of the virtual enslavement of a whole nation for centuries, and a tribute to humanity in its occasional beauty."

"What do you mean *occasional*?"

"The buildings, at least, and most of the interiors, are pretty horrible in their excess, but if you focus on the details — much like the abstractions you can produce by enlarging great paintings — there is often consummate beauty, lots of it, hidden in the whole, where the work of the craftsman as artist is

415

sheltered from, in the case of Versailles, the monstrous overall conception.

"And the gardens," she went on, enthusiastically and entirely on her own steam, "though a contradiction of nature because they were dictated by an overly vain human design, nonetheless are saved by nature. They're the real beauty. Versailles would be impossibly nauseating were it not saved by them, wouldn't it? Nature has the talent to soften, forgive, and remake, to create something beautiful out of our mistakes, paradoxes, and counterpoints — even when it comes to you invisibly."

"*Exact!*" Jules exclaimed, approvingly and to compliment her.

She leaned forward, modestly looking down, pleased with herself, and asked, "What shall we play?"

"Any piece you know well and would like to play."

"I've been working on *Sei Lob und Preis mit Ehren.*"

Jules was astounded that she picked this, the signature and emblem of his life. But he tried to check his astonishment, for it was a very well known piece and now quite popular. "Good," he said, "I'll fill in the second part."

"There is no second part." You could see in her face that she thought, how can he think there's a second part?

"I'll make one — following, echoing, rein-

416

forcing. After all, what we're dealing with is a transcription. We have a lot of latitude. And don't worry, I'll watch you. I've been doing this a long time."

She lifted her bow and, after counting to four, began to play. He joined in after the first phrases, offering a respectful but almost playful counterpoint. She was fully taken up by the music, and when they finished she had the satisfaction of having followed it beyond its explicable bounds.

"Beautifully done," he said, "with technical virtuosity, love, and — let's call it — *lift off.* But let me ask you this: when you held the bow, did you know that you were holding it?"

"Yes."

"And when you fingered, did you know that that's what you were doing?"

"Of course."

"Lastly, did you feel the cello against you?"

"How could I not?"

"Then here's part of my twenty percent and their not-even-one percent. Ideally, and it might take years — who knows? — you should be totally unaware that you're holding the bow, fingering the strings, that the cello is against you. You shouldn't be pushing the sound, it should be pulling you. That is, although you're the agency producing it, you should feel only that you're riding upon and within it as *it* carries *you.*"

"And how do I achieve that?" she asked

somewhat skeptically.

"By understanding but then forgetting it — after a billion hours of practice. If you think about how you walk or how you speak normally, you'll stumble. If you trust that the world has its own grace and that sound has its own life, you can enter into both. And only then will musicianship, theory, and the ineffable combine into something greater than the sum of its parts. For this I frequently use an analogy that, however, I feel uncomfortable about using now."

"Why?"

"Because it's about sex."

"Try it."

"Sex? I've already tried it."

She smiled, slightly. "I mean the analogy. I'm not going to scream as if I'd seen a mouse. I've seen plenty of mice and I never screamed."

"I haven't ever mentioned this except in a class full of people, and even then I cautiously introduce it."

"Well you didn't cautiously introduce it now. I'm *twenty-five years old,*" she said, as if that actually meant something. Immediately upon saying it, she felt keen embarrassment for trying to impress that her twenty-five years had conferred upon her a weighty maturity. She saw a faint and compassionate expression that he kindly tried to keep to himself.

"All right. But don't take it wrongly."

"I won't."

"First, wait. There are a few things I forgot to mention." He then referred her to the center of the piece by playing it himself. She was almost exasperated by his diversion, and yet fascinated by half a dozen points of musicianship that he conveyed as effortlessly as if he had done so thousand times before, which he had.

"I see, I see," she would say, and then play a few bars, repeating them until she got it. "That's interesting. That's good."

This lasted for about half an hour during which they both were fully absorbed. Then, thinking he had escaped, he said, "Now, to get the particulars right, you have to paint at first with a very broad brush. Technicians like Levin have no idea of what that means. The broad brush in this case, for this piece and for the classical era from Bach through Mozart, and partly into Beethoven although he marked the transition from classical to modern, is the spirit of the age. Human nature was the same, eternal and universal truths were the same, but conditions other than those of the natural world were different, and the difference must be understood."

"What does that have to do with sex?" she asked. "You want to skip it, don't you? All right, skip it."

"No. That's not so. It's just that when I say

419

it in class people twitter and smile stupidly. I hate the coyness."

"I don't twitter, I don't smile stupidly, and I'm not coy," she said, with an almost royal severity.

He loved it. "I'm not saying you would, or are. Clearly you aren't. All right. I'll go there. The layers I spoke of — musicianship, theory, and spirit — have equivalents of a sort in sex. From top to bottom, first you have just love, transcending mortality, when the physical is elevated paradoxically because it becomes unnecessary and pales in the presence of love. It's a perfect and rare experience, as fleeting and insubstantial as evidences of the soul. I would risk saying that both parties become, as much as is possible in this world, agencies of the divine.

"The next layer down is earthbound and more erotic, and yet not entirely so. Through eros, the other person is central and always in mind. The overwhelming feeling is one of truth and discovery, of knowing someone else intimately and beautifully. Though this is less refined and more common than the first layer, it's by no means accessible to everyone. It's pure love but without a connection to the divine.

"At the bottom layer you have independent eros, in which — somewhat like the highest manifestation but in an entirely opposite way — the particularity of the partners disappears. The sex runs itself and feeds upon itself, which takes you out of yourself in a different way than the other two ways, but it certainly does.

"Most of us stay mainly in one area, which might encompass, for example, the top half of the bottom band and a bit of the middle band. And the range oscillates north or south as slowly as a storm front. In music it's the same. You have the same progression from the base, which is rhythm more or less, through the middle, which is all those things of musicianship and even theory, that make one delight in knowing and feeling it. The highest level is ineffable, so refined that it cannot be captured.

"But ideally, and rarely, in both music and in love, there's a fourth layer, which is when one can exist in the three layers simultaneously — driven, orgasmic, automatic; then, more gently, simultaneously knowing, loving, discovering, sharing, holding back nothing; then, again simultaneously, spiritually, ineffably, even religiously. When all combine, you ascend to another band, whether in music or in love, and you're in heaven."

"Is that all?" she said, meaning the opposite, and, frankly, wanting to try it.

"Yes."

"It's not a line you say to a dressed-up girl in a hotel bar in Davos?" She didn't mean this at all, but she had to take the charge out of the atmosphere.

"I've never been to Davos," Jules said, blushing unnecessarily, "and besides, it's too long to be a line. It's something true that I said to a *beautiful* girl in my house in Saint-Germain-en-Laye. Perhaps I shouldn't have, but at my age you can say such things without being suggestive."

"Really?" she said. "You think so?"

"I hope so. I hope I haven't offended you. I apologize if I have. I look upon such things like someone who's pulling away from them. The fact of departure is now so strong that I no longer fear it. You can look upon them as someone who's arriving."

"Theoretically, and I'm not much one for theory myself," she said, "would it not be possible to meet in the middle?"

"Nature punishes the effort. December/May makes for a great story as long as you can skip the end. It's maybe what stimulated Goethe to write *Faust*. It's not that it's inherently evil, but that the way things are renders it impossible — except perhaps for a few bright moments contrasting with a sad decline."

Élodi took this as a rejection of an advance she was not sure she had either made or wanted to make, because like him she moved between strong attraction and a kind of repulsion that was, in fact, an artifact of attraction. It was confusing to both of them. His love for her was benevolent and giving, as it would be for someone much younger. At the same time it was a desire for her as a woman, pulsingly sexual, intolerant of anything standing between them, even the thinnest silk, or air. Like two positive charges, the magnetic attractions flared in alternation and were not compatible or even present at one and the same time. As one rose on the horizon, the other declined, but only to return and drive out what had driven it out before.

So teacher and student maintained their distance, each thinking that they would do so forever. This became so highly charged that, to escape, Jules took the lead and returned to the matter of music. "The difference in the spirit of one age with the spirit of another," he said, "despite the constancy of both nature and human nature, is legible in music. Death, pain, and tragedy still rule the world, though in the rich countries of the West we insulate ourselves from them as never before in history. But when death, pain, and tragedy were as immediate as they were to everyone, even the privileged, in the time of Bach and Mozart, you have darkness and light coexisting with almost unbearable intensity. Which is why in all of these great pieces — although neither in dirges, which I cannot stomach, nor in silly, triumphal marches — you have the tension between the most glorious, sunny exultation, and the saddest and most beautiful mourning.

"The Bach we did today is just that. It was my father's favorite piece, on this very instrument." He held it out, and brought it back. "He knew how joyful it was, and yet how sad. It was the first piece I heard him play, and the last."

"I do love it," Élodi said, after which followed, to their surprise, their satisfaction, and even to their excitement, a perfect, contented, extended silence.

III.
LOYAL À MORT

THE SUN COMES OUT FOR ARMAND MARTEAU

Edgar Auban had been kind enough to extend the probation of Armand Marteau to March the first. This was because although Armand had failed miserably during the fall — moving not a single policy from mid-October until Christmas — in the week between Christmas and New Year's Eve he had sold a half-million-Euro policy to someone old enough and in ill-enough health to generate a decent premium.

But as the new year crept forward and he moved not a single contract, he began to talk to himself a lot. Although he disguised it by pretending he was on the phone, you could tell by his expression and the fear in his eyes, as well as the fact that he had no earpiece, that he wasn't selling anything but rather making imagined exhortations and asking imaginary questions.

As he went, the way his insurance colleagues across the Channel might have put it, 'round the twist, he became even more isolated and reviled, which is what happens to herd animals when they limp, suffer, and cannot keep up. That no one looked at him gave him the kind of privacy no one wants, every second of which is shame and torment. The worse it got, the worse it got. They still called him hippo, elephantus, *le Titanique,* butter blob, and other such names — Cherbourg in pants, wonder whale (they thought they were creative) — but now it was less with amusement than with hatred, as if each insult, whether to his face or behind his back, was intended to cut a piece off him and batter him down until there was nothing left and, to their intended relief, he was gone.

In February, when in France there is not a single holiday to relieve the gray weeks, long nights, and wet cold, some genius had hypnotized the office staff into believing that the eighteenth was a semi-holiday because it was the feast day of St. Colman of Lindisfarne. Although no one had ever heard of St. Colman of Lindisfarne, everyone took a long lunch with a lot of drinking in an ugly restaurant in La Défense: that is, everyone but Armand Marteau. He was the only person left in the office, charged with taking messages for three hours, in the time slot when new business seldom came in, because people went home to eat. Four to six were the hot hours, as were ten to eleven forty-five in the morning.

In twelve days he would be gone. The Marteaux were practically starving. He had a toothache and could not afford to go to the dentist. His wife cried at night. The children cried during the day. They acted up in school. That morning, as he slept on the way in, someone getting off the train at a stop somewhere where it was drizzling in the dark had slapped him hard on the side of his face, either just for fun or out of hatred. He hadn't been able to see who it was except that when the train started up again some excited youths on the platform were laughing and sticking their tongues out at him as the train pulled from the station.

Then, at the office, they had all slipped away. Everyone. Armand had just unwrapped his sandwich and flattened out the wax paper around it when the phone rang. Assuming that it was someone else's client, for whom he would only relay a message, he wouldn't have answered — out of spite, fastidiousness, and misery. But he hadn't begun his sandwich, so, expecting yet another blow to his pride, he picked up, announcing the name of the subsidiary.

"You're a subsidiary of Acorn?" asked the voice on the other end of the line.

"Yes, we are Acorn."

"Am I in the right place for term life insurance?"

"Yes," Armand replied, cautiously tensing

429

the way a fisherman stays still as he sees a fish approaching his baited hook. The fish hadn't asked specifically for anyone, which meant that Armand was free to take the call. "I'd be happy to serve you. We're the division that deals with policies of a minimum value of five hundred thousand Euros." He expected that to be the end of it.

"I'd like to buy a policy."

"May I ask in what range?"

"Ten million Euros."

Armand's heart thumped in his chest as if it were a cat frantically trying to escape from a cat carrier, but he strained to be nonchalant. "Your age, sir?"

"Seventy-five in June."

The premium would be beyond anything anyone in the office had ever snagged, and the commission would be life saving. As far as Armand knew, although nothing would prevent writing a policy of that magnitude, there was no such policy in effect not only in his location but in any of the others throughout France. If he could do it, he would outshine everyone, he would save his family, get revenge, and secure his position. Outwardly, he remained magically calm. "I'd be happy to discuss this with you at your convenience. Where are you located?"

"Saint-Germain-en-Laye."

"We're in La Défense."

"I know. It's convenient, part of the reason

430

I called you."

"Would you like to come in, or shall I come to you?"

"Why don't you come here?" Jules asked.

"Are you free this afternoon? I can suit your convenience."

"What about now?" Jules proposed.

"Your address?"

Jules recited it.

"I can reach you in less than an hour, certainly. The weather was so bad I didn't take my car," Armand lied. "I'll have to use the train."

"Don't rush," Jules told him. "Take your time. I'll see you when you arrive." He hung up without saying goodbye, like Jack, or the generic kind of person who might buy a ten-million-Euro life insurance policy.

In near shock, Armand gathered his brochures, calculator, and forms, automatically put them in his briefcase, left the office, locked the door, and walked into the elevator like someone who had been hypnotized. He knew they would be mad at him for deserting his post. They would think that this was the final dereliction, the failure that would at last put him under. And if he couldn't sell a policy, they would be right. The thought occurred to him that the call wasn't genuine, and that he would find himself in the rain in Saint-Germain-en-Laye, standing in front not of a house but a butcher shop or police station. Because of this, waiting on the platform, riding on the train, and finding his way through the town was a torture such as one might feel on the drawn-out path to one's execution.

But as Armand Marteau, in dread, left the station and walked through the lovely gardens of Saint-Germain-en-Laye, the sun began to disperse the clouds, which had been no more than a thick mist settled upon the country-side. As it was February 18th, the sun strength was roughly equivalent to that of October 23th. The day had not been too cold, and there was no wind. So, all of a sudden, something like spring arose. The sun came into the clear, surrounded by blue. Remnants of fog, which in the absence of strong light had been gray and dull, now shone in white as they fled upward and disappeared. Evergreens and the stems and branches of deciduous bushes were covered in droplets of condensation left behind as the fog lifted, and they sparkled like a hundred million suns. Best of all, the air was soft and forgiving, as it is when light returns to the world after the dark of winter.

He dared to take this as a sign, but, still, he imagined that nature was merely cruel, and that, as so often it did, it was setting him up the way it does with farmers, who after a glorious summer redolent of perfection then find in drought or hail or pests that they have been tricked. Because so many of his father's crops had failed, Armand Marteau was expecting to see that the address he had been given was in fact a graffitied storefront, its iron gate long rusted and closed.

At the Shymanski gatehouse he didn't know what to think, because as camouflage it was deliberately modest and decrepit. Only when the gate was opened and one could see a small palace set in its own meticulously landscaped park would one realize what splendor lay beyond the nondescript walls. As he knocked, he knew it could go one way or another. And as Claude the now discreet gardener, happy at the prospect of earning twenty Euros, opened the gate, Armand Marteau knew that he had finally been given his chance.

Jules had sold the piano, a small Picasso ceramic that he had always hated, his Volvo, a few first editions, half a dozen Krugerrands, and the little Daubigny. He had consolidated the proceeds of the sales with all his cash and savings into a single checking account, the new balance of which was more than €236,000. Shymanski had gone to the South of France forever, but for the moment his furniture and decorations remained in place. Except for the gardeners, the servants were with him, but the house was alarmed with every beeping and blinking contraption known to man, including nets of laser beams suitable for a great museum.

Jules had disarmed the alarms. Greeting the awestruck Armand Marteau in the main hall, he was dressed in his characteristic blazer but with one of Jacqueline's Hermès silk scarves made into a cravat, which made him look both ridiculous and the part of a billionaire. Shymanski wore cravats. Had Jules not been standing on marble parquet in a magnificent hall with Renaissance oils on the walls, but on some street corner in Paris, he would have looked like an idiot who thought he was David Niven. Here, it was just right.

"Thanks for coming on short notice," he told Armand.

"The client is our reason for existence," Armand stated, trying not to let his knees knock.

"Good, good. I like that," Jules responded as he acted the part of a man imbued with confidence and kindness. "Come in and we can talk." Armand followed briskly. He tried to walk deliberately so as not to thunder against the floor and draw attention to his weight, but the floor was marble so solid it would have remained absolutely silent even had he jumped up and down like a child on a hotel-room bed.

Almost open-mouthed at the decor of the

salon, with its Fragonard, tapestry, eastward view, and extraordinary surfaces made all the richer by carefully designed lighting, Armand tried as hard to pretend that he was calm as Jules tried to pretend that he was in control of his life.

"Subsidiary of Acorn?" Jules asked.

"Directly owned — and backed — by all the resources of Acorn. I'm Armand Marteau, by the way" — he gave Jules his card — "of the La Défense office, high-value, one of two we have in France." He then launched into a general description of Acorn, its reliability, and its history of payment to beneficiaries, explaining that though it was expensive it paid out much more readily than any other company.

"That's why I chose Acorn," Jules said, smiling invisibly. "What is the cost of a ten-million-Euro policy?"

"First, I have to ask why you might want it. We ask that of all our potential clients, so we can know their desires. In your case, it's not readily apparent that you would need such a policy."

"I haven't moved any substantial sums out of the country since Hollande," Jules said, truthfully, thinking of the cash he took to America for use whenever a credit card wouldn't do, "and I don't believe in tax avoidance even if I find the regime of taxation to be punitive and unfair. However, great wealth is often deliberately tied up in distasteful complications that cannot be fully understood except by experts. Upon death, a gate falls on your assets, and the wealthier you are, the more time it takes to lift that gate."

Armand nodded. Everyone knew, or at least suspected, that this was true.

"Except for insurance proceeds. When I die, I want my daughter to have some money immediately, to tide her over until the estate is settled."

"Who would argue with that?" Armand asked. "It's entirely reasonable."

"So then, what's the cost of a term policy for ten million?"

"It's a very large policy, and at your age the premium changes every year, settling somewhere between a base cost (the minimum you'll always pay) and a maximum. The premium determination is made taking into account the investment proceeds of the previous year, but in the first year you pay only the minimum, which is, nonetheless, considerable, and which, in turn, depends upon your health. Do you smoke, or have you ever?"

"Never."

"How would you characterize your health? Excellent, good, fair, or poor?"

"Excellent."

"You're not in treatment for any diagnosed disease or condition?"

"Not at all, fortunately."

"Let's say then that you are in excellent health, a non-smoker, etc. If you meet all the criteria and rate high in the physical, your first-year's premium, payable in quarterly installments, would be two hundred and thirty-five thousand Euros. But in the second year, with the worst possible investment assumption, you might have to pay as much as a million fifty-nine-thousand Euros." He pulled out a laminated chart and unfolded it. "You can see here how it gets crazy. At age one hundred, your premium could be nine million, two hundred thousand Euros, but that's just for illustration, because at the maximum rates by then you would already have paid many times the value of the policy. No one's ever done that."

"Two hundred and thirty-five thousand, divided into four installments?" Jules said. "Why so little in the first year?"

"To bring customers in. Suicide is precluded in the first two years, as are death in a self-piloted aircraft, accidental death in mountain climbing, car racing, and quite a few other pursuits. Statistically, if you're top-rated on the physical, charging the minimum is even a bargain for us. The physical is comprehensive. We write the policy at these rates only if you pass."

"I'm sure I'll pass, and so I'll take this," Jules said as routinely as someone buying a newspaper.

Armand felt a surge of elation. Suddenly it was as if he had no weight. "For ten million?" He could still hardly believe it.

"Yes." Jules acted detached and unconcerned.

"We'll need bank references."

"Of course." Jules went to Shymanski's desk and took out a leather portfolio, into which before Armand Marteau's arrival he had placed copies of his own bank statements and other documents. "My checking account number at BNP Paribas, the branch here" — he threw his right hand in the air, as if directing traffic, pointing to — "thirty-one Rue de Paris, is seven three, eight one, four nine two, eight six. That account is for everyday expenses."

"The balance?"

"I don't know, really. Somewhere between two and three hundred thousand."

As Armand Marteau wrote, he said, "Is there another financial reference, perhaps of greater substance? Not that that's not of great substance! But I ask only because the policy is so large."

"Again, the money is tied up. But, yes, I can give you another. Unlike the checking account, it's not in my own name. It's a trust linked to the house here. The title of the trust is my address."

Armand Marteau wrote the address as Jules

gave it to him, reading it back to make sure it was accurate.

"Exactly, followed by 'Nineteen Sixty-Eight Trust'."

"Numbers or written out?"

"Numbers. We established it at the time of the student revolts, because we didn't know what was going to happen." Shymanski had indeed established it then, and for that reason. Jules knew the account number at Société Général because for years he had made symbolic ten-Euro per month payments into it so as to be included in the insurance coverage pertaining to the house.

"It's *not* in your name?"

"No, it's a trust. Just the address. I fund it periodically, of course." That was entirely true.

"The balance?"

"Again, I don't really know." He knew roughly. It was the last Shymanski trust not to have fallen to the monster boys, and Shymanski had stuffed many of his remaining assets into it. They would have it, Shymanski had told Jules, disclosing the amount, by the end of the year. Meanwhile, it was frozen. "But it's certainly north of fifty million," Jules told Armand.

"Fifty million?" Armand Marteau repeated as a question, his eyes almost bulging.

"It serves real estate needs, here and in many other places. Commercial as well."

"You *will* pass the physical," Armand said, almost as an order.

Jules took this graciously. "Of course I will. I run and swim every day. I don't know how long I'll stay in good health, given my age, but, right now. . . ."

"That's another thing," Armand said. "The high-value policies come automatically with disability. If you become legally disabled, you get five thousand Euros a month. The benefit is part and parcel of the life insurance. You can't choose to reject it."

"Why would I?"

"Ah! Well, here's the problem — for some people. Obviously, you wouldn't need it, but you'd have to take it for the whole policy to remain in force, and you can't work. You could manage your personal investments, but you'd be forbidden to practice your profession, whatever that might be, in any form whatsoever. But you're retired, is that not so?"

"No. I'm on a reduced schedule, but employed by the University. I teach privately as well. I compose. Surely I could sit in my house and write music?"

"You could. But if you were found out, the policy would be voided."

"I couldn't continue to have private students?"

"No."

"What if I didn't charge them? I don't need

440

the money."

"It wouldn't matter. It's the customary activity that figures in."

"I couldn't write a sonata for my own entertainment?"

"Have you, in the past, ever sold a musical composition?"

"Yes."

"Then, no."

"How would anyone know?"

"They might not, it's true, but if they did. . . ."

"What? Do they, that is, do you, have detectives?"

Armand let seconds pass. He inched forward on his chair, and leaned in toward Jules. Then he raised his head so as to look at Jules directly. "They have a *lot* of detectives, whose incentive is a percentage of whatever policy they can void."

"What percentage?"

"Ten. That is, ten percent of whatever you've paid in, if fraud is discovered before the policy pays out. If it has paid out and the company can claw back the money, the incentive is still ten percent, which in your case, with your policy, would be a million Euros. If after the policy goes into effect there's a hint of irregularity, you'll be very popular, I assure you."

"So I couldn't even write a little ditty?"

"Ditty, symphony, sonata, song, to them it

would all be the same."

After an hour and a half of filling out forms, obtaining the proper signatures, and receiving a check for the first quarterly payment when the physical was completed and successful, Armand exited onto the street and turned left into a golden sunset spreading across a powder-blue sky. His round and ruddy face was orange and glowing, his blue eyes like aquamarines.

He breathed hard and held his briefcase tightly. Perhaps it was a dream, but no. Now he felt that he could sell such policies quite easily, maybe even several a month. Assuming that Jules would pass the physical, Armand Marteau would be the top performer. Edgar Auban would reprimand and threaten him the next morning, and Armand would say, nonchalantly, "Yesterday I sold a ten-million-Euro policy to a man who's going to be seventy-five in June. I have his signature. I have the check." And then he would watch Edgar Auban either faint or float up to the ceiling.

Walking through Saint-Germain-en-Laye, through air that despite the date was balmy, and in light that was magically bright, Armand thought, is this what it's like to be thin? To be handsome? To be rich? To be admired?

Spring Fire and Smoke

Jules went into the physical for which, without intending to, he had prepared all his adult life. But as in war, preparation was no guarantee. Things go wrong in the body independently of will, devotion, discipline, or virtue. It can happen any time, but is sure to happen to the old, then to cascade, and then to end. The tests would bring to light processes and balances that he could neither read nor directly influence. As there was only so much he could do, he entered the assessment in a state of calm and with a prayer that he didn't pray but felt. For the Jews of Eastern Europe, who for ages had their synagogues in unheated hovels, there were cathedrals in the air, which amplified modest prayers, if heartfelt, into a choir of confirming voices. If perhaps the assimilated Lacours of Holland and France had thought themselves different from the Jews of the East, the war had made them one.

Cathérine and David were now prepared

for Luc to die, and as he declined they crossed into despair. All they could manage was to take care of him day by day. Everything else was defeat. Death, their own as well, seemed very close. Both of them had come to look much older than they were. Jules understood only too well that were Luc to die it would be the end of the line for a chain of life that had started at the beginning of time. It happens every day, but is no less painful for being commonplace.

Although his possessions — paintings, photographs, books, letters, clothing — were only material, they had received the impress of his life and of his little family when it was young. These things would all be dispersed and destroyed. How many photographs of people who were deeply loved ended up in junk shops and flea markets, curiosities treated without respect for the souls that, were one to look closely, one could see in them? Photographs and letters would go to Cathérine, but then where?

Though he hardly knew Élodi, he loved her as if he were twenty, but he wasn't twenty. So she, like the composition for the Americans, like his career, his works, his whole life, he accounted his failure. The one thing left to him, his last act, might yet fail as well, although he was certain that, like everyone else, he would succeed in hitting the center of the black target to which he felt himself rushing faster and faster, the target that, once struck, ends the game. Not only would he not resist the increasing acceleration, now he would push it along, aiming himself at reckless speed, a missile in love with the point of impact.

With such thoughts, he submitted to examination at the Clinique de Grève, a neglected and secondary facility where, to be in residence, the doctors must have done something wrong. Maybe they weren't even doctors, although they said they were. Jules was sure that, given the circumstances, his blood pressure would be the kind of number that could break the bank at Monte Carlo.

"Unbelievable," the doctor said, after the third measurement. "One ten over seventy. I thought there was something wrong with the machine, or that the cuff was not on right. No medicine?"

"No medicine."

"Are you sure? For someone your age. . . ."

"I don't take any medications whatsoever."

"How can that be? It's crazy. Your blood work is in the normal range except for bilirubin, which is high — Gilbert's syndrome. You'll live forever."

"I've been told that," Jules said, "but I think it's optimistic."

The doctor was Russian, bald, thirty-eight, and amazed. "And I've never seen anyone over fifty with normal liver function, especially a Frenchman. It's always at least a little out of whack."

"No medications," Jules said, almost like an idiot or a fanatic. "I hesitate to take aspirin. Virtually no alcohol. No caffeine. Chocolate, yes. Never tobacco even once. Exercise like an athlete in training. Sleep like a dog. Spend hours on the terrace, doing nothing. Play music." He began to laugh because he sounded insane, and his laughter made him seem even more so.

But the doctor was Russian, so it didn't matter, because they can't tell the difference. "Terrific," he told him. Then, "*Horosho*! You must have good genes. How long did your parents live, assuming they're no longer with us?"

"They died in the war." This, the Russian doctor did understand. "I'll never know how long they might have lived. They certainly would not be alive now. When they would have been a hundred, I felt a kind of relief, as the years that were taken from them were finally over."

"Okay. Lie down."

After a thorough and uneventful physical exam, Jules had an uneventful EKG, a chest x-ray, and an assessment of his mental acuity. He passed. Then, with the EKG leads still attached, they put him on a treadmill.

"You do this to old men?" he asked.

"Gently," was the reply.

It started that way, but as he adapted to the increasing pace and elevation, it wasn't so gentle. He hadn't run as hard since his collapse, but he didn't want to quit, for fear that they would think he was in distress. In fact, he had easily passed earlier in the test, but the doctor was scientifically curious about such an intact specimen at such an advanced age, and given that the pulse and the EKG were clipping along as orderly as those of a young man, speed and elevation were increased until, sweating as if he were running in the desert, Jules was racing at the ramp's peak elevation and at fourteen kilometers per hour. He didn't want to die, but he couldn't ask to stop.

"Feel good?" the doctor asked.

Jules nodded as if it were true, but his expression was too pained to convince. Then, he thanked God, the machine was stopped.

"You passed for someone much younger. How do you like that? Leave the EKG on and have a seat. We'll watch until your pulse returns to normal, just to make sure."

"I passed?"

"You did a lot more than pass."

"I mean, the whole thing?"

"They won't go beyond the actuarial tables for your age, but they'd write you a million policies if they could. They like people like you. They like Gilbert's syndrome. They like

447

non-smokers. You're good business. What company?"

"Acorn."

"High-value?"

"Yes."

"Then you'll live forever."

"Actually," Jules told him, "I'll live till I die."

A week later, Armand Marteau delivered the policy in person. He had been saved, and the weather cooperated with his happiness, bursting into premature spring. He brought four copies. "Most people," he informed Jules, "put one in a safe deposit box, keep one at home, and give a copy to each beneficiary. Thus, I've brought four for you, and a card you can carry in your wallet. Let's go over it for your consent so you can sign off on a seven-sixty-A to show that the terms have been explained and accepted."

The policy was locked-in — for Luc, for Cathérine, and a portion (ten percent: a million Euros) for Élodi, who wouldn't receive a copy. The insurance company would find her. Cathérine had to have the policy in hand so as to get the money as quickly as possible. Her copy would be in an envelope to be opened only after Jules' death, but he would push her to plan for what they wanted to do. She would protest that it was impossible and therefore senseless, but she would accede —

not because of him but because of Luc.

Armand Marteau carefully went over the terms. Ten million Euros. Everything else paled in the face of that. "Euro five million to be held in trust for Luc Hirsch by Cathérine Hirsch, née Cathérine Lacour, Trustee. Euro four million to Cathérine Hirsch, née Cathérine Lacour. And Euro one million to Élodi de Challant. It would be good for you to provide me with addresses, contact information, and, if possible, a photocopy of their identity cards, although none of this is required."

"I'll see what I can do. I don't think I'll be able to copy the card of Mademoiselle de Challant. Did the physical rank me highly?" Jules asked. He knew. He wanted confirmation.

"The highest for your age."

"The bank references?"

Armand Marteau reddened. "Yes, they were fine."

"But?"

"The trust. The bank can give no information as to its owners. The money in it was as you said, the numbers and titles correct, but no names are accessible to me."

"Taxes," Jules said. "You understand."

Armand looked around, lowered his voice. "Yes. I gave you the benefit of the doubt. The normal procedure would be to pursue it until there was an answer, but I passed it through."

"And what if, purely hypothetically, I were not the owner of the trust? What would happen? Would that be fraud?"

Because of his interest in the matter, Armand may not have been the most meticulous examiner possible, although as a salesman he was not an examiner. "No, it would not be fraud. When we vetted that provision the responsibility became ours, as we are obligated to exercise due diligence. Fraud would be more in the nature of misrepresenting your health, or anything that occurs after policy acceptance, such as a faked death. It's our job to determine if you qualify for the policy, not yours. After all, there's no law that says we couldn't write a ten-million-Euro policy for a Gypsy."

"A poor Gypsy?"

"Most of them are poor. I think maybe all of them. Just as long as you pay your premiums. . . ."

"Armand," Jules said. Armand was young enough that Jules could be familiar. "Why didn't you pursue it?"

"Because of this house," he said, looking up and around. "It suggests that pursuing it would be unnecessary. Your manner and bearing, and your kindness, also suggest that it would be unnecessary." By now, Armand knew that something was out of kilter. He saw it in Jules' eyes and expression. "And because, Monsieur Lacour," he said, "I have a family."

"You have a family."

"Yes."

"Who would, otherwise," Jules asked, feeling his way, "be in distress? If you had not sold this policy?"

In briefly closing his eyes, Armand Marteau confirmed that this was so.

Neither of them said anything until Jules asked, "What would happen to you if they discovered that I was not the beneficiary of the trust?"

"They won't. They can't."

"How is that?"

"The verification is done with emails, and every six months the servers are wiped clean. That's Acorn, worldwide, if the law allows. Certain records we have to keep, but we keep only those. There have been too many investigations, I suppose. No one ever bothers anyway to check the appropriateness of the sale. It's the premiums that count, and, as you saw, suicide is excluded, as would be hiring someone to murder you, or anything such as that. If you die tomorrow, that's too bad for them. They'd fire me, that's for sure, but I received a two-hundred-thousand-Euro bonus just for writing the contract, I get another two hundred thousand when the policy pays out, and they can't touch that either."

"You don't like them."

"No," Armand answered nervously, "I don't."

Jules smiled slightly. "Neither do I."

Now they stared at one another somewhat in shock, having discovered, although not daring to speak of it, that they were accidental co-conspirators. Because of this, they both became extremely polite and distant, as if they were afraid of one another.

"So," Jules asked as he saw Armand out, "tell me again. When do they dump the servers?"

"August."

"What date?"

"The first."

"You're sure."

"I've been there a while."

"You've been a great help, Monsieur Marteau."

"And so have you, Monsieur Lacour. Thank you."

Halfway down the drive, Armand Marteau turned back to wave to Jules, who was still watching him from the doorway.

Now that Jules knew approximately the time of his death, he felt truly free for the first time in his life. Although he didn't believe that he would actually come to see his parents, Jacqueline, or the Mignons, he took the greatest comfort that he had ever experienced, in knowing that by following them, he would be like them. He didn't look forward to death, but he was happy that it would come, if it would — according to his plan — when he was straining at his utmost, flushed and red, in the sun, and in the open air. On the path above the Seine, in the heat of summer, he could hit the gravel hard and go down fighting.

In the time remaining, he had Paris past and present, with colors and light, and layer upon layer of sound and music drifting over the whited city like the smoke of spring fires.

As Light and Warmth Put France at Ease

As light and warmth put France at ease, winter elided gracefully into spring. Cathérine thought her father had lost his mind. Because she hadn't enough strength left to pity him, she was frightened instead. David counseled patience, but she had none to spare and would lash out at Jules when she felt he was acting crazily. That he was insistent and unrelenting convinced her only the more that he was out of his senses. When she begged him to see a psychiatrist he laughed, and said, "I saw one. He was riding in a bus around and around the Rond Point. Or maybe he was chasing a hamster in the pet store, 'round and 'round on the wonder wheel." After he said things like this he would laugh like a crazy person. It rather shook her confidence in him.

Luc had stabilized but not improved. The prognosis remained the same. Cathérine couldn't bring herself to banish her father from the house, but every time he came she wanted to strike him physically, because he brought information about clinics in Switzerland and the United States — in Boston, Baltimore, Ohio, Texas, and Minnesota — and information from the Internet that covered real estate, climate, schools, immigration, banking, etc. It enraged her.

"If you're going to be so stupid as to show us real estate ads for these places, why is every house over two million Euros? We can't qualify for a visa to live in these countries, or even afford to visit, and the course of treatment wouldn't be covered in any one of them. Why? Why?" And then as often as not she would break down in tears, and despite the fact that he was the cause of it she would go to his arms as she had when she was a little girl. Her hair was still red — many shades lighter than her mother's deep auburn — and she still had the freckles common to both Celts and Jews, although no one knew why.

"Make these plans and be ready to go," he said authoritatively.

She pulled away, took in a long breath, looked at him in frustration and astonishment, and replied, "It's cruel of you. We don't have the money. You don't have the money. Is Shymanski going to give it to us?"

"No."

"Then, what? You don't have secret wealth. Did the grandparents have diamonds? Are

455

you going to rob a bank?"

"I just think that you should plan on taking Luc to one of these places, living there as he gets treatment, and — because of the situation here — staying. In the middle of August."

"That's impossible."

"Have everything ready to go just in case. Promise."

"We don't have the time!"

"You have the time."

"False hope."

"Cathérine, I respect you greatly, but I've seen much more than you have. I know more. There are things in the past and in the present that I absolutely cannot tell you. You'll have to trust me. Why would I hurt you?"

So Cathérine did as he asked, but it hurt to fly up in such a dream when her bonds held her so tightly to the ground.

Although Jules knew that in regard to Luc, Cathérine, and David he was anything but mad, he admitted to himself that in regard to Élodi, quite apart from his now damaged relation to Jacqueline, to whom he had remained loyal nonetheless and whom he would always love no matter how painful it might be; quite apart from his morals, ethics, and concern for the girl herself; apart from his contempt for professors who fell in love with their students; apart from his strong suspicion that a single kiss would shatter not

456

only the illusion but that all feeling on his part and any on hers, if indeed she harbored any, would cruelly vanish, leaving as punishment emptiness and a sense of sin; and apart from the unseemliness of it, his knowledge of his failing body, and his rapidly approaching death; apart from all that, he loved her — inappropriately, wrongly, foolishly, and hardly knowing her. He had touched her hand, once.

Though on one level he thought he was suffering a delusion or perhaps a fall into schizophrenia, in his mind Élodi had somehow fused with the city, the low, gray and white, undulating city that over a long history had fallen as softly and soundlessly as a blanket across its rounded and submissive terrain. Like the women who had led the surging crowds at the Liberation, at whom he had stared in photographs as a child, hoping and believing that they were angels who could make whole what had been lost and that they might bring back his parents, whose bodies had never been found. . . . Like the women in white at the head of jubilant waves on the streets of Paris in the shock of freedom, Élodi appeared to him in white as well, suspended above the ground, her form and presence indistinguishable from music in the same way that pure energy, which is not matter, is what matter is made of. It was as if she flew, as if she were with him even when she was not present, the angel he had once hoped for. It was a sad thing, because he knew that, as much as he might want to, he would never ask her, so early, to share the burdens of age.

Spring, however, is the season of benevolent surprises. The air is soft, the soil is warm, colors bloom in the sunlight, and the world is again like a garden, though when night falls winter comes halfway back. The alternation of rich, warm days and cold nights sparkling with stars is like a declaration that everything is possible but nothing is promised, that what is given will be reclaimed.

Because Jules had turned cold to her, Élodi stopped the lessons. She thought that, angry because of her forwardness, he had pulled away. In the painful and embarrassing position of having opened herself warmly and courageously only to be rejected, she quickly came to resent him, but she didn't understand that it was only with the most agonizing discipline that he was able to resist her attraction. She felt as if he were punishing her, so she transferred to another teacher — to Levin, his rival — and broke off all contact. Though it was what he wanted, he found it impossibly difficult. He tried not to think of her, but thought of her all the time. She tried to put him out of mind, but she thought of him sometimes with overpowering love.

Now he had no individual students, and only one class every week, sparsely attended.

His reputation among the up-and-coming and those in mid-career was that of someone who was used up and on the way out, as most certainly he was, even though he retained every quality, skill, and talent for which students once had sought him. But he was suddenly older, and it seemed useless for him to focus on and repeat things he had known and practiced for most of his life. That which to the public had formerly been exciting was now forgotten.

Many years before, as he struggled to support his young family, he had had a job in a quartet playing at a Swedish Embassy reception. During a break in the music he rested quietly on his gilded chair, unnoticed by the British and American ambassadors in conversation nearby. The American asked the Englishman if he had seen an editorial in *Le Monde* the day before. "I don't read the papers," the Englishman replied. "They're not worthwhile."

"Cables are enough?"

"Cables are too much, and I read them only when I must. We have a low-level person who stands on the cliffs at Dover and barks across the Channel." Understating while overstating, he was perfectly in character, and, still holding his bow, Jules cocked his head to listen.

"But really," the American said. "You have to know what's going on. I spend hours and hours each day keeping up."

"I don't."

"How is that? How can you not?"

"There are only so many plots of action," the British ambassador said, "and they repeat themselves. If not exactly, still closely. I've been in the diplomatic service for almost fifty years, and when something comes up, as it does every day, I need know only the one or two details that depart from the same thing I've seen a hundred times before. My young aides are surprised as each situation unfurls. That's how they learn. But I know what's coming already and can save a lot of effort. They look to us not because we're smarter — we aren't — but simply because we've been there. It's all very neat, and given that when you get to be my age you have to conserve your energy, it dovetails."

"I'll try it," the American ambassador promised. But he was thirty years younger.

"You can't. Not yet. It wouldn't work. Eventually, however, it just comes to you. You slide into it without even knowing, and it's a wonderful way to end up, because it's like looking back at the world as if it were a play. You see things as a whole."

Upon hearing this, Jules had looked forward to when he might have calm, clear vision, and equanimity. But he'd had no choice other than to plunge back into getting and spending, striving, struggling, and all the things appropriate to his age at the time.

Perhaps because of something in her early life, the way she was raised, her loneliness, or a quality inherent to her, Élodi had passed those things by and was already in the state of those whose appetites have largely disappeared and their lifelong desires become just a flicker or a dim memory. At an inappropriately young age, combined with the resilience, strength, and sexual heat of youth, she had the outlook of a woman who had lived a long and full life. In that way, Jules was appropriate for her, though cruelly appended was that it could only have been for a very short and perhaps unhealthy few years.

Having passed by and passed up just about everything, and now, in a sense, actually rich, because he knew he would make only one more quarterly insurance payment and had therefore more than a hundred thousand Euros left to spend before August — more than one thousand a day — Jules decided that he would try to let down his guard. The insurance proceeds were set to go where they were needed. He had thinned out his possessions and organized those that remained for Cathérine to keep. He paid no rent, owed nothing to anyone, and had dissolved his friendships not out of anger but because it was time for them to end. He would not even have remained friends with François Ehrenshtamm would that have been possible. Unlike the British ambassador, François was still enmeshed in the details of life. He was ambitious and craved reward. Jules didn't know whether François' youthful energy upwelled to fulfill the needs of his continuing appetites, or if his continuing appetites were the result of upwelling youthful energy. But it didn't matter, because, like Jules, François was in a boat with no oars.

That boat was rapidly approaching falls within a stone's throw. The mist from torrents of water had already sparkled down on them as it arced back and rose from the edge. Beyond the edge the world was blue, the drop infinite, and no one had ever seen beyond it. Now that it was so close, Jules was fixed on what was ahead, but François was still blindly concerned with his position in the boat, fighting with anyone who would fight with him about definitions, words, economics, justice, and ideas, all so that he might continue to accumulate that which he soon would not at all need.

Jules taught his one remaining class just out of habit, like making his bed when he got up in the morning. Some people, because no private person must make his bed, don't. He did, always and always meticulously. Apart from continuing certain lifelong routines and bringing expensive gifts to Cathérine and David — they thought he had robbed a bank, which fit intriguingly with his insistence that they plan for Switzerland or America — he spent his days walking through Paris and Saint-Germain-en-Laye, in the forest there, and the gardens, where he would sit in the spring sun for hours, resting, still, and listening to the wind.

Although he went as much as possible to parks, high overlooks, and other beautiful places, he found beauty even in commercial quarters and industrial districts — in the spring sun shining on a wall, or in small bits of greenery clinging to nothing or having arisen from cracks in crumbling concrete. He delighted in form, warmth, and the breeze, in shades of color, and in changing light. He sometimes walked all day, stopping in a restaurant and, without looking at prices, ordering exactly what he wanted. He didn't care if, when walking through a dangerous place, as he often did, he would be attacked or even killed — although he thought it best to stay alive until the second day of August, after the Acorn servers were purged. He slept when he wished, ate when he wished and what he wished, and did what he had always wanted to do from the time he had first learned music but had never found the courage to start: he began to write a symphony.

It came naturally, if slowly because of all the parts. He would dream the music with fidelity that exceeded that of music in the world, awaken to note the themes for all the instruments, and later in the day or evening fill them in note by note. He had always dreamed music but never written it down. Not only because he had never seemed to have had the time, but because it had always seemed too close to Beethoven — not Mozart or Bach — and he assumed that no one was interested in a symphony-length, Beethoven-like cadenza by Jules Lacour. Now it didn't matter who was interested or not. He wrote it because it called out to be written, and he calculated that if he kept up the pace it might be finished by the end of July.

He would talk, sometimes for hours, to his mother and father, whom he hardly knew; to Luc, imagining him as a young man; to Cathérine; and to Jacqueline. He paced the huge room, gesticulating and speaking out loud especially to Jacqueline's photograph, not quite as if she were there but rather as if he were communicating with someone on the other side of a glacial crevasse or a small river. He spoke to Cathérine in a way in which he was unable to speak with her when he was with her. He told his parents what his life had been like, and that he had never forgotten them and never would. And he spoke to Élodi, apologizing for allowing himself to take her lead or having led her on — he was not sure which.

Early in May, he decided to go to the Louvre. It was not for edification, to study, or to learn, but rather to look at the paintings and marbles without intellectual exercise and let their colors and forms flow through him as if someone in charge of the museum had ordered the opening of windows and doors to allow the fresh air of spring to pour into the galleries.

Though Paris was immense, he hoped at every turn of every corner to see Élodi coming down each newly opened prospect. He dreamed that he might then finally embrace and kiss her, the gift of coincidence enclosing them briefly, as if in parentheses. It hadn't happened, and he ached to think that it would not.

A lifetime of profession and practice allowed Jules to hear music without any kind of electronic device. The stores of his memory and his precision of pitch enabled him to reproduce the sound of music without physically hearing it, although the inexplicable thing was that even so, without the actual sound it did not have the same transcendent power. He had always been annoyed by speculations about Beethoven's deafness. How could Beethoven have continued composing if he couldn't hear? The answer was simple. He heard music despite his deafness as precisely as if he had had the ears of a newborn. It was all inside. But whether or not at that point in his life he could enjoy it was an open question.

Without benefit of the implements stuck in the ears of entire upcoming generations, Jules listened to whatever music he wished, and wherever he was it enhanced form and motion. Clouds scudding by were fine enough, perhaps even captivating, but with music they seemed to hint at the answer to all questions in their graceful obedience to the rhythm, syncopation, and counterpoint present in all things. The pulsing of electrons, flashing of stars, harmonies of orbiting planets, the apparently disjointed movements of traffic coursing through the arteries of a city, or of blood faithfully flowing throughout the body for a hundred years without cease, were set to one elemental interval of motion. All the variations were only the symphonic components weaving in and out of the main theme. Music opened up and made apprehensible everything as it ran together and pointed in one direction too distant and bright to be intelligible but perfectly comforting nonetheless.

As he walked through Paris, music deepened the sight of everything. From jets inscribing white lines across a powder blue sky, to leaves shifting only a few millimeters in bright sun, or the grace of a woman moving through a garden, never had the world seemed so beautiful and forgiving.

■ ■ ■ ■

At the Louvre, Jules was not conventional. His approach was somewhat like experiencing a sauna in reverse. In the Finnish style, you heated yourself to almost boiling, then plunged into ice water, which clarified and calmed. But rather than hot followed by cold, Jules would spend half an hour in the statuary hall, staring at the marbles until everything dissolved into motionless white. Cleansed, as it were, he would move to the painting galleries, where form and color would rush in, the wealth and density of the imagery as overwhelming as being taken by the wild surf of a remote ocean.

Given a limit to what he could absorb, he always had to rest, which he would do in the Louvre's bookstore. Every time he visited Cathérine and David he brought presents: books and prints for them, toys for Luc. Because Cathérine didn't know that everything would end in August, and he had recently spent more than three thousand Euros on copper engravings and reproductions of Greek marbles, she was on the verge of having him committed.

With his arms full of books and toys, he moved toward the cash registers. Standing off to the side in a passage that led from the center aisle, was Élodi. As he approached her, without taking her eyes from the book in which she was absorbed, she stepped to the side and politely excused herself, until she saw that it was he, and then it was as if she had walked into a wall. They looked at one another for a wonderfully long time.

"What's that?" he finally asked, about the book she was holding.

She held it up: *Les Maîtres du Marbre, Carrare 1300-1600,* by Christiane Klapisch-Zuber. On the cover was a picture of a quarry.

"Carerra marble is a most interesting subject, isn't it," Jules said, gently teasing. "The last — I would guess — thirty or forty cellists I've taught always had a book about marble with them during their lessons. When I'd leave the room and come back, they'd be reading it, and I'd have to clap hands to get them out of the trance."

Never at a loss, Élodi replied, "Okay, that's me. And you? You're buying toys?" It was an affectionate and emotional accusation.

"You've heard of second childhoods? This is my fourth."

She looked at the pile in his arms. " 'Babar Goes Fishing Magnetic Catch and Release Game?' " She read further, " 'Ages three to five?' "

"Did you ever play it?" he asked.

She shook her head.

"Then how would you know? It's very calming if you play while listening to Erik

Satie. It makes you feel like Daubigny painting on his boat. That was always a dream of
mine, that on a boat drifting down the rivers
of France I would paint what I saw on the
banks."

"Then why music?"

"It's superior, and more discernible, in that
it fully occupies you until it ends. Then it's
gone. It's linear, it vanishes, it leaves you both
sad and fulfilled. And I inherited it. It was
my father's profession and now it's mine.
Also, I draw like a two-year-old. You stopped
coming."

"You made me stop coming."

"I know. I can explain."

"With your arms full of toys?"

In the Tuileries they paused to sit by the first
fountain west of the Louvre, the one almost
embraced by the wings of the palace but
slipped from their grasp like a dropped ball.
The green metal chairs littered about the
gardens were new and had little of the feel of
the essential Paris that Jules once had thought
would remain fixed throughout his life. Since
his youth, someone had invented an epoxy or
other compound that kept the slats shiny and
smooth without wear. Like civilization itself,
they seemed frictionless and unworn, with no
story except things to come. Their time had
just begun, there was nothing rough and
knowing about them even though eventually

they, too, would be old.

"I have to rest," he said, despite the fact that he could have run, however slowly, all the way to Saint-Germain-en-Laye, but he wanted her to know by way of warning, to remind her, that he was old. This was because, as they walked, they walked together with the rhythm of a man and a woman who are in love. There was a lightness, an expectation, and an exactitude to their step, an excitement that carried them forward as if gravity had disappeared from the world.

"I have to rest, too," she said. Obviously she didn't. They moved their chairs east a few meters when a south wind carried the plume of the fountain out beyond the rim and sprayed water across the gravel. It wouldn't have been disastrous had it wet them. For the first time that spring, the evening was so warm that they might have heard the few tree frogs in the park, awakened after having slept since October. In fact, except sometimes at four o'clock in the morning in the middle of a hot and empty August, the traffic on the Place de La Concorde made it almost always impossible to hear tree frogs or crickets in the Tuileries. But they were there.

"Are you all right?" Élodi placed a hand on his arm. He wondered if it were as electric for her as it was for him, or, for her, more like petting a dog.

"I'm all right, but I don't think I've ever just walked past this fountain. I don't really have to rest, I just like to sit here. Even when I have an appointment and have to rush, I'll sit down for at least a moment, like genuflecting, before I go on."

"Do you genuflect a lot?" she asked mischievously.

"No, but I know how to do it. When I was young the churches were full and it was part of the culture. Even Jews could genuflect perfectly. I think it's a lovely gesture and I've always admired it. Especially when a woman does it, it's extremely graceful and beautiful."

"I do it," she told him, "in church."

This difference between them arose only instantly to disappear, to their pleasurable relief. To check the excitement relief generated, neither said anything, which, in silence, brought them closer. "Why are so many children crying?" Élodi asked. When she saw small children, she felt love for them that was very strong in view of the fact that they were not her own, and a desire to have children that filled her with both pleasure and longing. Jules had the same surge of love — which a foolish person might think inappropriate — but rather than prospective it was an intense remembrance of things past and lost, and the natural emotion of someone in the process of leaving life.

Amidst the crowd at least two children were

471

screaming unhappily. Remembering Cathérine at that age, Jules answered, "They get excited by the playground, but eventually they have to leave. They get tired from the Métro, scared by the crowds, or they're hungry, their clothes are too tight, or the wind blows in their faces. Sometimes they're scared by what they see, and you never know what it is: a face, a dog, it could be anything."

"You have children?"

"A daughter."

"How old is she?"

"She'll be forty soon."

"My," said Élodi, taking in a breath.

"Yes, that's what I say. I don't know what's happening here, but I don't want to walk away, not yet. Perhaps we should have dinner. I know a place nearby that's practically invisible because it's in a courtyard with no sign on the street. It's been there since before the war, and the food is good."

At dusk, the streetlights had begun to come on over the bridges and along the boulevards, and the restaurant was warm and dark, with islands of light. When they entered they were hit by a wash of conversation as cheerful and unintelligible as the sound of a waterfall, and as they walked to their table they smelled bread, wine, candle smoke, perfume, linen, good leather, and gin. The owner seated them near a fireplace in the back and left them with menus. A conical blaze was dancing above four splits of oak that after having spent the winter outside crackled like gunfire. The people who looked at Jules and Élodi thought that she was either his granddaughter or that it was scandalous even for France. As they scanned the menus, Élodi asked, "Why are the Tuileries always so packed with people? Is it just overflow from the Louvre?"

Jules could not converse and read his menu at the same time, so he looked over the top of it to answer. "Overflow from the Louvre is part of it. This area has few parks. Tourists not going to or coming from the Louvre come here to rest after walking around. And I think the French are repeating what their forbears did. For some, a very few, it's atavistically promenading with their aristo-cratic ancestors. For others, it's strutting through the domain of the king they be-headed. In revolutions the populace goes mad with a desire to view the king's real estate. It's always the same. Which one are you?"

"I suppose I'd be promenading like a low-level peacock, which is ridiculous of course. And you?"

"We weren't here."

"Where were you?"

"Germany, Holland, I really don't know as far back as the Revolution. Our family records and memorabilia were lost during the war. It doesn't matter."

"Yes it does."

"No, not compared to what else was lost."

They ordered soup, bread, cheese, but not wine. "Just Perrier," Jules told the owner, and looked over to Élodi, who followed his lead after he said, "I've come to believe that Badoit is too salty."

"No wine?" she asked.

"What I have to tell you I want to tell you without wine, which would make it less difficult. But it must be difficult, because it must be exact."

"Sometimes water is better than wine," she said. She looked around. "The tourists don't come?"

Glancing in the direction of the proprietor, Jules said, "He keeps it out of the guidebooks. How he does that, I don't know, but it's almost like a private dining room. I've always preferred modest restaurants. They're somewhat like women in uniform. Clothes can be a great frame for beauty, but when a woman is in uniform — military, police, nurses — the only thing that matters is her face, and you see the real person, freed of plumage. Although sometimes, I admit, the cut and tailoring of clothing adds to a woman's beauty in a breathtaking fashion." Élodi was reddened from having been in the sun, and she was wearing the dark navy-blue dress with white piping. Jules never smiled in photographs, because he felt that he looked like an idiot when he did. But when Élodi smiled — he had seen pictures of her in chamber music programs tacked to the bulletin boards and kiosks in the Cité de la Musique — she looked not merely beautiful but brilliant.

Like a sinking swimmer grabbing the side of a pool, he returned to the subject of restaurants. She was aware that when he had spoken of the beauty in a woman's face he had not been able to take his eyes off her, and she was also aware that she herself was almost glowing.

"I like station restaurants, cafeterias, the places where truck drivers and construction workers eat, or fishermen, or poorly paid clerks."

"No Michelin stars?"

"Not a one, and very few deathly sauces. The same simplicity for hotels. For years we vacationed in Contaut. . . ."

"Where is that?"

"Do you know Hurtin, or Hurtin Plage?"

"Normandy?"

"Aquitaine, the Gironde. North of the cut above Arcachon are beaches and forests that are as empty as if they were on the coast of Africa. French and German tourists crowd Hurtin Plage, but south of it for sixty kilometers there's nothing. When you get to Contaut you can turn north to Hurtin Plage, or south on sand roads into the forests and dunes. For eight or nine years it's been a national reserve, but before that there were a few shacks near the beach. We used to stay there for two weeks in August, returning in the last two weeks, when Paris is empty and quiet.

"No running water or electricity — kerosene lamps. You could hear the waves and the wind day and night. There's no sleep like sleep lulled by the waves. Other families vacationed in nearby shacks. The fathers were street cleaners, road workers. Our daughter played with their children, we shared fish that we caught, and we watched out for each other. It was a kind of paradise, and if you compare it to a five-star hotel in Nice or Saint-Tropez it would rank so much higher in every way that is truly good that it would make you wonder why people try so hard to dress up and impress — when heaven is to be had in simple things."

She knew that his difficulty in getting to what he wanted to say was because of her. It was wonderfully dangerous.

"I still don't understand why you have no boyfriend," he said from out of the blue — awkwardly, insultingly — hoping and yet not hoping that she would contradict him and say that she did. "Why?"

Her answer was mysterious. "Facial hair." But then he got it.

"You mean the studied, three-days' growth,

as if they think it's what makes a man? I suppose it hides their callowness. Instead of pretending, they should wait until they've suffered and endured. Until they've raised a family, faced death, lost the ones they loved. Then, effortlessly, their faces would show character. Hair is not character."

"Exactly," Élodi said.

"But they're young, and you're young."

"I prefer character. Life is short. I'm not interested in a man who has to costume himself as a man. Besides, it strikes me as dirty. Did it used to be like this?"

"No. People looked like that only when they were shipwrecked or in battle, which is, I suppose, the look young men who have hardly lived want desperately to cultivate."

"I mean everything: civilization."

"Yes, more or less. It's not worse, but it's not better. It depends on the duration of the sample. With a broad enough perspective, things seem to stay the same: periods of advance and decline, peaks and valleys. It's as if we're in an exquisite jungle with pools of fresh, aerated water beneath white waterfalls, colorful and fragrant flowers, calming greenery, fruit on the trees. But there are also tigers, jaguars, and snakes lying in wait. To forget that they're there and may at any moment rip you apart is to live in an illusion. And for fear of them not to see the paradise all around is a greater illusion still. The white

477

froth of the falling water, the fragrant blooms, the tiger burning bright, waiting in the tangle of waxy green, are together necessary and complete. In the gap between them is the spark that makes life."

She looked at him for a moment in which nothing was spoken. "I'd like to go to Contaut someday, and live as you describe."

"You can't. The shacks are gone. It's a national reserve, regulated for the public good. Those days are over for me, but you'll find other places."

"Is that what you wanted to tell me?"

"In a way, yes. But, as difficult as it may be, I have to be more specific."

"You don't, really. I think I understand."

"I know, but I've said it so many times to myself — and I'm so practiced — that I want to tell you." He paused. "You know about votive candles?"

"Of course."

"Have you lit them?"

"When I was little. Not since."

"I noticed this about how a candle in a glass jar will burn. For ninety or ninety-five percent of its ever-diminishing life, the paraffin is white and opaque. But at the end, just before it burns out, it becomes entirely transparent. Just before the end, everything clarifies."

"That's true, as I remember."

"To tell you exactly would be the right thing. I want to."

She waited. He couldn't divine anything about what she thought, except that she was still, and breathing lightly. He tried to remember that she was so much younger, and probably would be in uncharted territory, but on the other hand he himself felt a certain terror. "I'll be matter-of-fact," he said.

"The first instant I saw you I fell in love. It's not right that I did. I don't deserve it, and nothing can or should come of it. I'm three times your age. My own child is much older than you. I've always had contempt for men who reach for life through the agency of a young woman. It's understandable that they would as their lives are rapidly vanishing. But it's unmanly, I'd even say cowardly. Better to tie yourself to the mast of your convictions and loyalties and receive your death without trying to escape in the arms of someone as fresh and beautiful as you, because there is no escape.

"But I wanted you to know, just so that you would know, that when we shook hands when we first met, I didn't want to let go. I saw you extend your hand — do you remember? You were wearing this dress — I don't think I've ever seen anything as beautiful. That I wanted it to last forever is not just my own lunacy, but a testament to you."

"But it happens all the time," she said.

"People falling in love with you when they touch your hand?"

"Love between people of vastly different ages."

"It's a mistake and it doesn't work."

"You could have twenty-five years."

"Really? Have you ever seen a hundred-year-old man, naked?" She laughed, sadly, but she laughed. "Taking it to an even further extreme, my father's great grandfather lived to a hundred and six. That was deep in the nineteenth century. So, if I were a hundred and six, you'd be fifty-six. You'd still have a beautiful, lithe body, and could run and leap, and make love for hours. Besides, I'm not going to live to the year twenty forty-six. Hardly."

"Maybe ten good years?" she asked.

"Unfortunately, it's not a negotiation. I'm not even going to see September."

"You're ill?"

For fear of statements that might be subpoenaed and prejudice the insurance payments, he could say only, "No."

"Then how do you know? At first I thought you were fifty."

"Very kind of you."

"Really."

"Even so. I know because . . . How can I explain it?" He sought something to say other than the truth, but what he did say turned out to be truth that he had felt but not recognized. "It hangs over me. Certain things I've done."

"In the war? Have you killed anyone?"

What he said was, by necessity, veiled. "I think that one would only kill another man if it were to protect the innocent from evil. And that God would forgive saving lives by taking others, if the lives taken were those of the aggressors. And if one doesn't believe in God, then it must seem strange that conscience acts just like Him. But no matter how morally correct or urgent killing may be, you can't escape having done it. The way the world is may have forced you to it, but although you may try, you can't wash away the sin. Good deeds afterward don't compensate. You've ended a life that God has given, extinguished it. You've put paid to a soul that by definition is far beyond anything you can comprehend, and nothing you can do or think can make up for it. If something like this were so, if it were with me all the time, how could I ever bring someone as lovely as you into it?"

"What if you were loved back? Couldn't that hold it in abeyance?"

He thought, she's young. Any feeling she might have for me can vanish in a day or two, which is as it should be.

"What if you're loved in such a way that it doesn't matter how old you are, or if and when you die?" she persisted. Her generosity was beautiful in itself, but he had to answer the question honestly.

481

"It would be the same," he said, expecting her to dissolve in hurt or anger, especially when he went on to say, "There's a tradition in this faculty of young, magnificent girls who get involved with decrepit old musicians like me. It's not right." Now he was sure he had been cruel, and he expected anger.

But Élodi was most unusual. Without either giving way or showing signs of confusion — emotion, yes, you could see it in her face — she said, "I see. I switched over to Levin when I felt you didn't want me to come. Frankly, I play better than he does, because he has no feeling. He's great for pure, technical musicianship, and I do have to finish up with him."

Jules was taken aback by her calm. "After how I just said what I just said, I expected something else, maybe an explosion."

"From me?"

He nodded.

"Not from me. I don't explode. But I want to resume with you, privately. At your house, through the middle of July, when I leave Paris for Lyon. You may remember that I came to you. That I wanted you to teach me. I still do. I can pay, but I won't offer to, because I know you wouldn't accept."

"I was surprised that you came to me."

"And why do you think that was?"

"I don't know. Scheduling? Someone said I was a good teacher?"

She shook her head to indicate that it was something else. "I heard you play. Then I saw you one time as you left the building in the Cité de la Musique. I was on the corner, ten meters away. You stopped to stare at a tree as the wind was shaking its leaves in the sunlight. I was amazed to see that because of this you missed the bus. It was then. I understand what you've told me. You're right. Nothing will happen between us except the music. But some people fall in love with a touch while shaking hands, and others, just as inexplicably, in other ways."

If, at Its End, Your Life Takes on the Attributes of Art

As if she were talking not to her father but to a splinter she was digging out of her flesh, and with a bitterness such as he had never directed toward her in all her life, Cathérine lashed out at Jules. "It's spring," she said, "it's not close to Christmas, and we're *Jewish.*"

"I know that," he answered, slightly afraid, because he knew the danger when a woman with red hair is angry. "In fact, I knew it decades before you were born, and, believe it or not, I had something to do with it."

"So why this? He can't even do puzzles."

"Yes he can. He's doing it. Okay, it says 'three and up, twenty-four giant pieces'. But look, he's got half of it done already."

Oblivious of his mother and grandfather, Luc removed puzzle pieces from the box one at a time and, as slowly and carefully as someone assembling a hydrogen bomb, fitted them — though not always at first — into the right place.

" *'Babar et le Père Noël'*," Cathérine said resentfully as the charming, gentle elephant, airborne in the blue and costumed in the red suit of Père Noël, took shape.

"I also got the fishing game. It's not specifically Christian," Jules said.

"Fish?"

"Well, not 'loaves and fishes' anyway, and look at that elephant's face. It's what every child needs — so kind, unthreatening, and colorful. Another world, and a good one. So what if he's Père Noël?"

"It's not appropriate," Cathérine said, weakening as she saw Luc warmly entranced by the gravity-less Babar.

"It is appropriate. What's not appropriate was the Peter Pan." He was immediately sorry that he had said this, and expected a hail of anger from Cathérine. But instead, even as she held herself stiffly and controlled her breathing, her eyes filled with tears, which she did not want Luc to see. Jules held out his arm, and, after a moment of hesitation, she sat down next to him and buried her face against his shoulder so Luc would not hear her cry. Soon it was over.

A few weeks before, as they were waiting for dinner, she had put on a Peter Pan movie in English. Her command of English was not strong enough to allow her to comprehend the song lyrics. They bothered Jules, but he said nothing until, as he thought about it, he had to turn off the movie even though Luc was literally wide-eyed. And Jules did turn it off, despite making Luc cry as if he had fallen. The combination of Never Never Land and the repetition of the lyric, "I won't grow up . . ." was what did it for Jules. Of course, Luc didn't understand, which somehow made it all the worse, and even Cathérine hadn't understood until it was explained to her, but then she did, and she said, "Okay. Okay, we can't have this in our house. Not now."

So it was, in their house, and their household, where the real danger came from within, mysteriously and improperly choosing as its target the most vulnerable and innocent. Fighting it was not made any easier by a sense that there was a battle outside as well, a danger that seemed to be everywhere in the air.

When, only months before, the massive crowds had marched in Paris, chanting "Death to the Jews," many of the demonstrators were smiling and laughing. This was easy for some to dismiss. Other than in rare exceptions, in France death was not brought expressly and en masse to the Jews as it was at the beginning of Jules' life. In fact, despite his history and despite his defense of the Orthodox Jewish boy on the bridge, Jules himself felt unthreatened. The high national unemployment, crime, riots, and the occasional massacre in France notwithstanding, the center of Paris and regions west were welcoming and safe.

Even during the war, the theaters had been open, bakers baked, waiters hustled, mothers took their children to the park, and pigeons washed their wings in puddles. Now, as everyday life continued, even Jews could easily forget the chant of "Death to the Jews," which was anything but ever-present. This was especially true if like Jules one was blond and looked German, English, or Scandinavian. From his appearance alone, no one had ever taken him for a Jew. So, like Marcel Marceau in a film Jules had seen as a boy, he could walk through walls, or be invisible. And, besides, for him death was not feared, but what he sought. Not only would it correct being alive, which he had always thought a betrayal, but now it had other purposes as well.

Alone, he was immune to the chant, but not when he visited Cathérine and her family. They were young, identifiable, and, most of all, beleaguered from within. The angel of death fluttered against their dwelling like a bird stubbornly beating its wings against the window, and all they could do was watch it quietly, hardly taking a breath, hoping that the glass would not give way.

The evening of the *Babar et le Père Noël*

puzzle — which lay ninety-percent finished as Luc slept in Jules' arms, his body limp and conforming, his skin sweet despite the almost marine smell of his medications — Jules wanted to recommend a movie to Cathérine and David. They were eager for that, because he often came up with interesting choices and because, as they never went out and were so often too exhausted to read, they watched a lot of movies.

Jules could not, however, think of the title. Nor could he remember the names of the actors, all of whom were famous and many of whom were his favorites. "You know," he said. "I can't . . . I just can't think of his name." He was obviously disturbed by this. And more so when he found himself unable to recall the name of a single person in the cast."

"Who's the director?" David asked.

"It's. . . . I know who it is, but I can't summon it."

It was then that Cathérine said, "I don't know why we're acting like idiots, bookmarking pages from the MD Anderson Cancer Center, apartments in Geneva, *houses* in Geneva. Why are we doing that, when you can't even remember Fabrice Luchini?"

"It wasn't Fabrice Luchini."

"Who was it?" she demanded.

"I don't know."

"You don't know? You don't know the title, you don't know anything. Why do we let you direct us?"

"One thing has nothing to do with the other, and I'm not directing you. As far as Switzerland and the rest, I'm begging you to trust me." A moment passed. "And I'm grateful that you have."

"What I'm saying," Cathérine let fly, now not so much in anger as in sadness, "is that you're not all there."

"Of course I'm all here," Jules told her, smarting at first. "Memory has nothing to do with judgment. Don't you understand what happens with memory? I can remember every note and rest in a long piece. I can remember exactly certain things that happened more than seventy years ago."

"But you can't remember something that happened yesterday."

"I'll tell you why, Cathérine, and maybe you can learn something."

"Go ahead," she challenged.

"The Internet," he said.

"The Internet," Cathérine echoed mockingly. "That explains it."

He forgave her. He would always forgive her. It was all right if she gave whatever it was that she could not handle, to him. This was his job after all. He was supposed to be the redoubt in which those he loved could find protection. If not admirable, it was okay that she was angry.

"Bandwidth," he continued.

"Bandwidth?"

"Yes. You know how politicians brag about bringing bandwidth to poor people and out-of-the-way places?"

"So?"

"It costs a lot of money. But what part of bandwidth is used for text — all the emails, chatting, encyclopedias, books, etcetera — on the Internet?"

"I don't know," Cathérine answered.

"About one percent."

"What are you getting at?" she asked, more convinced than ever, and more upset and alarmed, that he was losing his mind.

"The rest is visual: movies, television, games, photographs. Why do you think that is? It's because the densest form of information perceptible to humans — other than the spiritual and metaphysical, for which there is no proof within the realm of reason — is visual.

"What does this mean, in turn? With your eyes open you can look at this room and perceive, down to the smallest detail you are able to resolve, everything that's in it. Close your eyes, and you have only an approximation, notes. Now, think of all the visuals you take in within a few seconds, walking from room to room, or watching television, or flying above the city and looking down at its ten million lines, colors and angles, all of which you can remember only as a sketch, and only an instant later. Take the train from Paris to Marseille, and through the window, because you can receive the image of every blade of grass and every stone in a stream, you take in more discrete information than can be packed into a thousand — ten thousand — national libraries. Think of all you've seen, in full color, high resolution, and motion, in your entire life. Do you remember it? Only imprecise sketches of a very limited part of it.

"In terms of volume and processing, the mind's chief activity is taking in visual information. Its second-most active function is getting rid of it. It's as if there are a billion little clerks who continually sort, identify, and jettison. We cleanse, dump, and dispose of most of what we receive."

David was intrigued. Although doing her best not to be, so was Cathérine.

"What happens when you're as old as I am? To begin with, I've taken in twice as much information, useless and otherwise, as you have. By definition I've exercised the facility for erasing things twice as much as you have. Also, as the time left to me rapidly narrows, I reject with greater and greater vigor that which isn't important — just as, because I can't take them with me, I lose attachment to my possessions. I'm also clearing out the attic in here," he said, pointing to his head.

"The facility for getting rid of what I don't need is working at high-speed and not always flawlessly. In general, I hardly need to know about movies. How could whatever is helping me clean house have predicted that this evening it would have been useful had I remembered this one?

"I'm not embarrassed or disturbed that I've lost so much, anymore than a farmer would be embarrassed or disturbed that the wind has blown the chaff from the threshing floor and left only the wheat. You may not understand this until you're much older, but to people of my age it's given, if one will take it, that things become at once more beautiful, more intense, and more inexplicable. You learn to see with your emotions and feel with your reason. If at its end the life you're living takes on the attributes of art, it doesn't matter if you've forgotten where you put your reading glasses."

"Please," David begged. "I can drive you. There's no traffic, and I'll be back in an hour."

"That's not necessary. I like to walk, and the trains are running."

"When you change at Nanterre you might be standing in the cold for an hour."

"It's not that late, David. I won't have to wait more than ten minutes, if that. And I don't mind the cold."

"At least let me drive you to the station. And this time of night, Jules, the trains are not necessarily safe."

"Here? They're perfectly safe. And I don't have to worry about such things anymore."

"Yes, yes, I know. Nor did you worry about such things when you were younger. I know that, too."

"I didn't, especially when I was a soldier."

"You've never been bothered by. . . ."

Jules interrupted. "Only in the middle years, when my family was in tow. Then I'd worry a lot. Now that's your job."

The train ride was smooth and dull. Unlike the old cars that creaked because there was so much wood in them, the new ones whined. Everything inside was plastic, glass, or steel, and fluorescent light reflected coldly from the glass of windows blackened by the night. Part of the coach ceiling, slanted over the steps leading to the upper-level seats, was a color that did not exist in nature, at least not in the temperate regions: a pinkish, melon color, neither cantaloup nor orange, that was at least faintly nauseating. Every time Jules rode the RER, there it was. And every time he saw it he thought of the immensely tall African he had seen, wearing pants of exactly the same color, who had bumped his head ascending to the second level. Angry at himself, he had hit the plastic panel with one fist, swearing at it in an African language as if it were alive, before striking it with the other. Jules was in total sympathy.

He didn't want to miss his stop, but in the hypnotic rocking of the carriage he was half asleep even though the closely set ties were concrete and the welded rails had no joints. Brilliantly colored, moving images from his past rose in rapid, random succession.

In August of 1966, on the train from Paris to Bordeaux, he had finished with the army, Jacqueline was twenty-two, the windows were open, and fragrant air rushed by. Every color outside glowed as in a medieval miniature, even the flags at military bases, whipping in the breeze. At an American base next to the rail line a thousand tanks were visible in row after row. As Jacqueline and Jules were served *framboise* in the dining car, they watched them in their endless ranks. A huge American flag and the Tricolor furled and unfurled above the base, both the colors of blood, snow, and the sea.

Another image, from years later, when Cathérine was a little girl and they stayed in a shack between Contaut and the sea. Always high strung, Cathérine had had trouble sleeping, but not at Contaut, where the sound of the waves allowed her to find deep rest a minute or so after she closed her eyes. The first time she returned to Paris from Contaut she thought she'd never fall asleep again, and would lie awake for hours. They took her to a doctor, who gave them sleeping pills, which they accepted out of politeness but then threw away. Instead, Jules bought forty jewelry chains with tiny, delicate links, and a box of Cuban cigars. He gave the cigars to anyone who wanted them, and put the chains into the wooden box, which, when rocked back and forth sounded remarkably like the ocean. After a few minutes, she would be fast asleep.

Perhaps because at Contaut they had left their worries in Paris, and for two weeks were relieved of making a living, paying bills, going to school, and answering mail or the telephone, parents and child made a bond as strong and yet as invisible as the forces holding fast in the atom.

Contaut then was still a naval base. Seaplanes that patrolled the Bay of Biscay made their home and found shelter on the enormous lake that stretched south, and the German fortifications on the Atlantic beaches were as intact as if squads of infantry were still inside. But they were empty, forbidding, dark, and piled with sand. The biggest one was shaped like a German helmet, with firing slits looking out at the surf, its massive concrete the color of gunmetal and pinstriped with impressions of the long-vanished wooden cement forms.

One summer they ran out onto the beach the way one does arriving at the open ocean after a long drive. Turning from a distant blue so deep it was painful, they saw that, undermined by the tide, the fortress had rolled over onto the sand. Firing-slits pressed against the ground, steel doors ajar, the interior full of seawater and echoing like a shell that holds the sound of the waves, it could no longer stand in what its builders had vainly conquered only a generation before.

The only other occupants of the train car on the RER were a boy and a girl in their teens sitting across from Jules, two seats behind. They had been there when he got on, and he had taken note of their fast, jerky, almost violent movements, which he knew did not seem that way to them. To him, their gestures were explosive. Their arms flew around and their speech was loud and rushed. He hadn't been like that when young, but then again he had had a special maturity that he would never have wished upon anyone.

For these kids, Jules didn't even exist. That is, until he was seized by rapidly advancing confusion and darkness and could neither move nor speak, nor hear, nor see. In the seconds in which he remained conscious he was sure he was dying. Keeling over to his right, he fell into the aisle. The boy and girl stopped their talking. "Drunk," the boy said. A moment passed.

"Maybe he died," the girl added.

"No," her boyfriend added, as if he knew. "Go see."

"I'm telling you, he's drunk."

"You should check."

"Do I have to?"

"Yes."

He got up, walked up the aisle, and stepped over Jules as if stepping over a log. Peering at him, he said, "He's breathing. He's not drooling or anything, and I don't smell alcohol. Maybe he had a heart attack."

"What can we do?"

"Call it in. I don't have my phone."

"My battery's dead."

"Why do you do that all the time!"

"It's too old. You know it's old. I'm waiting to get the new one. What are we going to do?"

"At the next stop," the boy said, "we'll tell someone. What else can we do? I'm not a doctor."

The train rolled on for five minutes, and when it stopped, the boy and his girlfriend ran out to look, but found no one. Then they watched as the doors closed and the train moved on. Eventually they found two policemen, one of whom asked, "How do you know he wasn't drunk?"

They argued, but the police were stubborn, they were just about to end their shift, they were tired, and they didn't want to complicate things. So the train kept moving, just as it was supposed to, into the center of Paris.

The Patient, Barely Alive, Had Collapsed on the RER

For an instant after he fell and just prior to his loss of consciousness he had seen something extraordinary and comforting. The world is full of stories and reports about the brief impressions that flash before the eyes of the dying and those who have come close to death. It's easy to say that these are nothing more than the creations of minds under extreme stress, dreams and desires coming forth in an instant as images of a life's hopes and loves — no longer held in check — break their ways to the surface. But is it possible to create a new color, in new light?

Jules saw a horizon of three hundred and sixty degrees. Dark gray clouds circled like a low wall. But it gave way to a glow above it in a color that did not exist on earth. It was simultaneously all but none of the known colors of white, beige, and platinum. It had the texture of mother-of-pearl or alabaster, but no veins, imperfections, or spectra of interference. It glowed as if the source of illumination were behind it, and pulsed almost imperceptibly. Its light immediately banished all fear and pain, washed away all regret. As it seemed to exist independently of time, and though he saw it for only a second or two, he felt as if he had been bathed in its light for eternity.

When he awakened in the ICU at La Pitié-Salpêtrière he felt disappointment at having once again re-entered the world. No one else was in the room, only the beeping machines, illuminated numbers, and dancing lights that these days keep watch over the sick and the dying. How easy it would have been to fall back into the gentle off-white glow. He tried to summon it by closing his eyes, but he couldn't. He'd been thrown back, and would have to see it through. Coming awake, he assessed what was left to him and prepared for the useless tests, questions, and examinations that he was sure would follow. Having had them in New York he knew more or less where he stood.

After neurological workups, consultations, and visits from Cathérine and David, he discovered to his great relief many hours of happiness and contentment in La Pitié-Salpêtrière, a place he had hated but now loved, because it was the gate to the road upon which he would follow Jacqueline. Even if he would never find her, following was enough.

Things leveled off, the doctors were done with him, and he would be going home the next day. He didn't know how he was able to adjust happily, but he had gotten used to the food and the routine, and even watched a movie on television. It was about a dog who, to find a female dog he had seen in a crate on a train, crossed the Australian continent to ask for her paw. Jules liked it. He loved dogs. The only reason he hadn't gotten a dog was that he knew that the central component of a dog's emotions is loyalty, and he didn't want to break its heart when he died. But even dogless he looked forward to going out once again into Paris at the end of April.

Lying quietly propped up in his bed, he heard the well practiced knock of nurses and doctors about to enter a patient's room. What did they imagine? That he would be with a tart? In fact, imprisoned in the hospital, all he could think about was sex. He tried not to include Élodi but he did, often, imagining every part of her body and how he would be lost in his love of it. Now he realized that Dante had been playing a double game when he created the eternal kiss of Paolo and Francesca, because when Jules thought of touching, holding, and kissing Élodi, he wanted it to last forever, and in the way he perceived this it would not have been punishment but paradise.

After the knock, a nurse half-entered the room, her right hand holding the door. "You have a visitor," she said.

His obsession having tricked him that it was Élodi, he started with pleasure and fear. "Send her in."

The nurse was puzzled at first, then said, "A man, I assure you. A Monsieur Marteau. As big as an ox. It's okay?" She saw Jules' disappointment.

"Okay."

Armand Marteau ducked slightly as he came through the doorway, although he didn't have to.

"How did you know I was here?" Jules asked.

"You were responsible enough to carry the card I gave you. Still, it wasn't so easy to find you. This is a big place. *Neuropathologie, Bâtiment Paul Castaigne, Secteur Vincent Auriol, Hôpital Universitaire La Pitié-Salpêtrière, quarante-sept à quatre-vingt-dix e trois Boulevard de l'Hôpital, Treizième Arrondissement, sept cinq zero un trois, Paris.* Geographical coordinates to the second would have been a fifth as long. But I found you."

"Why would they, without my permission, contact you?"

"It says so on the card. It says 'death or disability,' and you're disabled."

501

"I am not disabled."

"Medically and legally, you are. Your diagnosis. . . ."

"How do you know my diagnosis?"

"Don't forget, you signed waivers. Full transparency, and with a basilar aneurysm that is both on the edge and inoperable, you are technically and legally fully disabled."

"And what does that mean?"

"It means that your disability benefits started as soon as we received official notification, and that you cannot any longer work. It means you must resign your post and refrain from any activity related to either ongoing or future compensation, or even without compensation, from any activity related to your previous career or careers."

"I can't teach?"

"No."

"Not even privately, without compensation?"

"Perhaps you don't remember, but we've been over this before."

"I can't write music, without compensation, for my own pleasure?"

"No. If you write it down or record it, it has the potential of being sold."

"May I play the cello?" Jules asked, sarcastically.

"Yes, you can, as long as it is unrelated to compensation, performance, or teaching."

"How would anyone know?"

"They might not," Armand said patiently, "but if they do, the policy would be voided and you'd be sued for the costs of its implementation."

"What if I give up the policy, or don't take the disability payments? Can I refuse them?"

"You can give up the policy after two years if you've paid the premiums in full. If you refuse the disability payments, the policy is voided, with the consequences I described. Given your economic status, you have many options. For some people, the conditions might be a kind of trap, but if money is of little consequence you can more or less do what you wish. And how did you end up here? I would have thought you'd gone private immediately. Switzerland. England. The U.S."

"That's not important. What about you?" Jules asked.

"Me?"

"How would you fare with the various options that you relate?"

"Since you bought the policy, they've directed me to much more than my share of high-value business. They think I'm magic. I've purchased new equipment for our farm in Normandy, paid off its debts, and reacquired the land we had to sell to meet previous obligations. I'm going to go back there. You saved me. If there's anything I can do. . . ."

"I'm happy that it's been good for you."

"I want things to work out, and I don't want you in trouble," Armand said. He moved closer so he could whisper. "Everything would be fine except for the fact that when you were brought to the emergency room, and were in and out of consciousness. . . ." Armand looked around to make sure that no one was there, "you diagnosed yourself. Correctly."

"I did?"

"You did. You said, 'inoperable basilar aneurysm.' It took them an MRI, a radiologist, and two neurosurgeons to come to the same conclusion. This was noted in their report, the supposition being that you had received a previous diagnosis. When we got the report, all ears pointed up. Our chief has referred it along."

"To whom?"

"Merde!" Armand said.

"What?"

"He. . . ."

" 'He'?"

"You will be scrutinized."

"On everything?"

"Probably just the medical, although they can open up the whole case. I wanted to let you know," he whispered. "That's why I came." Armand turned away, then back again, still whispering, and with urgency. "You'll be getting a visit from our investiga-

504

tor. *Terrible!*"

"What do you mean, 'terrible'?"

"His name fits him to a T. He hates every-one."

The last thing Jules needed was a dogged investigator. "What's his name, then?"

"Damien Nerval."

"I guess it sounds satanic."

"A little, yes. He likes to fight. We used to call him Flagellons, until someone did and he hit him with a stick."

They wanted to bring him out in a wheel-chair, the standard procedure, but he jumped up and ran down the hall, with the nurse call-ing after him in panic. What would they do, arrest him? For walking? Running? *You are forbidden to run, because you're not supposed to be able to walk.* If he actually needed a wheelchair he would sit in one, but as long as he didn't need one, he wouldn't. In so many ways already outside the law, he didn't care about rules.

Just before exiting the hospital he saw a young doctor in surgical scrubs, a stethoscope draped around his neck. "Excuse me," Jules said. "The way the stethoscope hangs, it looks like mink heads."

"I beg your pardon?"

"When I was a boy, women went around in furs with the heads attached and hanging from their shoulders. Minks, nutrias, baby foxes. They — the minks, nutrias, and baby foxes, although maybe some of the women, too — had whiskers and glass eyes. Sometimes they'd be three or four in a bunch, even five. That was only seventy years ago. You see how things change? But don't get on your high horse. Now they go around with bare breasts, like the women of the Germanic tribes at the time of Caesar, or Cleopatra's bath attendants, at least in Italian movies. *'Oh, Hercules! Cleopatra enters the bath!'* "

The young doctor was struck dumb.

"You don't believe me about the minks, I can tell. Look it up. 'Google' it."

"Okay."

"But first, where can I buy medical books?"

"Where can you buy medical books?"

"I asked *you.*"

"For laypersons or physicians?"

"Physicians. I know how to read. I have an education. I know Latin and Greek. I once took chemistry, organic chemistry, even histology. But that's immaterial. Where do you buy these books?"

"Try the Librairie Vigot Maloine. They have something like a hundred and thirty thousand books on medicine, thirty thousand in the store. They have everything."

"Where is it?"

"On the Rue de l'École de Médecine, right off Saint-Germain, near Métro stop Odéon."

Jules took out a ten-Euro note and pressed

it into the young doctor's hand. "I don't . . . that's not necessary," the young man said.

"Yes it is," Jules said. "Lunch."

"You really don't have to do that."

"Why not? You just saved me ten-million Euros."

The bookstore was bright and colorful. "I need a summary," Jules told the clerk — a devastatingly attractive, thin, dark-haired girl wearing glasses, "a handbook that will cover all the diseases and conditions, not just internal medicine, or oncology, etcetera, but something comprehensive. More or less an outline of the whole thing, not for laymen."

"What you need then," she said, is *Le Manuel Merck,* Fifth French Edition, more than four thousand pages. It's just what you want."

"The cost?"

"Ninety-nine Euros."

"That seems like a bargain," Jules said, "for every disease in the world."

He couldn't resist looking into the book, so at the end of the alley he sat down on the steps near a statue of Vulpian, a great nineteenth-century French physician, the spitting image of Robert E. Lee. Jules, who had never heard of Vulpian, felt painfully ignorant.

At home, the quiet and stillness were oppressive. He wanted to write a symphony, to sleep with Élodi, to be with Jacqueline. He so much wanted to live, and he so much wanted to die, but the conflict would resolve itself, because, without fail, he would do both.

The symphony, a full, over-spilling cadenza on the theme of the Bach *Sei Lob und Preis mit Ehren,* had to be written, as a homage and in the face of the barbarism that neither for the first time nor the last assaulted the West. It had to be written, with need of neither name, nor credit, nor claim, to complete a song that was started in Reims at the Liberation. Jules had needed his entire life, event after event, test after test, failure after failure, finally to understand that he had been meant to do this from the time his father had played the last note, and that, if he did, somehow, without explanation, beyond reason, there would be enough justice and love in his life so that he could finally let go.

He could allow neither the necessity of obtaining the money for Cathérine and Luc to block the writing of the piece, nor the writing of the piece to block the necessity of obtaining the money. And he would be perfectly happy to write it not for audiences, the world, or posterity, but only and simply for Élodi. He was unsure that he could compose something worthy and vital enough to bear the weight intended to appeal to a beautiful young woman with most of her life ahead of her. And given Damien Nerval, if indeed that was his real name, it would have to be physically untraceable to Jules himself.

On the lowest level of the bookshelf was a neatly stacked half-meter pile of paper: odd groupings of bond, graph paper, letterhead, and musical notation pads. It had accumulated since the Lacours had moved to Saint-Germain-en-Laye. And near the bottom of the stack, wrapped in yellowed, partially disintegrating cellophane, were two hundred pages of music paper he had bought in the sixties. He pulled it out. It was slightly jaundiced but not disintegrating. He put it on the desk, from which he pulled the wide, shallow, center drawer. Several bottles of ink had been sitting there since he had stopped using fountain pens long before. He took out a bottle of navy blue, dated 1946, to see if it had dried. It hadn't. Although almost seventy years old, it was perfectly liquid.

He opened the leather box that was the sarcophagus of his Mont Blancs, seized what once was his favorite, a type from before the war and before he was born, and found that the point was encrusted with the ancient residue of the same ink that had survived in its heavy Mont Blanc glass bottle. At the hot water tap after ten minutes of filling and emptying the reservoir and wiping the nib with paper towels, Jules had given himself the means to find shelter many years back in time, there to fulfill a task that when he was

509

young he had felt but could not identify. Paper, ink, and pen had been waiting. They knew nothing of what had happened in the years between.

Someone who always ate alone in restaurants, preferred rabbit in beer, dressed in shiny black silk, was as bony and tall as a chain-link fence, and took stairs with aggressive rapidity preceded by the stiff-legged hop that midgets have when they begin to ascend a ramp, would, perhaps not surprisingly, be named Damien Nerval. Who could tell if he had become the man he was because his name was Damien Nerval, or, because of the man he was, he had changed his name to Damien Nerval from something like "Mouton de Bonheur". But, for whatever reason, he was the man he was: hostile, intimidating, hateful, tortured, and yet obsequious — his studied way of putting prey off guard. He was able to exist because most people want to avoid confrontation, and he always gave them a prescribed way to do so — a narrow exit they could take only if they left behind exactly what he had come to obtain. But he had never encountered someone quite as damaged and devoted as Jules Lacour.

Jules Lacour, whom Nerval assumed had neither much testosterone, time, nor muscle tone left. A music teacher. A hospital patient, barely alive, a man who collapses on the

RER. He would be quick work. Nerval, at forty-five, the sweet spot between strength and experience, was backed by the great, indefatigable, trillion-dollar machine of Acorn, a *dispositif* with neither soul nor conscience but rather a thousand lawyers and a good many laws that over the years it had cooked up in legislatures all over the world. Jules Lacour could not make a credible stand against such combined powers. And yet professionals take nothing for granted, and Nerval was nothing if not professional.

Jules had thirty years of experience beyond Nerval's, and much else, not least the spirit of the survivor who believes his duty is to die. He had lived his life in an alternate moral dimension: that is, where day in and day out love and loyalty forge the soul into a steel capable of resistance unto annihilation. More than a decade before Nerval's birth, Jules had been, summer and winter, a soldier in the mountains of North Africa. He had been immune to the terror of death since the age of four. In his child and the life of his grand-child he had a devotion that drove him on. Since infancy, he had been fighting with God in an argument that surpassed the demands of prayer or interrogation. And though he loved much, he feared little, and had always met superior power, its arrogance, and its self-enjoyment, with a direct challenge and a rising within that fed upon and strengthened itself.

In the days before Nerval showed up, Jules studied medicine. It wasn't hard, as the way he planned the encounter meant that he would decide how it would proceed, not Nerval, who would have no inkling of the advance preparation. So when Claude nervously announced Nerval, Jules was pleased even if it meant another twenty Euros gone.

Nerval was wiry, dark, and sharp-featured, with sparkling eyes and a half-jack-o'-lantern, bent mouth. The muscles of his face tensed when he met Jules, in an expression that said, 'I'm looking through and into you, I accuse you, and won't let go.' This was intensified by a tic that, although neither Parkinson's disease nor any other malady, involved the near-continual short oscillations, like the action of a fishing lure, of his head upon his neck. Left, right. Right, left. Ad infinitum. He impolitely refused the offer of something to eat or drink, instead sitting down opposite Jules in Shymanski's study and, without the normal human curiosity that might have caused him to note or appreciate his surroundings, getting right to business.

He loved to catch people. Some hunters hunt for food and regret that they must kill. Others enjoy and take pride in it, the ones who become elated after a day in the uplands in which they've left two thousand birds dead on the ground. Nerval believed that he was doing justice as long as he followed the rules, and he gave not a moment's thought to the fate or motives of perpetrators of fraud against the company. No one could fault him for doing his duty according to the law, but as he did so he never tempered his view of what he did by taking into account that Acorn itself was a perpetrator of fraud — in bribing legislators and bureaucrats to allow premiums far in excess of covering costs and reasonable profits; in fighting savagely to deny claims, especially to anyone with neither much education nor a lawyer; in greasing judges; in accomplishing illegal trades and rigging markets with the vast capital it controlled; in false accounting; paying off auditors; and stiffing independent contractors; not to mention false advertising, impenetrable contracts, monopolistic control of certain sectors, and billing statements as easy to comprehend as hieroglyphics. In short, Nerval was so heavily un-nuanced he would have made a happy executioner.

He opened Jules' file and laid it out on his lap. Reading for a moment, he said, both contemptuously and with the enjoyment of a fisherman who sees a fat trout about to swallow the hook, "We know exactly what you're up to."

Absolutely still, without a blink or a twitch, as if he were made of stone, Jules waited and waited and waited, unnerving Nerval. "Who's *we*?" he then asked quietly.

"Acorn," Nerval answered. "Our agents, officers, and investigators — like a sock around the ball of the world."

"Oh," said Jules, amazed at the metaphor — it was too strange to be just a simile — "I see."

"What do you see?" Nerval pressed.

"What do you think I see?"

"I think perhaps you see, or you should see, that we know what you're up to."

"And what am I up to?"

"You tell me."

"No," Jules said firmly. "You brought it up. You tell me."

"I don't have to tell you anything," Nerval said aggressively.

"Yes you do."

"Why?"

"Because you came out of the blue. You have to initiate. All I have to do is sit here."

"What other than guilt would prevent you from answering my question?"

"What question?"

"What you're up to."

"You didn't ask me what I'm up to. You told me that you know. That's not a question."

"All right then, what are you up to?"

"Nothing."

"That's not true."

"How do you know?" Jules asked.

"Because we know exactly what you're doing." Frustrated, Nerval then assumed the position not of the interrogator but the interrogated. "You have a ten-million-Euro policy. Weeks after the start of coverage, you suffered a cerebral aneurysm. Upon admission to the hospital, semi-conscious, you made an accurate diagnosis — inoperable basilar aneurysm. The attending emergency physician, a radiologist, and two neurosurgeons were able to reach that conclusion only after imaging and consultation. How, exactly, were you able to do that?"

"Did I do that?"

"Yes, you did."

"That's remarkable."

"It is remarkable, in that it has fraud written all over it. Are you a physician?"

"No."

"Were you trained as such, or in any related field?"

"I'm a cellist, although in University I ranged widely, including in the sciences, and now I read widely, including in the sciences. I resent when scientists assume that because I'm a cellist I know nothing of their subject matter. I read scientific journals and have done so for . . . let me see . . . fifty-seven years."

This unnerved Nerval. "Do you have them?"

"The journals?"

"Yes."

"I discard them. I found that I never reread magazine articles. I don't think I've ever done so more than once or twice in my life. I used to save them, but then I realized it was unnecessary."

"Can you prove that you've read these?"

Jules let seconds go by, long enough to see satisfaction, a slight reddening, and relaxation in the face of his tormentor, whom Jules allowed to rise a little before slapping him down. "Yes."

"How?"

"Just enquire of the two or three journals I've read over the years as to whether I've subscribed. And, to protect myself in an examination of the tax authorities, I've kept my financial records, including my checks, which will document my subscriptions."

"Beginning when?"

"Beginning after I got back from the war in Algeria."

"You have your records since then?"

"Yes, don't you?"

"I wasn't born then. It's ridiculous."

"That you weren't born then?" Jules asked.

"No, that you keep such records."

"They will prove what you asked to be proved, if you wish to look."

"You claim that on the basis of having read scientific journals you were able to make an accurate diagnosis, without imagery, that four

516

physicians required a day to make, in consultation, only after test results?"

"I don't claim that. It was you who did. You may think whatever you wish."

Nerval now wanted to kill Jules, or at least beat him physically. "You know that we're carefully checking your medical records. Nothing will pass."

"And you'll find nothing you seek. I'm not quite sure what that is."

"In all of France?"

"In all of France and in all the world."

"We have a very wide net."

"How nice to have a wide net."

"Have you traveled abroad in the last ten years?"

"I was in America in the fall."

"We can't look there without a judicial determination, both French and American, which, eventually, we can and will get."

"You don't have to do that. I'll sign any release," Jules said, pivoting from resistance to overwhelming cooperation. It amazed Nerval.

"You will?"

"Of course, to speed your investigation. What else can I do for you?"

"You can explain how you did what you did."

"The diagnosis?"

Nerval nodded. Now he was the sheep, and Jules the shearer.

"That's easy," said Jules, enjoying, without showing any sign of it, that the medical question distracted Nerval from the trust account Jules had used as a bank reference. He needed only to last until the first of August, baiting Nerval with the bullfighter's cape of the complex medical situation, which had the irresistible air of a scheme, because that's what it was.

"Okay. How?"

"Winston Churchill."

"Winston Churchill?"

"*Exact.* Like most geniuses, he was indifferent to what didn't interest him. 'Good' students are like good dogs. They can fetch what their teachers want them to fetch. Churchill was not made to fetch. He was, as he once said, 'Bloody Winston Churchill'."

"How does that possibly . . . ?"

"It does. The entrance examination for Sandhurst had a geography component. He wasn't interested in geography and hadn't prepared. A list of all the countries in the world was given to the candidates, and most spent months studying them as intended. Having neglected to do this, Churchill began the night before. His eye was drawn to New Zealand. Realizing that in five or six hours he couldn't master the geography of the entire world, he stayed with New Zealand and arrived the next morning an expert on the geography of that country and no other. By the grace of God and for the salvation of England, the West, and France, the sole topic on the exam was . . . New Zealand."

"So what you're saying is that by the grace of God you studied basilar aneurysms?"

"Not exactly, but I do have time to read. I'm pretty old and my body is failing. How long does it take to train in medicine, including preparation for medical school and the professional training afterwards? Ten years, fifteen? One must tackle an enormous body of knowledge. And yet I'm interested in the subject. So, like Churchill, I threw a dart. I chose one topic each from a number of areas — esophageal diverticula, insulinoma, spasmodic torticollis, idiopathic pulmonary hemosclerosis, autosomal recessive Von Wellebrand's disease, Ehrlichiosis, dystonia, orthostatic hypotension. . . ."

"Enough!"

"And, for the brain, only one thing — *inoperable basilar aneurysms*. The point is not that I know a lot, or that I'm accurate. I know just a little. If it had been something entirely different I still would have said inoperable basilar aneurysm, I would have been wrong, and you would not be sitting in that chair."

"Nonetheless, we've not finished with you," Nerval told him.

Jules sat back and said, "Ah! But you are for today."

This did not sit well with his guest, but,

then again, seldom did anything.

Jules returned to his own quarters where for half an hour he stared across the terrace and over the Seine toward Paris. Claude had moved the potted trees and bushes from the greenhouse back to their warm-weather stations, and there they stood guard in a light drizzle. It felt like a summer morning when the day should be bright and hot but is gray and warm, and the lights in stores are gleaming through the rain as if on a winter evening. He loved such summer mornings, with the sound of water dripping peacefully from lush foliage, and the special noise, a swoosh, that cars and buses make as they push across wet pavement.

He picked up the telephone, conscious that he would be calling Élodi on his landline and she would answer, like those of her generation, wherever she was, on her cell. With a landline, holding the phone to your ear as you dialed, you would not have to race to get it before someone hung up. You didn't have to position the instrument so it faced you, like the mirror mirror on the wall. And the buttons on a landline — no hope anymore of a dial — were a lot bigger, although thanks to his profession Jules had no lack of manual dexterity. Landlines did not double as television sets, pedometers, encyclopedias, atlases, travel agents, or teletype machines, not to mention several types of cameras, alarm clocks, blood pressure monitors, and a thousand other things that he had spent his life quite happily not carrying in his pocket. But, still, as Élodi's phone rang, he felt old and wrong.

When she answered, she had read on the screen that it was he. "Where are you?" he asked.

There was a silence. It sounded as if he were checking up on her. "Why do you ask?" she asked in return.

"I always ask when I call people on the cell phone. They could be on a boat in the Mediterranean, riding a horse in Australia, or at Buckingham Palace. That's the best thing about cell phones, I think."

"I was in a bakery on the Rue des Rosiers, and now I'm just about to sit down in the Place des Vosges." Somehow, he took comfort from the fact that she had been in the Jewish Quarter. "I live on the Boulevard Bourdon."

"I didn't know that."

"Yes, I was lucky. Maid's quarters, with a separate entrance." She sat down, happy that he was, in a sense, with her, but wishing that he were actually beside her.

"Isn't it raining?" he asked.

"It was, but it's fine now. The sun is out."

"Maid's quarters."

"One tiny room in which I can, and have, stretched out to touch two opposing walls at the same time — with the tips of my fingers and my toes. But it has a minute kitchen, a bathroom, and the best part is the view, and that I can see water, which is wonderfully calming. The house is almost at the north end of the canal, not far from the Place de la Bastille. I'm nine storeys up and almost level with the top of the column. The gilded statue on top blazes like a chemical fire when it's struck by the sun. My father told me that when old British warships left port some of the sailors would stand on the knob at the top of the fifty-meter masts, with no support. Every time I see the statue, I think of that.

"And he would be happy, because although he would think Paris is now very dangerous, I live just up the street from the *Hôtel de Police, Quatriême Arrondissement.* Almost every parking space on this block is taken up by a police car, a dozen or more at a time."

She didn't tell Jules that the young police officers would flirt with her, and that though she found them attractive in their smart uniforms she would blush and hurry on.

"My two dormer windows are very small. From the street they look like tank periscopes. The canal is always full of yachts and barges, many of them Dutch. On the east side there's a park with lawns and trees, and one luxuriant willow close to the water. In summer, the Place des Vosges is my garden.

"*Chambres des bonnes* are all over Paris,

and no one knows what to do with them. The rich don't want strangers in their buildings, and regulations and architecture often prevent conversions. The wonderful part is that when you get one it's usually on the top floor. Under the roof it's hot in the summer and cold in the winter, but I can see a hundred square kilometers and a huge sky. I was lucky. The people from whom I rent are classical music patrons. They like it when they hear the cello from upstairs."

What she described, and the way she described it — in her language, in her voice — was so lovely and seductive that he despaired that he was not half a century or even just thirty years younger. He would have liked to have spent another lifetime with her, starting out in a room so small he could touch opposing walls, with a view of the water, and the Place des Vosges as their garden. But the energy, anonymity, and hope of youth were not his to have again.

"Do you still want to resume the lessons," he asked.

"Yes."

"Can you come here?"

"When?"

"At your convenience."

"Tomorrow."

"What time?"

"Late in the afternoon? Around four? I have ballet until two. I started when I was little.

There's no future in it for me, but I've kept it up because I like it and it keeps me fit."

"Don't bring your instrument."

"No? Why not?"

"We'll use the one here."

ÉLODI, JULES, DUVALIER, ARNAUD, AND NERVAL

That evening, Jules was driven and possessed. Though he would see Élodi the next day, he went to a website that he could enter as a faculty member, and saw her address on the Avenue Bourdon. He was shaking as he did so, as if committing a crime. "That's enough," he said out loud, thinking it would stop him. But it didn't, and he left the house to walk to the RER.

Increasingly nervous all the way to Paris, he went not to the Place de la Bastille but, pulling against himself, to his office, hoping that whatever was driving him would dissipate and that he could then return home. He sat down at his desk and turned on the lights, but in the sudden glare all he could see was her face. Alternate surges of magnetic pull, fear, excitement, and a kind of dizziness ended up getting him on his feet and eventually walking fast toward the Bassin de l'Arsenal, where the barges were moored in front of her building.

It was possible to walk from his office to the Cité de la Musique, which for reasons of self-preservation he had never done even in daylight. And the bridges crossed the Seine in such a way that it was plausible that in going there he would pass by her house. But not this late. Driven on and feeling the terrible pleasure of madness, he thought at one moment that there would be none but happy consequences and at another that it would be the end of everything. And yet he kept going, even past La Pitié-Salpêtrière.

His thoughts raced until he was giddy with guilt, hope, and pleasure, and he moved as if falling forward. He had at least to look at the building where Élodi lived. He hoped to ring the bell if he could bring himself to do it. He found himself loving — to the point where it reverberated throughout his body like a warm wave — the innocent and artless charm that she could not contain, and which had caused her to write *"dernier étage"* after her address. It had carried into the computer. She hadn't had to supply such detail. It was a sign, somehow, of her goodness.

Pushed and drawn as if against his will but entirely as a result of it, he went directly past La Pitié. At times, memory was so strong it was as if Jacqueline were still there and alive. If he turned into the ancient and depressing precincts of La Pitié might he not be able to go past the yellow awnings, the banana trees, the tired nurses and doctors coming off shift, ascend to the room in which Jacqueline had died, to find her there, alive, to speak to her, even if just for a moment, to tell her how much he loved and missed her, that above all he wanted to join her, and that now he knew he would? She would smell like the sea, which was what had happened with the intravenous liquids that had flowed into her before the end, but it wouldn't matter. The question was answered by his legs, and soon he was crossing the Seine.

Once on the Right Bank, and with guilt so sharp it had become physical, all his emotion turned toward Élodi. He wanted her as if he were young, as if after making love there would be no "Now what?" but rather a magical subtraction of the fifty years between them. Twenty-five again, with time not a dying horse but a young one, full of unconscious energy and ignorant of what was ahead except that the very end could be neither seen nor felt.

Walking along the canal, on the west side of the Avenue Bourdon, he passed the police station and came to her address, closer to the Place de la Bastille than he had thought. What if he encountered her on the street? What would he say? He feared but wanted it. Everything was quiet. On the highest floor, one in a row of tiny dormers — the tops of which were level with the peak of the roof —

was lit, her light. She was right there. All he had to do was press the buzzer, and she would come down. It would be either the end or the beginning.

One thing among the many things Jules didn't know about Élodi was that she wore contact lenses and was extremely nearsighted without them. When home for the evening she took them out and put on glasses, the clear lenses of which in magnifying her eyes brought to them a strange perfection and clarity — in blue of course — and the frames of which, in combination with her hair falling past the temple bars, added another irresistible attraction. Perhaps had he seen her relaxed on her bed — her legs folded beneath her as she read — slowly and carefully reaching for a cup of tea while keeping her eyes on the book, deeply absorbed, utterly beautiful, he might not have tried so hard to keep his promises.

He took a step toward the door, but then he thought how shameful and ridiculous it was for an old man to pursue a young girl, and he knew he was old, and he knew it was unmanly to do such a thing, for it showed that he was unable to face what he had become and what was in store. He turned away from the door and toward the empty street, and with deep, inconsolable regret, he walked on.

■ ■ ■ ■

Murder is one thing when a distraught lunatic kills his wife and children, sits in his car for two hours pointing a gun at his head and, before anyone gets wind of what he has done, pulls the trigger. Case closed, except for the sad and difficult gathering of evidence and stories, but it's mainly paperwork after the first few days, and is usually wrapped up in a week or two. An idiot high on drugs robs a little grocery store and kills the old Moroccan woman behind the counter. Witnesses see his beaten-up Fiat and get a partial license plate. They notice that it has a little flower on the aerial, to help the idiot find the car either in a parking lot or after he robs a store. Ten minutes later, he's speeding and running stop signs, a tail light is out, and his muffler is dragging. Two patrol officers pull him over. He bails. They chase. He turns with a gun. They fire. Case closed and, again, wrapped up in a week.

On the other hand, a carefully plotted murder or the murder of a stranger can take years, might never be solved, and, if you are a police officer, can assume for you the character of a job you go to month after month where you work hard most of the time, although sometimes not, and sometimes find a break, but never quite get there. It makes

529

you feel that your life is a waste, that the world is cruel, dangerous, and impossible, and that you will always be unhappy.

It had been months since Duvalier Saidi-Sief and Arnaud Weissenburger had begun the case of the Bir-Hakeim Bridge. Their prime witness, Raschid Belghazi, who believed the Comédie-Française was a pornographic movie house, had said he told them everything he knew, and been cleared to leave Paris. Now he was gone. The families of the murdered boys were voiceless and oppressed. They had no special pleading anywhere, much less in a ministry, and their communities had recently rioted anyway about something else and quickly settled back. It was the kind of case that was forgotten, or at least pursued halfheartedly.

But, Weissenburger, because he was a Jew and the evidence pointed toward a Jew who had murdered two Arabs, was absolutely determined, in the name of fairness, objectivity, and *laïcité,* to solve it. Saidi-Sief, hating his own people's lower orders who disgraced their long traditions by embracing rootlessness and delinquency, suspected that the events had a twist no one had envisioned, and was just as eager as Weissenburger. Further, their devotion to their work dissolved their differences and brought them together in a way that both hoped could be the future of France, even if both were highly skeptical that it would be.

They went over the surveillance footage too many times, looking for something they might have missed. They stared at the lab reports until they could dream them. They used every informant they could contact, and begged other officers for favors that in the end turned up nothing. At one point, Houchard called. "How's it going?"

Duvalier said, "For several months we spent eight to ten hours a day looking at traffic surveillance tapes. It was fun."

As the time passed, the only thing they really had was the rowing club. What were the chances that whoever killed the two boys and jumped into the river was a member of this club, and knew he could pull himself out on its dock and seek shelter there until morning traffic would camouflage his escape? Did he plan it that way in advance? It was a thin and unlikely thread, but as it was the only one they had, they followed it.

The judge was adamant that he would not give them blanket authority to collect DNA samples from all the members. Theirs was astoundingly too broad a request, based on a highly improbable supposition. But he did agree that if they narrowed it down enough he would issue warrants, and he did agree that if they needed to go outside Paris, he would arrange it. Houchard, the *OPJ,* wasn't doing anything, and the judge liked that the

531

two young *APJ*s were so stubborn. So they investigated each member before they would seek an interview, make a visit, and ask for a cheek swab. Then they went ahead. As they suspected, most people were cooperative. It all had to be done politely and diplomatically, which took time.

They learned a lot about rowing clubs. You can hardly buy real estate on the river, so no matter how rich you are, if you want to row in Paris you have to join one and move among the musty lockers and garbage cans that tend not to be emptied because no club member thinks it's his job to do so. There were some billionaires or almost-billionaires who racked their boats in the drafty, rough-hewn boathouse, as well as semi-impoverished rentiers who would eat or not, depending upon interest rates. There were horribly arrogant lawyers; obsessive professors; dull-as-paint businessmen; a few women, some of whom were young and beautiful, with goddess-like, lithe bodies; retirees who could barely get their boats in the water and wouldn't have lived through the fight on the bridge; even a policeman; and a bus driver.

It would have been easy had Arnaud and Duvalier had some mechanism with which to sort out the Jews, of whom there could not have been that many, but this was strictly forbidden. Arnaud did it anyway, using computers in Internet cafés, but other than names and the occasional suggestion in an article or posting, which left little certainty, there was not much to go on over the Internet. They had to approach the subjects one by one. The few who refused a cheek swab were put on a list for heightened attention after all the subjects had been examined.

One thing they discovered was that athletic people who had single shells tended to live in beautiful places, mostly in houses, but, if in apartments, the kind that take up whole floors or more than one and have expansive terraces with colorful awnings, lots of geraniums, and distant views. It was an education, and their visits were interesting. They always went together. Both the innocent and the guilty were able to conceal much less when faced with two questioners, on opposite flanks, two men of different character supporting one another and observing. It was human nature not to lie as well to two people as to one, because it was human nature to be jangled by two sets of eyes at two different angles.

When Duvalier and Arnaud got around to Jules they had found out what they could about him, checked his address, and looked on Google Earth to see where he lived. Because the estate was shielded by many layers of trusts, they had no idea that it wasn't his, and thought he was, in fact, their biggest billionaire, as he would have been had he had Shymanski's wealth. Looking forward to seeing the gardens and the interior, and to being offered refreshments as in several other luminous houses they had visited, they were curious to see the compound.

They thought it highly unlikely that an aging billionaire would smash someone's head against an abutment, slide down stone stairs on top of someone else, kill him at the bottom with a martial-arts punch in the throat, and escape by throwing himself into the Seine. But they were open to the possibility. And because they were detectives they had the habit of scoping things out before they moved. The more information in advance, the more time to think, to give play to intuition, the better prepared they would be. There was a kind of magic in it, or, as Duvalier liked to say, an art.

After Élodi had arrived, they did. Not wanting to be noticed, they parked on the street and waited, hoping that the feel of the place might give them something unexpected to go on in the interview.

Élodi, who was wearing the yellow silk print, had some music in a portfolio, and no cello to burden her. As Jules watched her walk from the gate to his door he realized that from a distance he'd never really seen her move without the cello. Although she had been graceful even with it, when she was without it he witnessed something of extraordinary beauty. If someone walks when she knows she is observed it can make her stiff and awkward, but Élodi took not a single, self-conscious, unbalanced step. In the fading, primarily reflected light, with the sun, now high over the Western Atlantic, draping the eastern parts of Saint-Germain-en-Laye in shadow, the color and sheen of the silk made it glow. As he had noticed before, it was tight on her. But now he didn't avert his eyes, and as she came closer he saw her body moving against the material, and the slight shuffle of the fabric as she made her way forward. He knew that were he to cup his hand around her side as he pulled her into an embrace, what he would feel through the silk would be intoxicatingly firm and strong.

When they were sitting down in the same places as before, she asked, "Why not bring my instrument? Is there something wrong with it?"

"No, it's perfectly fine. But I can't teach anymore."

She looked at him questioningly.

"Or, rather I mayn't teach anymore. I have a cerebral aneurysm, and I collapsed on the train. The aneurysm is wrapped around my brainstem, partially at least, and inoperable. I shouldn't quite say that. It is operable, but the risk of damage or death is so great that it's better just to let it run its course and see how long I can live."

This recalled for Élodi the deaths of her parents, and the nausea and terror it had brought. Now whatever she had felt for him, confused as it was, was intensified.

"I have an insurance policy that covers disability, and they tell me that I'm now disabled. I'm not, but if I do any kind of work it voids the policy. I can't have that, because I need it for the people I'll leave behind. So I can't write or teach, even privately, even without compensation. Bureaucracy, public or private, is both stupid and monstrous."

"If you can't teach, why am I here?" she asked, thinking that although she herself had flirted with it, now it was he who was being what people of his age — unlike many of her contemporaries, she knew the expression and understood its context — called being 'too forward'. She both wanted him to be forward enough to make love to her, and not to be forward at all, which was exactly the way he felt. When they were thinking the same way, with a bias to attraction and risk, it made heat as if by induction: they could actually feel it between them. But when thinking the same way, with a bias toward caution and regret, they felt an internal, physical coldness. And when, as often happened as things changed between them in rapid oscillation, one was hot and the other cold, it made for a turbulence they could not master. But one kiss, one embrace, would have clarified everything.

"I'm not allowed to work, it's true. However, nothing prevents you from trying out my cello with the prospect of buying it," he said. "That's not work, but the sale of personal effects."

"And you can give me tips on how it should be played."

"Absolutely. The older the instrument, the more idiosyncratic."

"But you know," Élodi told him, losing her footing and out of character, "I can't afford it."

"Oh? I haven't set a price. How do you know? You haven't made an offer. And most instruments like these are passed down, with never a price."

"But you have a family."

"A daughter who doesn't play — and it must be played. That's why it exists."

"How much would it be worth if you did sell it?"

"I have no idea, but it's not one of those things to which a high monetary value is attached. If it were, I would have sold it to help my grandchild, who's sick."

"Is that what the insurance is for?"

"Yes."

"I see. Jules?" It was extremely pleasurable when she addressed him that way for the first time. It changed things and relaxed her. It also made him seem very old, so she thought that perhaps she shouldn't have done it. "I'm interested, perhaps, in purchasing your cello, as you cannot work. . . ."

"Ah," he said. "What a surprise."

"Yes. May I try it? And will you guide me in playing it, because things that are aged are so often idiosyncratic?"

"Very much so," he answered, meaning, also, yes.

She leaned forward and asked, not in a whisper but quietly and skeptically, "Are they watching you? Would anyone care?"

"They questioned me. They were here just recently. As unlikely as it seems, I wouldn't rule it out. But don't worry." He gestured toward the cello.

She took hold of it. "What would you like me to play?"

"Play what you brought."

"The Bach."

In what followed, they passed the cello back and forth, and in so doing, touched lightly. Although this might have made them less comfortable with one another, it made them more comfortable, particularly because after each touch came the Bach. Sometimes he had to cross the gap and sit next to her, and when he did she reddened and her perfume rose. She was life.

He wanted so much to stay with her that when she had to leave he saw her to the gate and beyond. As soon as they stepped into the street he saw the spectre of Damien Nerval catercorner in a car and pointing a large telephoto lens in their direction. Undoubtedly the camera had a motor drive, and the interior of the car now sounded like the inside of a cuckoo clock just before the cuckoo pops out.

Jules placed his hand against Élodi's left side, pivoted so his back was to Nerval, and said, "Don't look. They are watching. We should talk a while." He had been right about what he would feel — the silk, taut musculature, lovely breathing.

"They can find out that I'm enrolled, that I chose you as . . ." she began.

"I know. But if we talk . . ." he said.

"So what?"

"Perhaps," he dared, "we should pretend to kiss? That might put them off."

She thought it was funny that, suddenly, he was as awkward as a preadolescent. As seductive as she had ever been, with intense physical pleasure coursing through her as she spoke, she asked, "What level of verisimilitude do you have in mind?"

"I suppose it would have to be unambiguous."

"I think that's right."

He had never intended to kiss or embrace

her, and was afraid to do so. "I'd be afraid of joining my imperfection to your perfection. Afraid that I would be like someone who's just gotten up in the morning."

"I know what you mean," she said, "but I get up in the morning, too. So let's by my perfection find your imperfection out."

And they kissed — holding close — and it lasted for almost ten minutes.

Floating and in love, Jules went inside to work on his homage to Bach's *Sei Lob,* and found that he couldn't. All he could do was vibrate with pleasure and love as he replayed the kiss again and again and again. Although he knew it would never happen, Jules wanted to return with Élodi to her tiny apartment and forget everything that had kept him from her. He felt and imagined this so strongly it was as if he were with her in a new life that other than in dreams was impossible. And on the train, numb all the way home, hardly turning her head, Élodi would feel intense pleasure echoing through her entire body, with sadness following insistently in its wake.

But on the street outside the Shymanski compound, reality was still in command. After Élodi turned the corner on her way to the station, Arnaud and Duvalier simultaneously and explosively opened the doors of their car. Arnaud spoke for both of them as he alighted onto the pavement. "Who the hell is that?" For as Jules and Élodi had embraced and kissed, Nerval, in his nondescript Peugeot, was using the motor drive on his camera, and the two detectives had watched him, unable to move until Jules and Élodi had left.

As if it were a person to be interrogated, Arnaud approached the Peugeot at an investigative forty-five-degree angle. He was massive enough that it seemed as if he could have actually blocked the car had it tried to drive away. Duvalier rapped on the driver's window. Nerval calmly turned his head and sneered. Duvalier rapped again. Nothing.

"Open the window," Duvalier ordered.

Nerval stared at him without moving, "Why?" He asked so quietly that Duvalier knew what he said only because he read his lips.

Duvalier yanked open the door. "Who the hell are you?" he demanded to know.

"I am," came the answer, royally, "Damien Nerval, *investigateur.* Who are *you*?" He was still sneering, not because he wanted to, but because his face was constructed that way.

Duvalier held up his identification. "I am," he said, echoing and mocking Nerval's tone, "Duvalier Saidi-Sief, *flic.* If you don't want to be arrested, you'll tell me what you're doing."

"Arrested for what?" Nerval asked, and actually laughed.

"For obstructing an investigation. You're

ten seconds away."

"Me? You're investigating him, too?"

"Who?"

"Lacour," Nerval answered. "What are *you* investigating him for?"

"That's not your business," Duvalier told him. "What are you investigating?"

"I asked first."

"Get out of the car."

"All right, all right, irregularities in the purchase of an insurance contract."

"Really," Duvalier said. "That's fascinating, but we take precedence. You'll leave now and if I see you here again you'll be lucky to be arrested, understand?"

"No no no," said Nerval. "You don't get it. My employer is . . . well, I won't say anything. Believe me, you can't step all over our investigation."

"No no no no no," Duvalier echoed, wagging his finger. "My employers are . . . well, I will say that they don't have to bribe, trade, or ask for favors, because they're the people of France. Get it? Remember the Bastille? Yes? Good. Fuck off."

"We'll see," Nerval said, starting his engine. "We'll see what the minister says. I believe he's your employer, although at such a high level he could not possibly have heard of you."

"He can fuck off, too," Arnaud said.

Nerval tried to close the door, but Duvalier

blocked it, pulled him out of his seat, pushed him up against the side of his car, and hit him in the face — not half as hard as he could have. "Give the minister that message for me. And if I see you here again, I'll shoot you." He pushed the finally ruffled Nerval back into his car.

After the Peugeot sputtered up the street, an amazed Arnaud asked Duvalier, who was still shaking with anger, "Is that how you do it in Marseilles?"

"Yeah."

"I've heard."

"We have to."

It was dark, almost time for dinner, everyone was hungry, his visitors had pulled Jules from the music he was writing, and he had to receive them in his quarters rather than Shymanski's study. But he didn't care, because kissing Élodi was still with him.

They thought he had a saintly nature, because at this rare moment he was as beatific as a Tibetan monk. He offered them food and drink. They refused politely. He told him that the apartment was a study he had built as a private retreat. Would they like to go upstairs? No, they said, not·necessary. They had a feeling that something was off, because he fit the profile and because he didn't. They had already eliminated almost everyone else in the rowing club. Of course this alone had elevated their suspicion, although logically it should not have.

"We're investigating an incident," Arnaud said. "We'd like to ask a few questions."

"Certainly. What incident?"

"We'll get to that later."

"That's strange."

"We're roundabout," Duvalier stated.

Jules countered, "I'm roundabout too, and I have all evening. I have all day. Whatever you'd like. We can have dinner. We can go bowling." He was elated.

"You seem quite happy."

Jules just laughed.

"The girl?"

"You saw?"

"Yes. She's young for you."

"Far too young," Jules agreed. "Impossible. I don't understand. This kind of thing is happening to me now, when life should be quieting down."

"You're not taking it further?" Duvalier asked. "I saw her. I would."

"I would, too, but she's half a century younger than I am. That's insane. I do love her, but I don't know if she feels anything for me other than curiosity and, perhaps, respect, or, who knows, pity."

"People carry such things further every day."

"You mean, like the one-hundred-and-twenty-year-old man who married a young woman of twenty? I'm not that stupid."

"Well, in your case it's only fifty years. What have you got to lose?" Duvalier asked. Everyone was amused, certainly Jules, who understood the humor better than did his guests.

"Listen, there are two ways of meeting death."

"Death?" Duvalier asked. This alone was enough to wake up a policeman.

"I collapsed on the RER and lay there half dead for as many stops as it took for someone to suspect that I might not have been a drunk. It was at the Gare de Lyon, very convenient to the hospital. Had I gone to the end of the line I'd be dead. I have what's called a basilar aneurysm, and could go at any moment. The guy on the street with the camera? Suddenly I attract scrutiny, because I bought an insurance policy just before it happened."

"He's not there anymore."

"You met him?"

"We did. We told him to get lost."

"Oh."

"So, the girl. You'll keep yourself from her?"

"Yes. It's crazy that I love her, but I do. Still, I know that to meet death, and for me death is near, you either strip all things of their value so as not to regret too much, or you learn distance."

"What do you mean, 'learn distance'?"

"With distance, as things recede, you need

not reject or devalue them to protect yourself. If you achieve distance, that which you might otherwise betray for fear of losing it still seems benevolent, loving — but gently dimming, going silent. Life recedes gradually until all that was bright and startling is like a city seen from afar, the noise of wind and traffic a barely audible hiss. You glide away without pain, and you love it still. She's in the bright world that I have to leave."

Duvalier and Arnaud hardly knew what to say, but they had a mental list and they went through it. "You served in Algeria," Arnaud said. He could not help but think of Duvalier.

"You've been looking into me?"

"Yes."

"Why?"

"We may get to that later. But you don't seem especially surprised."

"What should surprise me? An idiot from the insurance company is taking pictures of me as I kiss a young woman I love but cannot have. I collapsed on the train. I have to deal with a detestable man whose name is Rich Panda. My grandson has leukemia. Classical music is as popular as hoopskirts. Two policemen show up at my door. Look, I wouldn't be surprised if aliens came down and chopped me up for cat food. What did you say?"

"Algeria."

"What about it?"

"What do you think about Arabs?"

"I don't."

"What do you mean, you 'don't'?" Duvalier asked.

"I don't think about Arabs, per se."

"What is your opinion of them?"

"I'm a Jew," Jules told him. "My parents were murdered by the Germans because they were Jews. The gravest, most persistent sin of mankind lies in not treating everyone as an individual. So, in short, I take Arabs as they come, just like everyone else."

"But as a group?"

"As a group? They have a very high incidence of killing innocents with whom they disagree. It's part of the culture, part of Islam, part of their nomadic origins. But no individual is merely a reflection of a group. That's the injustice that ruins the world. So, my answer is that for me an Arab is the same as a Jew, a Frenchman, a Norwegian, anything you'd like. If I were to judge people by their identity, I'd be like the people who killed my parents. Those were called Nazis. Do you think I could ever be one?"

"Did you have the same opinion in Algeria when you were at war with Arabs?"

"In Algeria, officers — before you were born — I had very little contact with Arabs. I was surrounded by French soldiers or alone in the forest. Even had I been prone to developing prejudices, I had very little material with which to work."

"But now," Duvalier pressed, "do you think they're ruining the country?"

"Yes," Jules answered, "along with everyone else. If you must speak collectively, they don't get a pass. Some people burn cars, sell drugs, and rob passersby. Others buy drugs, live off the state, or, in airy offices at the top of skyscrapers, allocate capital, as they say, which is playing *Chemin de Fer* with other people's money. Non-Arab *politichiens* take bribes and thrust their grossly inferior selves into positions they're not competent to fill. And, may I add, pretentious, dissolute, beatnik philosophers sleep with the wives of their best friends."

"I'm not going to let you get off that easy," Duvalier announced. "What you say is anodyne. But I want to know what you think of the Arabs in France, one in ten of the population — as a whole, a community, a culture, a polity. Good for France? Bad? Indifferent?"

"Why would you want to know that? You're not an opinion survey, you're a policeman."

"It bears upon the incident we're investigating."

"Am I a suspect?"

"No. We have no suspects at the moment."

"I don't understand, but I'll be happy to offer my opinion. It was wrong for France to try to make Algeria a little France, to construct a replica of itself there and in other countries. We became a foreign master that destroyed the rhythms and tranquility of those places — both their qualities that were good and their qualities that were not. And it's just as wrong — because we did not by and large assimilate in the Arab lands, and the Arabs do not by and large assimilate here — to have a little North Africa in France. Those who are here already should be made more welcome than they have been, but they must become French."

Duvalier, because he agreed, played the devil's advocate: "Why?" He expected a long essay. François would have supplied one, in impassioned, bear-like tones, with Italianate gestures.

But Jules replied, "They must become French, because this is France."

"You enjoy this," said Arnaud, who had been quietly observing, ready to be either the good cop or the bad cop.

"Sometimes I enjoy everything, but what do you mean by 'this'?"

"The questioning."

"Certainly," Jules told him. He couldn't resist adding, in English, *"I'm having a whale time."*

Arnaud, whose English was only elementary, thought that whatever the reference to a whale, it was very sophisticated. "The people we interview usually hate it. They get jumpy, tortured. Why are you having fun like a whale?"

"A lot of it," Jules said, "is left over from what you saw on the street, but it's not just that. My wife is dead, my only child long married, I have no more students, and my oldest friend is a quisling and a liar to whom I will not speak ever again. I can go a whole day saying only five or ten words to a human being — a waiter, the man who sells newspapers, the guard at the swimming pool. Now you show up, two cops, and you're asking me interesting questions purely out of left field — what do I think about Arabs, am I going to make love to the girl you saw me with at the gate. And, then, maybe, we'll get to why you're here. Of course it's fun. Stay all night. Have you had dinner? We don't have to go out. I can fix you something. I have a big American steak, enough for three, even him," Jules said, meaning Arnaud. "I can barbecue it. . . ."

"Please," Duvalier said, holding up his hand like a traffic cop, which for a while in the beginning he was. "We won't be long. Now, moving on, you row on the Seine, is that correct?"

"How do you know that?"

"But you haven't rowed since October."

"You know that, too?"

"According to the log in the boathouse."

"I went to America. Then it was winter.

Then I learned I have an aneurysm. The doctor told me that I shouldn't row, and that means I'll have to sell my boat. If I die suddenly, I don't want to be lost in the Seine. It's deep, turgid, and flows fast. I don't want my daughter not to know where I've come to rest."

"But," Duvalier said, "after winter, *before* your aneurysm, you didn't row. Others have started up again, months ago. Why not you?"

"No mystery," Jules said. "I got out of shape. Every new season you have to begin again, and the older you are the more difficult it is."

"Fair enough. How long have you rowed on the Seine?"

"Sixty years or so."

"You must know it as well as a harbor pilot."

"That's an interesting point. You'd think that after sixty years I would. When I first took to the river I thought that, with practice, without turning to see where my bow was pointing I could chance gliding between bridge piers and hewing to the center of a channel, or taking the bends in the river while not hitting the bank. Align the stern tip on a waypoint, count the strokes, and have confidence that you won't ram a stone pier. It doesn't work that way, and I've never done it. Granted, I navigate well and don't veer off course, but I have to turn my head and check all the time. It was a disappointment through all those years. I used to think, ten more years, and I'll be able to do it without turning to check. No."

"You're familiar, however, with the currents."

"They vary with the season and the rainfall."

"You know the Bir-Hakeim Bridge?"

"It's where I make my turn. I used to row, sometimes, when I had all day, all the way to Bercy, but now I turn at Bir-Hakeim."

"So you'd know how the river ran from the Île aux Cygnes to the boathouse."

"You have to know. You're pushed at sometimes ten kilometers per hour, and to keep the prow properly oriented in such a current you have to row at about five kilometers an hour at a minimum, so your speed below Bir-Hakeim on the return can be up to twenty, if the Alpine regions are gushing water into the Île-de-France after big storms."

"How do you keep from slamming into the dock?"

"You go past it, turn, and approach from the west in almost slow motion."

"After the Île aux Cygnes, what does the river do?"

"It veers south, pushing you toward the south bank. You have to keep away, because traffic can run against you there, and when you get to the boathouse you don't want to try to cross against the current. Why do you ask? It seems very odd."

"So if someone were to fall in the river at the Île aux Cygnes, he would be swept West and South?"

"Yes."

"Could he manage to stay on the north side enough to get out at the boathouse dock?"

Jules furrowed his brow, as if trying to plumb the reason for this question. "You know what a vector is?"

Arnaud, an engineer, did. Duvalier, a student of the humanities and Korean, did not. Jules saw that he didn't, and even though Arnaud nodded, Jules explained for Duvalier. "Simply put, if you want to go straight ahead and the current is pushing you to the right, you pull to the left enough so that you end up where you intended to arrive in the first place. When I pass the Île aux Cygnes, I row with a heavy bias to the north so as to compensate for the current taking the boat south. The wind complicates it further."

"What if you're in the water?"

"I *am* in the water," Jules said, as if they were idiots.

"Not in a boat, swimming."

Now looking at them as if they really were idiots, Jules said, "Nobody of any intelligence swims in the Seine. It's filthy and dangerous."

"If you capsized?"

Jules smiled. "You've given me an opportunity to boast. In almost sixty years I've never gone over, so I wouldn't know. Everyone else goes over — once a year, twice, certainly in the beginning. Ask them. But it hasn't happened to me. I've never been in the Seine."

"Why is that, do you think?"

"Balance, caution, luck. Over the years I've had close calls. I've been out when the wind was so high there were whitecaps. The wakes of barges and motorboats have washed over me. I've been attacked by fat swans running across the water with outstretched wings. But I've never capsized."

"Hypothetically, then. A swimmer south of the Île aux Cygnes, who wants to get out at the boathouse dock. . . ."

"He'd better be a strong swimmer and he'd have to vector north, or he'd end up slammed against the bank of the Île Saint-Germain. If he tried swimming directly across he'd be washed to Sèvres. The Seine runs strong. Geography has made a narrow channel, and the embankments narrow it further. When the flow of a wide river is narrowed, it must take on speed."

"All right," Duvalier said. "We're almost finished. Two more questions."

Jules waited. He looked neither apprehensive nor disturbed. What they didn't know was that he could feel the touch of Élodi as if she were still held against him. She was small-breasted and firm. It had seemed that when she was pressed to him the feel of her body was something that answered all questions by making them, for a time at least, irrelevant. Although Arnaud and Duvalier were unaware of it, now and then traces of her perfume on his clothing would drift up and absent him from the scene.

Duvalier asked where he was on the night of the murder, specifying the date.

"How could I possibly answer that?" Jules said. "Who remembers that way? Do you?"

"No one does. But that was the last day you rowed. Does that help?"

"Not really. I could look at my calendar, my checkbook, credit card statements."

"Would you do that please?"

Jules went to his desk and opened some drawers, taking out his calendar of the previous year, 2014, and his check ledger. The day in question was blank except that he had recorded the number of the row, its distance, and the cumulative distance. He had written no checks that day, the day before, or for several days thereafter.

"Credit card statements," Arnaud said. "May we see them?"

From a filing cabinet nearby Jules fished out the proper month's statements. On the date in question there was nothing. François had paid for dinner that evening, in cash.

"I see," Duvalier said. "Did you know that, that night, there was a double murder, on the bridge and on the Île aux Cygnes? The murderer jumped into the Seine. We have contradictory descriptions. One fits you approximately, and from all we can tell the perpetrator left the river at the boathouse dock."

Jules looked momentarily stunned. Then he laughed. "You think it's me?"

"It could be you."

"I don't know what to say. Why would I murder anyone? Who was murdered?"

"Two boys, or, depending on how you look at it, young men," Duvalier told him. Then, observing very carefully and speaking precisely, he said, "The murderer met resistance and left a lot of blood. Therefore, we have his DNA. Would you object to giving us a sample — just a cheek swab — so that we can eliminate you as a suspect?"

Duvalier and Arnaud saw a momentary break in Jules' composure. For just a moment, he looked like someone who was caught. But only for a moment, the time it took him to reflect that he had not been wounded, and to remember that the boy he had saved had bled profusely.

"And I might add," Arnaud did add, "that the DNA tells us that the murderer was an Ashkenazi Jew, like me, and like you. Am I not correct?"

556

"That's true," Jules said. "I am. And I'd be happy to give you a cheek swab, or blood, if you'd like."

"The swab is enough."

"By all means," Jules said, opening his mouth wide, and, they noted, suppressing a laugh, which they could see in his eyes and because he shook like someone who is laughing.

"Well," Duvalier declared when they were in the car, as he held up the plastic envelope that contained the cheek swab, "that takes care of him, one way or another."

"Yes it does," Arnaud answered.

"He fits the description, Arnaud."

"Except that he's forty-five years older, he has hair, and he's not as fat as a hippopotamus."

"You can't have everything."

"I know. God works in strange ways, doesn't He? What do you think he's doing now?"

"God or Lacour?"

"Lacour. It would be easier to figure out what God is doing."

"I don't know. If I were he I'd be sitting in a chair, eyes closed, breathing deeply, remembering again and again how I kissed that beautiful girl."

ÉLODI ALONE

Years before he died, Élodi's father, explaining that he no longer wanted to argue, left the practice of law. He preferred to trim the hedges, cut the lawn, and sit on the terrace in the sun — a terrace distinguished by its healthy geraniums in long-lasting, vivid red. In the summer season, from its balustraded expanse one could watch white clouds riding on the wind over snow-covered mountains high enough not to feel the heat of May or June.

He told her — after a while repetitively — that when he was young he loved the sight of things so much that he needed nothing else, and found extraordinary happiness in color, a graceful line, the sun on rippling water, a strong wind waving through the wheat. When by necessity he had had to make a living, pay taxes, pass exams, fight opponents, this had left, and he wanted it back.

Neither he nor her mother was able to convey to her the common quality of knowing how to get along in the world, to read what people said when they were saying something else, and to withhold the truth when it had to be told. This was fine in the lush park where she grew up. There, she had music, mountains, and even a rushing stream in the sound of which she heard melodies that she could later repeat as she played. But in the society of others she was at sea. She went to Paris to study music so she could work as a musician and have the ability to live, if not on a grand scale, for the music itself.

Music asked nothing, required nothing, needed nothing, betrayed nothing. It appeared instantly when called, even in memory. It was made of the ineffable magic in the empty spaces between — and the relation of – its otherwise unremarkable components. It arose ex nihilo to encompass and express everything. It fled into silence most modestly when it was done. It seemed to have a mind and a heart of its own. It teased with its perfection and led right up to the gates of heaven. Even at rest it was always ready to be called, it had existed forever, and it would last as long.

She practiced for many hours a day, but as she had to break them up she walked a great deal, and rested in parks, sitting still — as she had learned from her father — and harvesting strength and well-being from form, color, and light.

She knew it was sad that she was in love with a man who, although he was still strong and virile, was so ancient it was absurd. And unlike the love that would be appropriate to a woman her age, it ebbed more than it flowed. At times she was infilled by it, but it would always flee and leave her empty. Even at its strongest, it was dying.

Paris in July is frenetic and hot, but unlike the heat of August, when everyone leaves anyway, the heat of July doesn't slow the pace that builds to a frenzy in spring and early summer, and is still a great encourager of hopes, actions, and sex. Summer dresses, light clothing, bare arms and shoulders, the ease of a hot afternoon, open windows with warm breezes sweeping over white bed linen turned back, work done, the telephone not ringing. . . . But Élodi was still alone.

Her infatuation with Jules was ending in nothing. That he would not take the lead, she knew, was in large part out of consideration for her. Had he slept with her, as he and she wanted, it would have been easy to end. Instead they had had weekly lessons that were tense and exciting for what they withheld, which was somehow poured into the musicianship.

"Because we perform," he said, "we've become addicted to praise. At an early age we look not to the music but to a teacher's approval, and later to the applause of the audience, the reviewer's sentence or two, or perhaps, eventually, to the world tour, posters in front of the concert hall, the wide-eyes of hotel clerks and managers as fame knocks them back like a wave. The object seems to be to become so revered that you have to build a wall around your house — except where its lawns meet the Lake of Geneva or the sea off Antibes. And as you seek approval, praise, position, wealth, and fame, the music becomes the means rather than the end."

"For me, music is the end," she replied, "as I have and likely will have none of those other things."

"You don't have them, yet," he insisted. "If you do have them, as I think you will, you'll be pointed in the wrong direction whether or not you want to be. And when those things fail, as they must, you'll have been diverted from the music after having betrayed it. Grocery clerks, railroad workers, farmers, private soldiers, and street cleaners expect neither praise nor fame. Their reward comes quietly as they pass through life unrecognized. Learn to live like them. The music is all you need. And if you stray from it, it won't have you back."

At the end of July, when heat and diesel fumes had begun to push the city into the slough of August but there was still enough of the freshness of summer to sustain the excitement of the month's last days, Élodi had practiced all morning, had a picnic in the Place des Vosges, returned home to practice until three, and then walked to the Jardin du Luxembourg. She found a bench with an open prospect and took a seat next to two elderly women miraculously in coats and hats.

Élodi placed a bottle of mineral water between herself and the adjacent old lady, and put a folded newspaper on her lap. She tried to read it, but instead her eyes fixed on a ridge of palaces and domes beneath a sky in full and turbulent motion. She was in the yellow dress. It was hot enough that her skin glistened, and parts of the dress that pressed at her sides and beneath her breasts were wet enough that the silk clung to her body. In the direct sun, strong in July even at four, her hair shone blindingly gold.

Perhaps she was the first one in all of Paris to see the beginnings of a black-and-purple thunderstorm coming in from the east. The clouds were as massive as alps and would bring cooling rain and wind. She knew and was sure that they would rescue her from the heat even though she hadn't hoped for their aid. She thought back to the mountains she could see from her room when she was a girl. Snow pouring down like a torrent over a fall,

with musical rhythm, filling the world: furi-
ous, joyous, suicidal, glorious. Stop the trains,
stop the cars, cloak the trees and telephone
wires in white, clear the paths of cracks and
imperfections, silence footfalls, quiet the
world, and amplify light until day lasts into
night.

She almost forgot where she was and that it
was summer, but then the wind picked up. It
fluttered dresses, and it ruffled newspapers,
making them hard to read. But because it offered relief in evaporation no one seemed to
understand that it was the emissary of an approaching storm.

Though she was far from her apartment
and knew it would rain, she held her place,
remembering distant thunder rumbling
through the mountains, in hairpin echoes
twisting along the valleys, like replicas of the
jagged lightning that made it. Weak but long-
lasting at a distance, the sound left no doubt
that in the mountains themselves the crash of
thunder was deafening. She used to hear it as
it emerged in the night from a crucible of
distant flashes, and she could track it in the
crackling static on the radio. There was nothing quite like a Beethoven symphony from
Bern or Berlin cast over the mountains in the
darkness of a storm and landing in her room,
wounded by lightning but playing on. The
glowing plastic obelisk on the radio dial was
yellowed and warm as it locked on to music

riding on the rain.

With clouds north and east of Paris rising to take up more and more of the sky, the wind picked up and distant thunder could be heard as little curls of lightning jumped from cloud to cloud. People fled. The wind gusted, and took a hat or two. Knowing that the storm wouldn't arrive for ten or fifteen minutes, Élodi remained seated. She would have time to get to a café and watch the downpour scouring the streets and sidewalks until it passed as quickly as it had come, leaving in its wake ten minutes of humid air that would dry in the sun.

The old ladies struggled up, gathered their things, and waddled off. As she watched them go she discovered that a young man was sitting as close to the other end of the bench as he could get, deeply absorbed in sketching on a newspaper-sized pad. Because of the angle at which he held the paper so as to fight the wind, she couldn't see what he was drawing, but she lifted herself a little higher and craned her neck. He glanced to his left, and after their eyes met he was slow in turning away, but he did, and reddened so much it looked like apoplexy. He was tall, he had a sensitive face with fine features, he was as young as she was, and so shy that, though he tried, he couldn't unredden. To her, this meant that he was good. It meant as well that he would probably not approach her.

So she moved next to him to look at what he was doing. The effect was extraordinary. He reacted so strongly to her presence that his pulse beat in his neck as if he were running a hard race. She herself was stunned by what she saw. "That's beautiful," she said. "It's so beautiful. It looks like a Leonardo. It's magnificent."

"It's derivative," was his modest answer, "and there's no demand for such things now."

"Don't worry about that," Élodi told him. "We're in barbaric times. What is supposed to be and is no longer art has fused with publicity like a dead tree wrapped in ivy, and anyway, you don't find your own voice 'til you're older." (Jules had said these very words to her.) "If you do find it early, it will likely be insufficient — unless you're Mozart."

"Are you a musician?"

She nodded. "Cellist. Just a student."

"I'm a student. Given your appearance, I would think you were a lawyer, or a banker. Maybe you were ENA, and are high in a ministry."

"Really? Why?"

"Your elegance."

"Oh no, I'm not like that. My apartment is the size of a broom closet."

"My apartment," he said, remembering what it was like. "Let's see, the bathtub is in the living room, as is the kitchen, as is the

565

bedroom and the hall. But really, you look like you live in Passy in a penthouse of a thousand square meters."

"No," she said. "No penthouse, no bank, no ministry, no money. This is my best dress."

"Why did you wear your best dress to the park on a day when it's likely to rain? If I may ask. Sorry."

"You may ask, and you needn't be sorry. Although I don't know why, I wanted to look my best. And I don't have many others."

The air was full of electricity, light, and shadow. She felt an excitement she had never felt. Unlike what she had experienced with Jules, it was divorced entirely from sadness and obligation. The whole world seemed to be opening before her with a benevolence, excitement, and ease — as in the most beautiful music. She had waited too long, and now it started to rain in huge drops, almost the size of grapes, spread few and far between, but that was all right. The wind picked up, and lightning echoed north of Paris. Élodi and the art student left together to find shelter. And they would stay together, for the rest of their lives.

AUGUST

Because they had come up with nothing, Duvalier and Arnaud decided upon a tactic they had been taught in training and that they and every recruit had hoped never to use. If everything you have is unavailing, the foundation of your investigation must be faulty. Therefore, you remove the strongest support, as upon it the rest of the edifice depends. In the bridge murders, the strongest element was negative. The DNA evidence ruled out all the suspects, including, most recently, Jules. What if the blood that had pooled on the bridge deck had come not from the perpetrator or any of the victims but from someone else? The blood at the bottom of the stairs didn't match the blood on the deck. The killer rode the second victim down to the Île aux Cygnes as if on a sled, but even if he left no blood on the way, had he stopped bleeding enough so as not to leave a trace on the second victim, or a trail as he ran? The forensics people had grid-searched a meter on each side of his path as reported by the witnesses and police, and found not the tiniest droplet.

Ignoring the DNA led to an even deader end, so they started over, which involved viewing the surveillance tapes and investigating more thoroughly each member of the rowing club who might have been physically able to mount the attack, take to the Seine, and survive. That it was a rowing club meant that nearly everyone was strong enough to have done so. They combed databases and started the long process of re-interviewing their prospects, from the top of the list down, even though, purely from intuition, they had drawn redlines under four of the names. They wanted to take these — of which one was Jules — as they came, so as to disallow a bias and yet not disallow anyone who might seem unlikely.

They started in May, alternating the numbing review of tapes (though these were hard drives, they still called them tapes) and doing interviews. Often they walked to the interviews, for exercise and to be in the open air, and so that they could have lunch in various interesting restaurants and sit in parks afterward, as they read the paper, discussed the case, or just took in the sun. Sometimes they did necessary shopping. They knew the case so well that they could read one another's thoughts about whatever passed before them.

In the first days of August, with Paris largely empty of the French, they persevered automatically. Most of their subjects had left the city, everything was slow, they were almost forgotten, no one was looking over their work, and it was so hot that the birds sang less. Finishing in the middle of the afternoon of August 10th, a Monday, they returned to the office in a half-trance after the blazing light of the street. Dead leaves littering the parks because of heat kill were a reminder that fall would soon bring bright colors and cool wind.

Arnaud went off to splash water on his face, and as Duvalier, not even trying anymore to think of the case, sank into his chair he noticed a manila envelope on Arnaud's desk. When Arnaud came through the door, Duvalier told him that something had arrived from his *commissariat.*

Arnaud sat down. "Probably changes in regulations. They're always pestering us with crap like that and more things to do." Leaning back in his chair, he opened the envelope the way one deals with the tenth piece of junk mail in a stack, his chief concern being to avoid a paper cut.

"What's this?" he said as an envelope fell out, and a note from the *commissariat.* The envelope had Turkish stamps on it. "What is this?" he asked Duvalier, holding up the envelope.

" *'Türkiye Cumhuriyeti.'* That's just like Arabic — *jumhuriyatu:* meaning republic."

"And this building?"

Duvalier looked at the picture of a building on one of the stamps. "I don't know, but it says *'Askari Yargitay,'* and 'a hundred years.' It's the hundredth anniversary of *Askari Yargitay. Askari* were soldiers. *Yargitay* I think is a court. Maybe it's some sort of military court. So what? That's just a stamp. What does the note say?"

"It's from Koko," Arnaud answered, displeased.

"Who's Koko?"

"He's the idiot who. . . . They can't send him on patrol so they keep him at the office. He does secretarial work. I don't know how he got through training. The second or third day he was on duty, he was sitting in a patrol car and he shot himself in the thigh and calf."

"Through the thigh and into the calf?"

"No, two shots."

"How can you shoot yourself by accident, twice?"

"He said he thought someone had shot him so he shot back. He limps, of course."

"He says, 'My dearest Arnaud. . . .' "

"What's his native language?"

"French. 'This letter came to you about two weeks ago from the DGSI, with no explanation. I left it on your desk but you never showed up so I'm sending it. They opened it and sealed it with the kind of tape you try to fix tears with when you mistakenly tear a letter or something. I didn't read it. No one did. Hope to see you soon, Koko.' "

"Maybe you should try to transfer to this *commissariat*," Duvalier said.

"Maybe I should." Arnaud cut through the tape but before he took the letter out of the envelope he read the postmark. "It came into France in the middle of April. This is August, so it's undoubtedly urgent."

In the envelope was a letter and a folded receipt from a restaurant in Paris: Chez Renée, 14 Boulevard Saint-Germain. Arnaud swept his eyes to the bottom of the letter. "It's from Raschid Belghazi. He was cleared to travel. He wasn't at all a suspect."

"I'll bet he went to Syria," Duvalier said. "Am I right?"

"Yes. What does this say?" He passed the letter to Duvalier.

"It says. . . ."

"I thought you didn't know Arabic?"

"I know enough to know this. It says, *'La Allah illa Allah, wa Muhammadu Rasul' Allahi. La qanun illa ashariyatu.'* 'There is no God but Allah, and Muhammad is the prophet of God. There is no law but the *shariya.'* " He handed it back to Arnaud.

"And this?" Arnaud turned the letter and held it up for Duvalier to translate.

" 'In the name of Allah, the merciful, the

compassionate.' The Arabic handwriting is pathetic, like a five-year-old's — not that I can do much better."

The rest was in French. Arnaud read, haltingly. He hadn't much practice reading aloud, in that he was a policeman and he had no children. "He writes: 'By the time you read this, I hope I will be a martyr. The caliphate is growing. In your lifetime France will be Muslim. There will be no unbelievers. Notre Dame will be a mosque of Allah, and the only book will be the Holy Quran.

" 'You gave me your card to tell you if I thought of anything. Now that I am waging jihad and will be a martyr I am proud to say that the three of us went to rob and kill a Jew. We found one on the bridge and beat him, but before we could cut off his head a man came from behind, the one you're looking for. He was older than I said, and his description was what you said. He did yell something in German, but I don't know what. I made a lot up because I didn't want you to find him. Then he would have said that he saved the Jew, so I changed things. I threw our knives in the water and picked up this, which he dropped. Now maybe you can find him so he will die in prison at the hand of the brothers even before the armies of the Caliph enter Paris and clean it of all such filth when they come. And they will, God willing.

" 'Raschid Belghazi.' "

Arnaud and Duvalier were still for a moment before they turned their attention to the receipt, which they handled by pinching it at the edge. It was stained with blood.

"Get a plastic envelope," Arnaud said.

"Why don't *you* get a plastic envelope?" Duvalier asked.

"Because I don't know where they are."

"After all these months?"

"In which I haven't had to use one."

"They're right next to the DNA pouches, in the cabinet," Duvalier told him as he left, "the one near the copy machine."

"Good to know," Arnaud said, "for the next time we get a bloodstained restaurant check from Syria."

When the evidence was encased, they examined it more carefully. In a rapid, feminine hand, it read: *'Crécy, boeuf, eaux gaz 2g, saucis, pain, mousse choc 2, tasse, serv.'* The whorls of the letters looked like roller-coaster loops and pigtails, and after each entry was a number, the total being €83. Not surprisingly, the date was the same as the date of the murders, although the waitress had not written the year.

"Two people, Duvalier, one of whom is ours."

"Maybe they paid with a credit card. Let's go."

"Later," Arnaud said.

"Why Later?"

"I have to go to the dentist. The restaurant will be open in the evening. It might even be closed now."

"All right. I'll copy the check to show them, and give the original over for blood and prints. How can you wait? How can you stand it?"

"Because my tooth hurts. We've been at this for months. Nobody's going anywhere. He says to eat fewer things with sugar. He's right. I don't even like it, really. It's too sweet. I like flavor. I should be able to do without it, don't you think?"

When they arrived at the restaurant it was early and almost no one was there. An old lady who had to have remembered the conquest and liberation of Paris was drinking red wine at a corner table. She wore a blocky black hat of the forties and, in the heat of August, a dark coat. Someone like that, both detectives sensed, whose husband was probably long gone, whose children, had she any, were old, and whose life had wilted, had reason to drink in a corner as she waited for nothing and knew it.

The head waiter's pencil mustache made him look like he should have been in a silent film. As Renée's husband or father, or whoever he was, approached them, menus in hand, they took out their identification.

"Is this familiar to you?" Arnaud asked, handing over the receipt.

"It's our *addition.*"

"Did you write it?"

"No. Josette."

"Is she still employed by you?"

"She's right there," he said, pointing to a woman polishing drinking glasses. All the two detectives had to do was pivot.

"Yes?" she said.

"Did you write this?" Duvalier asked. He handed her the receipt.

"I did."

"What can you tell us about it?"

"It's an order for two. *Purée Crécy.* We serve that in season due to the quality of the carrots harvested at Crécy. *Boeuf Bourguignon,* twenty Euros. Two Badoits. *Saucisson de Lyon,* fifteen Euros. Bread. Two *mousses au chocolat.* Tax. *Service.* You know, we don't use carrots from Crécy, but no one can tell the difference. Perhaps I shouldn't say that, because you're policeman, but he didn't know the difference."

"Who?"

"The guy who ordered it."

"Did he pay with a credit card?"

"Cash. We note credit cards."

"Do you remember who he was?"

"Of course I do. He's famous."

"He's famous?"

575

"Yes. I've seen him on television. Sometimes on the news, sometimes late at night. Once he was on for an hour, just talking. I don't think I could talk on television for more than a second."

"Who?"

She looked at them with contemptuous sheep eyes. They could see that she thought they were really stupid for not knowing the person she was thinking about. Then her expression changed to one of happy superiority. "François Ehrenshtamm." She smiled as if to say, 'What unbelievable idiots!'

Duvalier answered, "François Ehrenshtamm, really?"

"He comes in."

"Do you remember whom he was with?" They were excited, because they were narrowing it down: Ehrenshtamm, perhaps, or his dining companion.

"*Who* he was with," she corrected (she thought). "Different people. Sometimes alone."

"But this time?"

She shook her head to say that she didn't, and added a shrug of the shoulders as confirmation.

The overwhelming color in François' apartment was red. It was as if he and his young wife and the beautiful, blue-eyed, baby girl in her arms lived inside a rose in summer. It

must've been on purpose, part of his philosophy — while one was alive, at almost any
cost, to seek heat, warmth, blood, vitality,
fecundity. Who else would paint walls deep
red? It was simultaneously comforting, envel-
oping, and exciting — just full of life. The
baby's aquamarine-blue eyes against the red
made Duvalier and Arnaud feel that they had
exited the world they knew, and they envied
the beauty and warmth of that into which
they suddenly had come.

Like most famous people, whose many
surpluses allow them to be generous, François
welcomed his visitors graciously. He brought
the two detectives into the living room —
where immense bookshelves stretched from
floor to ceiling four meters high — and,
because dinner was over, offered them dessert. The rules didn't oblige them to refuse,
so they didn't. Young Madame Ehrenshtamm
— the baby content in a sling in front of her
and curious enough to turn her head to the
guests each time her mother changed direction — brought chocolate mousse and tea.

"Your favorite," Duvalier said.

Only somewhat surprised, because it was
not exactly a wild guess, François answered,
"Yes."

"You like it at Chez Renée?"

"Absolutely." Unthreatened, François
waited for the line of questioning. He enjoyed
the prospect, as he was used to questions,

challenges, and verbal sparring, and justly thought himself at least the equal of even the most skilled advocate. He had triumphed once at a trial, emerging from hostile cross-examination the complete master of the proceedings.

"And you like *Purée Crécy?*"

"I do, yes. It's a childhood food, like *madeleines.*"

"Proust," Arnaud said.

"Proust," François echoed, not quite condescendingly.

"So," Duvalier went on, "do you remember the last time you had *purée Crécy,* and *mousse au chocolat* at Chez Renée?"

"Not really. It must've been quite a while ago."

"Last fall?"

François looked like it was coming back to him. "Maybe."

"And your dinner companion had *boeuf Bourguignon.*"

"How do you know that?"

"We have witnesses and documentation."

"You have witnesses and documentation? For my dinner at a restaurant?"

"Yes. We know the time and the date, that you were there. All we need to know is who was with you."

"Why?"

"That's the subject of investigation."

Feeling that he had already done enough to damage Jules, François grew reticent.

"Who was it?" Arnaud asked.

"It was a long time ago. I often eat out with friends, colleagues, interviewers, editors."

"Yes, but you know who it was."

"How do you know I know?"

"Your expression. You're covering."

"You're sure of that?"

"I am. This is what we do. Sorry," Duvalier told him, "but the penalty for obstructing an investigation is not nothing."

"The investigation is not about something serious, is it?" Madame Ehrenshtamm asked.

"No," Duvalier lied, "just a stolen car."

Knowing that Jules could not be possibly have stolen a car, and with his own interest and that of his new family in mind, François told Duvalier who it was. But when he saw the stunned, pleasurable look on the faces of his guests, which, though they were professionals, they could not suppress, François knew that he had betrayed Jules once again.

Determined to die within a week, Jules had already made a partial step into another world. Had he felt a need to describe this, which he did not, he might have said that it was like heading out to sea with only a glance at the land left behind. The rhythm of the waves was smooth and reassuring. He had no fear. The music he heard, rising from a lifetime, was seductive and comforting. He had discovered that to die with a purpose made death far less daunting than merely to die at its whim.

It was nine or ten — he was not sure — but it was dark as he sat on his terrace, near the row of pines, breathing steadily and calmed by their scent. He had said goodbye to Cathérine. He had embraced and kissed the baby, whose skin was flushed and salty. He loved Cathérine very much, but he didn't give her the slightest reason to suspect that she would never see him, alive, again, except to say that he would be making arrangements that would help Luc. Cathérine's expression was that of the child to whom the parent is once again the mystery that the adolescent imagines she has dispelled.

Lost in thought and remembrance, Jules didn't notice that someone was knocking on the door. But because the gardener, who knew François, had told him that Jules was in, François persisted until Jules was roused. He walked slowly through the big living room to the hall, and opened the door with so little energy it suggested disdain.

François thought Jules was looking past him. "Jules?" he said, as if it were not Jules.

"François."

"I'm sorry. I'm so sorry."

"That's all right," Jules said dispassionately.

"May I come in? I have something important to tell you."

Jules turned and, without closing the door, led François into the living room.

"Where's the piano?" François asked.

"I sold it. Shymanski is finally out. I have to leave by the first of September."

"Where will you go?"

"I have the perfect place to go, really, the most perfect place."

"I see. The house is nearly empty. Have you begun moving already?"

"I sold a lot of stuff."

"The cello," François said, eyeing the cello. "You'll carry it out yourself?"

"The cello will be the last thing to go, just before me, but, no, I've arranged for it to be sent."

"Where?"

"The fourth *arrondissement.*"

"That could be expensive."

"Yes. Remember the girl I told you about? She lives there."

"Oh. You're going to start a new life?" François was surprised and curious, and was about to ask more questions when Jules, who had much the upper hand, cut him off.

"François, why have you shown up, at night, without calling?" Jules never would have said that to him before.

"They told me not to, the police. They threatened me."

Jules nodded.

"You know?"

"I think so."

"You stole a car?!"

"No, I didn't steal a car. Do you think I would steal a car?"

"Of course not. They must be crazy. They really threatened me, but I owe it to you. I hope they haven't followed. I took an extremely roundabout route. I went all the way down to fucking Disneyland."

"Did you have a good time?"

I didn't go in. They couldn't have followed me, I took so many turns."

"François, you're a philosopher and an intellectual, so I suppose it might not have occurred to you that to see if you contacted me, apart from tapping your telephones they would just park outside my house and spare themselves a trip to Disneyland."

"I didn't think of that. I must be an idiot."

"You're not an idiot, you're a philosopher. You don't fix enough faucets or do enough laundry. Those things teach you the kind of things you never learned. Why did you come?"

"They showed up at my apartment."

"Arnaud and Duvalier?"

"You know them?"

"They came here as well. What did they want?"

"Last fall, in the rain, after we ate at Renée and you walked home, you dropped the check from your pocket. I paid for it only after a struggle, but you wouldn't let go of the check."

"I dropped it in the restaurant?"

"I don't know where. The restaurant sent them to me. They wanted to know with whom I ate. They say you stole a car. I knew that was impossible, so I gave them your name. I didn't think it could hurt. Are you sure you didn't steal a car?"

"Maybe I stole a car while I was sleeping. Why would I steal a car? François, I have a car. I'm a cellist. Cellists don't steal cars."

"I really didn't think so, but I went out in the hall as they left and I heard them talking. They're going to get a warrant, but the judge in the case is in Honfleur for August, so they're driving up there tomorrow. The next day, they said, they're going to arrest you. One of them thought they should bring other men, but the other told him you weren't dangerous and they didn't need to. What's going on? What are you going to do?"

" 'It's of no account."

"No account? They're going to arrest you!"

"No, no one's going to arrest me."

"How do you figure that?"

"The past will arise and the pace will speed up. In the gross and scope of things, it'll hardly be perceptible. I have eternity on either side, so how much can it matter?"

François looked at Jules in complete perplexity, not because he didn't understand what he called "the Bergson stuff," but because Jules seemed as happy as if he had just been injected with morphine.

"I'll look down upon Paris, the traffic on the streets and boulevards, the city breathing like something alive, and Arnaud and Duvalier will seem as small as grains of sand. Past and present will combine into one. I'll see troop trains going to Verdun, Hitler on the empty Champs-Élysées, the Liberation, century upon century overlaid all at once."

"Jules, are you all right?"

"Yes, and I can see. Music is the only thing powerful enough to push aside the curtain of time. When it does, everything becomes clear, perfect, reconciled, and just, even if only for the moments when we rise with it. Nineteen forty-four, François. The world is still alive."

After his visit to Jules, in which he had wanted to think of himself as a kind of French Paul Revere, François believed that Jules had gone mad, but that, despite this, Jules was safe.

The next day, Arnaud and Duvalier drove north to Honfleur, taking Duvalier's Volkswagen Jetta instead of a police cruiser. It was light, and even though the engine was not powerful the acceleration was like that of a sports car. And it had a sunroof, as police cars do not. On their way, just east of Lisieux, they passed Armand Marteau, who was heading toward Paris. They wouldn't have known Armand Marteau, and he wouldn't have known them had they been stuck in the same elevator or elbow to elbow at a bar, even though the three of them were focused on Jules. Still, when their vehicles passed at a collective 190 kilometers per hour, only ten meters apart, had there been a little bell devoted to marking such things it would have sounded.

The judge was an elegant old man with, nonetheless, gaps between his teeth. They caught him completely by surprise as he was returning from the beach, dressed in shorts and a Dr. Seuss T-shirt. They were in summer suits, with ties. Less embarrassed than they were, he invited them into his garden, from which they could vaguely hear the waves. The judge pulled out of his flip-flops and swung his feet onto a big ottoman with a square cushion. His wife brought out caviar on toast, and a pitcher of sangria.

"We have to drive home, *Monsieur Juge,*" Arnaud said upon his third glass.

"Why don't you stay for a swim and work it off. *Do we have enough chicken?!!*" he screamed so loudly that Duvalier's drink spilled.

Because the judge had been looking straight at Duvalier when he shouted the question, Duvalier said, sheepishly, "I don't know."

"I wasn't talking to you, I was talking to my wife. I have arthritis and I can't turn my head. *Do! We! Have! Enough! Chicken!!!*"

"For what?!"

"For four!"

"No. But we have ham, too!"

It was a very strange hearing, which ended when the two policemen — a Muslim and a Jew, who had had a nice lunch of ham — left their guns with the judge and went off to the beach. The judge's bathing trunks fit Arnaud decently enough, but to keep the pair loaned to him from falling off, Duvalier had to use a rope tied around the bunched-up waistband.

Before they went swimming, however, they told the judge what they had, including the most recent information, which was that the blood on the receipt was the same as that on the ground, that Raschid Belghazi's prints were on the receipt, as were two other sets, one of which they were sure would be Jules'.

"But you don't know," the judge said.

"When we take him in we'll know. Our theory about the boathouse seems to be correct."

"And if you're wrong?"

"We're very sure. We accept the risk."

"Before you arrest him, it has to be cleared with the DGSI."

"We would have broken the case much sooner had the DGSI not intercepted the letter from Belghazi."

"They didn't. The letter was caught by the DGSI, who got it from the Turks before it even left that country. And what do you mean, it shouldn't have been intercepted by the DGSI? That's their job. We'll have to wait until tomorrow. Do you think he's a flight risk?"

Arnaud expressed skepticism. "He's old, he's lived all his life in Paris, he has no one to go to and nowhere to go. The old almost never run."

"I'll sign," the judge told him, "but only after I run it past the DGSI."

"Can you reach them now?"

"Not the person to whom I speak. Tomorrow. Why don't you stay overnight? It's not a weekend, and there won't be much traffic going back. Once I have clearance, you can be in Paris in time to arrest him."

"You can't do it independently of the DGSI?"

"No. Your Raschid Belghazi is with Islamic State. They take that very seriously, and the DGSI has much more information than we do, so we've got to defer. Besides, I promised them."

"You knew?"

"Of course I did. The letter was forwarded to you a while ago. I thought you were working on it."

Armand Marteau drove around Saint-

Germain-en-Laye for almost an hour trying to find a good parking space. He had driven from Normandy to tell Jules something he could have related in a phone call of less than a minute, but he didn't want to leave a record. Yes, someone might have recorded his appearance, but he knew that it wouldn't be Nerval. Even were no one watching Jules, Armand didn't want an accidental parking ticket to mark his whereabouts, so he took the time to find a good space.

When he appeared at the door, Jules wasn't surprised. "Marteau," he said. "Come in."

"Better to walk in the garden."

"All right," Jules agreed, closing the doors and starting out in that direction. "Why?"

"Bugs."

"It's August," Jules told him. "There are more bugs in the garden than in the house. Or is it the other kind of bug?"

"It's the other kind."

"In my house? There aren't any."

"How do you know?"

"Who would do it?"

"The DGSI."

"Why?"

"We don't know. First the police then the DGSI ordered Nerval to lay off. The police were crude, and threatened him. He was going to work around them, but as soon as he started the DGSI flattened him. It came from above, in our company. Evidently you have

588

the attention of ministers, which made sense to everyone, given that you live here, and would be the kind of person who would — excuse me, who could — pick up the phone and call the Élysée.

"I came here to tell you that Nerval is off your case, and the DGSI's on it. There was a delay in wiping the servers because of vacations in August. It can happen. But they did it at the end of last week. Your policy exists only as it is written. The investigative materials and notes are gone forever."

Armand looked back at the palatial house. "You don't live here, do you. I mean, it isn't yours."

"How did you know?"

"By accident. We're fixing up our farm, and I've been there since late July. There are a lot of old magazines lying around, and in one of them was an interview with Shymanski after he was accused of bribery. They didn't show the outside of the house or say where it was, but I recognized the study where you received me, and the painting. It's his house, isn't it?"

"Now it's his sons', and they're selling it."

"So you have to move. But you're not going to move, are you?"

"No."

"This is your last stop, and where I come in."

The fate of Cathérine and Luc now depended on a rotund blond farmer from

Normandy, whom Jules hardly knew.

At times of stress and danger, the truth always shone out to Jules, which was partly why he had never quite succeeded in the world. Truth had always been more alluring than success. "Yes," he confirmed. "This is my last stop, and it is where you come in. What are you going to do?"

"I'm going back to Normandy, to work my farm."

AMINA

Jules crossed the Pont des Arts, where recently scores of thousands of padlocks fastened by hopeful couples to the grills beneath the railings had glittered in the sun. Now that the locks were removed, the panels that replaced the grilles to which they had been attached were covered with graffiti: "Dojo loves Priam," "Jean-Paul loves Anneka from Groningen." Though the locks, in being too heavy in their collectivity, may have endangered the railings, they had been a boon to local hardware stores, and as if the gold were real their brassy finish seemed not to fade. He remembered how not long before he had stopped to examine one of these locks. It had a chromed bolt, it was of foreign manufacture, with "333" engraved upon it, and hot to the touch. He had wondered if the two people who fastened it to the bridge to commemorate their love were still together, and how long it would be until not a single couple thus commemorated was intact or living. If both partners made it to the end, would that count as perpetual? Would they have to die on the same day, or at the same instant? If separated by years, would the loyalty of the one who was left count for perpetuity?

He was walking to the Quartier latin to take the last few things from his office, give the key to the new occupant, and, if desired, acquaint him with the idiosyncrasies of the room, the problematic radiator, and the almost stuck window. Jules would inform him of where the sun struck in different seasons, the restaurants nearby, and whom to call on the custodial staff.

Jacqueline had been in this office, of course, when death and parting were hardly a thought, and her presence as a young woman had remained, an invisible and ineradicable undercurrent stronger than even the exciting presence of Élodi. When Jules thought of Élodi it was like waking, and he would arise as if he were weightless, but then the excitement would drift away like a wave that would fall back and with the salute of its crest disappear into calmer waters.

Élodi was now like something in the light when seen from the dark. He could neither love nor not love her, even after she had ended something that hadn't really begun. He was neither puzzled nor determined, and knew exactly what was happening and what had to be. There was no answer or resolution. The one thing that seemed to be getting stronger was the reality of Jacqueline even as she receded into the past. She may have been dreamlike, but as he himself faded, the dream was becoming more real. The comfort of fading dovetailed with the illusion of rising and the hope of returning. The more Élodi receded, the more Jacqueline came to the fore, like an image on photographic paper emerging as if by magic from what according to logic and the senses was only empty and white.

As he had ten thousand times before, he climbed the stairs, experiencing a momentary illusion that the years had not passed. Jacqueline was in a library somewhere, and would meet him for lunch. Cathérine, age six, was in school. They loved her as nothing else.

Waiting for the new tenant to show, he gathered up the few things left and put them in a shopping bag: some books to be returned, stationary for the departmental office, journals to be discarded. He sat down. The replacement was due in a minute and a half. As if to hold the new man to account either for being late or so rigid as to be exactly on time, Jules stared at his watch, ready to form an opinion. Thirty-five seconds before the appointed hour, there was a quick, soft series of knocks, as if a woodpecker had a boxing glove on his beak. Jules got up, went to the door, and opened it as slowly as if it had been the heavy door of a vault.

Across the threshold was a trim, beautifully dressed woman, neither tentative nor reserved. As Jacqueline once had been, she was in a gray suit, with pearls. Although beige, her blouse was blessed with pink, her hair reddish blond, down almost to her shoulders.

She had the most extraordinary expression, such as he had never seen even in Renaissance paintings and a millennium's representation of angels. It was at one and the same time mischievous, knowing, innocent, forgiving, loving, comforting, challenging, proposing, curious, seductive, and enthusiastic, all of which ran together to knock him back into the world. One could say it was all in her eyes, or all in her smile, and one would not have said enough.

And it had to happen on the day before the day he had chosen to die. This woman, though vital and fit, was so much older than Élodi, probably in her early sixties. But though she was past the age of creating it anew, she possessed the fuse of life.

She introduced herself. Amina Belkacem — in origin Algerian for sure, Muslim most likely, charming and beautiful without doubt. Her French was that of a highly educated, upper-class *Parisienne*. Her eyes, like Élodi's, were blue. She asked politely and diplomatically if this was the office to which she had been assigned, and when he responded that it was, she said she hoped she hadn't inconvenienced him in any way, and although what she said was pro forma, it was also remarkably and absolutely true, the genuineness of it shining through.

"Not at all," he told her. "I'm happy to retire. At seventy-five," he added as reassurance and confession.

"I suppose that in twelve years or sooner, I will be too," she said, graciously informing him of her age — with, he thought, unmistakable flirtation. Why not? Maybe she was as crazy as he was. It was the last thing he wanted, needed, or expected. She went even further.

"The distance between us is not that great." This may have been just charity.

The distance between them was in fact not that great. She was marvelously attractive, enough that he was distressed to discover that his plans now had competition. He hoped that she was married. "What faculty?" he asked, businesslike but observably rattled.

"History."

"You'll be near enough to the libraries. The Bibliothèque Nationale is nearby."

"Of course." She smiled forgivingly.

He felt foolish. Obviously she knew where it was. "My wife," he said, as if to put Amina off, "made good use of the libraries. I'm in music, so not so much."

"Is she retired, too?"

"No. She never retired. She died."

"I'm sorry," Amina said, and it was clear that she really was. "I'm very sorry. My husband is gone, but he's still alive, so to speak, and stupid." She couldn't help but laugh.

"Why did you marry someone who was stupid?"

"He wasn't stupid to begin with. I think he started taking stupid pills. There's no other explanation."

"Oh," Jules said. Slightly scared by her declaration, though it was delivered with only traces of bitterness, Jules then took her around the little office the way a bellboy gives hotel guests a tour of their room. "You have to turn this thing here," he said, pointing to a valve at the side of the radiator, "to regulate the heat. But steam escapes, so you must do it with a rag. They haven't fixed it since de Gaulle.

"Monsieur Gimpel, the custodian, is a communist, which he will let you know every time you speak with him. If you ask him to attend to something he'll tell you he can't, but then he does. Except the radiator. That's for the engineers, he says, as if there's a picket line around it.

"To open the window, you have to bang the top of the frame with the heels of your hands because it swells shut, but that always works. In winter, I move the desk a meter to the left, or otherwise by mid-afternoon the sun shines in your eyes. There's not much else." He paused. "*Sandwiche Miche* is popular for *emporter* if you want to eat at your desk, but if you go left from it and down the first alley, there's a bistro that hasn't changed since before the war. It's quiet, simple, and the food is good. What's your specialty?"

"France and its wars of the twentieth-century. The little ones in Africa that continue to this day, the Great War, the Second World War, Vietnam, Algeria, the Cold War. Although people generally and even historians tend not to think of it this way, France suffered through, and its history was shaped by, more than a hundred years of war."

"Do you know Vietnamese?"

"No. German, Italian, and Arabic. And English. I lived in America for fifteen years."

"Where?"

"California."

"I was in California, recently. It's like taking drugs," he said, "although how do I know? I've never taken drugs."

"You're exactly right. It's because its past is as thin as ether. The dream that surrounds you there is from hypoxia. It kills brain cells, fairly slowly, but by the end even the nonagenarians carry around skateboards."

"Well," Jules said, pulling himself away,

though e wanted to talk to her forever, "I have t   o. I hope you have a productive time here. I   a good place to work." He paused. "I've   en here most of my life."

All he way home, he pictured her face and rem nbered her perfume, her hands, the clo   of her suit, and the way she moved.

V ile Jules had been cleaning out his office d had met Amina, Arnaud and Duvalier ad arrived in Saint-Germain-en-Laye. Jules iad just left and the gatekeeper wasn't there either, having cut the lawns and begun a five-day vacation. For the first time in many years, the great house was empty, except for Jules, who slept on the floor of his bare apartment. In the main residence most of the hundreds-of-millions worth of paintings and other valuables had been removed, but everything was still alarmed to the hilt.

They waited. With nothing to do at home, and because he was so unsettled after he met Amina, Jules wandered around Paris and arrived home in the dark long after Arnaud and Duvalier had given up for the day.

"He'll show. He's not going anywhere," Duvalier had said. "We'll come back tomorrow, early."

"I can't," Arnaud said.

"What do you mean, *you can't*? We have our case, maybe. An arrest hardly means a conviction, and he may even be innocent. But it looks good."

"I have to go to the dentist to get an implant."

"What's the matter with you? This thing is like neurosurgery."

"A tooth is not so easy," Arnaud said, pulling back his left cheek to expose a prominent gap among the rear molars. They're going to put a titanium plug into my jaw. It's almost general anesthesia. I can't drive or carry a weapon for two days, and if I still have to take hydrocodone, I'm off for as long as I do."

"We need you for this even though he's an old man. He's seventy-five but capable of taking down three much younger men with knives, and I don't want to call in anyone else, because it's our case. I don't know the cops in Yvelines and what they might do. It's a murder case so they might send in a SWAT team, which would be ridiculous and demeaning. Okay, it's not in our jurisdiction, but we can bring him in for questioning – we have the order — and when we cross the line into Paris. . . ."

"I know."

"Promise me that no matter how much it hurts you won't take any pills after day two. We'll get him then."

"All right."

"Meanwhile, let's go home. We didn't have to rush up to Honfleur, but that's the way it is. Sometimes I wish I worked in a bank."

The weather turned cool for a day or two as the heat wave broke. Paris was to have a short respite before the virtual sirocco that had been blowing across it returned, but now it was remarkably like Denmark, Sweden, or Scotland in August — high, bright sun; cool air; and sparkling, dappled light. Newly cut lawns were cold to the touch. At night in the chill, people dressed as if for the excitement and relief of autumn. Paris awoke.

And so did Jules, his mind and memory working with concentration and illumination. He knew he was irrational and in love with a woman with whom he had spent all of fifteen minutes. He was as much in love as he had been with Élodi, but this was different because it was possible, because Amina knew what he knew, because separately they had come to the same place in their lives. He said to himself that he was just crazy, that she could not have possibly fallen in love with him as he had with her. It was a lesson he had learned many times over, in many infatuations. And yet he could not help but continue to believe that she had.

As he concluded his affairs — the forwarding address at the Post Office, the last bills to be paid, the final items removed from the apartment so that now everything he possessed would fit in a small rucksack — a strange thing happened.

The music he was able to summon in full fidelity took on a life of its own, contrary to his will. He had structured much of the past, and especially these last days, on the *Sei Lob.* As it had been for seventy-one years, it was still his magical and forgiving path into another existence, God's voice lifting away heartbreak. It would be the accompaniment to that which would close the circle and make the past once more the good and beautiful world that a child remembers for a time after he has emerged from it with inchoate knowledge of the perfection from which he has been separated (or, sometimes, ripped), a memory that fades in the crib and for which there are no words.

Now a new music, not what he had intended, arose in apposition. Sometimes they played at the same time and he could hear them both, but then one would overcome the other. Opposed to the *Sei Lob* that would take him from life was a Couperin piece he had always loved. It was music he had associated with Paris as time motionlessly passed through it: *Les Barricades Mystérieuses,* and indeed they were. It was supposedly a play on virginity, but the power of the music elevated it far beyond such things.

The harpsichord is a very strange instrument. It plucks and stops, attacking its sonorousness at each note by refusing to let the note sustain and fade. In that sense, it refuses death — by jumping, as if from one ice floe to another, to a new note and a new life. It can sometimes be stilted, but if done right the chain of sound becomes as beautiful as the sparkling of stars. The Couperin exceeded this in that it was like a continuous waterfall of golden light so promising and overwhelmingly bright that it could startle even someone about to die. As it and the Bach closely contended within him, Jules had a compressed, comprehensive, detached, but nonetheless deeply emotional view of all his days.

He was sure he would never see Amina again, and that she had been only a test of his willingness to exit. He was old enough and experienced enough to conclude that he had exaggerated her qualities, that, because he was now separated from reality, this was his affair alone, and that the salvation he saw in her and hoped was mutual was merely something he had manufactured to keep himself alive. Luc was failing, and had one more, slight chance. Jules had to try to save Cathérine as well. Perhaps France would not go the way it had once gone. But though his intellectual appraisal told him it wouldn't, it had happened before, it had happened in history, and it had happened to him. The insurance, dearly purchased, was to give Cathérine and Luc what he had been unable to give his mother and father. Amina was life's last emissary, but he would have to leave her behind. He didn't know her, and would never see her again. He hoped she would simply fade away.

The day after they met was the last day of cool weather, and in the morning, in a gentle and insistent shower of cold, thin raindrops, Jules had gone to the pool to see if swimming five kilometers might kill him. He thought that giving up the ghost as waters swirled around his strokes and his attention was taken up in the rhythm and exhaustion of the swim would be easier than running in the heat until he died. But several hours after entering the water he emerged feeling, if a lot more tired, as healthy and powerful as a young man. As Jules left, his nemesis the guard said, "Are you training to swim *La Manche*?"

"Why do you ask that?"

"The lifeguards were talking about you. They almost got to the point where they were taking bets as to when you would get out."

"Actually," Jules said, "I'm going to swim to Peru, but it won't be that far, because instead of going around the Horn I'm going to take the Panama Canal. Or maybe the Suez. I haven't yet made up my mind."

In Saint-Germain-en-Laye is a tiny alley, unknown to almost everyone, that right-angles from another tiny alley off a narrow cul-de-sac that as it proceeds becomes entirely residential, and because of this has little foot traffic. To get to it you would have to veer off a fairly quiet commercial Street into a narrow way, walk past a travel agency, an estate agent, and a lawyer's office, continue on past the blank walls of the back of a school, make a right down another narrow street, with only the featureless school walls on either side, until at the end, half hidden, is the covered Passage Livry. If you dared follow it — because it looked like it would lead only to a back courtyard full of refuse bins — you would discover that it opened to a little garden with a fountain, teak benches, pebble paths, and a small bar and *tabac* run stubbornly and un-economically by a very old man who kept at it even after the municipality built a garage that closed off his little square from a busy street that had then been quick to forget that he remained.

There are many hidden courtyards in France. It might be said that the whole country and its culture is a form of architecture that protects private life. Almost all of its large buildings surround an interior garden as delicate as the stone walls around it are strong. Jules had discovered this one only after being present late one night when the proprietor of the bar, having had too much to drink, fell down on the street and bloodied his nose. Jules took him home, at first unbelieving that he was being guided correctly. Then, for thirty years, he had returned fairly regularly, often with Jacqueline, and Cathérine, who would play alone at the edge of the fountain.

And after they were gone he would go there to sit in the garden, read the newspaper, and enjoy a *complet.* Now he did so again, and due to the great swim he felt perfectly fine about having two brioches, two croissants, and a cup of scalding chocolate with whipped cream floating on top like Mont Blanc. It was the last time he would enjoy such things, for the next day the sun would be blazing and the temperature was predicted to surpass 35°C. That day, he would run until, in the battle he had always sought, he would bend time and loop back to the unfinished business of 1944.

But at present it was cold, and despite the steaming chocolate he was beginning to get a chill as he ate and tried to read a story about drilling for gas in the Eastern Mediterranean. The Jews had found gas and oil offshore. The Turks would try to take it from them. The Syrians would try to take it from them. The Lebanese would go to court. Hizb'Allah would attempt to blow it up. Such a nice windfall, and a fight to the death to keep it.

In the fading periphery of his vision, he saw something over the top of his newspaper, and lowered it to see directly. A woman was walking around the perimeter of the square, checking the few house numbers, looking for something. She walked like someone who is irritated, stopping and starting, unsatisfied. Jules took in a breath, and thrust his head slightly forward as stupidly as a pigeon, because it was Amina.

He jumped up suddenly and ran to her, thinking on the way that soon he would have to apologize to a stranger. In his early life and sometimes even of late he had often rushed toward people when he thought that they were his father, his mother, or Jacqueline. But he had always managed to catch himself. He would look at his watch, snap his fingers, and turn around. Still, the breathless shock of thinking he had caught sight of them, none of whom had aged, was something that would take half an hour to dissipate. Rushing toward this woman, he didn't have to snap his fingers, feign looking at his watch, or turn, because it really was Amina.

After she had joined him at his table, doubling the old man's customers at a stroke, she saw that Jules seemed suspicious. "I didn't track you, if that's what you're thinking," she told him. This amused her.

"Of course not. I didn't think that."

"It *is* extremely unlikely that in all of Paris and environs we would end up in this little place at the same time, but I was at the estate agent around . . ." she twirled her left hand

and index finger as if stirring something ". . . the corner. And he said there was a listing in, or, rather, off, the Passage Livry."

"You're moving here?"

"I am. I hope to. Do you live here?"

"For most of my life — that is, in Saint-Germain-en-Laye. Tomorrow I'm leaving."

"Where?"

Instead of answering, he took a sip of his chocolate, and softened his non-reply with the kind of expression — a concentration, a quarter smile, a slight narrowing of the eyes — that compliments the person upon whom it is focused.

"I think I told you that I've just returned from America," she said. "I want to live here because of the gardens, the forest, the quiet, the amenities. I can feel my blood pressure drop when I get off the train. I want to find a quiet place that I can make beautiful, prefer- ably one with a view. I suppose the estate agent sent me here because if there is in fact anything available in this little square it would have a view onto it, and it is quiet. But I'd rather see out toward Paris. My experience has been, in real estate and other things, that if you look hard you can eventually come up with something good."

"The change is unexpected?"

"Yes. Six months ago my husband and I were at Stanford. We were somewhat isolated, but we had friends, and we were always busy.

In retrospect, I suppose that was not good, but at least I thought I was happy for the first fourteen years, even though it was like living in what they call virtual reality. They use the word incorrectly. *Virtual* means it's real but doesn't seem so, but they apply it to what isn't real and does seem so."

"Then what?"

"My husband, who, unlike you, has lost most of his hair and is quite fat . . . decided to write a book. With one of his graduate students."

"In what?"

"Sociology. I'm a historian. There's a conflict right there. Purely by happenstance, his graduate student is six feet tall, the top of her legs are at about my shoulder height, she has blazing, naturally blond hair, balloon-sized breasts that — like a paint shaker in a hardware store — jiggle before her at high speed as she walks, and ridiculously white teeth."

"Your teeth are white."

"Of course. I've been in California for fifteen years. But not like hers. When she opens her mouth the beam picks you up and slams you against a wall. She's a human lighthouse."

"Is she a Muslim?" Jules asked.

"From North Dakota? I should go there to get my teeth whitened and my breasts jiggled."

"Is your husband a Muslim?"

"Oh yes, especially now that he's discovered his polygamous side."

"So you're separated."

"Divorced. In Nevada, just across the line, it takes a minute and a half."

"Children?"

"He was infertile. I stuck with him. Now, of course, I'm too old."

"I have a daughter, and a grandchild," Jules said. "They're probably going to leave France."

"Why?"

"We're Jews. That's one thing."

"I understand. We left France, too."

"And the little boy is sick, desperately so. When you're that sick, sometimes the only hope is another country, whether that's true or not."

The way she looked at him, and he knew it, it was clear that she was seeking someone she could love, someone who would love her as if she were once again a girl and the world was young. There was no question that he was capable of such a thing. She could see it in his face and read it in his every expression.

On the Grand Terrace at Saint-Germain-en-Laye

Things go faster toward the end, and at the very end as fast as light. Not only because of the relation of time passed to time left, but because life, like a wide, deep river flowing into narrow shallows, is compelled by natural law to accelerate. And accelerate it did.

Empty of all but the most devoted runners, the white path shimmered in the morning heat. Even the fanatics, breathing hard, had finished up. At home they would shower in relief, bathroom windows open, fragrant steam rushing out and up, and, except for the flow of water, silence almost ringing in their ears.

The long terrace high above the Seine stretches for two and a half kilometers as straight as a rule, forests and gardens flanking it to the west, Paris floating dreamlike in the east, and, descending toward the Seine, vineyards, pastures, Guernsey cows, trees, roads, and bridges across the river over which tooting trains rush to and from Paris.

Cathérine grew up here. At evening the family would walk on the long roads and the wide avenues through the trees. Louis XIV had been born on this hill with its view east, but had turned with the rest of Europe to look west, the westward-oriented canals at Versailles symbolizing the maritime routes to the New World. In that sense, Saint-Germain-en-Laye was part of the age that made the French Revolution necessary, and still held magically encapsulated in its topography the peace and languid pace of the centuries in which clocks and machines had not ruled.

Almost since sunrise, Jules had been sitting on a bench near the circle that divides the Allée Henri IV from the Chemin du Long du Terrace. Decades before, shortly after they had moved into the Shymanski house, he had paused before the door and reflected that one day, after what he hoped would be many long years of going in and out without thinking about it, he would close it behind him, or it would be closed behind him, for the last time. And even then, in the beginning, he knew that when that happened, the time from the first to last crossing of the threshold would be compressed into absolutely nothing, all gone.

He was tired of life, but full of love. Though he had long believed that only God was capable of infinite love, the love he had for so many people and so many things seemed nonetheless to have no limit. Ashamed and surprised, only on his last day and in his last hours had he discovered that one can love infinitely not as an attribute of one's capacities but rather as an attribute of love itself.

Such thoughts ended suddenly when he heard a loud crunching of gravel behind and to his left. An ice-cream vendor on a bicycle attached to a white freezer chest had peddled from the park. He was deeply disappointed that the Long Terrace was empty. You could see on his face that his gambit had not paid off. "Oh goddam," he said to himself as he stopped. Then he saw Jules on the bench. Pedaling over, he looked hopeful.

"How about an ice cream?" he proposed, smiling like a child or a salesman.

"It's eight o'clock in the morning," Jules told him.

"Get an early start."

"I, I don't. . . ."

"Don't be ridiculous. In summer everyone eats ice cream in the morning. People have it for breakfast."

"I'm just about to run. I don't want to have a full stomach and unbrushed teeth."

"Don't be ridiculous," the ice cream vendor insisted. "It melts and goes right into your cells to give you energy. And there's water all over the place. You can rinse."

"I'm sorry, but I don't even like ice cream that much. I like cookies," Jules said, as if justifying himself.

"I like cookies, too, but everyone loves ice cream, even monkeys. I can give you a chocolate bombe on a stick — it has raspberry and cherry inside — ordinarily two-and-a-half Euros, for one."

"That's the other thing. I don't have any money."

"Don't you have a credit card?"

"No."

"What about your watch?"

"I don't have a watch, and if I did I wouldn't trade it for an ice cream."

"Your socks?"

"You want to trade an ice cream for my socks? Say that again?"

"That's right."

"I'm not giving you my socks."

"You don't really need them to run. Lots of people run without socks, I see them all the time."

"Not me."

"Okay. Then will you be here tomorrow?"

"No."

"Why not?"

"I'll be dead."

"Yeah, sure. If you pay me tomorrow, I'll let you have the ice cream today."

"I won't be here. I told you."

"All right. I'll just give it to you." He opened the thick top and reached down. Mist arose from dry ice. The top slammed closed, making the idiosyncratic sound of freezer doors big or small, whether on a bicycle or set in a wall. "Here, take it." He pedaled away, crunching over the gravel, and as he did Jules heard him say, "Fucker."

On the morning of his death, Jules was holding in his hand a raspberry-cherry chocolate bombe. He took time out to eat it. It was extremely good, and for a moment he thought of nothing else.

Élodi awoke in the arms of her young man, happy as she had never been, the whole world in front of her and hardly a hint of what was to come as she made her way. In the remnants of summer they were going to Portugal — knapsacks, student fares, second class, staying in hostels, taking most of their meals on benches or sitting at the edge of fountains or on rocks by the side of the sea. But now, in the morning with the sun flooding in from the east, someone was downstairs and the intercom was buzzing. As she left the bed she took the top sheet, which had been cast aside because of the heat, and wrapped it around her.

"Yes?" she said to the box set in the wall. She had never ceased to think it strange that people talked to walls.

"Hedley's, Madame."

"Mademoiselle."

"Mademoiselle," the box repeated, corrected.

"What's Hedley's?"

"Specialized couriers. We have a delivery
for you."

"I've never heard of Hedley's. How do I
know . . . ?"

"If your windows face the street. . . ."

"My window does."

"You might look out."

"Okay. Just a minute." She looked magnificent as she crossed the floor, her hair dishev-
eled, buoyant, and golden, the sheet draped
about her more beautifully than the rarest
gown. Clutching it to the top of her chest,
not that anyone was looking, she peeked over
the sill. On the street was a most impressive,
highly polished truck, with a man in a pressed
uniform standing attentively on the sidewalk
beside it. She returned to the intercom. "You
have a delivery for *me*?"

"Élodi de Challant?"

"That's right." She pressed the button to
unlock the street door, then raced to put on
some clothes.

Soon enough, standing in front of her door
were two uniformed men, one carrying a
cello case, the other, two bankers' boxes.
When she saw this, she thought, he's gone or
he's dead. After she signed and they left, she
opened the cello case. The instrument was
old and worn, but, as she knew, it had had an

extraordinary sound. On a note placed beneath the strings Jules had written, "This is left to you for the beauty of its sound and for the advancement of your career. You'll see in documents that will follow in a few weeks that you must never sell it, only give it. But as you'll soon discover, you won't need to sell it."

Élodi opened the bankers' boxes. They were full of music. On the top of one pile was the symphony Jules had written only recently. It opened unconventionally with a cello solo that laid down the theme. She put this part on the music stand, took the cello out of its case, and tuned it. Then she played from sight. It was a simple theme — and to her it was as beautiful as the *Sei Lob* itself, as beautiful as anything she had ever heard.

In Saint-Germain-en-Laye even though it was still rather early it was very hot in the direct sun. Jules glistened with sweat, and had fused with nature as if he were comfortably a part of it. He had never wanted to die in bed, but, rather, like an animal, on the ground, in the sun, after struggle. Without fear, animals take death as it comes. They feel the earth, see the sky, and know they have fought.

But Jules was not quite ready either to run or for the last few seconds in which one may or, he suspected, may not see and feel the justice, love, and satisfaction for which one has struggled all one's life. In the increasing heat, he was content to forge his past and his present, his desires and his regrets, into a molten alloy that might if he were lucky be something bright and new right before the end.

Perhaps because of history, his own circumstances, or his particular nature, he had, like so many others, spent his life unhappy to live. It had been a disservice to Jacqueline, to Cathérine, and to everyone he had known, and yet another reason to regret that he hadn't been murdered in his infancy. But, now, in his last hour, he was finally happy to live and unafraid to die.

To the east, Paris was obscured in a mist of heat and whitening light. The sun was directly over the city, making it almost impossible to see. But he knew that as the sun rose its rays would flare against every building entry, every window, every gilded fleur de lys, sculpting them in three dimensions, adding depth by shadow, painting in color and detail. Although no jets were weaving contrails in the blue, Jules heard the drone of a propeller, as in his youth when it carried no suggestion of the antique and set just the right tone for a summer morning or afternoon.

He longed for his mother, his father, Jacqueline, Cathérine, Luc, Élodi, and Amina, even Amina, the last woman he would love. And he did love her. He had tried and failed to do right by each and every one. As he aged, everything was eroded away but love and conscience, which were left sparkling and untouched in the stream. Paris was beginning to come clear as the sun began to cross west. He decided that as soon as he felt the breeze, he would start his run.

Arnaud and Duvalier thought they had set out early enough from the Passy *commissariat* to catch Jules at home. They had assumed that between shifts it would be quiet, but because it was a Friday in August the shifts had been rearranged and the *commissariat* was busy, the street in front of it clogged with uniformed police striding this way and that. Then, as Arnaud and Duvalier drove west, heavy traffic brought them to stop in a tunnel echoing with horns and cloudy with exhaust.

"Everyone's leaving Paris because it's Friday," Arnaud said. "Why don't they leave on Thursday night? What's the difference?" He was irritated and jumpy.

"People don't like to drive in the dark," Duvalier answered. "Especially older people, who can't see as well. I've heard they can't smell as well either."

"Then they should leave on Thursday morning. They don't have jobs."

"Why don't you tell them that? The next time Hollande speaks, push him from the lectern and command old people to leave for vacation on Thursdays. Mussolini could have done it. Putin could do it. Why not you?"

Traffic started moving again, and because Saint-Germain-en-Laye was not far, soon they were pounding on Shymanski's gate. Claude was south of the house, planting flowers, in his element, his hands in the loam, and the best loam it was, for billionaires can afford to buy the very finest dirt — light but perfectly dense, of the consistency of a good chocolate cake and the color of dark English bridle leather. Flowers that grew in it seemed to detonate in the air like the bloom of fireworks. The perfection of a well-planned and tended garden is a message that says life has purpose. So when Claude heard them he said, "I'm not answering. To hell with them."

Duvalier, however, was as stubborn and as resourceful as he looked. That no one answered he took as a challenge, and kept at it for ten minutes. Then he got Arnaud to knit his hands together and give him a boost. Arnaud was so strong that he was able to extend his arms straight up and support Duvalier standing on his palms, like a circus acrobat. Duvalier easily saw over the wall. "He's in the garden," he said.

"Lacour?" Arnaud asked in a strained voice.

"The gardener. Hey!" he shouted. "Hey! You!"

Claude threw down his spade, spat, and

619

started toward the gate. When he got there and opened it, he was not happy. "Why didn't you call for an appointment?" he asked impolitely.

"We don't have to call for an appointment," Duvalier said. "We're the police."

"Yeah yeah yeah. Calling for an appointment would be efficient, and, I forgot, you're the police, so you can't. What do you want?"

"Lacour."

"You missed him."

"He left?"

"Yes he left. That's what 'you missed him' means. He went out this morning. He'll be back."

"When?"

"In the afternoon sometime. He goes out every morning, even in winter. He exercises like a maniac. He swims, he lifts weights or something, and runs. He's crazy, because he's way too old for that. Then he gets the paper and reads it in a café. Then he comes home. Like a clock."

"Which was he doing today?"

"I don't know. Usually he does them all, unless there's so much snow on the Long Terrace that he can't run."

"Can't you tell by what he was wearing?"

"He runs and swims in the same shorts. I didn't see if he was carrying his goggles. They help you see underwater. That's how they can take pictures of fish on television. Start at the pool in the park if you want to look for him. We have a pool here, and Shymanski is gone. But when Shymanski lived here, out of respect for him and his family, Lacour never swam in it. He used the municipal pool instead. When he comes back, if you haven't found him, I'll tell him you were here."

"Don't," said Arnaud.

"Why? Is this serious?"

"Just don't."

"There is no law . . ." Claude began.

"Yes there is," Duvalier informed him, "and you can go to jail."

"I'm not afraid of jail."

"I am," Duvalier said. "I've seen what jail is like. If I were you or anyone else I'd be very afraid of jail. You like food? Be afraid of jail." As they were leaving, Duvalier turned back and asked, "Who's Shymanski? Shymanski the industrialist? This is his house?"

Amina Belkacem was numbingly pretty even as she aged, and her face did not in the slightest cease to convey goodness and love. With the same driven, breathless trepidation Jules had felt when he walked to Élodi's house, Amina returned via the *Passage* Livry to the hidden square where she had discovered that in the few minutes in which he had shown her around his office, and even before that — at first sight — she had fallen in love with Jules.

621

In near-adolescent delirium she imagined marriage, happiness, and contentment. But as she had lived a long life, she knew that she had to take one cautious step at a time. If he found her in a place he frequented, it would be obvious but also a touch deniable. She hoped that if he thought as she did he would return there at roughly the same time they had met. So she sat down at a little table and, when the old man came out, ordered tea. After he brought it to her she opened the newspaper and didn't read it. Instead, as she stared at it, other things passed before her eyes.

Because her father was a Muslim and her mother a *colon,* apart from a few secret, tearful visits of the grandmothers, both families had rejected their children forever. Though Algerian by birth, her parents had met in the Paris Resistance during the war. It mattered little to them then and afterward that he was Muslim and she a Catholic. They lived in Algeria with great difficulty until, when Amina was seven or eight, the war there drove them out. Life in France was hardly easy. Her father was attacked on the street, Amina spat upon in school. Partly because her only friends were books, she never relinquished first place in her class.

But as she grew it was not enough to be alone and first. She had to have something to love independently and apart from her parents. She chose for that the inexact but intense memories in which the emotion and contentment of childhood were recollected in colors and sensations.

"I can bring you an umbrella, or help you move to the shade," the old man who owned the bar said. She was in direct sun and even from inside his café he had seen that her arms glistened with hundreds of sparkling droplets, and her fresh white blouse was beginning to cling to her transparently. "It's extremely hot, you know: you can get sunstroke."

"I'll be cooled by the breeze," she answered.

"There's no breeze here. Only in winter when the wind is strong. They enclosed it. There was a time when I couldn't keep up with the customers. They came from the street that is now on the other side of those buildings."

"I won't be long," she told him. "There'll be a breeze on the hill above the Seine."

In the beating, aggressive sun, she closed her eyes. Her family of three, because they didn't fit in, anywhere, was isolated and close. At first, she thought this was the way every family was, and her childhood was a paradise of innocence. On summer holidays they would drive along the coast almost to Tunisia, doubling back on the road west from the village of Chataibi to a deserted beach south of the Cap de Fer. Several kilometers long, it went even more kilometers deep inland over dunes of the purest, whitest sand. There were only a few farmhouses just north of it. The Belkacems would camp for a week or ten days in August, carrying in many trips across the sand to their tent the food and water they brought with them. But the main course was always fish her father caught while casting from the beach. Year after year, they never saw another person, and were free there: free of allegiance, free of fear, free to love as if throughout the world Christians married Muslims and Muslims married Christians and no one thought twice about it.

Eventually the war drove them out and to Paris. Now, in Saint-Germain-en-Laye, Amina felt the heat almost like the driving heat of North Africa. Eyes closed, she saw the sea surging in dark blue. She could see into the distance and along the bleached strand undulating in rising heat and disappearing in a confusion of vision before it reached the horizon, white glare over the blue, the colors of innocence and love. She had them still, as richly saturated in heat and light as when she had first seen them.

"Do you know Jules Lacour?" Arnaud asked the guard at the pool.

"Why wouldn't I? He's been coming here since the beginning of time."

"Is he here now?"

"No."

"Was he here?"

"Yesterday he swam five kilometers. He says he's going to swim to Peru. He's a liar."

After a pause to take this in, Arnaud asked, "Do you vote?"

"In elections?"

"That would be a good place to start."

"What do you mean?"

"I mean, when there is an election, do you vote in it?"

"Of course I do."

As they left the pool they both knew where they were going and didn't need to speak. Nonetheless, Duvalier voiced what they were thinking. "If he runs in the forest, he'll come out in the park, but maybe he just runs on the Terrace. If we don't see him, we'll wait in front of the house."

"In this heat?"

"We can park in the shade."

From the pool, Arnaud, Duvalier, and from *centre-ville,* Amina, came onto the Allée Louis XIV, Amina a hundred meters or so behind the two policemen. A great formal garden gives a certain elevation to the soul if the paths and plantings are laid out according to proportions known since classical times and as inexplicable and ineffable in their effect as the measures of intervals and tones in music. All the more so if the garden is on a height overlooking a distant prospect of varied colors beneath a dome of clear sky. The two men and Amina walked slowly in the heat. A breeze crested over the hill, as Amina had thought it would, and continued evenly down the straight Allée.

Arnaud and Duvalier came to the bench where Jules had been sitting. Jules had gone into the park to find a spigot, where he would feel water for the last time, holding it in his cupped hands again and again and bringing it to his face. He knelt at the gray pipe, not caring that he wet his clothes as he brought double handfuls up to his face. The water was clear, cool, and pure, its sound beautiful even as it issued from a spigot to which gardeners, without thinking much about it, attached their hoses.

Arnaud and Duvalier straightened themselves so as to rise slightly higher in the hope of seeing a little farther down the glimmering white path disappearing northward along the Terrace as straight as a rule. They shielded their eyes almost in salute, and saw just an empty road. Independently, each felt that he had glimpsed something on the long white prospect that said Jules was gone, and that, somehow justly, he was out of their grasp.

When they turned to go back to their car and find a place to park in the shade, they were relieved. They looked forward to going home that evening and relaxing, they hoped, as if just after a graduation. If they had him or if, as they expected, he was gone, the case would either be closed or tabled, and they would be free until assigned to the next. They sensed that it was over.

As Arnaud and Duvalier left the park, Amina arrived at the bench on the circle between the Allée Henri IV and the Long Terrace. She was entirely alone, and hadn't come in search of Jules. In fact, she had more or less given up. She looked toward Paris as the cooling breeze lifted her hair, ruffled her blouse, and made her skirt luff at her legs.

As Jules emerged from the lawn at the edge of which he had knelt at the spigot, he saw the trim form of a woman standing next to the bench. At first he appreciated her for the firmness of the way she stood and her colors in the sun. He kept walking slowly toward her. Then he recognized her, and stopped. Staring at her, it was as if everything in his life rose and burst within him. The contention of equally balanced forces was unlike anything he had ever experienced. The weight of loyalty, obligation, and faithful love fought against the promise of life and love anew.

If she walked away — when she walked away — what would he do? If she turned toward him to get to the RER, he would have no choice. If she went left toward the Long Terrace, where he had been just about to begin his last run, the plan would be shattered at least for that day. Or perhaps forever, because, although he didn't know it, Arnaud and Duvalier were waiting for him.

As the breeze died down she was ready once again to start her search for a place to live. Without having seen him, she turned right, to the town, and went up the stairs at the southeast corner of the circle, rising toward the five great ornamental urns flanking the steps. The scene seemed to Jules like something on as unreasonably grand a scale as in a dream — that she would go, and he would let her go as she branched off from his life, closing his course, in such a monumental way. And yet her diminutiveness, her self-containment, and grace made even the grandeur of the exit close and warm. Had he been next to her, and touched her, it would have changed everything.

But he just watched her as she disappeared among the ordered ranks of closely cropped trees and the long banks of flowers in the August sun. She was gone. Everything was silent except the wind rising from the east and curling over the battlement-like retaining wall of the Grand Terrace. Wood smoke came from beyond the vineyard. A little girl with blond hair raced ahead of her parents, crossing the circle of grass. They followed, the father holding an infant who squinted in the sun, before this family disappeared as well.

A distant church bell rang, and when it did, as if right before his eyes, he saw its whitish-

628

gray metal. Things don't vanish, he thought. If they exist once, they exist forever. Nothing is lost. It's all somewhere, permanently engraved on the black walls of time. He took a few breaths, and as his much needed courage began to return, he set off to find them.

Although there was not even a single cloud, it seemed to him as if there had been a stroke of lightning in the sun and a clap of thunder in the clear. Suddenly, and as if from nowhere but the past, he felt utter fearlessness and resolution. As a soldier, he had come to know the courage that comes on the heels of anxiety. Always anxious before a patrol, when he took his first step into the darkness he accepted death, and from that point forward he left all fear behind and experienced a lightness and joy as if he were invulnerable.

Morning heat had driven everyone from the long path, and he was alone as he watched the trees shimmer in the sun. From memory and as if to match his excitement came the *allegro* of the *Third Brandenburg*. As it twinned with the heat and light, he began to run. He would run faster than a man of his age could run on a hot day and remain alive. He would force it upon himself as if he were fighting for life. At first, things came wonderfully clear. The years of the fifties and sixties became images that, like the petals of peonies, fell suddenly and easily and almost at once,

629

still white and unmarred but now littered on the grass.

Although he had not bidden it, he was grateful for this music as a perfection of art and a summation beyond the power of reason. Music had been the oxygen that had kept him alive. He hadn't become a great musician or a great composer, either of which would have diverted him from the essential task of his life. But he remembered, he never flagged, and he had lived for more souls than his own. As he ran, the music gathered everything he knew and had known in his life, and everything seemed to turn in a massive whirlwind of red and silver light.

Then the red and silver, which seemed to him like a lion of fire, the sun's leaping corona, or a city burning but not consumed, turned to gold, and, somehow, this was France in all its history, rising like a sun. As in massive forest fires after which come years of young and tranquil green, the golden air and light that floated above the combustion were a promise of the silence and peace to follow.

The running became more and more difficult. Though he tried not to slow, he was forced to, and, as he slowed the music changed, as he had always expected, to the *Sei Lob und Preis mit Ehren.* Now his mother and father were close, Cathérine would have a chance, and Luc might be healed. It had been Jules' duty and obligation to stay with his mother and his father, Philippe and Cathérine Lacour — when he said their names it brought them close — not because of sense, law, or logic, but to follow the illogic of love. Now at last he would go where he was always supposed to have been.

As he ran, the red and the black crept forward from the periphery of his vision until it enveloped him and he was blinded. He lost touch with his body. His senses were almost gone when he heard himself crash against the white stones on the path and felt them, for a moment, cutting into his left cheek. He lay there, knowing that at the last he might have, as he had been told, thirty seconds more, thirty seconds when all threads were braided, all feeling risen, all memories recollected not in detail but in sum, in a miraculous density, in a song too great to be heard by the living.

Events that would not be suppressed rose from the dark and broke the surface to pull Jules Lacour back to the place he had never really left. Here, in balance with all he had seen since, was what he had always longed for. Wanting in equal measure both life and death, he would cross over easily and unafraid from one to the other, finally at peace as he had not been since the first and last time he had heard his father play the *Sei Lob* and, as riddle and solution, it had been impressed upon his heart, waiting for his life to come.

As it had for Amina, a cool breeze arose. It traveled up the hillside, over the vineyards, and across the path where Jules lay. When it got to the forest it gently raised the canopy of leaves, and then relaxed. The last thing he heard, when supposedly there was silence, was the distant music of Paris — the sum of footfalls, the sound of engines, of horses and bells, of voices, laughter, water flowing, the movement of traffic, the wind in the trees. Sound lifted from the streets, from the procession of the Seine and the roll of the hills. Sound that was filtered and shaped by the form of little things such as a rail or a cornice, sound that was made by the wind sweeping down a wide avenue. These ever-present and underlying sounds, of which he had been aware from his earliest infancy, these forgiving sounds that now were strong and overpowering and came from the inter-weaving paths of the living and the dead, were music as beautiful and compelling as the masterpiece of life itself.

And so it was, that day, when a detail of history finally came to rest in Saint-Germain-en-Laye, and the music of Paris bathed the city in a rain of gold. Jules was free and gone, but the music remained — sonatas, sympho-nies, and songs present even in silence, wait-ing to be heard by those who might stop long enough to listen on their way.

ABOUT THE AUTHOR

Mark Helprin is the acclaimed, bestselling author of *Winter's Tale, In Sunlight and in Shadow, A Soldier of the Great War, Freddy and Fredericka, The Pacific, Ellis Island, Memoir from Antproof Case,* and numerous other works. His novels are translated into more than twenty languages and read around the world. He lives in Virginia.

The employees of Thorndike Press hope you have enjoyed this Large Print book. All our Thorndike, Wheeler, and Kennebec Large Print titles are designed for easy reading, and all our books are made to last. Other Thorndike Press Large Print books are available at your library, through selected bookstores, or directly from us.

For information about titles, please call:
  (800) 223-1244

or visit our website at:
  gale.com/thorndike

To share your comments, please write:
  Publisher
  Thorndike Press
  10 Water St., Suite 310
  Waterville, ME 04901